# WAR WITCH

## LAYLA NASH

Cover design by Satyr Media

# CHAPTER 1

*T*he buses never ran close enough to where I wanted to go. The rain held off as the bus lurched to a halt, still a mile from where my best friend's birthday party had no doubt kicked into high gear. The bus driver grumbled as he descended to check the engine, and I checked the window for any precipitation. Saints blast it.

The three of us on the bus grudgingly departed after the driver indicated we were better off walking. "Some of you," he added with a sneer as he looked at the two shifters, "more so than others."

He looked to me for solidarity, but instead of participating in his hostility, I ducked my head and started walking as fast as I could toward the safety of the bar and Moriah's friendship.

I didn't know either of the shifters on the bus, and it wasn't my job to convince the human driver that his bigotry against Others was wrong. Perhaps he'd fought in the war against us, and no doubt lost friends and family, probably been injured or at least displaced. Besides, if a human caught me in public without a ring that identified me as a witch, he could report me.

That guy sure as hell would. I'd end up arrested and fined, maybe jailed since it wasn't my first offense.

Or maybe the bus driver belonged to one of the humans-first, humans-only militias that hunted nonaligned Others. I wouldn't have to worry about jail, but being strung up and murdered as a testament to how deeply the humans could hate.

I hustled to get past the half dozen blocks outside the Slough where the streetlights never worked properly and the sidewalks cracked and crumbled underfoot. The humans blamed the magic in the witches' memorial for all the disrepair, but in reality it was just a shitty neighborhood. No one cared enough to renovate. Some of the buildings still showed signs of the war, unrepaired after five years. The two shifters from the bus headed in different directions, so almost immediately I was alone except for the stars.

A muffled yelp broke the quiet and the reek of burned magic drifted from a nearby alley. It was far enough out of my way I could keep walking if I wanted, though, and almost no one would blame me for ignoring trouble that had nothing to do with me. A flash of light, tinged blue, and muttered spells convinced me to turn my back, consigning the perpetrators and victims alike to their fates, until the magic intensified. Magic coalesced and darkened, and coated the back of my throat with old memories. Hints of blood and sulfur and demons ran through the magic like snarled threads.

The choking sobs, pleas for mercy, stuck my feet to the broken pavement.

I focused on the mouth of the alley where the magic pulsed. Walking away from two shifters and a bigot was excusable, particularly since the shifters could handle themselves, but no witch walked away from dark magic. Even a retired war witch. *Especially* a retired war witch.

I edged closer, searching for traps, although the intensifying magic urged me to move imprudently. A smart witch would have called the police or the Alliance and let them deal with it —and for a second, again, I considered it. It wasn't my job anymore. None of it was.

But the conscience I inherited from my parents, along with their magic, kept me walking into the alley until it was too late. The dark witches didn't turn from their work as I approached, and I gathered up some of the cleanest magic they manipulated. The stickiness of corrupted power made my toes curl, but I had no desire to introduce my own magic into the mix. Leaving my magical fingerprints all over the alley would only cause more trouble.

Two witches stood over a writhing victim on a makeshift altar made of knotty lumber balanced on crumbling cinderblocks. There should have been three. Dark witches always worked in threes. I glanced over my shoulder, wary of the errant one sneaking up on me in the dark alley. I rubbed my nose as the sulfurous smoke curling around my ankles billowed up, and I gagged on the stench of rotting garbage and old blood. One of the dark witches muttered in bastardized Latin as she gestured with her right hand, a book held open before her, while the other positioned a gleaming knife over the human woman tied to the boards.

Blood pooled on the ground and the altar, collected in a small chalice. It stained the hands of both witches. Their magic twisted and combined, descended to the demons and oozed back up, warped and forever changed. The breeze of its return stirred the smoke, and I sneezed.

Both witches turned to stare. The short one looked on the verge of saying, "Saints bless."

I rubbed my nose again as I studied the altar. "You shouldn't be doing this."

The one holding the book recovered her composure first, but the charming smile never reached her eyes. "She hired us for healing and then refused to pay. This is the price, just a little bit for us. Evens things out."

The victim flailed against the restraints, eyes bulging as she screamed around a gag and tried to get my attention. If the witches used anything but demon magic, I might have believed the story—health insurance didn't cover magical fixes, and most humans couldn't afford the Alliance's exorbitant prices for legitimate healers. The truly desperate went in search of downmarket sawbones for procedures on the cheap, sometimes literally in back alleys. Often the price of the healing was not money but energy or memories—only gray magic and a fuzzy line, blurred by desperation on one end and greed on the other. Blood, bone, and hair crossed the line into dark magic, any way you cut it. Though the woman's blood on the table could have been explained by a clumsy surgery prior to actual healing, collecting her blood in a chalice hinted at much darker intentions.

The scent of blood and angry magic resurrected flashes of the war and started sweat trickling down my back, even in the cold night air. The smell of spent ammunition competed with their dark magic, and the low rumble and ear-piercing shriek of artillery echoed in the past, but still too real as my heart began to pound.

I tried to steady my breathing despite a rat-a-tat-tat refrain of machine guns in my head, and glanced back toward the street to make sure a third witch didn't approach. The short one, standing over the girl, also smiled, eyes too wide and unblinking. A hint of red flashed near her irises. "She tried to back out of the deal. We're not here for charity, so we... convinced her. You understand."

My fingers twitched with the urge to hex them, if only for doing sloppy magic in a back alley where anyone walking by could have caught them. The militants adored discovering that kind of mess; it was a propaganda goldmine. I didn't know either of the witches from the war, and they both looked old enough to have fought—which meant one of two things: they were cowards who hid, or dark witches who protected themselves and then stole magic from the dying.

"You should let the girl go," I said. It was a warning, though they did not seem inclined—or intelligent enough—to hear it.

"Sure," the one with the knife said, resting the point against the smooth skin of the young woman's abdomen. "Right after we—"

"Now," I said, enough oomph in my voice that their magic wobbled, and the one with the book snapped it shut.

Her eyes narrowed as she made a fist, her sapphire ring winking as magic flared. "Mind your business or we'll strap you down next. Little witch like you would give us enough power to last a couple weeks."

"Brave girl," I murmured, heartbeat steadying as my magic rose unbidden. It quieted the memories, stilled the shakes. Old habits died hard, and a threat like that brought the Morrigan to the surface. I'd die fighting or take my own life before I'd let a dark witch touch me again. My magic curled around in a protective embrace, but I used only their contaminated power to create a rift behind them, hiding the effort in their magical firestorm. I didn't even have to move my hands. "I'll give you one chance to—"

"Go plant some herbs," she spat, waving to dismiss me with a sending spell.

The one at the table laughed and drove the knife into the human's stomach, blood swelling up in a surge over pink, pulsing flesh. I ignored the woman's terror, the leeching paralysis of flashbacks that reached through even the indifference of magic to echo people I loved screaming and begging when I was too far away to help. Instead, I reversed the sending spell, aimed it back, and gave the tall one a nudge with her own magic.

5

The cool disdain of my power was a gift from the saints, shielding me from the past and the regrets that would no doubt haunt me in the morning. The witch mocked me with "Is that all you—" and stepped back to regain her balance. Her ankle hit the rift I'd opened, though, and her eyes widened. Her arms windmilled, the book falling to the ground with a thud, and she tumbled backward into darkness. She disappeared without a sound into what I knew from personal experience was a particularly cold hell.

The one at the table squared off as her colleague's disappearance unbalanced the spell they'd built. A skilled or powerful witch could have recovered from the disruption of the magic, but this one was neither—and had already succumbed to demon madness, by the red circles around her irises.

It didn't take much to shove her after the first witch, knife still clutched in her fist. I closed the rift behind them without bothering to look into it, and dusted my hands together to get rid of the last of their ugly magic. Technically I hadn't killed them. Technically the demons would.

It still left the human woman, gray-faced and losing blood, tied to the altar. I kicked through the salt circle that contained the rest of the dark spell, and waited until the bound magic dissipated to approach her. The septic reek of punctured bowel made me gag, and I struggled to hide my reaction from the girl's wide-eyed terror. My scarf, balled up and pressed against the wound, did little to slow the bleeding. Not for the first time, I wished I was half as good a healer as Rosa. I considered calling her, even glancing at my watch, but it was too early for her coven meeting to have ended. We met earlier in the night, at the memorial, but the coven was likely still busy chanting and arguing. It wasn't worth the risk of interrupting—with the kind of magic their coven threw around, distracting Rosa could destroy the whole neighborhood, if not half the city.

I pulled the gag away and the young woman, barely more than a teenager, sobbed for breath. "Help me."

"I'm trying to," I said. I'd already helped more than any sane witch would, but I tried to find sympathy through the lingering numbness of magic. "I'm calling the police. They can help you."

"My parents are going to kill me." A whispered confession, though the blood bubbling at the corner of her mouth hinted that something else might kill her first.

I kept pressure on the wound even as the dark alley fuzzed out, replaced by a battlefield in rural Kansas, and I fought to stay grounded in reality. The war ended years ago. It was the Truce. She was an innocent stranger; she wasn't one of my witches. She wasn't my friend. It wasn't Gina's blood on my hands.

Bile rose in my throat as I struggled with the double reality, the retreating magic taking whatever poise I might have patched together. Breathing through my nose helped but not enough as her heels scraped the splintered wood. Lightning flashed in the distance, or maybe just in my memory.

The expensive cell phone I dug out of her pocket made me shake my head; a rich girl like her could no doubt have afforded real magic, in a real hospital, without resorting to downmarket healing. Stupid of her to have tried saving a few dollars by going with the lowest bidder. I punched the number for paranormal emergencies, knowing she was too contaminated with dark magic to ride in a human ambulance. They'd refuse to take her and the delay meant death. My lips pursed as I studied her unfocused eyes, as I leaned and felt the whisper of breath against my cheek. There was no telling what they'd done to her before I intervened.

"Saints preserve you from your own stupidity," I said.

Rich or poor, everyone looked the same as they died: scared. Alone.

A disinterested voice said over the phone, "Bureau of

External Affairs. Is the nature of your emergency magical or involving a non-human?"

I used a touch of magic to disguise my voice, making it gruff like a stock Russian movie villain. "Couple of witches experimented on a human. They're gone but the kid needs help."

"State your name and the location of the incident."

"Ivan Darkwing," I said, glancing over my shoulder to search for that third witch as something scuffled the pavement. Nothing but shadows and a flickering streetlight in the distance, but it got my heart beating faster.

Ivan had been one of the more notorious witches during the war, claiming his family descended from firebirds and passed down ancient secrets from Zoroaster Himself. Ivan's infamy got him to the top of the humans' high-value target list, and the Chechen died dramatically in battle, in a blaze of magic and glory. Eight years later, he still hadn't risen. So those of us who remembered raised him from the ashes whenever we needed anonymity. I still hoped he would show up someday.

I cleared my throat, talking over the operator's disdainful snort. "The girl is in an alley off Cypress, three blocks south of Merrick. Magic and blood everywhere."

"Sending paramedics and a containment crew," the operator said, and the non-regional accent broke to reveal an exasperated New Yorker as she added, "You stay put, Darkwing. Provide a statement to officers when they arrive."

I hung up and wiped the phone off before returning it to the girl's pocket. Unlikely. I secured the scarf to her stomach with one of the straps binding her arms, and wiped my hands off on her shirt as best I could after drawing a protective rune on her forehead. As a nonaligned witch, if I were found at that scene, they'd arrest and convict me regardless of the evidence. A smart witch would have kept walking, but even a stupid witch wouldn't stick around for the cops.

Leaving her unconscious on the altar seemed unnecessarily

callous, though. No one should die alone, and if the sirens that rose in the distance were blocks away, she might not live to see help arrive.

I rubbed my hands together and braced for the comforting aloofness of strong magic, orders of magnitude more powerful and numbing than the stuff I'd stolen from the dark witches. Using more than the barest thread toed the edge of a dangerous precipice where more was always better. I'd been down that road before and barely survived. So I took a trickle rather than the beckoning sea and artlessly shoved it at her wound, hoping to stitch together enough of the damage so she survived for the paramedics. Sometimes all you needed was intent and enough juice to carry you through—spells and hexes were only window dressing.

Her eyes popped open and I jumped back. Her mouth flopped open like a stranded fish, gasping and choking. "Who are you?"

"No one," I said, still using Ivan's grumble as I backed up more, hoping the shadows would hide my face if her adrenaline-clouded memory did not. "The medics are on their way—can you hear? You'll be fine."

The hand I'd untied reached out, fingers trembling as she tried to catch my jacket. "Don't leave me. Please."

I chewed my lip, reality flickering around me as I struggled to breathe evenly. Another girl, another death, another plea: *don't leave me.* But in a basement, the last shelter we found as wards failed and boots kicked in a door upstairs. I turned away, pressed the heels of my hands to my eyes. Not real. Not real. *Breathe.*

"They're almost here. You'll be fine. Just concentrate on breathing." A message for the both of us, really.

The closer the sirens got, the faster my heart pounded. The more real the sensation of being hunted, being chased, being trapped became. Even guilt and shame as the strength left her arm and it flopped down, the blood staining her skin lost in the shadows, wasn't enough to unstick my feet. I should have comforted her.

"I'm Indira. Indira Modi." Her lips parted, red with lipstick or blood. "If I die, tell my parents I'm sorry."

"You'll be fine," I said. The dark witch's grimoire tripped me, and I crouched to pick it up without taking my eyes off her. A book like that couldn't end up in the open. Blue and red lights flashed near the mouth of the alley and I bolted.

I barely made it into the darkness of an adjacent alley before screeching tires and slamming doors filled the night. I didn't look back or celebrate the close call, panic rising in a tide from my stomach. Had to keep moving. The Externals would set up a perimeter and search for the perpetrators in ever-widening circles, maybe start a city-wide witch hunt if the girl had important parents.

The effort to remain at a purposeful walk probably took a few years off my life, but sprinting drew too much attention. Running from a crime scene meant immediate, absolute guilt. I shed my jacket, splattered with blood and demon magic, and shoved it into a dumpster once I'd made a few turns and gotten a little distance. I carried the book another several blocks before shoving it into a hidey hole I'd used for personal items when I had no home, and concealed it behind a rusty grate in a crumbling foundation.

A dog barked nearby but I didn't dare look back. It could have been a stray looking for scraps. Or it could have been an External or Alliance detective in animal form, on the hunt and following my scent. I dropped any hint of magic I held and wished for rain to clear the last of the blood off my hands. I couldn't swallow a knot of panic and adrenaline, shoving my hands into my pockets to still their shaking as I hunched my shoulders against the wind.

A few drops of rain plunked onto my forehead and the dark

night closed in around me, rumbles of thunder competing with rumbling memories. I clenched my teeth. It was the Truce. The war ended. We moved on.

A calming mantra Joanne taught me took the edge off as I started jogging, fleeing the cops and the memories alike, and I asked the saints for protection as the rain fell in sheets.

No good deed went unpunished.

# CHAPTER 2

*B*y the time I made it to Moriah's favorite bar, shifters and a few daredevil humans packed the Pug. Bass reverberated from the live band, audible from the street and teeth-shaking once inside, and only the shrilling guitar competed with the falsetto of the lead singer. My thumb gouged my palm, though the nail was so gnawed down it didn't distract me from the jostling bodies, flashing lights, and shouting partiers as I'd hoped. Focus. Had to focus. A handful of witches blended in; I studiously avoided looking at any of them, not wanting to risk a conversation.

I maneuvered around the crowd to see where Mo and her pack occupied the corner booths and high-top tables. She called out, wearing a birthday crown and already three sheets to the wind, but I pointed at the bathroom and she waved me on. I concentrated on the door to the ladies' room, trying to control my breathing. Memories crashed down on me with each punch of the bass, every elbow digging into my ribs. Strobe lights flashed like tracers. Cigarette smoke mimicked clouds of gas, creeping through a house.

I locked the door behind me and braced my hands on the

counter, ducking my head so I didn't have to see myself in the mirror. The mantra Joanne taught me in the fifth year of war promised stability as I whispered it over and over, fighting my racing heart and the headache beating behind my eyes. The coldness of witch magic might give me enough space from the memories to take a good breath, to calm down. To remember, or forget.

I shook my head, staring at the crumpled paper towels on the floor by my muddy boots. Magic could buy me calm but the price would be too high. Slippery slope, using magic as a coping mechanism. That was how I ended up spell-drunk and alone in an alley, unable to tell what day it was, only a few years earlier. The climb out of that hell was not something I had the strength to repeat.

It might have been an hour before splotches no longer obscured my vision, before my hands stopped shaking so violently I couldn't grip the chipped laminate counter, or maybe just a few minutes. I splashed water on my face before scrubbing the blood from my hands and arms, where flecks of red would draw unwanted attention. My reflection shook her head, couldn't stop shaking it, as I thought of the blood and the dark witches and a jacket I'd tossed away but couldn't afford to replace. Saints blast it.

I got rid of all the blood I could see, but wouldn't be really clean until running a cleansing spell on myself and everything I wore. That done well could take hours, and I couldn't occupy the only women's bathroom in a packed bar for more than a couple minutes. Already someone pounded on the door and shouted to hurry up. I dried my face and hands, pulling my hair back to keep it out of my face in case I ended up having to fight or flee. I wouldn't go quietly if the cops came after me, and the last thing I needed was a miscast spell because I couldn't see.

I leaned close to the mirror to stare at my own eyes, despite the woman shouting to hurry my ass up, and pulled my eyelids down to check for hints of red. The irises remained blue, thank all the saints, and the only ring was the black one I got from my father's family. Just blue eyes, no hint of red. I swallowed hard, blinking rapidly as I turned away. Using their smutty magic shouldn't have been enough to cause demon madness, but there was no telling how that shit worked.

Of course, no one would be able to tell what my eyes looked like in the dim bar as I unlocked the door and the disgruntled shifter doing a pee dance almost ran right through me. Panic receded, though returning to the chaos of the dance floor challenged my control until I slid into the booth next to Moriah. At least half her pack added to the scrum in front of the stage. She handed me a trio of shot glasses, full of shimmery blue liquid, and shouted in my ear. "You have to catch up."

"Happy birthday," I said, toasting her with a shot in each hand, and downed them both so I might eventually forget the look on that poor girl's face as the knife slid into her stomach. Alcohol could be just as numbing as magic, if you drank enough of it.

"Tell me something, Lil," she said, leaning close so her shrewd brown eyes could really see mine. The hunting look, we called it. Maybe she could tell if red tainted my eyes.

"What?" I gulped the third shot and shuddered. Downing that much alcohol on an empty stomach wasn't the first bad choice I'd made that day, and it wouldn't be the last.

Mo tossed her blonde braid over her shoulder, glancing around to see who might overhear before she went on. "Tell me why you smell like blood that isn't yours."

My heart sank. Even in human form, shifters had better than average senses of smell, and of course the bathroom soap was unscented to accommodate sensitive sniffers. I rubbed my mouth, looking across the bar instead of at her. Just in case. "How noticeable is it?"

"Not very. Only reason I noticed is because I know what you

should smell like. Everyone else will probably assume you're on the rag."

Ugh. The unfortunate, no-privacy reality of hanging out with wolves. You couldn't use PMS as an excuse for anything. I made a face, leaning to pillage a basket of cheese-covered something across the table. "Ran into a mess on the way here and tried to clean it up. Nothing to worry about."

She nodded, waving to someone on the dance floor before elbowing me. "But tell me before it gets to the worry-about level, got it? It doesn't do you any good to be a friend of my pack unless we know when you're in trouble."

"Oh, you'll know." Half the city would know, most likely, when I burned down the other half to cover my escape. I tried to laugh, not wanting her to see whatever remained of the memories from standing in the alley, blood oozing between my fingers, holding death back from someone I barely knew. Mo had seen me at my worst, through the ugliness of detox and recovery, so no wonder she wanted to intervene. It wasn't pretty when a war witch hit rock bottom and kept right on going. I pulled a small bag out of my pocket. "Anyway. Happy birthday. It's not much, but it should be useful."

She grinned. "I'd say you shouldn't have, but it's my birthday, by Hati, and I like presents," and she shook a delicate chain out of the pouch and onto her palm. She sniffed it carefully before touching it to a gift I'd given her years ago, an unremarkable watch with a linked band. She held the chain up, studying it in the pulsing strobe lights. "It's pretty, but I know it's not just a necklace."

I touched the watch band and sparks skittered across the table. "That detects active magic," I said, and it was bad news for me, since the sparks meant some of the demon shit still clung to me. "Stuff that's trying to do something to you. This," and I ran my fingers over the chain until it glowed a soft yellow and warmed to the touch. "Is something I've been working on to show passive magic—stuff that can ride along undetected until a specific time or event. I think I got the bugs worked out."

She paused with the chain halfway over her head, eyebrow arched. "You think, or you know?"

I laughed. "I know. I'm sure."

"I'm serious, Lil," she said, half a laugh and half warning. "I don't need some experimental charm of yours catching fire around my neck. Again."

I held up my hands in surrender. "I promise." But I choked down a giggle I could mostly attribute to the liquor, sitting like a warm rock in my stomach. "Really, it's good. I tested it. Just don't tell anyone what it does."

"Why not?" Mo draped it around her neck, frowning down into her cleavage as she fussed with where the charm would lie. "Seems like a really useful thing to have—Soren would pay good money for something like this."

"I know." It came out grimmer than I meant, by the look on her face, and to cover it I reached for a pitcher of margaritas a waitress dropped off. "As far as I know, none of the cops have something like that. Which is how it should stay."

"Or...?"

"Or we wouldn't be able to use passive glamours anymore," I said, rubbing my shoulder as it tingled, an old wound that ached when powerful magic approached. Far in the west, maybe the Slough, a coven raised a shitstorm of power. I tapped the table in front of Mo, trying to ignore the anticipation of that much magic—like the lead-up to a sneeze that never arrived but continued to intensify. "And not being able to use disguises would be bad news for us."

"Well, only those of us who hide our faces," she said, then took the sting out of it by winking. "But I get it, for someone who runs around smelling like someone else's blood."

"Totally not my fault," I muttered, and elbowed her for good measure. "I did a good deed. That's all."

Mo laughed as some of her wolves returned, carrying trays of shot glasses, and everyone stood to take a few, shouting toasts to the birthday girl. The wolves included me, more from obligation than because they liked me, and wolves took obligations very seriously. Long ago I tried to make up for a betrayal by other witches, and though I couldn't save their brother, Mo and her pack still felt they owed me blood debt. It was an uncomfortable burden to bear, particularly since there were some days I wondered if Mo truly considered me a friend, or if I was just another task she had to track and occasionally check up on.

I gulped a shot, reached for another. Maybe it didn't really matter. I'd saved her life a couple of times, helped her sister, stood vigil over her dead brother, and in return she pulled me out of an abyss after the Truce. It was a fair trade, as far as I was concerned. Witches did not like to leave debts unresolved, though the wolves maintained blood debts for years, sometimes decades.

The magic continued building, far away, and I focused on my watch, the numbers swimming under some of that shiny blue liquid. Closing in on the witching hour. One of Mo's wolves used me for a kickstand, giggling about a *ridiculously* good-looking feline shifter near the door who she wasn't supposed to like but no one said interspecies dating wasn't allowed. I started to look over my shoulder, needing a distraction from the building pressure and hoping the lion would do the trick, but she grabbed my face, shrieking, "He'll see you!" and collapsed into a chair, midway between laughing and howling.

I handed her a few more shots, said something trite about nothing ventured, nothing gained. My encouragement was enough, or maybe it was the liquid courage, because the girl announced she fully intended to make out with a cat and marched herself over to a startled young lion shifter with gold eyes and smooth olive skin. I banished the earlier panic, watching her both uninhibited and awkward attempts to flirt, and tried to forget about everything else in the world except Mo's party. Even if the coven met on the other side of the city, it wasn't my business. Even if they raised an obscene amount of magic on an inauspicious night in the middle of a storm. I wasn't the War Witch. Not anymore.

Drinking with shifters beat standing in a circle, chanting. Outside in the cold and rain, with the reek of bitter herbs in the air, the taste of one of Rosa's foul brews on my teeth. Waiting for everyone to catch up to magic I did without thinking. Constantly having to explain and help and teach.

Much better to be with the shifters. They at least believed in celebrating the here and now, regardless of what lay ahead. The witches were too busy mourning the past to enjoy the present.

I tossed back a drink as the room spun. The coven would cast their spell at midnight, and the consequences belonged to them. They weren't mine anymore; their mistakes weren't mine either. I had enough of my own bad choices to account for. I couldn't keep making up for theirs, too.

\* \* \*

THE LAUGHTER GREW MORE raucous and the jokes more raunchy as the drinks flowed. I concentrated on the wolves as the magic sweltered and seethed out of range, like a flash of light in my peripheral vision. The arrival of Mo's little sister, Mimi, was almost enough to distract me from surges of uncertainty any time another witch circled too close to our table. None talked to me, thank the saints, probably because I didn't wear a ring to identify myself as a witch and avoided eye contact. If they were smart, they wouldn't bother a witch who didn't want to be bothered. And if they recognized me... well. They had other reasons to avoid me.

Mimi, bright-eyed as always and wearing ankle-breaking high heels, slung herself into my lap and put me in an affectionate headlock. "Aunt Leelee!"

Surviving Mimi's drunken attention gave me an excuse to ignore the chill racing down my spine as the door opened across the bar, and stayed open as a group of men shoved through. I started untangling myself from Mimi, thinking to avoid whatever trouble arrived that late at night, but by then the group cut through the dance floor and I saw Mick, Mo's younger brother and alpha.

The wolves all bowed their heads or nodded as their pack leader approached, shoving over to make room so he could sit at the main booth, the other men dispersing through the bar. Mick winked at his sister, about to tease her, but caught sight of me first, his expression changing.

During the war, Mo was the strongest leader after Martin's death, and we all knew it. But the wolves weren't ready for feminism then. They still weren't. And Mick knew what I thought about that, knew as well that I'd helped his brother when he couldn't. He managed to be friendly most of the time, but there was always an undercurrent that I reminded him of a shameful failure, of misbegotten gains. Mo would never tell her brother he didn't deserve to be alpha, but something made me think Mick waited for me to say it instead.

Mick recovered quickly and managed to insult Mo about her age while nodding to me. I hid behind Mimi, although that only lasted until the band played her favorite song and she launched off my lap to the dance floor. Mo goaded her brother into catching up, and more trays of alcohol and every type of fried or cheese-covered bar food arrived in minutes. Mick's pack was close to Soren, leader of the Alliance, so Others curried favor with the Stone Hills pack, thinking it would get them in with the Peacemaker.

I mulled over how things sorted themselves out, and sought

answers in the bottom of a shot glass. Even the alcohol couldn't dull the rolling thunderheads of magic from the west. Too much, on the verge of uncontrolled and uncontrollable, and Anne Marie usually too proud to recognize it. I reached for my phone. Maybe if I interrupted them, the power would disperse before the entire city burned. I didn't have the courage or the focus to ward the entire bar.

I listed into Mo as I dialed Tracy's number, saying, "There's going to be trouble tonight," as I tried to find the right words to warn Tracy before Anne Marie got them all killed.

She looked a lot more sober. Mo got her hunting look again, "Trouble?" but before I could explain, the door to the bar boomed open.

Mimi crowed, "Leif!" and flung her arms around a tall man's neck as he edged through the crowd.

The entire bar hiccuped and looked, and Leif, Chief Investigator for the Alliance as well as its second-in-command, patted Mimi on the back and shooed her back to the dance floor as he scanned the bar. My heart jumped to my throat. The grim wolf did not look like he wanted to be in a bar; his demeanor screamed official business. The human cops weren't suicidal enough to try storming the Pug, but maybe they tracked me from the alley and sent Leif to bring me out. My hands knotted into fists under the table. He was the last person I wanted to hurt, but I would. I drew a deep breath and ignored Moriah jostling me as she demanded, "What trouble?"

Instead I planned the hexes to use, where to shield and where to cast. He would have a team outside. More out back. Humans and shifters and witches, all prepared for battle. Maybe using pre-set wards. Sound faded, distorted, and my mouth dried out as I focused on Leif with soda-straw precision. The door, and freedom, was a long, long way away.

# CHAPTER 3

$\mathcal{B}$ ut before I could do more than blink the alcohol blur from my vision, Leif smiled. He cut through the crowd like an Arctic icebreaker until he loomed over the booth. "Well, I'll be damned. You're turning twenty-nine for the sixth time."

"My birthday," Moriah said, half standing to hug him over me. "My rules."

The room spun as I held my breath and concentrated on the empty glasses in front of me. Leif reversed a chair next to the table and straddled it, disconcertingly close. He spoke to Mick first, a brief "How's business?" before addressing the lower-ranked wolves, all of whom offered him food and drinks. My heart pounded as he handed Mo a small box, shouting over the music, "I heard you needed a new collar," with a grin before he glanced at me.

His eyebrows drew together a touch, as if trying to place me, but no recognition immediately dawned. Or at least not the kind of recognition that would put me in handcuffs and on a short path to the executioner's stake. He said, "How's it going?" before Mo held up his gift—a beautiful pair of white gold dog tags covered in the angular script I associated with the Old North—and almost knocked me over in her enthusiasm to hug him. "You're a total jackass, but they're beautiful."

Leif smiled, giving her a one-armed hug as he caught my shoulder and kept me from being shoved to the floor.

Mo flashed her gift around to the rest of the pack, distracted by the shiny metal and intricate letters, and Leif leaned closer to say, "Sorry, I should have known that would get a reaction."

I tried to smile, about to tell him it wasn't a problem even as the alcohol and a decade of memories told me to say I loved him instead, when the stretched rubber band of magic in the west thrummed. I had a heartbeat to sit up, staring past his shoulder to the origin, waiting. Saints preserve them.

Held my breath as it stretched to the limit. Vibrated and held. Saints protect them. Then—

Snapped.

Recoiled in a violent surge, spiraling up and out and hungry, out of control, desperate—

The backlash succeeded where Mo failed, yanking me out of the booth, almost into Leif's lap. He caught my side to steady me, frown deepening, but I could only stare toward the Slough as the magic punched into my chest. Stole my breath. Stole the memory of breath, sucked the air out of the room, dried my eyes and replaced them with fire.

The other witches in the bar stumbled, collided with others, flailed around to find solid ground as all of that power sought a place to go, tried to rebalance the world. Even some of the shifters, particularly the ones allergic to witch magic, rubbed their ears or sneezed. I sucked in air, hands shaking, and thanked all the saints I'd been seated.

I gripped the table, trying to center myself as Mo made up excuses about how I couldn't handle my liquor to divert the attention of her curious packmates. I'd almost gotten myself together when a second wave of magic, more subtle than the first, rolled through the city. It carried the backwash from the first spell's breaking, a tidal wave of distorted power, and I shuddered at the greasy, clingy nature of it. The hint of sulfur in its wake. Dark magic. Maybe demon magic. Not unlike the magic I'd encountered earlier, but performed by more power-ful, more organized witches. A full coven, not two half-trained bashers.

My stomach lurched and for a second I feared I would deposit everything I'd drunk on Leif's dark jeans and perfectly fitted sports coat, but I white-knuckled the table and tried to think of anything but magic. It couldn't be the coven. Even Anne Marie wouldn't bring magic that stank of demons into her circle, no matter how desperate she was for power. I'd taught her better than that.

But if it wasn't them, that meant a very dangerous, very powerful coven had appeared from outside the city and could spark a conflict with Anne Marie, who hated sharing anything. Especially power.

Leif leaned closer, keeping me upright with a gentle hand on my elbow. "You okay?"

I fully intended to nod, make a trip to the ladies' room and excuse myself for the night. I studied his face as I fought the disorientation of ugly magic. The years had been kind to him. The newspapers always printed pictures of him, mostly as the scowling man literally at Soren's right hand, but sometimes because of what he did as top cop for the Alliance. The smudged ink never did him justice, and neither did my memory of late-night talks around smoky campfires. And it was the memories that had me shake my head in the negative, staring into his gray eyes and fighting back envy over the long blond lashes. Lucky bastard.

Half his mouth quirked up and he started to stand, almost shouting so Mo could hear over the pounding music. "Your girl isn't feeling well. We're going out for some air."

As he helped me up, Mo lurched forward and grabbed his wrist, yanking him off balance and pointing a perfectly-manicured finger in his face. It was an unacceptably aggressive move for a lower-ranked wolf, even while drunk, but her expression was stone sober. Not even a syllable slurred as she said, "She's my friend, Leif. I owe her blood debt. You better behave."

I blinked, glad Leif looked as surprised as I felt. He carefully freed himself, not seeming to notice Mick's efforts to intervene, and said, "A friend of yours is a friend of mine, Moriah. We'll be right back."

Her pointing finger didn't waver as she studied him, mouth compressed in a thin, disapproving line. Whatever she saw had her nod and fall back into the booth, snapping at Mick as he growled about insulting Leif's integrity. Thank all the saints the music swallowed Moriah's reply as I concentrated on walking a straight line to the door, rather impressed with how easily I managed it. Maybe I wasn't so drunk after all. Maybe it was just the shitty magic that made me feel off.

And then Leif caught my waist as I veered toward a post. "Whoa there, ace. Slow it down."

I concentrated on staying upright as we squeezed past the bouncer and plunged into the cold night air. A few hard-eyed men loitered outside the bar with degrees of unconcern, dispersing as they saw Leif. He made a few quick hand signs, too blurred by darkness and booze for me to decipher, and released my arm once we were on a flat stretch of sidewalk, though he stayed close enough to catch me if I fell. I wondered if it was just an excuse to get me outside, away from the crowd, so he could arrest me quietly. Keep Moriah from intervening, maybe starting a blood feud.

But when I stayed upright enough to search for the rest of his arrest team, Leif backed up a few steps, watching me with a critical eye as he took a thin cigar from a silver case in his coat pocket. I tilted my face skyward and let the clean air and cold quiet of the night roll over me, broken only by the thrum of bass inside the bar and a soft radio squawk, flavored with the scent of cigar smoke. The rain had stopped, which was too bad —it may have tamped down some of the nauseating magic, though a fierce wind did a fair job of moving the stench along. Except for the cloying sludge that clung to the back of my throat.

I searched the shadows around the bar, the alleys and streets stretching to nowhere, and wondered where the security team had disappeared. I shivered, more from fear than cold, although the wind cut through me and my jacket was in a dumpster too far away to do any good.

Leif drew on the cigar, watching me without expression. "Want someone to bring your coat?"

"It's at home," I said, trying to enunciate so he wouldn't realize I could barely feel my face. I almost expected a lecture— Leif never forgot his coat. He was responsible and sensible and appropriately dressed for the weather. Always. I hugged myself, turning slowly to look back at the door of the bar. Maybe Mo would storm out.

"Here," he said, and I turned, wobbling as my feet didn't move as fast as the rest of me. He steadied me, still holding out his wool overcoat.

I didn't take it. "I'll be fine, I don't expect—"

"It's what gentlemen do," he said, tossing the coat around my shoulders.

I laughed hard enough to slip, though it wasn't a happy sound. With my arms bundled up in the coat, I couldn't recover as my feet refused to cooperate. Leif jumped forward to catch me but we both toppled into a scraggly shrub next to the sidewalk. I frowned up at the stars as the heavens spun. Once upon a time, my dad and I rearranged the stars in the sky with magic, a good game until Mother found out. "All the gentlemen died in the war."

"No," Leif said, getting to his feet and dusting himself off before leaning to lift me to my feet. "There are a few of us left."

I was almost certain I heard laughter from the shadows, although it silenced when Leif's frown turned fierce. I picked his coat up from the crusty snow and dead leaves on the sidewalk, my cheeks heating. "Sorry, I'll—"

"Don't worry about it." He recovered the cigar from where it fell, putting the coat once more over my shoulders after retrieving a lighter from the pocket.

I tucked my hands in the pockets to enjoy the extra warmth of shifter body heat, like being wrapped up in a furnace, and studied his profile as he replaced the lighter. Blond hair covered his head, though his beard grew in auburn. The first time I met him, he had a full beard and a shaved head, a disconcerting combination when paint obscured the rest of his face. He came from a long line of Vikings, a family known for berserkers—the kind known as *ulfhednar*, "wolf-shirts." He and his fighters painted the skin around their eyes dark with a paste of oil and wax and soot, until it made their golden wolf eyes glow like the pits of hell. After years of war, he didn't need the paint to look terrifying. They still used it sometimes for ceremonies, though it made the humans nervous.

He glanced at me after a few heartbeats of awkward silence. "I remember you, you know."

"Oh?" was the only response I could conjure, the rest of my energy going into staying upright as the sidewalk tilted. Should have eaten more. Definitely.

"Yes. Lilith. It's been a while."

"I go by Lily now," I said, trying to keep the memories at bay. I'd been in a very bad place the last time we parted company, angry at the shifters and hating the deal they proposed with the humans. Feeling powerless to change the inevitable after Soren negotiated a deal with the humans that placed all the power in

28

him, left the witches to swear fealty or fend for ourselves. "Five years, I think. Since the Truce."

He made a face, the visceral reaction to an agreement most Others viewed as necessary but still a bad deal. A first step, a very small step, toward equality with the humans. After a moment to hate the Truce, he shoved his hands into his pockets and faced me. "I wondered what happened to you."

My heart stuttered, and I cleared my throat to buy time. "Why?"

He smiled, though he glanced once more at the dark street. A few bums loitered across the street, no doubt waiting to beg money and food from the inebriated shifters as they left the bar at last call. "The witches who survived joined the Alliance or left the country. Except you. You went underground but stayed in the area. We wondered about your loyalties."

The hope lifting my heart only gave it farther to fall—he'd wondered about a possible traitor, not a friend or anything more. I lifted my hands in an exaggerated shrug meant to show my ringless fingers, moving slowly since I didn't fancy dying in a hail of bullets because his security team thought I got aggressive. "Nonaligned."

"I know. Mo told us." He studied the coal on the end of his cigar. "War witches who can work with the packs are about as common as unicorns, we've found. There were times we needed you, the last couple of years. But I'm not surprised you stayed nonaligned."

I caught my breath to ask, wondering at how badly Anne Marie served if Leif wanted my insubordination over her obedience, but a flash of light froze the words in my throat. A dark car with red and blue lights in the grill rolled up. As it parked in front of us, a pair of Leif's security detail manifested out of the shadows right next to me. I resisted the urge to hide behind the burly shifters as two humans got out of the car, flashing badges. I swallowed hard. So this was how it ended.

I should have burned the jacket.

My hands balled into fists in the pockets of Leif's coat, and though I didn't reach for magic, it waited in a serene pool of blue destruction at the edge of my awareness—not unlike the alcohol burbling in my stomach as adrenaline and fear spun up. I definitely should have stopped drinking after the margaritas.

* * *

ONE OF THE HUMANS, tall and skinny despite a bulky trench coat, stepped close enough to shake Leif's hand, while his partner, shorter and rounder and almost jolly, leaned against the car. The skinny one glanced around as he shook Leif's hand, nodding to the two members of the security detail near me. "The front office said we would find you here. I hope we're not interrupting?"

Leif nodded to the fat human before shoving his hands into his pockets once more. "No interruption, Stefan, particularly if it's important enough to come to this part of town. What are we looking at?"

The skinny one studied me for a long moment, glancing at the bulky bracelet on his wrist before handing Leif a manila folder. "An incident about a mile from here. Someone calling themselves Ivan Darkwing phoned it in."

My palms went slick and my vision, wobbly though it was, focused on the skinny cop's wrist and the glowing alert bracelet. The liquor and bar food curdled in my stomach, along with regret, and I shuffled a little farther behind Leif. If my magic remained passive, they might not pick up on the dark witches' corrupted magic. For the human's bracelet to react, there had to be something stuck to me from Anne Marie's aborted spell or the earlier incident in the alley. Neither one would read well on any of the tests the humans used.

Leif ushered me behind him with one arm as he studied the contents of the envelope. "Good old Ivan. Seems he was a bit of a phoenix after all."

Stefan made an unimpressed noise. "Well, he left a hell of a mess this time. Might be dark magic."

Leif's posture tensed, the grim focus in his voice at odds with the booming music behind us and the cigar forgotten in his hand. "Dark magic. Why do you think that?"

"Witches strapped a human kid to a table and used her for sacrifice. Blood and magic everywhere."

"Sounds more like inexperienced healing to me." Leif frowned as he flipped through the contents of the folder. "Looks that way, too."

"Before she lost consciousness, the victim managed to say she paid for breast augmentation. There were cuts to her stomach, wrists, and thighs. Nothing near the chest."

The pudgy human watched me with a curious intensity as Leif and Stefan discussed the details of the girl's wounds, and it took every iota of courage in me to remain unmoving. The fastest way out of the city meant stealing a car. The buses all had cameras. Maybe the Externals knew they looked for me, and Stefan only delayed Leif long enough to get the quick reaction arrest teams into place. Maybe Leif played along, got me out of the bar and distracted so I wouldn't see it coming. I swallowed a knot in my throat.

Leif rubbed his jaw, stubble rasping against his palm. "The victim?"

"Seventeen. She managed to tell the first responders her name, but not much else. She's in surgery now, they're not sure when she'll wake up. If she'll wake up."

*Indira Modi*, I repeated silently to myself as I pictured the girl's face, but stopped before I could decide if her waking or not waking would be better for me. Intent mattered as much as power, with magic. Sometimes it mattered more. Hoping the girl never woke to give my description to the cops meant I might as well have put a knife in her. I said a prayer for myself to the saints instead—they could find me worthy, or wanting.

Leif shook his head. "This doesn't smell right. Witches tormented this kid damn near in public, in an Alliance neighborhood, and left enough evidence at the scene to actually support an investigation? I don't buy it."

Stefan shrugged, glancing back at the empty street. Even the bums had disappeared. "Dark witches, right? Nothing they do makes sense."

"But sloppy dark witches don't live long enough to do what these pictures show. They've been practicing for a couple of years, at least, and this tracks with the last few unexplained disappearances. Except this time they left evidence." Paper rustled as he fussed with the folder. "I'll check with the covens. One of them may have discovered it and decided to handle things. The witches have their own ... justice."

"Maybe don't alert the witches just yet," Stefan said, running a hand through his mousy brown hair. "Except the one behind you, of course. We want to run a joint investigation on this one, regardless of whatever extrajudicial efforts the Alliance may pursue."

The urge to vomit returned as the cop's attention landed on me with an indecipherable smile.

Leif didn't react, though the two security guards closed ranks until they were close enough to protect me, too. Or arrest me. But the Alliance's Chief Investigator only said, "Did the victim provide descriptions?"

"We have some details to work with."

The pudgy one piped up for the first time, straightening from his lean against the car. "But they're tracing where she met the perps, and when she wakes up, she'll give us more detail. Descriptions, timeline. We'll get them."

Leif grunted, then gestured at a patch of darkness as he

held out the manila folder. I jumped as a third shifter materialized and took the folder. Leif glanced at the man and said, "Call Nate, get him over to the scene. Send one of the witches, Andre if you can find him, before any evidence is destroyed."

The man disappeared so silently I didn't hear him move despite watching him jog off. Leif frowned as he addressed the human cops once more. "The victim's statement won't be any good after the anesthesia wears off. Too much time has already passed. She's not a reliable witness as it is, but the longer it takes for one of my people to interview her, the less credible her testimony. Get the doctors to wake her up."

"They're still trying to save her life." Stefan rubbed his charmed bracelet, watching me once more. "None of the witches at the hospital would touch her. Said she was contaminated with demon magic."

My knees wobbled and I reached out to steady myself on Leif's shoulder. Saints preserve me if any of those witches recognized my magic from trying to keep the girl alive. They could use my magic for identification, place me at the scene with the victim as sure as if they'd witnessed the whole thing.

Leif caught me, expression unreadable as he reached once more into the pocket of my borrowed coat to fish for the lighter. I concentrated on breathing, on not letting the panic bubble up higher, on keeping my magic back enough that Stefan's bracelet would never register it. Sometimes those charms recorded magical signatures like fingerprints.

And then the External spoke in a carefully disinterested voice. "It looks like your witch is not wearing a ring to identify herself."

My heart stuttered, and I resisted the urge to stuff my hands into the coat pockets again, not only because the humans would call it aggressive, but because Leif still searched the pocket himself. He drew out the lighter and focused on puffing

33

the cigar to life. I wasn't sure whether to hide behind him or make a run for it.

The Chief Investigator let the cop's subtle accusation hang in the air along with the cigar smoke, then carefully replaced the lighter. "Come now, Stefan. In this neighborhood, in this bar—that's not really a crime."

"Perhaps." Stefan's thin lips compressed, almost disappeared entirely. "And as a professional courtesy of course I won't write her a ticket—but it does raise questions about how many witches are not wearing their rings in this neighborhood. Perhaps the dark witches I'm looking for are hiding right inside that bar."

Leif smiled, a bit of an edge starting to show. "You're welcome to go in and check, of course. Although I can't guarantee your safety if you do so."

Stefan considered it for a moment, staring at the door as if waiting for the dark witches to trot out voluntarily in collars and chains. I gave him credit for even considering walking into the Pug. He might get a dozen steps into the bar, but he'd never make it back out. His reputation preceded him. The Bureau of External Affairs was not known for its even-handedness, and every Other in that bar had suffered at their hands at one point.

The External's attention landed once more on me. "Very well. We'll just test this one for dark magic, make sure she isn't going to carry tales to any of her covenmates. We don't want the perpetrators to get a head start, do we?"

I rocked back on my heels and my hands fell to my sides. I didn't intend to but that didn't matter as the Externals barked warnings and Stefan reached for something in his pocket. Leif pivoted before I registered what the cops meant, and put his back to the Externals as he gripped my shoulders. He walked me back several steps, the entire security team forming a half-circle between us and the humans.

Leif's blue eyes held sparks of gold, and the shadows across his face made his expression fierce, all angles and fury. My skin prickled as Warrior Leif confronted me, and I shrank away. His voice cracked like ice breaking on ice. "Are you out of your Skoll-blasted mind?"

"I didn't do anything," I whispered. A small lie. "I can't feel my feet. I lost my balance."

Behind him, Stefan smiled, a specialty taser aimed at me. My eyes narrowed, alcohol stealing what remained of my good sense. He mocked me. Thought me funny. Thought he could even slow me down with that ridiculous child's toy. Magic seethed and beckoned, just at the end of my reach, as the War Witch edged out of the past.

Leif squeezed my shoulders, his red pack magic flaring up and calling to my witch magic—reacting, no doubt, to my fear and the human threat, and driven by the protective urge of a leader. "You will get yourself killed, witch."

My teeth chattered but not entirely from the cold—anticipation and tension gathered in my stomach, the magic beckoning. I could solve all my problems in a flash of blue, and thank all the saints, I wouldn't even feel badly while I did it. I stared at the humans; Stefan would have to go first, the pudgy one would be slow enough I could leave him for second. Words hushed past my lips, unbidden. "They called me a dark witch."

"No," Leif said, and his scowl grew. "They implied it, hoping you would give them a reason to arrest you."

"I didn't—"

"Don't move a damn muscle." He released my shoulders and the fiery tingle of pack magic faded. He sent a dark look at his security team, so I had no doubt they would prevent me from getting Leif, or myself, killed. The Chief Investigator cracked the vertebrae in his neck as he faced the Externals. "Come on, Stefan. You know better than that."

"A simple request," the cop said. He lowered the taser to his side, though he didn't put it away. "And a ringless witch is required to comply, particularly in the vicinity of dangerous or unexplained magic."

"She's drunk." Leif sounded bored and dismissive, and heat flushed my cheeks. "And alcohol makes people stupid. So why don't you go meet Nate at the scene and he can start going through the evidence?"

The tall External's head tilted as he studied first Leif, then me, and then he smiled, putting the taser away. "Very well. As a professional courtesy. But I want a list of every witch in that bar, and this one's name at the top. So we can clear them from the egregious crimes committed tonight. Agreed?"

Leif's teeth ground loudly enough to make me shiver, but his tone remained so calm I wouldn't have known anything about the night bothered him. I envied his self-control. "Joint investigation, Stefan, per usual. Call my office tomorrow and we'll make arrangements."

He didn't move as Stefan returned to the car, where the pudgy External watched me with fierce concentration on his nondescript face. Something was wrong with him, as if he used a cheap glamour to disguise his face and body, and no human cop would do such a thing. The edges of his shape blurred, shrank, when I squinted. The short cop grinned, winking at me as he ducked into the car, and I swallowed unease as they pulled away.

Leif turned, gesturing for me to precede him into the bar as the security detail closed ranks behind him, and he flicked ash off his cigar. "Just had to get aggressive, didn't you?"

"A real gentleman would have been quicker to defend my honor so I didn't *have* to," I said, not looking back as I shoved the door open and almost clobbered the unsuspecting bouncer.

Leif snorted, as close to a laugh as I'd ever heard him. "Well, I'm a little out of practice."

I stumbled on my shoes or numb feet, and flushed from my toes to my hairline as he caught my waist again. "Easy, ace."

I shrugged out of his coat as I made a beeline back to Mo's table, trying not to notice my friend's raised eyebrows and pointed look. Leif either didn't notice or didn't care, retrieving his coat as he held a phone to his ear and disappeared toward the back door.

Mo lined up shots in front of me after I collapsed in the booth. "You look like someone just walked over your grave."

I made a face and pushed all but one of the drinks away. I'd passed my limit if attacking two human cops in front of the Chief Investigator seemed like a good idea. Getting totally hammered wouldn't be a good enough defense when the Externals kicked in my front door to arrest me when I got home.

Mick tapped the table in front of me, expression difficult to decipher as he canted his head at the door. "Trouble?"

A basket of fries seemed a good chaser for the shot, and I waved a handful of the greasy mess in the general direction of the door. "Externals outside, looking for trouble. Called me a dark witch."

His expression turned grim. "I'll register a complaint."

Mo leaned into me, eyes bright. "Then I guess you're coming home with me, tutz. So drink up," and she returned the shot glasses.

"It's not worth the extra attention," I half-shouted at Mick as a ruckus rose behind us. I didn't know if he'd heard as Mimi collapsed in my lap, and I drew breath to repeat myself, to beg him not to raise me any higher on the Externals' radar.

Before I could even lean forward, most of the pack crowded around the table, carrying a birthday cake covered in what looked like road flares. The band cut off and the entire bar started bellowing "Happy Birthday." I leaned back, trying to breathe. Saints protect and keep us. I said a prayer for Mo, three for the coven, and a couple for myself as well.

# CHAPTER 4

$\mathcal{B}$y last call I could barely see, and the earlier panic faded as no one tried to arrest me and the sticky magic from midnight dissipated like a bad dream. Birthday cake covered most of Moriah as she slid under the table, and even Mick had trouble keeping his head up. Leif rejoined the party eventually, but remained diligent about answering his phone. Some things never changed.

He checked up on the investigation but never said anything useful despite how much I eavesdropped. Accusation never crossed his expression on the two times he talked to me, so I had no idea whether Stefan pushed for more information or waited in the dark to arrest me. The memory of his hands at my waist, and the look in his eyes when he said he remembered me, kept me warm even after they propped the doors open at last call.

My watch read either three or four a.m., depending on how I squinted, and both were far too close to the devil's hour and when my alarm would go off for work. I didn't want to leave the warmth and comfort of the pack, particularly with wind and unknown magic howling outside, but they'd stay until the sun rose.

Moriah started singing show tunes, one arm waving from under the table. A few more drinks and the wrong word, and she would either pick a fight or burst into tears—neither of which was a good way to end her birthday.

Leif, perched on the same chair next to the booth where he'd started the night, leaned closer to speak to me. "You should stay with Mo for a while. Stefan will be looking for a chance to detain you, but he won't be brave enough to do it when you're with wolves." He glanced at one of his guys, waiting by the front door, and waved him over. Leif dropped a stack of cash on the table, ignoring Mick's drunken pleas that he wouldn't allow the Chief Investigator to pay, and instead Leif tilted his head at the exit. "We'll be driving past Mo's place. I can give you both a ride."

The world wobbled; no matter how much greasy food I ate, I couldn't shake the drunken blur from earlier. I gripped the table, weighing the risk of being around Leif against the possibility of that creepy External popping out of the shadows at my apartment. "Thanks, but I think we'll—"

Mo hoisted herself from under the table and slung her arm around my neck, almost knocking me over for the third time that night. She waggled her eyebrows at Leif. "Sure, babe. Take us home."

"Sure," Leif said, bemused tolerance in the lines around his eyes as he stood. Mo gathered her presents and purse and coat and a handful of hot wings for the ride, shouting goodbyes to whoever was still conscious.

I got out of the way so Mo could stagger upright, though I kept my attention on Leif. "It's not any fun, is it?"

"What?" He offered me his coat, eyebrow raised.

"Being you." I held onto sobriety and seriousness with my

fingertips, though only the alcohol made me brave enough to speak. "It can't be much fun at all."

He took a deep breath before draping the coat over my shoulders, leaning in as he tugged it together near my throat. Close enough that I could have lurched forward in a drunken stumble and kissed him. For a heart-stopping eternity, I thought he might meet me in the middle. "What makes you think this is actually me?"

"Because I remember you too."

His smile went crooked, and not in a good way. He didn't reply as he half-lifted Mo from where she leaned against the booth, sliding slowly to the floor. "Let's go, rock star."

"It's my birthday!" she crowed, arms in the air, and Mimi jumped up to hug her again.

Which led to an impromptu round of unintelligible happy birthday singing, only some recognizable as English. Leif tolerated it for a moment, then had his security guy help Mo stagger to the door.

His car waited outside. I'd expected a limo or an SUV, something large enough for the security team, but instead a sleek sedan idled at the curb. The guard helped Mo into the back seat and then got into one of the identical trail cars. Ready for an automotive shell game, perhaps, if the Externals decided to send a message to the Chief Investigator. Leif opened the passenger door and I paused, looking back over my shoulder at the Slough. Part of me still wanted to be with witches when I felt chased, hunted. The coven could protect me from the Externals, better even than Leif. Even if they'd been up to questionable magic, they could defend me with impenetrable walls of magic. Joanne and Tracy usually went for post-spell snacks at a diner not far from the Pug, I could—

"Something wrong?"

And again, I hesitated, instincts rumbling a warning. Yes, something was wrong. I opened my mouth to tell him everything, to admit I was Ivan Darkwing and tossed the dark witches into a demon realm and that one of his covens worked some very bad, very powerful magic, and as his head tilted and he looked more alert, I closed my mouth. He took things seriously; he would take those things seriously, and whatever happened next would get out of control very quickly. I didn't mind getting Anne Marie in trouble—would relish it, really— but I didn't want Tracy or Joanne or Rosa caught up in anything.

Leif's brows drew together as he leaned in close, dropping his voice as he caught my arm. "Bad news doesn't get better with age."

"I want pancakes!" Mo kicked at the window from the backseat, waving at us. "Come on already."

"Pancakes," I said, and slid into the car. I closed my eyes and relaxed against the warm leather—thank all the saints he had heated seats and someone thought to turn them on. Whoever it was deserved a medal.

"Right," Leif said under his breath, shutting the door.

As he walked around the car, I whispered to Mo, "This isn't a good idea."

"It's the best idea," she said with a sigh, and a heartbeat later, as Leif put the car in gear, she started snoring. I couldn't tell if she meant Leif taking us home, or eating pancakes. Either way, I found myself riding in silence through the city with someone I'd avoided for five years.

I studied his hands where he gripped the wheel, the battered alignment ring on his right hand and the scars crosshatching his skin in pale tracks. The ring's warm yellow gold, dented and smudged, cradled a ruby like old blood. The muscles stood out in his forearms, the sleeves of his dress shirt pushed back as he drove. The years had been kind to him— only a few extra smile lines creased around his eyes.

He shifted in the seat, about to speak, and I jumped, staring out the windshield as my cheeks burned. I willed myself to aloofness. I'd loved him from afar during the war, when I was little more than a half-grown kid masquerading as a war witch who didn't give a shit about anyone or anything but revenge. But a decade later – I was a grown damn woman. There was no reason his attention should still make me as nervous as a new witch at Beltane.

Leif glanced over at me. "If there's something I need to know, Lilith..."

He left the door open—I could walk through if I wanted, get myself and a dozen friends in trouble. My strategy of nonalignment only worked if I actually stayed uninvolved in the Alliance and all of the social and political drama that sprouted around it. The dark witches got what they deserved, and I would answer for it if the girl woke up, but Anne Marie's mistakes belonged to her and the Alliance she obeyed.

I delayed too long, could tell by his posture that he braced for some very bad news. Instead, I took a deep breath and offered another small lie. "Just a bad night to be called a dark witch."

"As opposed to any other day?"

I watched the trail cars in the side mirror, mesmerized by the headlights. "Full moon, or close enough, and an inauspicious anniversary."

He frowned, using a red light to lean back and jostle Mo until she lifted her head and insulted his manhood. Satisfied she still breathed, he faced me. "Next week is the first battle of Chicago, but—"

"The day the war started," I said. The words barely sneaked past the knot in my throat.

"Is in four months." His tone wasn't confrontational. He gathered data, trying to understand, storing it all away for later.

"For the wolves." I stared out the window, tried to pretend I talked about ancient history when it still felt like a very recent,

43

personal wound. "For the witches, it started today, fifteen years ago."

"Very specific," he murmured, hands whisper-quiet on the steering wheel as he turned into one of the nicer suburbs. "And yet we never knew?"

"You knew," I said, and the wound deepened. They ignored the witches, because as long as the humans hunted witches instead of shifters, the shifters gained time to organize, prepare, plan. Protect their packs and clans and prides as flames consumed the covens, one by one. And they wondered why there were so few witches left to help them, when the war got bad. "You let us fight alone until the humans started attacking shifters. Then your war started."

Even after ten years of fighting together, I refused to obey Soren or swear to the Alliance. Those four months convinced me witches would always be second class to shifters. And we were—no witches sat on the Alliance governing or advisory councils. Only Anne Marie and her coven were special advisors to Soren, but they had no real power. Once the Peacemaker made a decision, that was that. And his decisions always favored the wolves.

Leif made a thoughtful sound in his throat, forehead creased as he pulled into Mo's driveway and put the car in park. He turned to look at me. "I remember hearing reports of raids, arrests, that sort of thing right after the Breaking, but we didn't realize the witches observed a different anniversary. I'll inform Soren, perhaps we can—"

"No," I said, and it came out louder than I intended. Mo snorted in the backseat and muttered, "Pancakes?" before starting to snore again. "No," I repeated, fumbling with the seat-belt. "It's witch business. We don't need a bunch of shifters stomping into it with ceremony and flags and trumpets. No one got medals in our war, so we figured you wouldn't be interested."

"Ouch," he said, almost a laugh. "Good to know where we stand."

My face heated. Always smooth, I was. Not for the first time, I told myself that was the last night I'd ever drink alcohol. I shook my head, yanking on the seatbelt. "I didn't mean—"

"And kind of hypocritical for someone who received quite a few medals, if I remember correctly."

"Saints curse this thing," I said under my breath, the belt getting tighter and tighter against my chest the more I pulled on it. Maybe it was a security feature in the car. I struggled to breathe normally, stomach starting to clench as my palms grew slick with sweat. *Do not puke in his car* became my mantra.

He reached out and pressed the button, jiggling the belt for a moment before it finally came free. "There," and he looked at me, something in his expression telling me he was amused.

"I didn't keep them," I blurted out. "The medals. I didn't keep them."

"That's too bad," he said, still smiling. "More difficult for you witches to sneak up on us, if you jingle as you walk."

I pulled at the door handle, needing the cold night air to knock some sense into me. "I hardly think I would ever sneak up on you."

"A man can hope," he said, and levered himself out of the car before I could do more than blink at him.

He opened the rear passenger door and leaned in to jostle Mo. "Let's go."

I scrambled out of the car and opened the other rear door so I could gather up all of her stuff, except the chicken wings, though I almost fell into the grass as my balance pitched. Leif straightened to study me over the car's roof. "You need a hand?"

"Nope," I said, then marred whatever facade of competence I'd mustered with a hiccup. I put my shoulders back, gathering my dignity. "No, thank you, I'm well."

"Great," he said. The smile lines deepened for a moment as

he watched me, then he looked down at where Mo refused to cooperate. He waved at one of the cars when it became clear Mo had no intention of walking by herself, and one of the security team jogged over obediently to help Leif get her on her feet. "Then can you unlock the front door?"

"Sure." I fished through her purse as I bumped the door shut with my hip, watching them hold Mo up by her arms. "Can't you lift her by yourself?"

The other man snorted and Leif shot him a dirty look before jerking his chin at the front door. "Yes, I can, but the last time I threw Moriah over my shoulder, she stabbed me in the ass with my own pocketknife. I try not to repeat mistakes like that. The door?"

I laughed, having to concentrate on walking evenly to her porch and up the two steps, grateful she'd left the lights on. It took me three tries to get the key in the door, but I managed to shove it open just as Leif and his guy brought Mo to the porch. By then, she was wide awake and bright-eyed, but apparently content to be carried. "Lily," she said, reaching out to squeeze my face. "We need pancakes."

"We need water," I said, looking out at the street where two cars full of Leif's stormtroopers watched.

Inside, they put Mo on the couch in the living room, the guard nodding to me before excusing himself and disappearing outside. Not wanting to get in the way of his boss's chances with two women, maybe. I flushed at the thought and shrugged out of his coat, watching as Leif crouched to check on Mo. I didn't want to assume he would stay for whatever type of pancakes we managed to make, not with two cars of guys waiting, but inviting him to stay for food carried more obligations than I wanted to shoulder. The wolves had strange rules about food, and I couldn't handle the etiquette minefield that late at night. Besides, if history were any indication, the pancakes would be half raw, half charred, and totally inedible for someone as sober as Leif.

He made it easy, taking his coat and heading to the door. "Like you said, I'm no fun, and there's work waiting. You'll be okay keeping an eye on her?"

"That's not exactly what I said." I frowned at Mo. "We'll be fine."

"Good," he said, but paused at the front door. I followed him, focused on setting the locks, putting Mo to bed, and doing a quick cleansing spell before my alarm went off in five hours. Leif handed me a business card, blank except for a phone number in old-fashioned numbers. "Call if you need anything —or if you remember anything important. Stefan already filed the paperwork to request an interview, so I'll be by tomorrow. You'll be here?"

"Yeah," I said, even though it wasn't likely.

"Good. It's a date." But he flicked the business card I held. "In the meantime—call. For anything."

He nodded at whatever he saw in my expression, and left. I locked and re-locked the door behind him before stumbling back to the living room and collapsing onto the unoccupied love seat. Saints save me from myself, Anne Marie's machinations, and the External's questions. There just wasn't enough time in the day to handle it all myself.

# CHAPTER 5

ot even a minute passed before Mo sat up and fixed me with a jaundiced look. "I'm not as drunk as I look."

I laughed. "Yeah, okay."

"I was *trying* to give you an opportunity to work your magic on Leif, witch, but all you talked about was the war. What the hell is wrong with you?"

"*What?*"

"Oh, come on," she said, lurching up and weaving toward the kitchen. "You haven't gotten laid in forever. Call him back, say I got belligerent and you need help, then take him into the guest room and—"

"Moriah!"

"I'm just sayin'," she said, bracing herself on the wall next to the pantry. "You could use a little fun. He's serious as fuck most of the time, but he's a good lay." Rattling pots and pans drowned out whatever raunchy details followed.

I followed her, clipping my shoulder on the doorframe. "You—"

She handed me a bowl and the pancake mix. "Get to work.

LAYLA NASH

And yes, I slept with him. After Marty died, I was sad and in pain and I needed to feel something...not bad. Leif's a good friend, so—" She shrugged, then pointed the spatula at me. "He's too serious for me and probably for you, too, but he'll put a smile on your face."

"You are unbelievable." The fridge only slightly cooled my burning cheeks as I retrieved the milk, squinting at the measuring cup and trying to get in the ballpark of half a cup. "I'm not going to sleep with him."

"Oh yes you are," she said. She frowned at the puddle of oil in the cast iron skillet. "In two weeks or less."

The mixing bowl slipped out of my hands. "I beg your pardon?"

"There's a bet," she said. "And why the hell isn't this working?"

"You didn't light the burner." I wiped up the batter that splattered the counter and my sweater, licking my fingers. "What do you mean, a bet?"

"A wager." Mo crouched to light the burner, almost losing her eyebrows as the gas ignited with a whoosh. She sneezed, rubbing her face. "He doesn't give girls his coat, or walk them outside to get fresh air, or offer to drive them home. He has people to do that—he should have ordered Mick, or his security team, or ... Shit, he could have ordered anyone in that bar and they would have jumped through their own ass to do him a favor." She straightened, focused on the oil sliding around the pan. "Maybe not the cats. They're assholes just to be assholes. Anyway, while you two canoodled in the fresh air, a few of us made a small bet. Mick thinks it'll take at least a month for Leif to take you home. I'm not sure if you should be insulted or not."

I handed her the bowl. "Oh, I have pretty strong feelings about all of this."

She smiled toothily, again wielding the spatula like a machete. "There's a run on his personal life, so it's not about

50

you, babe. Still. I'll win four hundred bucks if you two go on a public, romantic date in under two weeks. Double that if you kiss."

Four hundred dollars, almost two months' rent. I leaned my hip against the counter. "Huh."

She caught my expression and leaned closer, whispering a conspiracy. "You can keep the money. I just want to see Mick lose."

"No." I pointed at the stove. "And you're burning breakfast."

She cursed, fumbling the skillet, and tried to rescue the charred remains. She threw it into the trash and surrendered the spatula. "You do it."

I elbowed her out of the way. "Go sit down."

She retrieved bottles of sports drink from the fridge, putting one at my elbow before she sat at the table. "So you're hiding here until the heat dies down? From the Externals?"

I concentrated on spooning batter evenly into the skillet. "Just tonight. I have to work tomorrow, and a few things to clean up at home afterward."

"They really said you're a dark witch?"

"Close enough," I said. "In front of Leif and all his guys."

"So you hexed the cop? Is that why Leif drove us back?"

I smiled at the pan, flipping the pancakes one by one. We'd done this many times, Mo and I, exchanging deep truths and gossip over breakfast late at night. "Leif stopped me before I got a chance. So I owe him one."

"Yeah you do." She waggled her eyebrows at me. "I can suggest some ways to repay him. If I remember correctly, he likes—"

"Stop or no pancakes for you," I said, turning my own fierce look on her.

She mimed zipping her lips, but after I delivered a plate along with syrup and forks, Mo spoke around a mouthful of mostly-cooked pancake. "And how was the anniversary thing tonight? Is that what went kaboom? That was the trouble?"

I double-checked that I'd turned off the burner—a lesson learned the hard way in my first apartment—before occupying the chair across from her. I didn't want to talk about the anniversary remembrance at the witches' memorial in the Slough. "That was something else. And it went okay. Somber, as usual."

"Did everyone show?"

"Most of them." I managed to claim a pancake before she finished them off. "And a couple of extras I didn't recognize. Kids, too young to know anything about anything."

She frowned at the plate, drawing spiraling mazes with the tines of her fork. "Is that a sign maybe you should take a step back? Let someone else carry the torch? It's been five years, babe. I don't think it's healthy for you to keep going back like this. And to them. You don't owe them anything. They didn't even try to help you. They—"

"It's more complicated than that," I said, glad I'd only eaten a little as nausea simmered low in my stomach. "They were my coven, and—"

"And they abandoned you when you needed help," she said. Her expression turned rocky, unmovable as granite. "There's no excuse for that. Pack is pack, even when things get tough. *Especially* when things get tough."

"Covens are different." I took a deep breath, pushing away regret even as I thanked the saints for Moriah. "They break up all the time. Leaders leave, someone new takes over, people have conflicts over rank or practice or whatever, and everything falls apart. People go their separate ways. We aren't obligated the way packs are."

"Then why do you keep going back?"

I took the plate to the sink to buy myself time, gathering the other dishes when it wasn't enough. I hadn't found an answer by the time I returned to the table, so I defaulted to the truth. "It's too late and I'm too drunk to answer that. Later."

She nodded, guzzling the sports drink as she watched me load the dishwasher. "Maybe you should call out from work."

I shook my head and immediately regretted it, vertigo making me hang onto the counter. "I need the money. Have to buy a new jacket. Mine was ruined."

"With someone else's blood?"

I looked at her sharply. Mo watched me without expression, waiting. When I said nothing, she flattened her hands on the table and studied them, voice careful. "Look, Lil. You are welcome to join my pack officially any time you want, if you align and swear fealty to the Alliance and Soren. I know you have your reasons for staying nonaligned, but... Tonight you ended up covered in blood *and* accused of being a dark witch. Between the kind of trouble you find on your own and the trouble the Externals will make for you, a pack's protection will come in handy. It might save your life."

I folded my arms over my chest. "I appreciate the offer, Mo, I do. I just can't. The price is too high."

"I know." She leaned her chin on her fist. "But things are changing. Open enrollment might not last forever. Just...think through whatever calculus you do and figure out what might make that answer change. Especially if you're mixed up in the kind of stuff that Leif personally investigates. It's better to be on the inside."

"Maybe." I shook my head. "But I'll think about it."

"Whatever you say, witch." She jumped to her feet, then braced herself on the table and squeezed her eyes shut. "Whoa. Maybe I am a little drunker than I thought."

"Uh-huh. No kidding, birthday girl."

I waited in the doorway to make sure she staggered through the living room without running into anything on the way to her master suite. She waved a hand at me, full concentration on her bed. "You can borrow the gray peacoat in the front closet until you get a new one." She paused in the doorway, blinking at me owlishly. "And you still smell a little like blood and a lot like Leif. You might want to wash it off before you go to the restaurant."

"Thanks. You smell pretty gross yourself."

She laughed, "Don't be such a witch," and flopped face-first onto her bed.

I dragged myself to the guest room upstairs that was unofficially my room after living with Mo on and off for a couple of years. She let me store clothes, shoes, toiletries, and a few keepsakes there, especially since staying at her place bought me an extra hour of sleep before heading to work.

I scrubbed every inch of my skin in near-scalding water before dragging the mattress away from the wall and walking a circle three times around the bed, weaving a cleansing spell into the circle as I paced. I crawled into bed with wet hair and activated the spell, closing my eyes after a green glow, shot through with pearlescent streaks from the demon magic, expanded into a dome around me. It would run as I slept, thank all the saints. Nine o'clock would come far too soon as it was.

* * *

BY THE END of the lunch rush, I still couldn't answer Mo's questions about why I kept going back to the coven. Folding cloth napkins into swans gave me time to reconsider, though my pounding head and uneasy stomach wanted me to crawl under a table in the breakroom to nap. Remembering the hoity-toity specials had almost been beyond my capacity for most of the day. A gallon of water and a handful of painkillers didn't even make a dent in the misery, but the relative quiet of the back room provided some respite. I concentrated on my swans, ignoring the shifters who ignored me. No telling if they'd been at the Pug the night before or got in on the bet Moriah mentioned.

Halfway into my stack of linens, one of the youngest witches at the restaurant crept in, supported by two others. The young one, Cheryl, stared wide-eyed as she sank into an empty chair, face pale and hands trembling. The shifters glanced at her, then at each other, and walked out without a word—witch business was witch business, and nothing they wanted a part of. I debated getting up as well, punching out, figuring out the fastest way to get to my bed. But I stayed, hands still on the napkins. I didn't know the girl well, but she looked how I felt and there had to be a reason.

She pressed her palms to her face, shaking all over, and her blonde friend brought her a glass of water. "Deep breaths, honey. What happened?"

"E-Externals."

"Have you called your coven leader?"

"Not yet. I thought—" She trailed off and looked up, confused.

The friend, Mary, pulled out her phone, dialing as she retreated to the hall outside. The other witch, an older woman named Lucy, sat next to the girl and hugged her close. "What did they want?"

Her hands fell to her lap. "They asked me about last night, about the magic. We had a coven meeting and the Externals thought we worked dark magic. They threatened to c-collar me and take me away."

I bit my lip. No worse fate for a witch, when an iron collar cut us off from magic. My mother put one on me once before the Breaking, to show me the price of getting caught working magic. The memory alone was enough to make my palms sweat. All color left the world without magic; all smells and tastes and sounds faded to sad watermarks of reality.

Cheryl sipped her water, shaking her head. "They just w-wouldn't leave."

Lucy hushed her, patting her back once more as she looked around, perhaps searching for answers. Her gaze landed on me and didn't stray as she went on. "These things go in cycles. We'll file a complaint with the Chief Investigator, and he'll speak to the Judge."

She and I both knew it wouldn't make a difference. The Externals had a good reason to investigate, partially thanks to me, and dark magic was scary enough to justify almost any measures. The only thing that inspired more fear than dark witches were the loki, unrestrained shapeshifters.

I studied the sign on the wall admonishing employees to wash their hands, and was about to offer a suggestion when the door opened and Mary returned. The grim tone only added to her normally sour expression. "It might be a while. It looks like the Externals raided across the city without informing the Alliance—any coven that met last night was targeted. The Chief Investigator's office is trying to straighten things out, but for now, they said to stay with your coven."

Lucy pinched the bridge of her nose as fat tears rolled down the girl's face. The older witch took a deep breath, the words dragged up from her toes. "What would you do, Lily?"

I blinked as all three of them looked at me, Mary's face puckering still more and Cheryl almost hyperventilating. I concentrated on making precise folds in a fresh swan. "Well, I'm nonaligned, so it's not like—"

Lucy leveled a schoolteacher stare at me and I trailed off. She knew me better than the other two, since we'd fought in some of the same areas during the war, and she was old enough to remember the world before the Breaking unleashed magic in the open. I held my hands up, fending off questions that never came. "Look. We have rights. They're not respected like they should be, but we do have rights. If it were me, I'd stand behind my wards and not let them close enough to touch me. Call the Styrma to make sure the Externals aren't acting alone, since they're not supposed to. But if they bother to talk to you, they don't have enough evidence to collar you. If they had the evidence, the Styrma would kick in your door first and they wouldn't bother knocking. You're probably fine. Just set stronger door wards."

"Easy for you to say," Mary said. "You didn't get woken up at six a.m. by a bunch of jackbooted thugs knocking on your door."

No, they tried to grab me on the street in front of the Chief Investigator himself. But I kept my mouth shut, offering only a shrug as I eased to my feet, picking up the swans and the flat napkins. "I'm nonaligned. If they can find me, they don't have to knock."

"Well, they're detaining whoever they want now, apparently, because Rowanwood coven can't find two of their members. They think the humans took them, but even Leif can't get the Judge to disclose where they are." Mary watched me with narrowed eyes.

"Rowanwood?" Lucy rose, forehead creased. "Who's missing?"

"Danielle and Cara. No one's seen them since last night, they aren't answering their phones, and they left their purses at home."

Cheryl patted her cheeks dry, and I fought down irritation that she was one of those women who looked prettier when she cried. Her voice wobbled charmingly. "The Styrma can't find them? What about the Morrigan?"

"No one knows anything." Mary rubbed her upper arms, still shaking her head. "It's like they just vanished."

My stomach dropped and my feet stuck to the floor, though I'd intended to walk away. Two witches who had vanished into thin air. Or through a rift into a demon realm. I unfolded one of the napkins, trying to sound disinterested. "What class are they? The missing ones?"

"Cara's a sender, Danielle is a basher." Lucy's head tilted. "Why?"

Saints preserve me. The two dark witches had been strong enough to be bashers, and the one used a sending spell to push me away. Typical. "Well, the Externals never arrest anyone over charmer without the Styrma present, and they can't hold anyone over mender class in their jails, even collared. Only Alliance jails can hold bashers or senders. So they're probably just hiding out somewhere."

Relief cleared Lucy's expression, but she still started calling people, trying to figure out where the missing witches could be. Mary comforted Cheryl after she started crying again.

I gathered my things, leaving the swans on the counter where someone in the dinner shift would get them, and paused at the door to copy my schedule. It looked like a busy week, but no telling if I'd make enough tips to buy another coat with the rent due as well. I stared blindly at the schedule for a long moment, and vertigo washed over me. I'd had more free time as a war witch during war than I did as a peacetime waitress. Maybe Mo was right. If I joined her pack, I could cut back my hours, benefit from the wider employment opportunities that Alliance members enjoyed, and pick up odd jobs with healing and mending or other magical chores shifters hired out.

I turned to leave, almost walking into the door as it swung in, and stopped dead in my tracks. Tracy looked at me, her eyebrows raised, then inclined her head and tugged on her earlobe as she did so. I nodded back, ignoring the tension in the room behind me—Lucy, at least, knew about my falling out with the coven. I edged the rest of the way out the door and into the hall to take a breath. Saints preserve me. There was no telling what convinced Tracy to break our agreement never to meet in public. I drew my borrowed coat tighter as I punched out and retreated to the alley behind the restaurant to wait for her. Chances were it wasn't good news, and might even be some of that bad news, getting worse.

# CHAPTER 6

*I*'d decided to leave at least twice by the time Tracy appeared. She looked younger than I remembered in the watery sunlight, but it could have been a glamour. I straightened from leaning against the brick wall, half-hidden by a dumpster, but stayed out of the line of sight of the street. "Hey."

"Hey." She tugged on her dark ponytail and hitched the strap of her messenger bag up on her shoulder. "Sorry it took so long, I didn't expect to take statements on External misconduct. They're pretty worked up inside."

"Not surprising, I guess."

She shrugged, dark eyes moving quickly, searching me and the background. "Some people don't know what it feels like to really be cornered, right?" She didn't wait for me to agree, instead offering an uneasy smile. "How have you been?"

"Worse than some, better than others." I smiled so she might believe me. "Seems like there's a lot going on lately. For everyone."

She made a face and glanced down the alley toward the

street. "You could say that. Look, I don't want to keep you from anything, but I couldn't do this over the phone. I need a favor."

A favor. My phone vibrated and I jumped, then glanced at the screen to buy some time before I blurted out the first response that came to mind. I'd have to be out of my mind to get involved with the coven again. When I didn't recognize the number on the screen, I tucked the phone away again. "What kind of favor?"

A smart witch always asked.

She rubbed her mouth, as if to hide a smile. "Nothing strenuous, I promise. I hoped you could come to the Slough tonight. We're meeting for the second part of the spell, and I wanted—I need you to observe what we're doing."

My eyebrows rose before I thought to school my expression into neutrality. "Observe? Observe what?"

She winced and edged closer, fidgeting with her earring and lowering her voice. "Look. I know you felt what happened last night. We were—most of us, anyway—surprised by how things worked. Anne Marie sort of explained it, but... We're casting again tonight and I'm a little concerned. Maybe not concerned, maybe worried, I don't know. Just...if it happens like it did last night, I don't know if we'll be able to handle the backlash."

"What were you doing before it went sideways last night?"

"A Calling." She chewed her lip, a trace of panic in the tension around her mouth, gathering around her eyes and in the way she picked at her sleeve. "A powerful summoning, but I can't get into why or who. I just...I'd feel better if you could watch tonight and tell me what you see."

My phone rang again, the same unknown number, and I frowned. Once was an accident, twice was a problem. I took a deep breath as I looked at Tracy. She'd been a good student, when I was still willing to teach, and a better friend. Almost a sister. As much as I hated Anne Marie, I couldn't walk away from Tracy. "What time?"

She exhaled, shoulders sagging. "Thank the saints. Midnight."

Midnight. Always the witching hour. "Okay. I'll do my best, but with the cops all over the place—" I shook my head. "I'll do my best. If anything changes, call me."

"We're not going to change anything for this cast. It has to be tonight."

"Well, call if anyone gets arrested," I said, and I canted my head at the door leading to the restaurant. "Or just disappears. Since that seems to be happening a lot these days."

She made a face. "There's no telling what's going on. It might be the humans flexing against the letter of the law, there could be a legitimate reason for it... Hell, it could be Soren cleaning house again."

"Cleaning house?" I leaned forward, heart in my throat. "Getting rid of witches?"

"Well," she started, then stopped, gaze darting away. "It's not really something..."

"Trace." I put a little Morrigan in my voice. "Cut the crap. What's going on?"

Her lips compressed in a thin line. "It's nothing to do with nonaligned. Not really your problem."

"Bullshit. At the Pug last night, two Externals called me a dark witch and tried to blame the shit you did on *me*. So between them and *you*, doing fucked-up magic again tonight and asking me to watch, it clearly is my problem."

She rubbed her temples, turning away for a moment. When she faced me, she looked older, more mature. Committed. "Okay, but this goes no further, got it?" She waited for my nod before going on. "Soren's been in charge for too long. People are calling it a dictatorship instead of the democracy we signed up for. The wolves are mostly content to go along because it benefits them. But there's a lot of dissent building up with the other canines, the bears, the cats... Even some of the covens are making noise. Everyone is on edge. A bunch of people were arrested a couple of months ago and it doesn't add up except that most of them challenged Soren's leadership."

And she looked at me, waiting.

My thoughts clicked too slowly, trying to calculate what it meant for Moriah and Mick. If Soren fell from power, a lot of wolves would fall with him. And his replacement would destroy anyone who supported the Peacemaker. Such was the nature of shifter politics. I pinched the bridge of my nose, ignoring the vertigo that had me reaching out to the grimy brick wall. "So this could be a purge. Or another civil war."

"Or an exodus." Tracy took a deep breath. "The Australians are offering sanctuary to Others, so are the Irish. The Russians, too, but no one's falling for *that*. Again. Or it could just be a new war with the humans, Lil—the Externals stir up the Alliance against the only man who kept it together through the war, get Others to depose Soren, then the humans can sweep in and tear us apart. Which is why I have to make sure what we do tonight is legit. If someone is setting us up, we've got to know."

"Could it be Anne Marie?"

She didn't meet my gaze, fidgeting instead with the strap of her bag.

I let the silence stretch, broken only by a honking car in the street. Finally, when it was clear she wouldn't speak, I nodded. "Not trusting your coven is the first sign you need a new one."

Her expression darkened. "Lily—"

"Trust me." I held my hands up, forcing myself to smile. "I know from personal experience. But that's between you and your coven, Tracy. So. Midnight tonight. Anything else I should know?"

She hesitated and I braced for the worst. I thought of what Leif told me the night before—bad news doesn't get better with age. Tracy cleared her throat, still not facing me fully. "I miss you. We miss you. If things go sideways, maybe...maybe it's a new opportunity."

A new opportunity that conveniently overlooked all the reasons it hadn't worked the last time. Maybe Tracy and Rosa and Joanne and I could put aside all of that. Start over in Australia or Ireland. But I only nodded, wanting to hug her, but not certain how she'd react. Jumping at another witch with outspread arms generally didn't end well for anyone. So I hugged myself instead. "Sure. Good luck tonight. I'll let you know if I see anything."

"Good." She paused, then tugged at my right hand, holding it up so I could see the bare fingers. "And if I were you, I'd find a ring. Any ring. If they come for you, it might buy you enough time to get away."

It hadn't helped any of the other witches, like Cheryl, although Tracy no doubt remembered my preference for fight over flight. I pulled free. "Sure. And I'll call you to bail me out when I get arrested for pretending to be aligned."

"You got it." She smiled, glanced at her watch, then lurched forward to hug me, hard enough to knock the breath out of me before I could even lift a hand. "Be careful." Then she turned and strode away, disappearing into the brighter sun of the open street.

I blinked. Pressure built behind my eyes as I squinted at where she'd gone. Saints blast it. Maybe staying with Mo another couple of nights was smarter than going home. I needed a few things from the apartment, but the safety of a pack promised better rest than even my wards could provide.

I TOOK the bus back to my apartment, looking out the window the entire time to check for anyone who might want to arrest me. A few hours separated me from Tracy's favor, and if I was going to stay with Moriah for more than a day or two, I had to get clothes and magical accoutrements. Just in case.

Despite being two stops early, I got off the bus at the last intersection before traffic thinned. Some habits faded with time and complacency, but I still knew how to check for an ambush. I needed plenty of time and distance to observe if anyone watched my apartment or me, which beat out the ache in my feet that made it difficult to get off the bus and walk. A local cult stood on the corner outside the shop 'n go convenience store, holding up placards that declared both the end of the world and the condemnation of non-humans to eternal hell. They handed me a pamphlet as I passed; I dropped it into the collection bucket of the love-everyone-love-everything group working the opposite street corner.

The war destroyed a lot of things, but it certainly revived religion—anyone and anything declared itself a prophet in the early days after magic revealed itself to the world. Panic and fear seemed to generate a lot of devotion, or at least lip service, to a whole suite of churches, temples, cults, revivals, and so on. Not many were organized enough to survive more than a few months, particularly when they relied on a single charismatic leader and the generosity of passersby. Not entirely unlike Soren and the rest of the Alliance leadership.

I pushed the thought away as I turned the corner and crossed an invisible border between the "mixed" part of the neighborhood and the area that Others dominated. No laws barred humans from renting in my apartment complex, but there weren't a whole lot applying.

The militias had something to do with it, but sometimes it was difficult to remember that we had a generation of children and families and young professionals who'd spent ten years fighting us as the monsters who haunted their nightmares. No human wanted to live next door to a witch or a shifter, unpredictable and following laws unlike anything the humans understood. Pack justice, coven trials, and blood debts didn't play well on the evening news. And the homeowner's insurance for Other-adjacent properties was astronomical, or so they said.

The apartment complex dominated several blocks, twelve and twenty-four unit buildings built in a square around a central courtyard. The buildings looked identical; even the giant green letters painted on the sides for identification purposes had long since faded. I took a shortcut across a side yard comprised of dead grass, dirt, and some dandelions clinging to life, and circled around to my building. Luckily even the most dedicated born-again sects wouldn't venture out to save souls in this complex.

The apartments shared open-air hallways and stairs in each building, so some of the small kids who should have been in school stood at the railings and watched my passage. The complex, with the only apartment I could really afford on my pay, was more like one of the shoddy roadside motels in the pre-Breaking horror movies—not even an open management office in case you needed maintenance. It was live and let live, so long as you paid on time, and it was the kind of place you stayed at if you didn't want to be noticed or remembered. The kind of place where, when the police came to investigate, if they came at all, no one ever knew anything about anyone else and fell back on, "Nice enough guy, quiet neighbor. Never caused any trouble." I counted on no one knowing my name, if the wrong people started asking.

And yet my neighbors challenged my commitment to that shared credo every time I passed their door. The witch and his human girlfriend fought, loudly and constantly. I paused in the hall, looking at their door as a crash disturbed the afternoon. Well, he fought. She took the punches. My feet refused to move, to carry me into my apartment and away from desperate "Please don't"s, repeated over and over. I'd asked her if she needed help and she always refused, made excuses, apologized for disturbing me. My stomach turned over. But I knew something of being so thoroughly entangled with someone that being untangled seemed impossible.

Another crash. I steeled my nerves, strode up to the door, knocked with authority and a heavy hand. Immediate silence followed, perhaps some whispered threats that I couldn't quite make out even through the shoddy door. Then the door opened and the witch, dark-haired and smiling, looked at me. "Hi there. What can I do for you?"

He knew I'd spoken with her, and he'd gone from being relatively friendly to overly friendly. Charming, as if he could convince me she was the liar through force of personality. I hitched my bag up on my shoulder, glancing past him into the apartment. "I thought I heard a noise, just wanted to make sure everything was okay."

"Everything's fine." The smile broadened, displaying even white teeth too big for his face. One of the other neighbors, a witch with an addiction problem, referred to him as Chompers once, and it stuck in my head until his real name escaped me.

"That's good." I cleared my throat. "The cops are coming around to all the witches, it sounds like. Arrested a couple, a few more disappeared. You might want to lie low, not give them any reasons to ask questions. You know."

His head tilted in a question, though the smile never moved. "Disappeared?"

"Two from Rowanwood. I've never met any of them, so I don't even know what they look like. Wouldn't be much help with a search party, I guess." And I tried a smile and a shrug, ignoring the way his girlfriend held her shoulder as she waited in the hall behind him. The look in her eyes hurt my heart.

The smile slipped into a frown, then returned. "That's strange. Is the Alliance looking for them?"

"Well..." I trailed off, let the silence speak for itself, then shrugged. "The witches are looking for them."

"Damn animals," he said under his breath, and looked over his shoulder. "Get my roster from the desk." He faced me again and didn't bother to verify his orders were followed, the girlfriend limping into the apartment. Chompers folded his arms over his chest, leaning against the doorjamb as he studied me. "Have you joined a coven yet?"

Small talk among witches always centered around covens—who was in one, which one, which was better, who was leaving. It was even more tiresome when one was totally nonaligned. But whatever roster he would show me was probably worth the small talk. "Oh, I heard a couple of bashers are getting together. I'm supposed to link up with them at some point."

"Bashers?" He snorted. "You're at least a sender, why would you want to go around with bashers?"

I tried to make eye contact as his girlfriend, Amber, slunk up. She wordlessly offered a stack of papers, and he took it without looking at her. She retreated. My chest ached for her. I wanted to stomp my feet, to hex the shit out of Chompers and drag her away. But she wore a glamour constantly, relied on him for some kind of magic, so it might not have been as easy as I wished. If he provided her medical help, dragging her away without a plan might do more harm than good. Or so I tried to convince myself.

He offered the papers to me. "This is my roster for the Alliance witches, at least. Do you remember the names of the ones who disappeared?"

I flipped through the covens until I came to Rowanwood, pausing to consider the nine yearbook-size photos on the page. "Danielle and Cara," I said, but it came out a bare whisper as the two dark witches stared back at me from their smiling, posed headshots. I repeated myself, then tapped their photos. "Those two, I think. I'm sure the Peacemaker will do something about it, at least send out a call. But in the meantime, they told everyone to stay low."

"Easy enough." The overzealous smile returned as he took his papers back, nodded toward the interior of the apartment. "Want to come in for a drink or something? My coven has an opening. You're welcome to sit in the circle a couple of times. See if you want to join permanently."

"Maybe later, but thanks." My skin crawled at the thought, but the shivers made smiling just a little easier. "Got to get to my other job."

"Well, if you ever want to cast with us, let me know." He watched from the doorway until I reached my apartment, a few steps away, and disappeared inside.

I locked the door behind me, set the deadbolts, and ramped up the magical wards that guarded my threshold. I glanced through the peep hole and held my breath—he remained in his doorway, staring at my door, and the smile had disappeared. A shiver ran through me. Damn witches.

# CHAPTER 7

$\mathscr{T}$he memory of Chompers' attention stayed with me even as I took the bus to the Slough after dark and made my way down the overgrown paths to the memorial. As much as I hated nature and the feeling of leaves and branches against my skin, it was a thousand times worse when it felt like something would jump out at me every other step.

The Slough contained the witches' memorial—three interlocked circles of trees, protected by magic and superstition. Each tree represented a coven that fought in the war. Some had been completely lost, so their tree was planted in memory and left to grow wild. The others showed some degree of tending, often with small offerings or candles or mementos left in the soil or among the branches. I got to the Slough early to walk the circles, murmuring a prayer to the saints to protect them all even though I'd done the same with Tracy, Joanne, Rosa, and Andre only the night before.

In the center of the center ring was a gnarled, twisted blackthorn. I couldn't remember it blooming in the last five years, since the night I planted it. My parents' coven tree had been the blackthorn, and I planted the tree in the heart of the memorial in their memory, and in the memories of all the witches who stood with me and perished. I stared at the twisted thorns and tangled branches, my vision blurring briefly in the moonlight. And to think, after ten years of war and five years of peace, we still weren't free. We still weren't safe.

I didn't linger too long in the open, nor did I disturb the detritus of the spell Tracy's coven worked the night before—some candles and salt, hints of burned sage. In the magically preserved clearings, the air felt colder, and I pulled my coat tighter as I headed for the edges of the forest.

By the time I found a hiding place outside the memorial circles, perched on a branch behind some lingering foliage, I'd developed a long list of things Tracy would have to do to make up for this minor favor. Nothing strenuous, she'd said. I made a rude noise and once more checked that my bag wouldn't catch on anything if I had to jump down in a hurry. A five-pound bag of salt, some sage, a mirror, oak twigs, and a few other things provided a comfortable counterweight on the branch so I could balance. Preparing to counter what Anne Marie and the others planned presented some challenges when I wasn't entirely sure what they wanted to accomplish. A summoning could have been a variety of things—finding a lost object, Calling a person against their will, summoning a demon from another realm.

The moon wasn't right for the witches to arrive, but Jacques, Anne Marie's second-in-command, had always had a pathological need to be early, to be the first, and I didn't want him to catch me wandering the memorial. From what little he shared of his childhood, apparently he'd been a late bloomer at every stage—walked late, talked late, read and wrote late, hit puberty late. I tried to find sympathy in my heart for him, but there were too many splits in that road, too many turns where he'd taken glee in making my life difficult.

The jade ring on the fourth finger of my right hand spun around and around as I played with it, an old habit and a nervous one. I'd taken Tracy's warning to heart and put on the ring of a mender and healer—a nonthreatening, relatively low-powered witch in the hierarchy of skills. Incredibly powerful witches could heal life-threatening wounds as if they'd never happened, but the witch hierarchy went by degree of power, not by proclivity or talent. What mattered was what you could do, not what you wanted to do. Rosa saved my life multiple times by patching me together when parts of me were nothing more than hamburger, but no one called her a mender—she was a war witch, whether she liked fighting or not.

The coven's work the night before left a distinct trail through the park, easy enough for other witches to follow. Especially with the overwhelming stench of burnt magic permeating the air, even after a full day. It drove everything away from that part of the park, until not even crickets chirped in the night. A blaze of powerful magic pulsed in the center of the memorial, around my tree, and revealed a complex spell combining a summoning and a Calling. The goal could have been anything, really—trying to find something misplaced, dragging someone back against their will, bringing something from another realm.

I checked the bag once more, but froze at the sound of approaching steps and disturbed vegetation. The full coven, all nine of them, entered the memorial. Magic connected them: they'd begun the spell elsewhere, carried it with them into the Skein. I held my breath. Of the threads that bound them, one shaded slightly gray, hints of intent that affected free will. Not precisely dark magic, but on the edge. Only the darkest of magics influenced the free will of a sentient being. That was a line that could not be uncrossed.

They spread out into the memorial silently, hands out at their sides to maintain the circle. Magic rose in sheets between them, condensing into blue ripples and waves. Anne Marie began to chant in a low voice, her eyes closed. A bad habit I'd tried to break her of, with no success.

Memories rose to the surface, unbidden. Nights laughing around a banked fire, none of us willing to admit we couldn't sleep because of nightmares, but none so brave we could risk the darkness alone. Rosa showing me how to cook proper rice and beans. Joanne teaching me the mantra I still used, lecturing me on mindfulness and meditation. Tracy comforting me as I sobbed over Sam.

Friends. Covenmates. A family when I'd needed one. Direction when I was lost.

I squinted, unmoving in my tree, at the warp and woof of their magic. It looked more like a summoning than a Calling, really, though focused on a person. Not Calling her lost car keys, that was certain.

The spell unfolded in complex connections, woven and built by powerful, capable witches. I searched for the intent but found little to guide me—whatever drove Anne Marie's spell, it wasn't evident in the magic. I resigned myself to not being able to tell Tracy anything interesting, but the magic flared unexpectedly, arcing up in a bright, blinding flash. One of the young witches stepped back, dragged the magic with her until it unbalanced. Tilted. Billowed up on one side.

Rosa made a sound, unwilling to form words that would disrupt the spell further, and leaned in to regain control. She and Tracy fought to pull it back into form as Joanne and Andre and Jacques crouched, anchoring the cast. Through the darkness, I couldn't see the young witch's face but imagined the stern talking-to she would get later. The slightest distraction during a spell of that strength made everything wonky. If it were bad enough, the coven would have to start over.

The fabric of the spell formed once more under the careful ministrations of the senior witches. It was almost back in shape, Anne Marie's droning voice undisturbed by the changes, when another flash pulled the threads apart. I leaned forward, gripping the tree branch. There. Right there.

In the woven pattern of intent and power and experience, a thread of darkness wormed through every layer. Saints above and below. Dark magic. Grimly shiny with opalescent malevolence—white for demon magic.

I swallowed hard around my panic. Demon magic corrupted their spell, but they didn't seem to know it. Rosa sure as hell didn't, else she would have stormed out of that circle fast enough to destroy the entire city. I inched closer, almost tumbled off the branch as I stared into the magic. There was no telling what would happen when the spell culminated, but I knew enough of demons to know the magic wouldn't be enough—it would need blood and bone and fear to feed.

Saints protect them.

No wonder Tracy wanted me nearby. She must have felt it during the first night, the imbalance from the dark magic's cloying, clinging hunger. It would draw from the pure magic, would work its way into the heart of the spell until intent didn't matter. Until whoever put that magic in the spell would control everything against the will of the others. I chewed my lip, searching for a place to intervene.

In every spell, there was an ideal place to turn, to change, to redirect. A natural pause, a hiccup. The magic warped, flowed around the darker thread. Anne Marie's voice gained volume, her hands pushed up, the coven following. If they finished, it would be too late, and the shockwave of magic that nearly knocked me over the night before would have been nothing compared to what would follow.

Salt and flame. I drew magic, hopefully soft and quiet enough not to draw attention. We'd worked magic together long enough that I knew how they built their circle, knew the right point to apply pressure. And they hadn't set a ward around the clearing, too confident in their own abilities. Rookie mistake. I'd taught Anne Marie better than that.

I sent an arrow of magic into the spell just before she tied everything off, the sliver enough to prevent the spell from culminating. The mess festered and seethed, pressed against the boundaries, but remained contained. The coven likely waited another night. But my magic hid inside their spell, would disrupt everything when they started again. Hopefully it would be enough to derail the disaster before it got them killed, even if I couldn't convince Tracy to call it all off.

The witches paused, arms raised above their heads, as Anne Marie shouted a final incantation. I leaned back. My elbow bumped the bag and it slipped into emptiness, almost dragging me over with it, and I grabbed at the branch. Shit and double shit. I held my breath, desperate. The magic should have distracted them, there was so much else going on no one could possibly notice—

When I dared look up, I found Joanne staring at me, head tilted and no expression on her face. She watched me from across the clearing as she anchored the circle. Her eyes narrowed, she mouthed, "Lilith?" and it rippled through the magic.

I shook my head, hunching down to make myself smaller. Joanne wouldn't do anything—she wouldn't blame or hex me —but if she outed me to Anne Marie, there would be hell to pay. I tried to ease back to the trunk and descend, but as I balanced, Rosa frowned in my direction as well. She opened her mouth, a question in her eyes, but Anne Marie suddenly threw her hands in the air, calling out the final part of the incantation. Magic flashed up in a blue column and I moved, dropped out of the tree, and shouldered my bag. They regrouped, milled around, both Rosa and Joanne looking in my direction. I shook my head, backing down the path until branches and dust obscured them from view.

\* \* \*

I HALF EXPECTED to find them on my doorstep when I got home. They had cars, after all, while I wasted time at the bus stop. Instead, only the flickering security light in the open hall greeted me. I shut the door and double-checked the locks before leaning against the wall, rubbing my eyes. Tracy and Joanne and Rosa would talk first, would at least ask what I intended. Anne Marie would act, and rightly so—what I'd done to disrupt their spell was close to an act of war. She was the War Witch, the leader of the War Coven, and the senior witch in the Alliance. She didn't need anyone else to approve her punishment of nonaligned witches.

Minutes passed before I felt them approach, the combination of their magic a wrecking ball swinging up the stairs. The magic practically vibrated the building, still active and intimidating from their coven work. Rosa ran her hand over the wards outside my door, a gentle touch that served as a wake-up instead of an aggressive breaking; I knew it was her by the green threads of healing magic running through the blue. She said, "Open up, *hermana*."

I pinched the bridge of my nose, but opened the door, letting it swing in until I faced a third of my old coven. Rosa stood on the battered welcome mat, arms folded over her chest. Joanne and Tracy stood behind her, expressions lost in the dark as the security light blinked out. Nothing broke the silence of the hall as we stared at each other.

Rosa arched an eyebrow as she looked at me. "So what's up, Lil?"

"Just wanted some fresh air."

"Witch, please," Joanne snorted, flipping her pin-straight black hair over her shoulder. "You hate nature. The only time you ever climbed a tree was when a wolf chased you up one. Come on."

77

I glanced at Tracy, hovering off to the side with a hint of panic around her eyes. She didn't trust them. Maybe didn't trust me. Either way, I couldn't tell Rosa and Joanne the truth. Not yet. I rubbed my temples. "Curiosity, I guess. Whatever you did last night felt wrong. I figured you had another two nights of casting and I wanted to see what you were up to."

"We did exactly what Anne Marie—"

"Come on," I said, interrupting Joanne with her own words. "You had to feel what happened last night. There's something wrong in that spell."

Joanne shook her head. "We have two new witches; we're trying to rebuild the coven. It's not easy balancing them when they don't have any experience."

There was no telling who introduced dark magic into their spell, but it had to be one of the nine in the coven. I didn't move from the doorway, didn't offer to let them in. Mostly it was shame at the peeling paint and shabby hand-me-downs inside, but my dad's long-ago lesson never to invite trouble inside also echoed in the back of my head.

A thump across the hall, followed by Chompers' muffled voice yelling, "Go ahead, call the police. Then what?" drew Rosa's attention. Her eyes narrowed as she looked back at the other apartment.

I cleared my throat. "So why risk something that big with untried witches?"

"The ones we trusted died or left," Rosa said. She looked at me with something like accusation, since I'd been one of the ones who left.

I held up my hands to fend off whatever might have followed, even though none of them added anything. We'd said all we needed to say about that... unpleasantness four years earlier. Or so I hoped. "What was so important it couldn't wait until you trusted the ones you have?"

"Information." Tracy spoke up after the silence stretched

and neither of the other witches looked inclined to answer. "We need answers, and this is the only way to get them."

"Answers about what?"

Another thump, and the sound of breaking glass reached us through the door. Rosa looked at me. "What is that?"

"He argues with his fists."

"A real man." Her voice dripped scorn, her hands clenched. The tattoos on her knuckles stretched, distorted. She didn't bother with a glamour to disguise them, and I didn't blame her.

"A witch." I shook my head, staring at the other door. "I tried to get her out. She won't leave him. Needs him for something, but she won't tell me what."

"You're a fucking war witch," Joanne said. She gestured over her shoulder, two-inch-long sharpened nails a flicker of red danger. She looked, as usual, like she should have been dancing in the trendiest club in the city. "Make him leave."

"Not my place." I winced at another round of shouting, another threatening, "Who would want you? Who?" I tried to concentrate, wondering when we would have to intervene. "He's aligned. If I do anything to him, the Styrma would crush me before I could explain. And Anne Marie would be out front."

Tracy started shaking her head. "She wouldn't—"

"You know it's true," Joanne said under her breath. She tapped those long nails against her perfectly white teeth, squinting a little as she studied me. Debating what to do about me, maybe.

When she didn't go on, I took a deep breath. "I don't know what information you need, but for what it's worth, please don't complete that spell. Walk away from it. There's something wrong."

"What's wrong with it?" Tracy said, just as Rosa started, "We have to finish."

"I don't know, exactly." A small lie, really. Small enough it

79

wouldn't hurt anything. "But it's not good. You can bind and banish it without completing the spell, it's—"

Joanne looked at me with an unnerving intensity. "If we don't finish, it will sap our magic for weeks. We can't afford to be weak now; there are too many threats. This will fix it, Lil. It's the only way."

The stairs creaked, almost lost in another thump-thump against the wall. I stared into the inky shadows, chest tightening. Maybe they'd called the Styrma on me anyway, just in case.

Rosa said, "Chica, you don't understand. For the witches to survive this bullshit with the wolves, we—" just as Leif stepped onto the landing.

The three witches froze. Leif's eyebrows arched. "You what?"

# CHAPTER 8

*S*hit and double shit.

Rosa remained unflappable, though Joanne had guilt written all over her face. Guilt over what, I didn't know. But Rosa, having spent her first twenty years surviving vicious gang wars, didn't even blink. Looking as serene as a tiger, surveying her domain, she arched an imperious eyebrow. "Must attend to witch business. Chief Investigator, dare I ask what you're doing here?"

"Investigating."

"Have you found Cara and Danielle yet?" This from Tracy, leaning forward into the light until her foot scuffed my welcome mat.

His lips thinned. "No one can track them. Has their coven found anything?"

"They scried," Joanne said, glancing down as her phone chimed. "But couldn't see anything. Which means the witches are dead or shielded by something pretty fucking powerful."

Or in another realm, I added silently. A demon realm. But still dead, so she covered it well enough.

"We're still looking." He tapped a small notebook against

his palm, his attention drifting to me. "You did not answer your phone."

I opened my mouth, about to spew excuses for missing whatever interview he'd planned, but Leif went still. A scream, quickly cut off, reached us. He raised a hand to stop whatever I or Tracy had been about to say, then did an about-face. His fist made a dent in the metal door across the hall when he knocked. Immediate, total silence rocked the hall. Even the crickets stopped chirping.

An eternity passed, as I held my breath. Chompers did not appear. Leif spoke in a remarkably even tone, despite the way his hands clenched and unclenched. "Open the door or I will open it for you."

"Is there a problem?" Chompers started, all smiles and teeth as the door cracked an inch.

My skin crawled.

"Yeah." The Chief Investigator reached into the apartment and caught the front of his shirt, yanking Chompers into the hall. "Shitbags who beat women."

"Fine talk from an animal," the witch snapped, fighting against Leif's iron grip. "And I didn't do anything. She's clumsy; she fell."

Rosa glanced at Tracy and Joanne, unspoken orders passing between them, and the younger women moved around Leif to enter the apartment. Rosa seemed to grow a foot as her magic buoyed her up, reinforcing her already tough shell. Chompers tried to meet her in kind, tried to summon his own magic to fight her and Leif off, but he was no match for a war witch. Especially one as vengeful as Rosa. She smiled sweetly as she hexed him, though, and froze the other witch against the wall. "Chief Investigator, release him. This is witch business."

"Rosa—"

"Release him. We will handle this."

Joanne and Tracy emerged, half-carrying Amber, who still

protested that nothing was wrong, she'd fallen, it was her fault. Her arm hung at a strange angle, and old and new bruises covered her arms and throat. Leif's expression hardened when he saw her, and he threw Chompers head-first into the door before propping the witch up in front of Rosa. "See that you do."

Tracy paused long enough to say to me, "I'll call you later. We'll take care of her," before she and Joanne helped Amber down the stairs. Leif started to say something about the Alliance hospital, but Tracy held up a hand. "Witch business," she said, and didn't turn.

The Chief Investigator looked about ready to strangle the next person to tell him something wasn't his business, which was tempting as his attention landed on me. Rosa still took up most of landing, though, and her blue-green magic tangled around Chompers and cut him off from just about everything —magic, light, sound, maybe air by the way he started turning purple. Her eyes narrowed and a muscle jumped in her jaw. Chompers contorted, flailing.

"*Hermana*," I said quietly, not daring to reach through my door ward to touch her. Her magic could react, or mine would, and all hell would break loose. "Don't kill him in the hallway."

"Why not?"

I sighed. "I'll have to get another welcome mat. This is already the third one this year. And then the cops will be around a lot, and there'll be a mess, and reporters. Saints help us if he leaves a ghost. Can't you take him somewhere else?"

She unleashed a string of the foulest Spanish I'd never been able to translate, but she eased the magical grip until Chompers sucked in air. Rosa gave me a dark look over her shoulder. "I will take care of this... *pendejo* now, but we will talk soon. *Claro*?"

"Yeah. *Claro*."

She frog-marched Chompers to the stairs, and damned if he didn't trip himself and fall all the way down.

Leif waited until she'd gotten Chompers out of sight, though her lightning-fast assessment of the witch's character and family tree remained audible for some time, then looked at me. "What will they do to him?"

"Well..." I chewed my lower lip as I leaned to see where their cars started, down on the street. Sometimes witch business was tough to predict. "I don't think she'll kill him."

"Wonderful," he said under his breath, then frowned at me as he held his phone to his ear. He spoke quickly to someone, telling them to send an investigator to "assist" Rosa with processing the perpetrator. When he'd finished, he shut the door to Chompers' apartment and gestured at mine. "We should talk inside."

I took a deep breath and a step back, for half a second wanting to shut the door in his face. He couldn't defeat my wards, would know better than to even try, and—I banished the thought and reached for the touchstone on the wall to amp down the wards. "Okay, but could we make it quick?"

My fingers were still a foot away as he stepped into the wards, attention on his notebook, "There's a warrant—"

"Wait," I said, lurching forward as he hit the invisible divide and blue sparked out in a lightning spiderweb from where he made contact. Shit and double shit. I grabbed at the ward, dragging as much magic out of the defense as I could and redirecting what remained into a childish hex as thunder boomed from the broken ward. He launched backward, leaving a slight indent in the already-chipped plaster across the hall. Purple gooey glitter covered him from head to toe. The excess magic whirled through me, squeezing my heart.

Silence rocked the small landing, and as I stared at the unconscious Chief Investigator, collapsed and disjointed as an abandoned marionette against the wall, the door at the very end of the building opened a hairsbreadth. Another witch peeked into the hall, caught sight of who I'd just zapped, and said, "I didn't see anything, I didn't hear anything," before locking and chaining her door.

I steadied myself on the doorjamb, nauseated from the surge of magic spinning through me, disoriented and blinking through the double vision of that much power. The floor seemed the best option, though I didn't have much choice as my knees wobbled and gave out. I concentrated on breathing through the pain, ears ringing, but kept my attention on Leif. Watching his chest rise and fall so I could time my breath to the same steady rhythm. He still breathed, at least. I hadn't killed him.

My head hit the wall with a thud. Cold sweat broke out all over me, my hands shook as I wiped them on my jeans, and my vision darkened around the edges. Couldn't pass out. Couldn't. Bitterness coated my tongue and I tried to swallow as everything flashed hot and cold.

He came awake in a rush, eyes snapping open as he lurched halfway to his feet, and his gold gaze pinned me to the wall more effectively than my own magic as the wolf roared to the surface. Saints preserve me.

# CHAPTER 9

*H*e breathed through his mouth, wild-eyed and searching for the threat, and maintained a defensive crouch even as nothing else moved. I swallowed around the cotton in my mouth so I could explain to the beast that he hadn't been attacked, to maybe get him to think twice before he ran through the wards again and killed us both. "You hit the wards."

It still took a good thirty seconds for the gold to fade from his eyes and his breathing to steady. He straightened, grimacing as he moved his shoulders and adjusted his jaw, then looked at his hands. Looked down at himself. "What the f—" He cut off, eyes narrowing as he looked at me. "What is on me?"

He never swore in front of women. Ever. That he'd almost slipped was a bad sign. I took shallow breaths, not quite panting, wondering when the burn of misused magic would fade. It had to end eventually. I remembered that much. The wards still sparked and shivered, rebuilding after the impact. "Only way to keep it from killing you. Different hex."

"What's wrong with you?"

"Took as much out of it as I could," I said, attempting a

smile. Even that hurt. There wasn't enough ibuprofen in the city to dent the pain. "Magic had to go somewhere."

"So you just sucked up most of a Class III ward?"

"Class IV," I said, closing my eyes. "You're welcome."

He snorted, then winced again as he moved his shoulders, glancing up and down the hall. He turned to study the purple glitter dent he'd left on the wall. He shook his head, then gestured at my door. "Let me in, then. You don't want me standing out here like this."

That was for damned sure. My vision grew splotchy, though, and my hands shook as I tried to push myself up and everything went clammy again. I sank back, the hall spinning around me, and my stomach rebelled. "Just need a second."

A muscle jumped in his jaw. His voice, even and calm, provided simple instructions through the static in my brain. "Arms over your head. Breathe in through your nose, out through your mouth. The touchstone is on your right, two feet up. Your other right, Lil."

I would have blushed, but let my left arm fall to my lap, too miserable even for embarrassment. Tried again with my right, fingers searching for the magical spot.

"Up another two inches. Reach for it. Straight up."

I took a breath and shoved myself up enough to reach the touchstone and disable the wards. The blue lightning disappeared from the doorway, but he didn't move. Leif raised his eyebrows. "May I come in?"

A breathy laugh escaped as I leaned my head back against the wall, though I flopped my left arm out toward the apartment interior. "Be welcome, be at ease, find rest within."

"Right." He edged through the doorway sideways, frowning at the threshold, then stood over me with his hands on his hips after closing the door. "Okay, superstar. What's next?"

Leaving the hex on him seemed like fitting punishment for

such a smart-ass. I braced my hands on the floor, dreading the effort it would take to stand. "Well—"

He caught my arm and hoisted me upright, steadying me as I swayed with the rush of blood from my head. I looked at his chin from only an inch or so away, trying to breathe normally. I cleared my throat, but words didn't seem forthcoming as I stood there and resisted the urge to lean against his chest despite the purple glitter. The Chief Investigator half-carried me down the entry hall to the living room, shaking his head, and dropped me onto the faux-leather loveseat next to the television that hadn't worked in months. "At least you're not going to run off this time. Do you need water or food or something?"

"No," I said, too embarrassed to even suggest he go into my kitchen. No doubt his superior sense of smell and the dirty dishes in the sink had already revealed I'd eaten pizza and cereal for the last two weeks. My cheeks were almost as purple as his as Leif surveyed the apartment, silent perusal slow and measured. I cleared my throat again, struggling for words. "I just need a minute."

He said nothing as he stood near the overflowing bookshelf, hands laced behind his back. Measuring, evaluating, taking note of the peeling paint and shabby hand-me-downs and the burns in the worn carpet. Judging the titles I kept and the ones hidden in the back. He glanced at the purple slime coating his hands. "How do I get this off?"

"Soap and water. A little elbow grease." A small lie. Infinitesimal. A sliver of payback for calling me "superstar." My vision stabilized, the tremor leaving my hands. I glanced at the glitter coating the arm of my sweater from where he'd touched me, and frowned.

"Right." From the look on his face, he didn't believe me.

"It's okay. You look good in purple."

A Cheshire cat grin spread across his face, made more ridiculous by the glint of white teeth in a purple beard. "Do I."

I flushed, waving the implications away. "Just an observation. Was there something you wanted to talk about?"

"A couple of things, actually," he said, but the smile remained. After a moment of letting me suffer, he tilted his head toward the door. "What did the witches want?"

"Witch business," I said automatically, then bit my lip.

"Nice try." He studied me, arms folded over his chest. "They led us to believe you didn't keep in contact. That there wasn't a relationship anymore."

"We don't. There isn't." It hurt to admit. My failing, my fault. My coven, moved on without me.

"Then why were they on your doorstep?"

I took a deep breath, managing to sit upright as I searched for a socially acceptable lie that didn't out the coven for doing questionable magic. "They asked about the missing witches. If I'd heard anything."

"Why would they think you know anything about it?"

"Nonaligned," I said with a shrug. "Rosa thought I might have heard something that no one would tell Alliance covens."

"And have you?"

"No. Nothing." I stared unseeing at the floor near his feet, wishing there were a much easier explanation. And wishing as well that I didn't have to work the next morning.

"If you hear anything, call me. Not them. Got it?"

I glanced up, a little surprised that he would expect me to go outside the covens. "Why?"

"I have my reasons." He studied me a moment longer after I nodded, then went on. "We received the External request to identify all the witches in the Pug last night, with a special request to identify you by name, rank, and location. We're slow-rolling them as much as we can, but there are a couple of other issues brewing. If push comes to shove, the Judge will side with them and I'll have to bring you in for an interview."

I nodded. "I understand." Even though he knew it wouldn't be easy and I wouldn't go willingly.

"You'll have a day's warning," he added, and I looked up, startled. That sounded dangerously close to a head start. Leif smiled with only half his mouth. "Professional courtesy for a Hero of the Second Revolution."

I made a face. I refused to dignify the teasing with a response.

"Where were you yesterday, before the Pug?"

"Work," I said. "Then a memorial at the Skein for the anniversary."

"What time?"

I frowned, drumming my fingers on the arm of the chair. "I think we started at nine."

"Anyone else can verify that?"

"Tracy, Rosa, Joanne, and Andre." I took a deep breath. "Anne Marie and Jacques showed up after we finished, had a few others with them that I didn't recognize."

"The First Coven gathered last night?" His eyebrows rose and he made a thoughtful noise. "What were they up to?"

"I didn't ask, and they didn't say." I didn't quite meet his gaze. It felt too exposed, too vulnerable, to have him in my apartment. "I left for Mo's party."

A muscle in his jaw jumped as he studied me, measuring my response. I willed myself to calm. The wolves couldn't smell lies, of course—that was ridiculous. But they could hear an elevated heart rate, could see dilated pupils, could smell perspiration. Deception was a messy business.

He glanced at his notebook, leaving purple smudges on the cover. "Did anything out of the ordinary happen on your way to the Pug?"

My heart jumped, but I refused to move. "The bus broke down. I had to walk. That was it."

"Did you hear or see anything strange?"

Like dark witches performing a sacrifice in an alley? I shrugged again. "The bus driver was a bigot, but I didn't stick around to ask him why. It was cold, and I ran most of the way to the bar."

Leif waited, letting the silence stretch. He didn't move as his phone rang, gaze still on me, but eventually he pulled it out of his pocket and held it gingerly. "Yeah."

The conversation went on but his attention didn't waver from me, and after a few minutes I started to squirm. He hung up, tucking the phone away. "Anything else you need to tell me, Lily?"

And once again I was tempted. It would be easy to tell him everything. He could fix most of it. At least then everything was out of my hands. But I only shook my head. "Nothing I can think of."

His lips thinned as he frowned, studying me for another long moment before he tilted his head at the door. "I have to go interview someone at the hospital, but there are a few more things we need to clear up. If you're not staying with Mo, be careful. We don't know what happened to the other two witches. It's still possible the Externals have something to do with it. It would be a shame for you to be the next one to disappear."

"Yeah," I said, levering to my feet so I could walk him out and reset my wards. "A damn shame."

He snorted, waiting to make sure I stayed upright before heading for the door. "Seriously. Be careful."

"That guy—Stefan? The tall one, right? What about the pudgy one?"

"Eric? What about him?"

I shook my head, frowning at the floor as he opened the door. "He looked weird, didn't say much. Usually the quiet ones are the dangerous ones."

"Not in this case. Eric is ... odd, definitely, but he's slow.

92

Thinks things through, then acts. Stefan is the short fuse." His head tilted as he studied me. "Did Eric say something to you? Has he tried to contact you?"

"No, of course not." I bit my lip, trying to banish the memory of the External with the glamour. "And...hold on a sec."

He was halfway out the door when I reached out and touched his bicep, tugging the hex free until it recoiled and the purple glitter disappeared. He looked down at his clean clothes, then up at me. The smile returned. "Thought I looked good in purple?"

"Not *that* good," I said, cheeks heating. I caught the door, started to close it.

"Be careful," he said. "And call if you hear anything."

"Sure." I shut the door and leaned back against it, closing my eyes as I massaged my temples. Saints save me.

I amped the wards back up and staggered to my bedroom.

# CHAPTER 10

For a few months during the war, I forgot what I really looked like. I hid my face behind a glamour every day, every waking moment, and tweaked my appearance even when I used something like my real face. I avoided mirrors, fearing the demons who could appear within their depths and not wanting to see what the years had done to me. My real appearance faded from memory until, one day, I looked into a scrying bowl and didn't recognize the person staring back at me. It didn't bother me until a dream reminded me I had my father's eyes and my mother's cheekbones. Mammo's chin, Farfar's unfortunate ears. And then I dreaded losing even the smallest details of their memories—including my own face.

I got dark hair from my mother, long chestnut locks that she attributed to her old Irish roots and their fae ancestors. She told me stories of the Old Celts and their warrior queens, fighting the Romans and maybe even the Vikings. At which point she would laugh and claim that was why she and Dad were destined to meet, since his people had been chasing after hers for centuries.

My blue eyes came from Dad's side of the family, and he

joked a Viking princess stared back at him when he tried to punish me, chilling his blood to face a descendant of Erik the Red. Never mind that his eyes were just as blue and could be just as cold when he worked magic. The first time I saw my own Morrigan face, it was looking at Dad in the middle of a complicated, powerful spell.

Unearthing an authentic photograph took days of searching through boxes in our old house, most of Mother's meticulous organization overturned as the hunters destroyed everything. There was only one photo I knew of where all three of us used our true faces, so we would always remember what we really looked like. At the time I had more freckles than sense, so I whined about at least covering my complexion, but Mother insisted. Memories are tricky, she'd said. She was right.

The photo froze us just after the Breaking, as magic revealed itself to the world and humans realized Others walked among them, but before everything descended into the chaos and hatred of war. My parents sensed what was coming, though, and tried to hide it from me. And still the unspoken fear that none of us would survive the approaching conflagration haunted us.

Though I resented having my freckles immortalized along with my overbite, I treasured the glossy rectangle that preserved their memory. I carried it with me everywhere, even after the Truce, not because I feared losing my face again, but because I did not trust its safety anywhere. But as I jumped into an alley to avoid multiple External vans parked outside the restaurant, keeping a family photo of two executed witches and my real face seemed instead an unbelievably stupid thing to do.

I hid near the staff entrance, debating the best way to walk away from the restaurant as Externals in riot gear loitered outside in the street and crowds of humans lingered to witness heavy-handed justice being dealt the animals and witches.

Maybe Leif hadn't been serious about that head start. Saints preserve me.

A hand, weighty with authority, propelled me around the corner as I peered out of the alley. Something jostled me into a shadow and I fought back, kicking and punching because magic would drag the entire arrest team on top of me. We made fun of the humans' crude gadgets and inelegant efforts to understand and quantify magic, but some of their sensors worked well enough to give us trouble. I grabbed the hand and bent it back, bringing my knee up into their gut just to get some room.

The pudgy External, Eric, staggered back. "Just wait, just wait."

"What the fuck?" I put my back to the wall, trying to catch my breath as my hands shook.

"Hear me out," he said.

"You're not going to arrest me," I said, and meant every word of it. If he couldn't hear the warning, it was his own fault.

"Don't be stupid." He frowned at the mouth of the alley, where authoritative voices drew near, then gestured for me to ease farther into the shadows.

I edged in the general direction, eyes narrowed to study him and that weird glamour he used. "Who the hell are you? What do you want?"

"I want you to survive the next couple of days," he said under his breath, straightening his coat and tie. "And I'm a friend."

A rude noise was the best response I could manage.

"Here," and he held out a handful of metal. A necklace.

"No way in hell." I put my hands behind my back. If he tried to collar me, a killing hex was the only response.

"It's not iron," he muttered, taking a step closer. Held up a ring on the end of the necklace. "Wear it, hide it under your shirt, but let them see it. It's the only way you're getting out of that," and he nodded in the direction of the restaurant.

"I could just walk away," I said. "Kill you and be gone."

"Stefan has your name already, regardless of how the dogs are trying to protect you. The fact that they won't identify you only makes you a better target. He's bucking for a promotion and he'll get there by crushing you."

"He's your partner," I said, heart beating faster. "Why are you telling me this? What's in it for you?"

"I have my reasons, but this," he said, gesturing at the alley. "Is not the place to discuss them." He tossed the necklace and ring at me; out of reflex, I caught them both.

A delicate summoner's ring rested in my palm, done in fancy filigree with a dark blue lapis lazuli stone, threaded with gold. It was a beautiful ring, but I didn't recognize the coven symbol on the panel. "What...whose ring is this?"

"I'll explain later. But you have to wear that. They won't believe you're a mender." And he raised his eyebrow as I touched the jade ring on my finger.

I started to argue, confident in my deception, and he rolled his eyes, face slipping under an oil rainbow. "No one would believe that—you've got too much attitude to be a mender. When he questions you, show him the blue one. He'll let you go."

"Why?" I shook my head, backing up with the necklace clenched in my hand. "It's just a ring, it—"

"This is the only way. Trust me." Eric called over his shoulder, "Got one here," and then turned back to face me. "He doesn't have enough to arrest you yet. Don't give him a reason."

"But—"

I trailed off as two Neanderthals in utility belts and body armor approached, looking grim. Eric stood aside as one grabbed my arm and dragged me toward the restaurant, through a crowd of more Externals guarding employees waiting to be processed.

I had no reason to trust him. None. But he was still a question mark, and Stefan, at least, was a clear threat. If I could delay long enough, the Alliance would show up to defend at least their aligned members, and I could benefit from their presence. I clenched my jaw as the behemoth shoved me into a chair in the dining room of the restaurant and I faced a sour-faced young woman in uniform.

* * *

THE SILVER CHILLED my neck as I worked to control my breathing and look like a meek mender, not the War Witch. Scared girl, not guilty witch with reason to fight. The easiest way to keep Lily alive was to forget I'd ever been Lilith. But in the back of my head, anger at Stefan's hounding, at the targeting of young witches like Cheryl, at all the unfair treatment we dealt with since the Truce, began a slow burn.

The officer in front of me was bored with me before the interview even started, looking around with palpable envy at the Externals interviewing the far more dangerous shifters. Her cheeks puffed out as she exhaled. "Name."

"Lily."

"Coven."

I tried to remember the lies seeded into their files over the past few years. The fake coven I'd given them when I first applied for the waitressing job floated up through my memory. "Dogwood West."

Her lips twisted. "Rank."

My skin crawled as the burly External behind me shifted his weight and the steel chain at his belt sent a frisson of iron shivers through me, but I concentrated on the positives—the wolves all had two or three guards, so only having one was a good sign. I held out my right hand, the jade ring sufficient proof, and made my fingers tremble for added benefit. "Mender."

She sniffed, unimpressed. "Where were you last night?"

"At home."

"Can anyone verify that?"

For a hysterical moment, I considered telling her Leif, just to see her reaction. The Chief Investigator could be a useful friend, but more often he was a liability. Better sense prevailed before I opened my mouth. "No. Just me."

She retrieved a small black box from under the table, and my heart plummeted. A divireader, one of their damnable gadgets but unfortunately one that usually worked. It could be fooled, of course, since nonmagical humans designed it, but fooling the box required having a glamour already in place.

The jig was up, as Dad had often said, twiddling a cigar between his fingers.

I balanced my fingers on the edge of the table as she pushed buttons on it and the thing lit up. "What if I refuse?"

Her gaze drifted to the behemoth behind me, and cruelty chiseled a smile across her face. "Go ahead."

An unspoken "I dare you" lingered. Doubtless the guard would break my arms and they'd do the test anyway. I took a deep breath and put my fingers on the small metal pads on each side of the box, and said a brief prayer. Electricity jolted into my left hand, through me, and out my right, where it registered in the box. I yanked my hands away at the sting.

The box beeped and a blue light went on. She looked at the screen, then my ring, then her notes, then the box. She cleared the results. "Again."

So I did it again, and again the blue light went on. I held my breath. Luckily only the most sophisticated divireaders could detect war witches. There were so few of us that the majority of divireaders only read to summoner, the next-most powerful rank.

The woman scowled, shoved her chair back, and strode over to a thin External supervising another interrogation. He didn't look away from the Kodiak bear shifter who looked about ready to treat him like a salmon, but I recognized Stefan's mousy hair. Great. I slid away from the table, needing space, but froze as sharp steel rested against my neck.

My flesh burned as my magic reacted to the hint of iron. I leaned to escape the pain, but the knife followed. "Not another move, witch."

Blood trickled down my neck in a warm crawl.

I took a breath to argue or defend myself, or maybe just to hex him and run, but swallowed my objections as the woman returned. She straightened her papers with exaggerated care, squaring the corners. "You," she said. "Are not a mender."

"What do we have here?" Stefan sauntered over to stand next to her, the delighted smile on his face implying we were long-lost friends. He upended my bag, the contents sliding across the table, and all motion in the restaurant ceased as everyone noticed my interview deteriorating. Stefan poked through my things. "No Chief Canine to protect you today. How unfortunate."

"No, he had plans with your sister."

A fist slammed into my ear and I pitched out of the chair. I lay on the cool wood floor and tried to be grateful the knife wasn't on my neck when the goon struck, else I might have been beheaded. I wobbled to my knees, leaning against the chair and rubbing my jaw. It hurt almost as much as Leif running into my wards. The shifters scented blood, and filled the air with low growling.

Stefan didn't seem particularly disturbed as he hefted my bag of salt. "Really?"

I closed one eye to squint at him, hoping the room would

steady and at least give me one target instead of three. "Might have been your mom."

I ducked the first punch, but the second caught me in the kidney. "Or not," I wheezed from the floor, laughing at my own stupidity. Saints grant me the sense to keep my mouth shut. As I used the table to pull myself up, Stefan wrenched the jade ring from my finger. My head pounded and the world blurred around the edges, but I forced myself up. "No, that's—"

The guard hauled me back, shaking me hard enough to rattle my teeth. Stefan toyed with the jade ring, then held out his hand. "Your true ring."

I concentrated on breathing despite the stabbing pain in my side, and hoped I hadn't broken a rib. Saints guide my path, saints protect my cast, saints guard my fate.

But the ringing in my ear made it hard to hear whether the saints chose to speak.

"*That* is my ring." I didn't look away from it, desperate. It was all I had left of Sam.

"You're not a mender. That's one felony. You have five seconds to give me your real ring, or I will start adding to the list."

The goon shook me again and the necklace slipped from inside my shirt. I caught at it, stomach lurching, and the woman lunged for it as well. Stefan beat us both, announcing, "Summoner," as he seized the ring.

In a heartbeat, three more goons loomed over me and aimed juiced-up tasers at my head. The behemoth put his knife to my throat once more, doubtless for the pleasure of killing me personally.

Shit.

I locked my knees and straightened, no easy feat with my head swimming and Stefan pulling me off-balance with his grip on the necklace. I would not die quietly, even with four mountains of muscle at my back and iron at my neck. The shifters would join in if I decided to fight—if not because they wanted to help, then at least because all shifters liked a fight and the Externals were their favorite adversary.

Stefan scowled as he studied the ring. "Where did you get this?"

I clenched my jaw so a grin wouldn't give away my anticipation as adrenaline surged and good sense burned out in flashes of memory and smoke. When I hexed him, he wouldn't get back up. From there, I had to fight my way out of the building and disappear. I knew spells for that, too, and stacked them in my mind.

A quick calculus gave me a plan: Stefan first, then the four goons behind me, then the woman. The ten more nearest at the interview tables would be next, and another twenty or so after that, long distance. Thirty seconds to clear the room of humans, without any shifter help. A minute, tops, if I missed on the first try. My stomach burbled with a familiar squirm of nerves and giddiness and sheer terror: battle. Under it all, the whispered promise of oceans of magic lured me in—it would be so easy. I wouldn't be afraid ever again, I wouldn't be weak or alone. Using all of that magic made me invincible, something those humans couldn't understand.

Stefan dropped the ring and turned on his heel. "Come with me."

As if I had a choice. Two goons picked me up and carried me into the manager's vacant office at the rear of the dining room. There was no telling where Paul hid, or if he'd even been called. I swayed in front of the vacant desk as the goons released me. A flash of movement was the only warning before Stefan's fist smashed into my nose. I landed in a heap, and took a moment to reflect on the choices I'd made as my vision swam and blood filled my mouth again.

Stefan gripped my elbow as he leaned over me, his voice cold. "Do not ever talk about my family, witch." He hauled me up and dropped me in a chair, going behind the desk to watch me bleed. "Who do you work for?"

I staunched the blood from my nose with my sleeve, grateful for the black uniform. My nose throbbed in time with my racing heart, my eyes watering and blurring him further. "I'm just a waitress."

He pointed at the necklace. "Who gave you that?"

I thought of the odd-faced External. I was a dead witch whether I lied or not, and if I brought one of them down with me—more the better. "Eric."

"When did you last talk to him?"

I sat forward, unnerved at having so many Externals in the restaurant behind me, and thought of my jade ring. Probably disappeared into someone's pocket, since we all knew the Externals collected alignment rings as trophies. "Today."

"What did you report?"

"Nothing." I squinted as the room spun and he drifted from two to three figures, and pressed under my nose. Blasted humans.

The thin mustache twitched. "What did you see last night?"

"I didn't see anything." Nausea brewed in my guts, amplified by the adrenaline and the blood leaking down my throat.

"He trained you well," Stefan said under his breath. He leaned over the desk, jabbing a finger at me. "But the Slough is *my* area. He will not bungle this investigation. If you or he fucks this up for me, I'll put you both in the ground. Understood?"

I shook my head, though it set the world spinning more. "I don't know what you're talking about, I don't give a shit about—"

"Stop denying it." His eyes narrowed. "I'll let you go this time, but don't you dare leave the city. This isn't finished."

I tried to formulate a reply that wasn't incredulous of my good fortune or questioning what that damn ring meant, but froze as his face screwed into a ferocious snarl. I slid lower in the chair. Whatever he saw behind me wasn't something I wanted to face.

# CHAPTER 11

The door creaked and I braced for another knock on the head. Instead, a gravelly voice said, "Stefan. Imagine my surprise to hear you're behind these illegal interrogations."

"Leif," the External said, feigning surprise. "Why are you here?"

"An illegal raid, illegal detainment of Others without recourse to their packs and covens, and threats of reprisal without official charges. Dangerously close to violating the Truce. I don't want to call the Judge today. Let them go."

The External didn't budge. "We're almost finished." And he waited, as if Leif would simply turn and go.

"Right now, Stefan." Leif sounded tired more than anything. "Follow the process."

A vein bulged in the External's temple, and I held my breath. He ground out, "Very well. Agent Simons, outside, will assist you with—"

"This one too."

"She's not one of yours."

"They are all mine today. Release her."

Stefan made a sharp, shooing gesture at me, as if he could hurl me through the wall based on hate alone. I braced myself to rise, turning, and Leif registered the smallest amount of surprise at seeing me. Then his focus snapped to my broken nose and the blood no doubt crusting my lips and chin.

His eyes were gray when he was happy, ice blue when he grew angry, and gold when he was furious beyond all reason. They were molten copper as he crouched in front of me, catching my chin so he could examine my nose. His voice dropped an octave or two. "Who did that?"

Before I could answer, listing to the side as my brain throbbed, Stefan tried to wedge between us. "She refused to cooperate and attacked me. Worry about your own pack before she drags you down, too."

"She is a friend of my pack," Leif said, growling. I held my breath; that was a lie dangerous for us both. His words broke like ice on ice. "You've drawn blood, Stefan. You will pay in kind."

I faced two Stefans as he stood over Leif's shoulder, as he sauntered back into the main room and picked my bag up from the table. He said, unconcerned, "We're done. For now."

With Leif's help, I stood and shuffled after the External until I could lean against the table, staring at the pile of my belongings. The battered photo, half-hidden and unremarked-upon near the bottom, gave me courage. As Stefan turned away, I said, "My ring."

His lip curled, but he gestured at the female External. "Give it to her."

"She's not a mender."

I took the ring from her, tempted to hex her to demonstrate why antagonizing a summoner was a dangerous game. I imagined all the destruction I could wreak on them for drawing my blood, and swayed. Leif steadied me even as he barked orders at the grim Styrma overseeing the Externals' departure, and the tension broke. The urge for vengeance faded. I slid the ring back on, thinking of Sam instead. It was the only gift of his I kept.

I focused on my bag, ignoring the sidelong looks from my coworkers. Leif nudged me toward a chair. "Sit. I'll be back."

I shut my swelling eye as I tried to inventory everything, every movement deliberate to keep my head and stomach in the right place. The Externals dragged their feet as they packed up and departed, attitude broadcasting that they weren't driven away by the Styrma or Leif. I touched the family photo before tucking it away.

Leif pulled a chair up next to me. "Couldn't even go ten hours without running into Stefan, hmm?"

"If you say 'I told you so,' I'm never speaking to you again," I said, then rested my head on my arms. It hurt my nose, but it kept the room from spinning.

"I'll get one of the menders." A warm hand settled on my shoulder, comforting but laden with complications.

I lifted my head, "No, it's—" but cut off under the intensity of his gaze. I took a deep breath. "I just need to sit a moment."

"Perfect." He flipped open the ever-present notebook. "And I told you so, by the way. I distinctly remember saying to avoid Stefan."

Nausea burbled in my stomach enough I considered puking on his shoes to pay him back. Instead I only watched him with my good eye, pain and what had to be a concussion making me unwise. "And you promised me a day's warning, so that's the second time your chivalry failed me. Bad form, wolf."

He came dangerously close to laughing, ducking his head to hide a smile as he drew his chair a little closer. I'd forgotten what a force he could be when he turned on the charm: it nearly blinded me as he looked up, running a hand over his short hair, gray eyes still flecked with gold. "I'll make it up to you somehow."

Caught in his gaze, I couldn't look away. My heartbeat slowed and the headache receded and a sense of easy familiarity, of comfort, struck me. Like rumpled sheets on a Sunday morning, still warm and welcoming. I felt almost drunk as I said, "Promise?"

Sparks of red pack magic dotted my vision as he smiled, just about to answer when one of Leif's Styrma, standing next to us for the saints only knew how long, cleared his throat. He grinned and studied me as he handed a stack of papers to Leif. "The complaints filed by Agent Tyroler."

"Thank you, Adam." Leif took the papers, still watching me. The other man remained, rocking back on his heels as he glanced between us, until Leif half-turned. "Something else I can help you with, wolf?"

"Nope." He beamed.

"Then go take statements while I finish questioning this witch."

"Oh, is that what you're doing?" The grin spread more and I massaged my temples. Just wonderful.

The Chief Investigator's eyes narrowed and his voice, still quiet, held a knife's edge. "Get lost, Adam."

"Sure thing, boss," he said with no small amount of glee, and retreated to where more of the Styrma waited. Once Adam joined them, the whispering started and several pairs of eyes focused on Leif and me.

Leif rubbed his jaw. "They gossip worse than the jackals," he said under his breath, then tucked away his notebook. "What did Stefan want?"

"Something about unauthorized magic," I said, though for the life of me I couldn't remember. I studied his dark jeans. He looked neat and clean with a pressed dress shirt and a charcoal sport coat, while I was a bloody, rumpled mess. Again.

I contemplated the gleam of his barely-visible French cufflinks until Leif said, "Lily?"

"Sorry." I flushed at being caught staring at him as he waited for a better answer. "Having trouble concentrating."

"Me too," he said. "Did Stefan ask about anything else? Threaten anything?"

He wouldn't stay in one place, his face drifting back and forth in front of me no matter how much I blinked. I squinted, wishing I could just lie down. "I don't think so."

"What did you tell him?"

"Nothing." I gave up trying to see through my swollen eye, watching him with just one. "You came in before I could come up with anything."

White teeth flashed in his red beard. "I forgot the white horse, but next time I'll get it right."

I snorted at the ridiculousness, then regretted it as blood dribbled from my nose. I didn't need rescuing, but it was tough to remember that when he smiled.

Leif handed me a handkerchief—a real cotton handkerchief with a monogram—and was about to go on when a deep voice said, "Boss, can this wait?"

"We're almost done," Leif said, tension rising in his posture as Mick crouched beside us.

Mick dropped his voice, gripping the back of my chair. "A friend of my pack is bleeding in public. I can't have that. I'll take her back to my house so she can clean up. You can finish flirting there."

"This is an interview."

"Right." Moriah's brother looked dangerously close to rolling his eyes. "How could it be anything else, with the giggling?"

"There was no giggling," Leif muttered, but he stood. "Take her to the pack house. It's safer. The Externals might raid your place, but they won't try mine."

The Chief Investigator helped me stand, letting me lean into him as the room tilted. I closed my good eye as I braced against his chest, warm and clean-smelling under the crisp shirt and soft jacket. He was solid and real as the world swam around me.

Definite giggling started in the crowd around Adam. Leif's eyes narrowed when he spotted them, and a flurry of movement erupted as the shifters became interested in every other part of the room. Leif transferred me to Mick, saying quietly, "Take care of your head first."

I'd already turned my focus to the door when Leif cleared his throat. "Lily."

I turned, wobbling at the end of Mick's grip. The Chief Investigator raised an eyebrow. "And yes, I promise."

As I tried to comprehend what he meant, Leif smiled, winked, and then strode after Adam and his co-conspirators, barking orders.

Mick half-carried me to the front of the restaurant, nodding to a bunch of grim shifters waiting on the street, and put me in the front seat of his waiting car. "You certainly got him all worked up."

"Not my fault." I rested my head against the seat, fighting down the urge to throw up. It was only after he started the car and pulled into traffic that I realized what Leif promised. All the blood rushed to my cheeks, surging painfully to my nose as well, and I rubbed my temples.

"That's what they all say," he said, shaking his head. We'd only gone another block or so before he took a deep breath. "Look, Lily. You're in a lot of trouble, and it's not the kind of trouble that nonaligned walk away from."

"I'll be fine."

"You will be if you align and swear to my pack."

Scowling hurt my face too much, so I settled for a disapproving frown. "I'm not joining the pack or the Alliance, Mick."

"They can't hold the Externals off forever, and the longer Leif tries, the guiltier you look. Frankly, Leif is just waiting to get more evidence so *he* can arrest you. Blaming you is easier than having to do a joint investigation."

"More evidence of what?" At least the concussion and headache made me too tired to really care.

"Does it matter? There have been half a dozen felonies in the last four days; they can pin any of them on you. The only thing that matters is that all of it goes away if you swear to the Alliance. Soren won't let the Externals arrest one of his people."

"Good to know the Peacemaker isn't interested in justice."

His eyes narrowed, grip tightening on the steering wheel. "There's more justice for some than for others, Lilith, and you should know that better than anyone."

My mouth went dry. Everything went still and quiet. I kept my hands on my thighs, staring at but not seeing them. "I beg your pardon."

"If there was justice, you wouldn't be here and you know it." He pulled over, shoving the car in park and half-turning to face me. "Friends in high places kept you off the executioner's stake, and it would be helpful if you remembered that."

"You don't know what you're talking about." I touched the jade ring, seeing it even without looking at it. Thinking of Sam.

"Fine. We'll all keep pretending that never happened. But today, here and now—without Mo, you'd be in the Reserve's loony bin in a padded room, talking to your ghosts. So pay it back, Lilith—align. Join the pack. Start doing what you know is right."

I reached for the door handle. "I'm done."

He grabbed my arm, jerked me back into the car. "You're going to the pack house, witch."

Magic surged and he slammed back into his door, blinking and shaking his hand. I kicked the door open and got out, bending down to speak despite almost pitching face-first back into the car. "What I know is right is not supporting an organization that coerces people into joining it."

I slammed the door and started walking, not looking back. I half-expected him to come after me and throw me into the car, since most alphas weren't particularly happy about hearing no from anyone. But the only sound was the car pulling away. I turned the first corner I came to and paused, leaning back against the brick building so I could gather my thoughts. Saints above. Maybe he was right about joining the pack, that I owed it to Mo. Maybe she was right and I owed it to myself.

My head pounded, my nose aching and throbbing. I'd never been a very good mender or healer; we'd always relied on Rosa. The need to call her nearly overwhelmed me. She would fix things. I looked around for the first time, trying to orient myself. And paused as I recognized the sign across the street and half a block down—Morningfair Charms. A dark SUV sat outside in the no-parking zone, and as I watched, a familiar mousy-haired human cop exited, Eric on his heels. I held my breath.

# CHAPTER 12

*I* shrank back into a doorway as Stefan scanned the street, getting into the driver's seat only after he frowned back at the empty sidewalks. It seemed like forever and yet only a blink before they drove away, disappearing around the corner. I counted to a hundred after they'd pulled away before bolting across the street. Anne Marie. She could have been hurt, could have been arrested and handed off to one of their arrest teams, could have been a snitch feeding them information...

The sign on the door read *Closed* but that never stopped me. I shouldered through it and ran into a solid wall of magic, gritting my teeth as black and blue tendrils of magic blasted into my chest and knocked me back. Anne Marie, waiting behind the counter, looked up in time to say, "Saints blast it—" before the backlash whirled out and caught her. It wrenched her away as the warding spell unbalanced and shook apart, confronted by the equal power of my magic.

My teeth rattled as I forced myself through, collapsing to the floor once I was inside, and the door shut behind me with sweetly-chiming bells. Shit.

Anne Marie, looking rumpled and aghast, braced herself against an aisle of charms. "What the hell are you doing?"

"Thought you were in trouble." I shook off the pins and needles of agony from confronting that much magic, and wobbled to my feet. She'd gotten a lot better. Or she had the coven helping her set wards. The only thing stronger was a circle of salt and bone and wood, preferably of oak, ash, and thorn.

"Nice try." Her glamour slipped under the shock of breaking wards, and she turned from a white-haired granny to a dark-haired woman not too much older than me, with an expression like craggy granite.

Spitting nails would have been more grateful. I tried for dignity. "You're welcome."

"Did you send them?"

"Don't be stupid." I glanced around the store, biting my lip. She sold charms and fortunes of dubious accuracy to humans. Grew herbs and stocked cauldrons and even kept a black cat. She catered to human expectations, just short of wearing a pointy hat and stirring a smoky cauldron, but had the gumption to call *me* the traitor. I pretended to examine a twig broom near the entrance, though it helped me keep my balance as the room continued to wobble around me. "They just raided the restaurant. Leif sent them away. I thought they might try to —you know."

Her chin tilted up. "Your concern is misplaced."

"No kidding."

"Especially since they're looking for you. I know I'm innocent, and I'm just as certain you're guilty."

I staggered into one of the aisles of packets of herbs, picked up a pre-mixed potion for true love and waved it at her. "Really? Guilty of what? Interfering with free will through love spells? Isn't that still illegal?"

"The charm is for the purchaser, to reignite passion in a

relationship." She limped back to the register behind a long counter, bracing her hands on the polished surface. "And you're guilty of something, Lilith. I know you're the only witch who could have been Ivan Darkwing, night before last."

I buried panic in studying the potion. Herbs and twigs and dust, only a touch of real magic. Eye of newt, toe of frog. "What makes you think that?"

"I had the area cleared of all witches. In a square mile, you were the only one nonaligned and unaccounted for who could have done... what you did, and used Ivan's name as an out."

"Done what?" I dropped the potion, wondering if I dared purchase a healing charm from her. If it meant helping the damn concussion from Stefan's fists and her wards, it would be worth it. Maybe Rosa would help patch up the rest of me, if I could find her.

"Either hurt that girl or killed the ones who did. It's got your fingerprints all over it."

Fear clogged my throat, but something else nagged at me. "Why did you clear the area?"

"None of your business." Color rose in her cheeks.

"Couldn't have been because you were doing some dirty magic?" I watched her, eyes narrowed, as I meandered through another aisle. Essential oils and creams, a variety of scents and enough magic to make my eyes water, stacked up in neat rows and columns. "Didn't want any witnesses, did you?"

"We didn't want the memorial to be interrupted." But she didn't quite meet my gaze. She'd never been good at lying. "And stop trying to change the subject. I know it was you, Lilith. Keep your mouth shut and your head down, and I won't tell Leif."

"If you had any proof," I said, stalking down the next aisle. I let my hand trail over the herbs in planters along the windows, watching the leaves wilt at the residual magic trailing from my fingers. "I wouldn't still be walking around. So maybe we're even, AM."

"I hardly—"

"What would Leif say if I told him what you guys were up to? What would Soren do if he knew you were summoning demons?"

She recoiled, expression almost comical in its disbelief. "We weren't summoning demons. How dare you imply—"

"I felt it, AM." I picked up a poultice, recognizing the name as one of Rosa's specialties, and a bottle of head-cure. I tossed them on the counter in front of her, praying I had enough cash in my bag. Payday was still a week away, and I hadn't gotten any tips in a couple of days. "Whatever you summoned, it came from a very dark place."

"You're mistaken." She jabbed at the register, then threw the two items into a small plastic bag. "Twenty-seven fifty."

"Twenty-seven—?" I cut off, shaking my head. "Saints. I always knew witches didn't believe in charity, but that seems a little much." I dug through my wallet, putting a few rumpled bills on the counter before I started searching for change to make up the difference. "Look, AM. I'm asking you. Please don't complete the spell tonight."

"I don't know what you're talking about."

I leveled a look at her and she had the grace to look a little ashamed. My change purse gave me another three dollars in quarters and dimes, and I reached into the depths of the bag for all the loose coins jingling around. "Come on. I know what I felt when that magic reacted. It's dangerous. There's something going on and it won't end well. It can't end well. Please. Just tie it off, banish it, start over later."

"We can't." She hesitated, on the verge of saying more, then shook her head. "That is, we won't. It's not your concern, Lilith, and if you insist on poking your nose into our business, we'll cut it off for you. Although," and she gestured at my face, her eyebrow raised. "You seem to be having that kind of trouble already."

"Anne Marie." I kept my voice quiet, bracing my hands on the counter. Not because I had to, certainly not. "Please believe me."

"You are a liar and a murderer," she said, gathering up the pile of coins and bills with shaking hands. "Why should I?"

"Because we were friends." It hurt to say. Hurt to remember. Hurt to beg.

She handed me a receipt. "You're three dollars short, but consider it a going-away present. If I see you again, Lilith, anywhere near my coven or our work, I will have you arrested and collared for dark magic."

"You wouldn't dare." I shook my head, tempted to leave the bag on the counter and walk away. But then I'd be out my money and the cure. So I shoved it in my purse, concentrating on that instead of how much I wanted to strangle her. "You'll implicate yourself, and I will absolutely tell Leif what you—"

"It would be worth it," she said, eyes cold. Expressionless. "To see you collared for dark magic. Worth every minute."

I wondered where along our journey we'd become enemies. I'd trained her, rescued her, given her a safe place in the early years of the war. Believed her a friend, second only to Tracy. But Anne Marie was always ambitious, anxious for power after a childhood spent with none, and she turned against me. Jealousy and ambition were a terrible combination. It destroyed our coven, and it got Sam killed.

So instead I addressed the take-a-penny tray. "If you need my help, Anne Marie—"

"We don't. Please leave."

I pursed my lips. Nodded. I felt defeated but angry—unable to convince her, unwilling to fight it anymore. "Fine. I hope you live long enough for me to say I told you so. Thanks for the three dollars. I'll pay you back."

She called something after me as I left, maybe warning me

she'd turn the wards up after I left, but it didn't matter. There was no reason to go back.

# CHAPTER 13

*I* knew Anne Marie well enough to know she and the coven would finish the spell that night, regardless of what I told them. The head-cure and poultice did enough to ease the pain that I could almost see straight by the time I got back to my apartment to prepare. A new door secured Chompers' and Amber's apartment; I held my breath as I paused outside it, wanting to knock to see if she was okay. Rosa hadn't called to mention any additional trouble, so I consigned Chompers to his fate and made a mental note to drop some food off with Amber the next morning. If he'd provided her some sort of magical help, maybe I could fill the gap until she got her future figured out. It was the least I could do.

I didn't spend long at home before heading out again, though I gathered enough supplies to hopefully avert disaster before Anne Marie's pride got all of us killed. The bag of salt weighed heavily on my shoulder as I ran for the bus, cursing my lack of vehicle with every step. The bus didn't get close enough to Anne Marie's house, even though I didn't know where exactly she lived, and I had to change routes three times before my magical senses picked up her trail. She'd always been a creature of habit, and the silver-blue wake of her magic through a neighborhood led me directly to her front door.

Most powerful witches left strong signatures of their personal aura where they lived and cast. It grew stronger over time, particularly if they didn't want the inconvenience of relocating every few years. I'd moved every month after the war, afraid of the coven and older enemies tracking me down, but after a few years, I forgot to be afraid. I struggled against the chaos in my memory and my thoughts half the time, so consistency in my surroundings helped. It was a tradeoff, but I never worked powerful magic where I lived to avoid the distinct beacon that developed as a result. Anne Marie wasn't so stringent.

She lived in a nice neighborhood—not as nice as the gated communities outside the city—but solidly middle class, in a house that could have fit a family of four. I paused near the mailbox to evaluate the security, and frowned as I searched the perimeter. Reinforced windows, a solid metal door, but no wards around the property.

I had to have missed something. I remained on the sidewalk in the lingering dusk, staring at her house and straining to see the wards or curses that no doubt protected her home. No sane witch would live in an unwarded house.

Something rustled in the bushes and I tensed. But only a house cat appeared, a mouse dangling from its jaws, and it slanted a disdainful look at me as it prowled through the flowerbeds and disappeared under Anne Marie's porch. I edged my foot forward to the walkway leading to her door, wincing as I braced for the backlash of whatever wards she might have hidden, but nothing happened. Nothing.

I stepped onto the walkway and looked around, wanting to stomp my feet in disgust at her sloppy security, but maybe a neighborhood as nice as hers didn't allow wards. It looked too nice to be an Other neighborhood, so maybe most of the homeowners were human. Most witches couldn't differentiate wards between human and animal forms, and wards that liquefied a couple of pets—or delivery guys—wouldn't go over well with the neighbors. Shredded golden retriever was the first ingredient for a witch-hunt.

She was at least a little more careful with her home, although not by much—a few wards protected the door and the front windows, though they hadn't been activated. They detected dark magic, not intruders, so it was easy enough to fiddle the lock open with a touch of magic.

I stood in the foyer for a long moment after shutting the door behind me, waiting for the other shoe to drop. I needed to find enough evidence of what Anne Marie planned to do that I could prove to Leif she was the cause of all the trouble. If things went badly when the coven cast a few hours later, then I wanted all the blame to land on Anne Marie. The grandfather clock against the wall reminded me there wasn't much time, if I hoped to still make it to the Skein and disrupt their spell.

When nothing moved in the house and the air remained undisturbed, I strolled through the foyer into the living room. My eyebrows rose as I looked around; it was as obsessively neat as her living quarters during the war. My fingers trailed over a shelf of knickknacks, all squared at right angles. Tracy and I had often unorganized Anne Marie's workspace, mixing pens and pencils, turning things upside down, shuffling papers, setting everything just slightly askew.

Occasionally war was very boring. We had a lot of time to come up with ways to amuse ourselves, and watching Anne Marie line her pencils up in precise order was enough some days.

My nose wrinkled at the forced perfection of the living room, though. The place looked like something out of a magazine—posed, staged, fake. Like Anne Marie and her glamour.

I took a deep breath and let my senses open, and a blaze of

magic called me up the stairs to a nondescript guest room over the kitchen. I tossed a handful of salt from my bag across the threshold, and the glamour wobbled. Just leaning through the doorway cracked the wards, so the lightning shivers of magic didn't run through me as I worked on disassembling the glamour that obscured the room's true contents. Eventually I stood in her workroom, the space lined with tables, low shelves, and tools hanging from nails in the walls.

"What are you planning, Anne Marie?" I frowned as I looked around the immaculate room, a little impressed in spite of my dislike for her. There had to be a clue somewhere. She'd mentioned a Calling, a summoning, and I'd seen enough demon magic in their spell to know she'd need a book for reference. She hadn't known enough about dark magic to be able to wing something like that.

I poked around, studying labels on the neat jars of herbs and dried flowers and other ingredients for her potions, and smeared lavender oil across the surface of an ornate mirror hanging over her work table. Mirrors served as gateways for demons, and if Anne Marie had been summoning them or even just thinking about them, there was a chance one might pop out of the mirror when I wasn't looking. I shivered just thinking about it, and banished all thoughts of dark magic as I paused in front of the open bay that had been a walk-in closet. With the doors removed, it was the perfect spot for a carved wooden cathedral lectern to support a dusty book: calfskin with a Tree of Life on the cover and talcum on the spine, and a curious heaviness around it.

No wards protected it, not even from dust or moisture. No traps or hexes prevented me from edging into the closet, and nothing hid it from view once inside the workroom. I didn't want to believe that Anne Marie's complacency included relying on a single glamour to protect a very dangerous book.

I didn't dare touch it, instead letting my fingertips glide just over the surface of the darkened calfskin. It was a true grimoire, copied by a real witch using magic to adhere the spells to the pages. Power and age gave it weight. It was a valuable book indeed, copied many years before the Breaking, but it wasn't one I'd ever seen or owned. My parents' library had been extensive, but as I flipped the cover open, I didn't recognize the handiwork of the witch who'd copied the book or most of the spells inside. I checked my bag to make sure I had enough room to take it with me. No witch would blame me for borrowing it for a bit.

I turned the pages carefully, deliberate in where I touched the surface to avoid any markings or text, and searched for a hint of what Anne Marie plotted. A Calling. Summoning something she didn't want anyone to know about, since she cleared the area of witches before casting. Except for two dark witches she hadn't known about, apparently.

The section on summoning spells opened and something fluttered to the floor. I picked up the scrap of paper, thin rice tissue with a few ink strokes on it, but immediately dropped it as my fingers burned.

A beeswax candlestick from her work table helped nudge the paper to reveal a symbol used to call someone—or some*thing*—against its will. Dark witches often used it as an anchor when summoning demons, most of which didn't show up willingly. Usually they etched it on a mirror. I glanced at the one over her work table again, just in case, and debated using more oil to completely obscure the glass.

I covered the tissue in salt for a little peace of mind while I examined the pages it fell from. They contained a normal summoning ritual, although one strong enough to Call a war witch or an Ancient—one of the old shifters, pure of blood and likely more animal than human. A piece of unassuming notebook paper, covered in Anne Marie's neat, rounded letters, was wedged in the same pages.

My heart sank as I read and re-read what she'd written: *Lion family, from Barbary. Lavi the Younger, 1796. Algiers. Ibn Aurelius.*

An Ancient. I shook my head as I closed the book on the note, tucking it into my bag. A Lion Ancient, born centuries before the Breaking and raised in a foreign land. Possibly crazy, and certainly not pleased about being Called by a circle of pushy war witches. Stupid, Anne Marie.

I left the demon sign on the floor, covered in salt. Even touching it could have invited the evil eye to follow me home. I paused by the mirror, studying the room behind me through the oil-smeared glass, and wondered how Rosa and Joanne and Tracy could possibly have missed what Anne Marie intended. Something wasn't right. As I hesitated, the clock downstairs clicked and then started to toll the hours—just ten o'clock. Plenty of time to get to the Skein, and maybe enough time to call Leif on the way so half the Alliance would meet me there to observe Anne Marie's dangerous slide down the slippery slope toward dark magic.

I pulled out my cell phone and turned to the door, convinced the book and the demon sign would be enough to get the Alliance on board. The air moved downstairs, and the front door creaked as it opened. Then shut. The unmistakable hush of breathing echoed in the silent house, and I held my breath. My hands went cold. Anne Marie wouldn't have come home early. Unless, of course, she knew I was in her house and riffling through her stuff. The Alliance cops wouldn't move so quietly, though.

I retreated to crouch behind the work table and braced against the wall, sliding the bag down my shoulder so I could maneuver. I hated feeling trapped, but there wasn't time to run when the stairs creaked and fabric rustled, getting closer. My heart accelerated and lightning raced through my veins in anticipation. Danger. Getting closer.

The breathing moved through the house, searching. Floorboards groaned under the footsteps, and my heart pounded against my ribs, desperate to break free. I concentrated on the first hex to use as I clenched my jaw to silence my chattering teeth as my vision sharpened, focused into a soda straw on the door. It was difficult to imagine which enemy would be worse: Stefan and the Externals, searching for Anne Marie's guilt just as I had, or Leif and the Styrma.

My gaze went to the curled calligraphy buried under salt. All things considered, a demon trumped them both.

# CHAPTER 14

The carpet hush-hushed with footsteps in the hall outside her workroom. I forced my eyes open wide to face the threat. Couldn't hide. Strike first, as soon as they showed themselves, and then run. Just as I tensed and started to reach for magic, the front door opened and closed again.

Not just one of them, whoever or whatever they were.

"She's in here," someone in the hall said, and a hex crashed through the room and destroyed the work table I crouched behind.

Shit.

I bolted, rolling across the floor to the closet, and flung a few hexes back at the witch who stood in the doorway. She grunted and fell back as the blue magic swirled up and tangled around her, pinning her to the door. My feet slid in the salt spilled over the demon sign, and I scrambled to get up and out of the small room. Being trapped upstairs as more feet ran up from the foyer sent my heart into overdrive, and I could hardly draw breath as the world closed in around me.

They tried to help their friend, who croaked and coughed against the hexes that froze her, and one of the witches bashed a spell into the wall until drywall crumbled. My hands shook as I pressed my back against the closet door and forced myself to stand. The infinite ocean of power waited for me, beckoning. It promised calm indifference and protection from the helicopters echoed in my thoughts, mimicking my racing pulse and taking me back to a faraway battlefield.

One of the witches sent Anne Marie's carefully arranged shelves flying across the room, smashing to pieces against the wall where I crouched, and she snapped, "You bitch, get out here and fight like a real witch. You killed Cara and Danielle, and now you're going to pay for it."

That did it. If this was the dark coven, tracking me down to punish me for sending their covenmates into a demon realm, I wasn't going down without a fight.

I shoved to my feet and surrendered to the magic. It rose through me in a freezing tide, painful for only a moment until it numbed away everything else. I felt buoyant and free, untethered to any earthly concerned. I was above it all. I was a war witch. *The* War Witch.

Power gathered in my hands as I stepped out of the closet, already forming a mobile ward around me in a protective dome, and I flicked my fingers in the direction of the four witches gathered outside the door. Debris from Anne Marie's workshop exploded out, knocking them back, but I didn't stop. The strongest, a summoner, crashed blue magic hexes against my wards and only succeeded in sending a cascade of sparks through the air.

One of them hurled powerful breaking hexes and managed to crack the wards, sending a backlash through the magic that almost disturbed my equilibrium. I took a breath and concentrated on getting out of that fucking room. I drove them back as they dragged their injured friend, and as I lurched into the hallway, one of the witches looked up at me and froze. "Who the fuck are you?"

"You attacked me. Who the fuck are *you*?" I didn't really care, though, not with the comforting buffer of magic. They'd attacked me, and I was well within my rights to kill all four of them.

"We're here for Anne Marie," she said, breathing hard as she struggled to hold up the injured witch. "She did something with two of my coven members. Are you a friend of hers?"

"A friend? Definitely not." Something small and silver on the floor caught the light, and I bent to pick it up, no longer so concerned with what they might do to me. From the looks on their faces, they'd figured out from the wards that things probably wouldn't go their way. The basher still looked mad as hell, though, so I kept an eye on her as I examined what I'd found on the floor.

An alignment ring made of silver, set with a purple stone for basher and the Alliance crest on one of the panels. I frowned as I studied the other, and my heart stuttered even with the cold disdain of magic as I saw the other panel. Rowanwood. Those damn dark witches.

The talkative one straightened, her eyes narrowing as she looked at me. "That's Wendy's. Give it back."

It wasn't just the Externals who collected alignment rings. I considered pocketing it, but something moved downstairs, near the door, and I didn't want to have anything associated with demon magic on me. I tossed it at the four witches and held my hands up. "You should leave. Fast."

I'd be able to find them again and deal with whatever dark magic they worked. Having a knockdown brawl in Anne Marie's house, as time ticked away from my chance to interrupt their spell, wasn't a good idea.

"Who the hell are you? You're not in the First Coven." The other witches didn't release their magic, and they didn't budge, still blocking me from the stairs and the way out as more noise and some flashing lights disrupted the quiet night outside. The chatty one straightened her shoulders and drew herself up, more magic gathering around her. "And you don't have a ring, which means you're nonaligned. You attacked us."

"You attacked first," I said. The familiar unfairness of being a second-class citizen rose through me, just as strong as the dispassionate magic, and I clenched my fists. "Get the hell out of here."

She took a breath and raised her right hand, on the verge of hexing again, when the front door smashed in and chaos erupted downstairs. The witches looked away and I charged, shoving past them to jump down the stairs. Hexes and spells burst at my heels and the wards shivered, rippling out as I slammed into a wide male chest covered in tactical military gear and bounced right into the wall.

Guns clicked and popped as men and women in solid helmets shouted orders and aimed at me and the witches upstairs. At least I wasn't the main target. I didn't move, not wanting to hold my hands up and risk getting shot for aggressive magic, and focused the magic into gnarly wards. Class IV wards. The kind that had knocked even the Chief Investigator on his ass. The Alliance's stormtroopers, the Styrma, surrounded me in the foyer and flooded into the rest of the house, prepared to do battle.

Alarms went off on the gear covering the dark figures, and more than one abandoned their weapons for what looked like killing hexes, tied to small objects so they could be thrown from a distance. One of the burlier guys said, "Release the magic now and identify yourself, witch."

"You've got to be kidding me," a familiar voice said, and I froze as Leif stepped through the open door. "Lily?"

"Hey," I said, trying to sound normal despite the weapons aimed at me and the furious witches upstairs. "So, this is a little..."

"What are you doing in Anne Marie's house?" His forehead

creased as he studied me, and I didn't know how to feel about the fact that he didn't order his guys to lower their weapons immediately. Maybe whatever had been between us at the restaurant was already gone. I'd broken into Anne Marie's house, after all, and he was the law for the Alliance.

"It's a little hard to explain," I said. The demon sign upstairs, if it had survived all the hexes and spells thrown around, would finally prove what a bad witch Anne Marie was. I just needed to show him, then maybe take him to the Skein to show him that as well. Leif wouldn't be able to see the magic, but he could smell the demons more strongly than witches could. I glanced back up the stairs, shivering as I thought of the oil-smeared mirror in the work room. "Especially here. I'd prefer to talk... somewhere else?"

Leif looked at me for a long time before he glanced up the stairs at the four witches, then gestured at the Styrma team still ready for battle in the foyer. "Detain the ones upstairs. I'll speak with Lily."

One of the guys, familiar as Leif's right-hand man, straightened but didn't lower his weapon from where it tracked me. "Boss, that's a nonaligned summoner, you shouldn't—"

"It's fine, Jake." Leif's blue eyes met mine in a hard stare. "Lily's just about to let go of all that magic, and we'll have a nice conversation outside while you deal with whatever the hell Rowanwood was planning."

I took the hint and slowly released the powerful magic that held me up. The world came back in a cruel rush—everything too sharp, too bright, too loud. The sensations slammed into me all at once and my knees weakened; I held onto the handrail as I concentrated on staying upright. The Styrma eyed me as they stomped up the stairs, crowding me out until I had to stumble down the last few stairs or risk getting trampled underfoot. Jake scowled at me and kept close to Leif as the Chief Investigator caught my arm and helped me stand.

Leif kept a professional distance as I limped to the porch, and he pretended not to notice as I paused to catch my breath after only a few steps. Using magic was like a muscle, in some ways; though I had near-infinite power at my beck and call, I hadn't used it in so long it took more out of me than I could stand. Which did not bode well for trying to stop Anne Marie at the Skein, if it came down to an epic battle with war witches.

Leif propped me up against one of the columns and frowned out at the half dozen cars parked in front of Anne Marie's house, some of them with flashing lights and others so unremarkable they made my nerves twitch. He took the metal case out of his coat pocket and selected one of the thin cigars, fiddling with it as he spoke. "Start talking, Lily. Last I knew, you were in the car with Mick and heading for the pack-house so we could finish talking about what happened with Stefan. Imagine my surprise to find out you escaped from Mick. And now you turn up at Anne Marie's house in the middle of a burglary."

"I didn't realize Mick detained me," I said, taking refuge in a little bit of irritation. "I wasn't in his custody, so when I left—because he threatened me if I didn't join his pack—it wasn't an escape."

"He threatened you?" Leif's eyebrow arched.

"I'm sure it was a misunderstanding," I said. After what Leif said in the restaurant, I didn't want him going after Mick. Moriah's brother was a jerk, but he didn't deserve the Chief Investigator's hammer. "But after everything that happened at the restaurant, I didn't want to stick around."

"So why did you come here, Lily?" Leif lit the cigar and studied the smoke curling around his fingers. "If you're not in contact with the First Coven, like you said yesterday, then this doesn't look good."

"Anne Marie borrowed a book from me," I said. The lie escaped before I could think of a more plausible justification for being in Anne Marie's house, but the heavy bag on my shoulder was the only thing working in my favor. "She refused to give it back, so I came here to... take it."

And I patted the bag for good measure.

He didn't believe it. It was clear from the way he watched me and didn't speak. I remembered the watchfulness from the war, and it still made me nervous. Before he could speak or do more than tap the ash off his cigar, Jake leaned through the door and cleared his throat. "Nate just called. Two External response vans are on their way."

Leif shook his head, pinching the bridge of his nose, then carefully flicked the coal off the cigar and put it back in his fancy case. "Great. Take care of the witches here and figure out why they broke into Anne Marie's house, and I'll take this one back to the pack-house."

"Boss—"

"Jake." Leif's blue eyes went diamond-hard, though his voice stayed perfectly mild. "Do you really want to finish that sentence?"

The other shifter didn't look at me, but irritation radiated from him strongly enough to give me a sunburn. "After what happened earlier today, people will talk."

"Let them." Leif caught my arm and shepherded me down the two stairs and toward a sleek sedan in the driveway. "Call me if there's a change."

Jake grumbled and went back into the house, and I heard him barking orders before Leif opened the passenger-side door and shooed me in. I kept a tight grip on my bag and Anne Marie's book as he started the car and practically flew out of the driveway and down the street, almost colliding with an approaching van with blaring sirens. Leif evaded the van, as well as the one following it, and I stared out the window at the passenger in the second van: Stefan. His eyes narrowed when he saw me, and he reached through the open window as if he could grab me through sheer force of will. But by then Leif's lead foot whisked us out of reach and left the Externals to deal with Jake and his crew.

I felt like celebrating, though it only lasted until I glanced over and caught the expression on Leif's face. I held my bag a little tighter and cleared my throat. "Where are we going, exactly?"

"The pack-house. Soren is interested in some of the recent... happenings."

He sounded remarkably grim. And the Peacemaker didn't get interested in happenings for just anything—the petty squabbles of witches were normally so far beneath Soren's notice, I figured Anne Marie must have elevated the threat to his attention just to get me in trouble. I sank lower in the seat, trying to orient myself as he pulled onto a main road not far from my apartment. Out of the frying pan and into the fire, it seemed.

# CHAPTER 15

*L*eif didn't let the silence stretch for long. The car paused at a red light and he glanced over at me. "What happened with Mick?"

"He told me to join his pack or Soren would arrest me. Something like that." I stared straight ahead, debating whether I stood a chance of convincing him that Anne Marie was up to no good. The witching hour approached too quickly and magic gathered elsewhere in the city. "After what happened at the restaurant, and with the Externals harassing aligned witches, he seemed to think my only hope for survival was swearing allegiance to him and Soren."

"It's not a bad idea." Leif accelerated through the intersection and another block before suddenly pulling the car over to park on a side street. He half-turned in his seat to look at me, expression difficult to reach. "Why not?"

"I have my reasons." Even if it was tough to remember what they were, with the Chief Investigator watching me so closely. I remembered times during the war when I would have given anything for a conversation in close quarters with him, and other times when I did all I could to avoid him. The magical fatigue made my head ache and my bones hurt, and I wanted to curl up someplace to take a nap, not answer questions about my whereabouts and intentions. "And I'd rather save that conversation for another time, if you don't mind."

"Fine. Let's talk about why you're avoiding answering any questions about the night of Moriah's party. Are you aware that two witches disappeared near the Skein?"

"I heard from someone at work."

"And are you aware that the witches at Anne Marie's house belong to the same coven?"

"I saw one of their rings, but I didn't make the connection." My heart started beating a little faster and the feeling of being chased, and cornered, returned.

"I don't believe in coincidence, Lilith." He stressed my old name, and heat climbed my cheeks since I'd told him the same thing often enough. There was no such thing as coincidence in magic or war, or so it seemed at the time. Leif's fingers drummed on the console between the seats. "So help me understand why, every time I turn around and find more trouble, you're in the middle of everything."

"Bad luck."

He wasn't amused. "Lilith—"

"Please don't call me that. It's not who I am anymore." It hurt to say, since I'd been Lilith the longest. A witch's true name held unbelievable power over her, and so I kept my true name —the thrice-given name from my parents—close to my heart. I'd been Lilith throughout the war and into the peace, and though I tried to leave her, and all her crimes, behind, it felt like a chain around my ankles holding me back.

"Lilith was a hero," he said, a hint of sympathy in his eyes.

"Not everyone remembers it that way," I said under my breath. I couldn't take his gentle tone, the understanding. We'd both suffered a great deal, and yet he seemed fine. Perfectly fine. I hated the creeping weakness that burned my sinuses and threatened to spill down my cheeks in rivers of tears. "So I'd really prefer Lily."

"Is that why you refuse to join the Alliance? Too many people remembering you as Lilith?"

I shook my head, even if it was partial truth. The Alliance would have celebrated me for the worst parts of my past, the things I hated about myself. The things I'd done that haunted my dreams and occasionally sent me into panic attacks in the middle of the day, based only on a breeze or a hint of exhaust or the rat-a-tat-tat staccato of rainfall that sounded too much like automatic weapons. I tried to breathe normally despite the increasing tremble in my fingers. "No."

He waited, letting the silence stretch until the shivers moved up my hands and made it almost impossible to hold my bag. I felt the car shrinking around me and fumbled with the door handle, searching for the window control.

"Breathe," he said, and cracked the windows open. Cool air rushed into the car and I leaned toward the window, struggling to inhale. The Chief Investigator made a grumbly noise in his chest, one of those wolf sounds that sounded scary but was meant to be reassuring. "Just breathe."

It felt like an eternity before the pressure behind my eyes eased and the world stopped collapsing around me. I couldn't face him, though, and instead told my secrets to the window. "Today Anne Marie called me a murderer. For what happened with the coven, at the end."

"You're not a murderer, Lily. I remember that much."

"Cold comfort, I guess, from the Hellhound himself?" He made a face at the old nickname the humans gave him, but it was the least offensive among many. I rubbed my forehead, dismayed at the sweat slicking my brow, and wished he'd lowered the window more. "I killed people, Leif. It was war, but I still killed people. Anne Marie will never let me forget that, and I can't live with her judgment."

Leif studied me in the dim light of the car's dashboard, his expression hidden in shadows. "Then why are you still involved with the coven, Lily?"

"Tracy asked me for a favor." I wanted to tell him everything. I wanted to spill the beans on Anne Marie and the demon magic, and all the trouble that waited at the Skein. The words stuck in my throat.

"I'm trying to give you the benefit of the doubt, Lily. Maybe I shouldn't, but I suppose I can't put aside what happened in the war either. I owe you. The Alliance owes you. But that only goes so far in the Truce, do you understand?" Leif tapped his fingers on the steering wheel, though his gaze never left mine. "I have two witches missing in what looks like dark magic, a human girl still in the hospital and contaminated with something we've never seen before, and suddenly a lot of issues with all the witches in the Alliance. The only common thread is you."

"That's not entirely true." I cleared my throat to get rid of the knot of tears, still lingering along with memories from the third year of war, when I was too young to know who to trust. Sometimes trusting anyone—*anyone*—was a leap into an abyss with no light. No hope. Bad news never got better with age. "Look, Tracy told me—"

Before I could get any further, his phone rang and a radio beeped loudly enough to make me jump. Leif didn't look surprised, only irritated, as he picked up the phone and turned off the volume on the handheld radio as it continued to blare warning noises. He didn't look away from me as he held the phone up to his ear. "Yeah, boss?"

Boss. The only boss in Leif's life was Soren. The Warbringer and Peacemaker. Leader of the Alliance, alpha among alphas, and a first rate son of a bitch. I held my breath.

Leif's eyes narrowed as he continued studying me, and my heart sank. It could have been any number of things. Maybe Anne Marie went to Soren after I left her store. Maybe the girl

in the hospital finally gave them enough information to identify me. Maybe the witches arrested at Anne Marie's house
blamed me for the attack. Maybe they'd found the demon sign
in the workroom upstairs and attributed it to me.

"You're sure?" he said, unblinking, and hints of the old Leif
—Scary Leif—started to leak through the calm, human
features. "Who called it in? When?"

Some of the background noise of his call snuck into the
quiet car—shouting and sirens. Maybe it wasn't to do with me,
after all. I didn't relax. Leif's features sharpened and he gripped
the steering wheel. "Okay. I'm on my way."

He hung up and put the car in gear, reaching for the radio.
"Change of plans. I'm going to drop you at your apartment, and
you're going to stay there until I can send someone to pick
you up."

"What happened?"

"Another misunderstanding, I hope." Leif's expression
turned grim as he accelerated through an intersection and
flipped a switch so that red and white lights flashed in the front
of the car, illuminating the empty streets as he drove.

A misunderstanding didn't usually get Leif that worked up.
He honked the horn as a truck almost cut him off, avoiding the
slow vehicle with an irritated growl, and then suddenly we
were parked in front of my apartment complex. He cut the
engine and got out, muttering into the radio as he walked
around the car, and I shoved my door open before he could get
to it. A little chivalry had its appeal, but not in the middle of an
emergency.

I held onto my bag, thinking of the heavy book and all the
new things I could learn from it before he came back to arrest
me, and backed toward the sidewalk. "Thanks for the
ride, I'll—"

"I'll walk you up." He still frowned at the radio and his
phone as both chirped again, distracted.

"It's fine. You really don't need to."

He gave me a sideways look and started toward the sidewalk, putting away the phone. "It's late, Lily. I'll walk you to the door."

The phone rang again, and Leif frowned down at it. I pointed to the noisy device. "Go. If something's going on, you should just go."

"I'm walking you to your door. I'm a—"

"A gentleman, I remember." I retreated a few steps and flapped my hand at the closest apartment building. "But it's twenty feet and a flight of stairs. Soren needs you. Go."

He hesitated, glancing at the phone again before scanning the surroundings, as if searching for any trouble lurking in the weeds and cracked concrete. Only a few streetlights flickered and went out, and not even stray dogs disturbed the night. Leif shook his head. "Fine. But I'm sending someone to pick you up and take you to the pack-house. I'll call you when they're close."

"I'll be standing by." I tried to smile, as if we could joke about things like that.

Leif folded his arms over his chest. "Lily, do not run. Wait here until Nate picks you up. Running only makes it worse, do you hear me?"

"I've got it." I started backing up, not wanting to linger too long in the open with the Chief Investigator in case some of the nosy neighbors started paying attention. "I'll be here."

His lips thinned at he watched me, the debate clear in his eyes, but he finally shook his head and headed back to the car. "I'm serious, Lily. An hour, tops. Be here."

I waved him off and didn't look back as his car started up and peeled out, not quite burning rubber but also not dawdling to watch me walk up the stairs. My feet dragged with fatigue as I navigated the cracked sidewalk and the dark stairs, muttering under my breath at the lack of light. Another broken bulb and the landlord too cheap to replace it. Flies, too, buzzed in a cloud near the landing, probably having migrated from something disgusting in the dumpster.

The witching hour played tricks with the moonlight on the walls as I dug for my keys. At first I thought they were only shadows on my door, smearing in long streaks and puddling around the welcome mat.

It wasn't until I was a few feet away that I realized it wasn't. The smell gave it away, cloying but too familiar.

Blood.

# CHAPTER 16

*A* bloody handprint marked my door, and others smeared along the jamb and adjacent wall. The blood gleamed dully in the moonlight, congealed but not dry. A fly buzzed closer, bumping into my cheek, and I flinched.

My feet stuck to the landing as I stared at the door. Someone left bloody marks all over my home. Someone found me. Someone who had a grudge or a reason to hurt me. Maybe Chompers, maybe Anne Marie, maybe the dark witch. Maybe a half dozen others I'd managed to avoid for the past five years. I took a shaky breath as my heart started to drum against my ribs. I'd faced more frightening things, but I'd never much cared what happened to me until after the war. It was far easier to charge into chaos when it didn't really matter if you survived. Wanting to live made things a little more difficult.

Irritation gathered over the dread as I looked down. I had to buy *another* welcome mat.

I pressed my shaking hands together and dredged up power as fatigue weighed me down. Smart witches didn't walk through bloody doors without powerful weapons to meet whatever lurked on the other side. I closed my eyes as the world shimmered around me, and for a moment I teetered on the edge of passing out. I rocked back on my heels and might have tumbled into darkness if I hadn't caught a whiff of Leif's cologne, lingering from before.

The cold magic crawled through me as I stared at the door and considered calling Leif. I didn't want to go inside alone, and he would never make me. I would never have to see what waited inside, would never face what left bloody handprints on my door, if I called him. Then I shook myself back to reality and reached for the Morrigan, the unflinching persona who'd laid waste to entire cities. I was not a coward. It was *my* home. I'd never called for help before, and I sure as hell wasn't going to start then.

The cold indifference of magic helped. Rosa's mantra steadied the world as I repeated it under my breath, over and over until I could ignore the flies and the sickly smell of old blood. I forgot about his past and my present, let the magic have me, fill me up. Make me invincible. I cut away Lily and Leif and Tracy and fear, until there was only Lilja.

Lilja, who exacted a terrible price when wronged. Who still hunted the dark witches who stole from her after seven years. Who tames the Northern Lights and wrote her name in the sky. Anger flared red in the periphery of the magic, waiting for an opportunity to release hell, and I pushed it away as Mother's ghost whispered in my ear about that damnable Viking temper.

I opened the door with a whisper of air. The wards, damaged by Leif's artless entry the day before and broken again by whoever left the bloody handprints, flared weakly as I stepped over the threshold. I followed the trail of blood into my apartment, feeling nothing as I noted more smears on the walls, like someone dragged bloody fingers over the shoddy paint as they walked.

I breathed through my nose and avoided pools of blood, trying to sort out the myriad magical trails, and stopped in the living room as shock reached through the magic to steal feeling from my legs. Saints above and below. Whoever broke in didn't like me very much, although the blood was a pretty good indicator of that. A who's-there spell confirmed I alone occupied the apartment, although that didn't make me feel any better. I'd rather have found something to punish for wrecking my stuff and invading my home.

They'd eviscerated Moriah's old couch, spilling its cottony guts in clumps around the room. My beautiful camphorwood box was reduced to splinters on the shattered coffee table, its trinkets crushed under someone's heel. The fake leather chair smoldered in a melted black meteorite in the corner. Strong magic, tinged with something dark, curled throughout the apartment, coating nearly every surface in a greasy layer.

I blinked, trying to clear my vision as I catalogued the damage. Curtains bunched on the floor in tatters, soaked with something nasty, and blood spattered every wall. I stood over a pile of my books, most of them split down the spine and the pages fluttering loose. I toed through the mess, looking for a few specific titles that I wouldn't want anyone else to have. All three were gone.

My throat constricted until I couldn't breathe. No telling who had them. No telling what they'd use them for.

But I had to worry about that later. I picked through the mess to the bedroom, trying not to notice in too much detail what had been done to some of the knickknacks I'd collected, and felt only emptiness as I peeked at the destruction inside. The wards on my bedroom hadn't been broken accidentally, like the door wards, so doubtless the strength of the solid wards surprised the intruders. The War Witch smiled a little. Maybe I'd inflicted a little damage of my own.

The damaged wards rippled around me as I paused in the doorway and let the magic boost my reserves. My mattress had been thrown against the window and slashed open. Goose down from the torn pillows made a mockery of snow on every surface. The odor of stale urine from a pile of clothes dragged out of the dresser made me doubt I would ever wear them again.

It wasn't a garden-variety robbery. Normal thieves selected easier targets, and carried bootleg magic detectors to check for wards. They wouldn't have picked my apartment to rob, regardless of how drug-addled or desperate they were. And they would have stolen everything, not destroyed it.

I leaned against the only non-bloody patch of wall I could find to formulate a plan. The disaster in front of me blurred as I blinked and tried not to see too much of it. It hurt more deeply than I'd expected, as the objectivity within powerful magic weighed how much I valued some possessions. I'd let a lot of my memories grow around things, and without those things... Maybe the memories would disappear as well.

I shook off the growing sense of grief and instead focused on the next step. I couldn't stay in the apartment, waiting for Leif's people to pick me up or whoever destroyed my apartment to return to finish things off. And I wouldn't sleep among burnt feathers and strange magic, and I sure as hell wouldn't rest anywhere without wards.

No wards protected Moriah's house, despite my frequent offers to set them up, so even though I knew she would offer me a place, I couldn't stay there. Shifters were strong, but they weren't a good defense against whatever destroyed my stuff. The only other option wasn't a difficult decision, though I checked the clock before I dialed. It was past the witching hour and I hadn't felt the expected explosion of magic from the Skein, so maybe Anne Marie had taken my warning to heart and called off the cast. I dialed Tracy's number as I pinched the bridge of my nose, wondering what to say when she answered. *I did you a stupid favor and it nearly got me arrested, so let me sleep on your couch?*

After the phone went to voicemail, I hung up and chewed my lip. The coven meeting definitely should have ended. But it didn't mean anything that she didn't answer. I tapped the phone as I returned to the living room and searched for hints of the intruders' identities. A deep breath brought more of the strong magic, dark enough to turn my stomach. Sulfur tickled my nose.

The phone landed with a squish on the blood-soaked carpet as my hands went numb. I didn't bother retrieving it as I turned widdershins.

A witch wouldn't have left a mess like that. But a demon would have.

Recognition snapped into place as brimstone curled into my brain: the magic from the Skein. Someone from the coven loosed a demon in my apartment.

I turned another slow circle. Even Anne Marie couldn't hate me so much. No true witch would unleash a demon in another's home. Dread settled like a stone in my stomach and weighed me down until I crouched, just a moment away from kneeling in the blood. I wiped off the phone as best I could before hitting redial.

It rang once, twice. I crossed my fingers, an old habit from childhood but a useless gesture. By the fourth ring, I started praying. Not a real habit but probably just as useless.

Five rings. Then a click. Instead of Tracy's cheerful voicemail, a deep voice I would recognize anywhere in the world. "Who is this?"

Soren. Warbringer and Peacemaker. I nearly hung up.

As I hesitated, his voice gained an edge. "Who is this?"

I cleared my throat, forcing the words out. "I'm trying to reach my friend. Why do you have her phone?"

My heart pounded staccato beats against my ribs. I struggled to draw measured breaths. Hyperventilating would not help Tracy. Or me.

Loud voices drowned out his reply; he moved and it became quiet enough to hear. "What's your name? When did you last hear from her?"

My vision swam, even with the cold dispassion of magic. I desperately wanted to sit but I couldn't find a clean surface no matter where I turned.

Another familiar voice carried through the background noise, and Leif said, "There's a lot of blood for only two bodies. Whose arm is that?"

I shuddered. Saints protect them. "Why do you have her phone?"

"There was an emergency. We can't find her."

My knees buckled and I sank the rest of the way to the sticky, ruined carpet.

Soren went on, oblivious as my world started to collapse. "We need to know what you know. Where are you? Someone will pick you up."

That was not a good idea, with everything else that had happened. I stared down at my bloody hands. Too many things I couldn't explain and didn't understand yet. I needed to figure out what the hell happened. My stomach rebelled at the sickly sweet smell, the iron tang filling my nostrils until I tasted blood on my teeth.

Maybe I sat in Tracy's blood.

He kept talking, using his reassuring leader tone, but I hung up. I rose, brain out of sync as I wobbled on unsteady legs, and stumbled to the door. It was time to act, not listen. If Tracy lived, she didn't have long. I gazed around the apartment and the ruins of that life before forcing myself to move down the hall. I could mourn what deserved to be missed later.

I retrieved a few treasures from their hiding places, including the half dozen dangerous books I'd hidden better than the ones on the shelf, and drifted out of the apartment, not looking back. The War Witch took over, just so I could keep moving. Something violated where I lived, but I walked away unscathed. I took what I valued and left, one step ahead of whatever wanted to kill me. I didn't bother to shut the door behind me. It would save whoever came to investigate the effort of breaking it down.

I stared up as the stars wheeled overhead and the night grew more dangerous. Tracy was only missing, and missing wasn't dead. She could be with the rest of the coven, deep in a cast, or maybe meditating and beyond my reach. I could find her. I would find her, and whoever destroyed my home and hers would pay.

They would meet the War Witch, and very few people lived to tell that tale.

# CHAPTER 17

*I*n the hall outside my apartment, I looked at the new door that protected Amber's apartment, and hoped she was okay. Nothing stirred. But the witch who lived at the end of the hall, the one who conveniently hadn't seen anything when I hexed Leif, had stacked killing hexes into her wards. She'd never done that before.

I considered asking her what happened, if she'd seen anything, but abandoned the idea. She didn't want to be involved, otherwise she would have come out to help me before I walked into the destroyed apartment. The shock of the intruders breaking my wards would have woken her from a dead sleep if she was home, and I couldn't blame her for protecting herself first. I glanced around the landing at the other doors, then straightened my shoulders and headed for the stairs. "It's okay. I don't blame you for staying out of it."

And I hoped at least the witch heard me.

I'd barely staggered to the sidewalk, still holding onto the magic like a protective blanket despite the growing cost, when the chunky External jumped out of the shadows and grabbed my shoulders. I swore and lurched back, nearly shoving a hex in his face, as he said, "Where the hell have you been?"

"What?" I shook off his hands and some of the terror that set my heart out of rhythm, and tried to back away in the darkness, away from the uncertain clarity of a security light. "What the hell are you doing here? What's wrong with you?"

A siren rose in the distance. Eric caught my arm and dragged me toward a car idling on the street. "We have to get out of here before someone sees you."

I wrenched away, keeping a tight hold on my bag, and figured I might have to hex him anyway. He'd survived the last one, but I didn't make the same mistakes twice. I'd been a fool about many things, and I needed to stop adding to the list. Eventually luck ran out. "What is going on?"

"Those Alliance witches destroyed your apartment," he said slowly, like I had trouble understanding. Maybe he thought I did.

"That's bullshit." I didn't want to believe it, even if part of me knew that Anne Marie was capable of all that, and much worse besides. "That's not possible. It was someone else. There was demon shit in there, and—"

"We can't stay here." He tried again to take my arm and pull me toward the street. "Stefan and the others are on their way."

"How the hell do you know it was them?" I shook my head, a knot forming in my throat. Damn it. Anne Marie, and the saints only knew who else, stalked the night and looked for me. Maybe she'd killed Tracy, too. Maybe that was why the coven didn't cast—the others figured it out, and Rosa and Joanne and Tracy would never have gone along with it. Maybe they were sacrificed. I should have been there to help, but instead I'd been breaking into Anne Marie's house to make a point.

"No one makes a mess like that except witches," he said, his lip curled as he flung his arm in the general direction of my ruined apartment. "There's a trail of magic right to your door."

"Trail? From where?" The sirens grew louder and closer, multiplying. I wondered if it was Leif, on his way to arrest me, or the Externals.

"Across the city." He pointed in the general direction of the sirens and Tracy's house. Under the flickering lights, the glamour or whatever obscured his face slipped again and showed a young woman with a ski-jump nose instead. The world realigned itself and I tried to see what it was that changed his appearance. Her appearance? Saints above.

Eric shrugged out of his overcoat and held it out to me. "Put this on."

"Why?" I didn't take it.

"You're covered in blood. If anyone sees you, you're screwed. You have to get out of here." He tossed the houndstooth coat at me and I caught it out of reflex, almost dropping the books I carried.

"Why are you doing this? Who the hell are you?" I backed away more, debating where I could hide for the night. I didn't want to bring more trouble to Moriah's door, particularly if dark witches or demons chased me.

"We're alike, you and I, but there's no time to explain. I'll drive you wherever you want to go, Lily, but we have to leave now. Stefan will be here any minute."

"Why do you care? You're an External. You're the enemy. We'll never be alike." I started walking, shaking my head. There was one sanctuary in the city that I rarely used unless it was a last resort, but Mother's wards still held in the house where we lived before the Breaking. It would be safe to scry for Tracy and the rest of the coven from there. Then I could figure out what to do next. If Leif didn't find me first.

"You'll be arrested," he said. His voice lacked inflection, as though he only repeated the weather forecast. "The Bureau is following the magic from the witch's house here, to your doorstep and no farther. With the dark magic in the neighborhood earlier, both crimes become yours. Add in Stefan's grudge over what happened at the restaurant, and you don't have a chance. You'll be executed within the week, if they bother to wait for the Judge."

More sirens broke the calm. I stopped in my tracks, staring into the night. What he said felt like truth. And Soren was already at Tracy's house, answering her phone. "How do you know what happened?"

"Our people watch every strong witch in the Alliance," he said. "I saw a disturbance at the residence. I can explain more later. You have to get far away from here before they see you."

"Where are the witches?"

"I don't know." He didn't blink.

"I don't believe you." I stared over his shoulder into the undisturbed silence down the block. One place alone promised safety. None but the foolhardy dared go there. The humans weren't allowed in after dark, and Others avoided it unless no alternatives existed. The trick was to get there unnoticed.

"Fine. Don't. Just...lie low for a couple of weeks. Get out of the city. I'll call when it's safe to come back." He glanced at his phone as the screen lit up, then headed for his car. "Seriously. Get moving, or let me drop you off somewhere. They'll be here in a couple of minutes."

"What did you see? At the witch's house." I didn't want to know. I really didn't want to know.

He didn't look away from the screen, though his shoulders tensed. "Not much. The beast and his people showed up just as I did, so I couldn't get close."

No External would have been stupid—or suicidal—enough to challenge the Peacemaker and his people without serious backup. I still wanted to call him a coward. "The coven. What happened to the coven inside the house?"

"They're gone."

"Gone?"

"Gone," he repeated. "At least two bodies, probably pieces of others. Blood everywhere. It reeked of demons. They were not...pleasant deaths."

I bit my lip, hating his disinterest. Those bodies, with their unpleasant deaths, had been my colleagues. My coven. My friends. "Demons."

His phone rang again, and again he silenced it. "Yeah. The same demon shit that's all over your place."

All the air disappeared from my lungs. Saints preserve me.

Something like sympathy made tiny lines around his eyes as he looked up at me, the phone's light casting strange shadows across his face. "You need my help, don't you see? I'll try to redirect the investigation, but you have to disappear. I'll call you when there's news." He headed to the car, phone to his ear, and didn't look back.

My phone went off as well as I turned away, but I shut it off when I saw it wasn't Tracy or Rosa or Joanne or anyone I cared about hearing from. I hustled away, drawing his coat closer around me to cover the bloody clothes, and headed west, to my only guaranteed sanctuary in the city.

# CHAPTER 18

*B*efore the Breaking, I lived with my parents in a middle-class neighborhood called Misty Glades in the western suburbs. Two-story Tudor revival houses mixed with sprawling ranches set on manicured lawns. White picket fences kept in golden retrievers and kids throwing Frisbees, while minivans and tricycles cluttered the driveways. It was a protected enclave against the rougher elements of urban life.

It even stayed that way for a few months after the Breaking, the neighborhood balanced on a pin's head while the humans tried to deny magic existed. Most of our human neighbors remained confident that the conflicts bubbling up around the globe would never affect their upper-middle-class existence, not realizing Others already lived among them.

People grew cautious as the seedier side of the magical *demimonde* emerged, but no one in our neighborhood wanted to know who wasn't human. The primary concern remained whether people mowed their lawns in accordance with the homeowners' association guidelines. Even though we weren't invited to dinner nearly as much once rumors started that my parents were witches, it didn't occur to me that anything bad would really happen. I still had to go to school and wash the dishes and help Dad in the garden.

And then street battles between human police and Other freedom fighters, trying to escape the increasingly draconian monitoring imposed by the government, began to eat away at the idyllic daydream that normal life would continue uninterrupted. The war began and ended for Misty Glades in a flash of magic on a bright summer morning, six months after the Breaking. Dad scrambled eggs and asked if I wanted pancakes while Mom read the paper, hmming over the latest attacks against witches in Paris and Jerusalem.

Even sixteen years after that morning, nothing grew in Misty Glades. Human and Other scientists studied the Remnant, as it became known, and took air and soil and water samples in an effort to reclaim the valuable land after the war ended. They found no answers, magical or conventional. It remained a dead zone despite the best science, technology, magic, and prayer. Eventually the city grew up around the Remnant.

I crouched near an abandoned hut at the edge of the shantytown on the eastern side of the Remnant, staring into the eerie darkness of the dead zone. After the Truce, but before it became clear the land was ruined, a few intrepid souls attempted to rebuild as land grew too expensive elsewhere and neighborhoods segregated between Others and humans. Structures disappeared or disintegrated without visible cause within hours of being erected in the Remnant. Wood frames simply disappeared. Steel beams melted to puddles in the gray dirt. Concrete foundations turned to dust and blew away. The ghosts ran everyone else out.

Only six structures remained standing in the wasteland, five the residences of powerful witches with strong defensive wards. The sixth was my house, untouched by time or weather. Exactly as it had been sixteen years ago, when the war landed on our doorstep in jackboots and riot gear. I squinted at the house through a cascade of oily magic rainbows, present even in the dark; the poison magic remained all around and through the once-prosperous neighborhood, tainting even my memories of better days.

I gathered my courage as I gathered more magic to attempt the walk through the Remnant. It generally wasn't a good idea to imitate ghosts, as they tended to resent the living pretending to be dead, but there weren't many other options for sneaking into the Remnant. The Alliance occasionally kept witches on the watchtowers around the dead zone, since magical flare-ups occasionally erupted from the remaining houses, and the Alliance stopped anyone, human or Other, who tried to enter the Remnant at night. There were no good reasons for someone to try the wasteland after dark.

So I cast a simple glamour until I looked incorporeal and ghost-like, and edged into the open around the shack. Luckily one of the ghosts who still haunted the Remnant had a nasty habit of stealing from the shantytown, so a ghost carrying a bag like mine wasn't that unusual. I wanted to race to the two-story brick house where I'd grown up, but I forced myself to pace with as much dignity as possible even as my knees knocked together and my hands shook with fatigue on the long hike along uneven, cracked sidewalks.

Ghosts never rushed—the dead had no reason to.

After an eternity of fear-sweat trickling down my back, I eased through the back door into the house. Mother's wards, strong enough after almost two decades to deter the ravages of time and stymie intruders, zinged around me and boosted my spirits. Strength, certainty, power. Underneath it all, love blazed higher.

I dropped the glamour along with my bag in the kitchen on the way to the living room. I shed Eric's coat and tossed it over the books, and washed the blood off my hands as quickly as possible. Scrying for a missing witch while a bloody mess was a bit too macabre for me, and the blood and bad magic could have affected the spell itself. I crouched under the piano in the living room and rummaged through a steamer trunk until I came up with a perfectly round copper basin. Scrying worked better in mirrors, most times, but for me, mirrors would always be where demons dwelt. I couldn't look for my friends there.

Setting a protective circle took only a moment after I filled the basin with fresh water, collected from rainwater in a cistern off the kitchen, then I wrapped my magic around the basin until it vibrated through every molecule. The reassuring numbness of magic buoyed me until there was no doubt I would find her. I was the War Witch. When I sought someone, I found them. I concentrated on Tracy, locked her face in my mind, and sent the spell into the water.

It clouded, grew dark and viscous, but revealed no clues as to her whereabouts. I concentrated harder. "Tracy."

The water shivered as the magic reacted to her name, but the ripples showed me nothing. Maybe, wherever she was, Tracy heard me. Maybe it would comfort her, give her strength, to know I searched for her.

My vision blurred and I had to wipe my cheeks to prevent any tears from contaminating the water with salt. I rested my hands on my knees as I concentrated on breathing. She was alive. She had to be alive and well and I would find her.

I would find her.

I murmured, "Theresa," and the water swirled white and cloudy. But no guidance formed in the dense vapor.

Maybe that was what the Rowanwood coven saw when they searched for the witches I'd shoved into a demon realm.

I closed my eyes. Breathe. *Breathe.* I wrapped the powerful, numbing magic even closer around myself as panic bubbled up in my chest. I stared into the basin as if it contained the waters of Mimisbrunnr itself and whispered her third name. "Teodora."

The copper rang at her thrice-given names, but the water remained opaque with no hint of her face. Tracy had to have heard the echoes when I used all three of her names. I sent an arrow of power with her name into the world on that ringing, hoping she would hear. She would know. She would give me a sign. Maybe not immediately, but soon.

# CHAPTER 19

*J* woke up with a magical hangover. My head ached and my sinuses clogged with emotion and regret and some of the dust that sifted through the old house. It was a thousand times worse than drinking too much. Even my bones ached as I tried to roll out of bed. The tax for using that much magic lessened over time, but made it much harder to stop. By the fifth year of war, I never released my magic. It was always around me, always dulling the pain, always numbing the terror and grief and deep-seated anger. On the few instances when I was forced to drop the magic for a short period of time, it nearly crippled me.

Opening my eyes took more effort than I wanted to admit, and for a brief flash, I was back in an alley five years earlier, trying to survive a magical detox when I finally realized how much trouble I was in. Going cold turkey after sixteen years of magic left me afraid and alone, terrified and unable to tell the difference between the past and the present and things that never happened at all.

I shook off the memories as I found my cell phone, the battery nearly dead after a night in the dead zone. The

Remnant drained any electronics that passed the border, and even getting close to the perimeter could play tricks with the circuitry in every sort of device. At least my phone still worked, though it showed several missed calls from Leif. But his wasn't the number I punched into the keypad. He had too many questions for me, but I had quite a few for someone else.

Eric answered on the first ring, voice uncharacteristically deep. "This is Zeibart."

"It's Lily." I hesitated, unsure of what to say next since I didn't even really know what I wanted from him.

"Hold on." It sounded like he moved, some of the background noise growing quiet until all I heard was his breathing. "Did something else happen?"

"No. But I have questions for you. About what happened, and why you keep showing up where I am."

"This isn't something to be discussed over the phone," he said. "Meet me at the diner at Wilson and Lake. Can you be there in an hour?"

I checked my watch and bit back a groan. The devil's hour had barely passed, and he wanted to meet at seven. "I'll do my best."

"Good. It might be best if you disguise yourself, given everything else that's going on."

"I know." Tension gathered in my chest as I dreaded the relief and eventual misery of using more magic. "I'll be there."

Getting out of the Skein in the early dawn was trickier still than making my way over the broken ground in the middle of the night, since far more people were up and about in the outskirts of the shantytown. The ghost glamour wouldn't work in the first hints of dawn, so I settled for a glamour based on a witch who'd died in the war and a don't-see-me spell to direct attention away from me.

It was still a long damn walk until I could blend into the

foot traffic in the shantytown, and longer still until I reached a bus stop.

By the time I arrived at the diner, I half-expected Eric to have left already. When I scanned the booths and breakfast bar, I didn't see him right away. I looked again, though, and something drew my eye to the back corner and a booth with a single male occupant. The face was different, an adjustment of the glamour he'd used earlier, and the gut he'd created bumped against the table. I didn't know how I knew, but I knew it was Eric. He was as eye-catching as a bowl of oatmeal, even with a hint of oily magic around him.

He didn't look up as I eased into the booth, the plastic-coated menu screening his expression. "I don't have much time."

Thank all the saints. A few hours of sleep remained a possibility, if I could find a safe place to rest. I squinted at his glamour, though, and tried to figure out why a second glamour, of a young woman with a ski-jump nose, hovered underneath. "How are you doing this?"

He didn't answer as the waitress approached, and he ordered only a cup of coffee. After all the energy expended in the last few days, pancakes and sausage sounded divine. My long, manicured fingernails distracted me as I handed the waitress the menu. No one local would recognize the witch whose face I borrowed, except the coven—and the coven had bigger problems than seeing a ghost. It was disconcerting to know I wore a dead woman's face, but it was safer than my own.

Once the waitress sashayed out of earshot, a conspiratorial grin bloomed on Eric's face. "There was a development in the investigation."

I unfolded and refolded my napkin, reining in curiosity borne of desperation. "They found the coven?"

"Oh no. No trace of the witches. We have a few leads, but we identified the bodies." He pulled a notebook from his jacket pocket and licked his fingers to flip through the pages. "Rosa Marquez and Joanne Park."

The room spun in echoing silence, broken only by the slow thud of my heartbeat. I leaned my elbows on the table to keep from sliding to the floor. I took deep, measured breaths as I focused on a water-spotted spoon on the table. Two good witches. Good friends. They'd fallen in with Anne Marie at the end, but I couldn't blame them.

They deserved more than a bloody end. More than being murdered and used to fuel some demon spell. More than betrayal from the coven.

But under the bitter grief lingered a hint of relief that Eric didn't say Tracy. Which was immediately followed by a backwash of guilt and disgust for being grateful that someone else died instead.

The sound of Eric's voice came from far away; I shook myself, and tried to muster the energy to care about what else he had to say. Saints keep them.

Eric poured half the pitcher of cream into his coffee. "You knew them well."

I stared into the liquid abyss of my own mug. "Yes."

"Mm." He stirred, watching the eddy and flow around his spoon as the coffee turned caramel. "They cast some kind of spell on the premises, using some of the blood, but the Bureau can't identify what it was. No connection to the witch who worked at the Skein, as they'd been hoping."

"Of course not." I dragged my gaze from my mug and stared out the window at the people walking with purpose in the chill air. They didn't know and wouldn't care that Rosa and Joanne were dead. It meant little, in the grand scheme of things, that two more witches perished. I cleared my throat again; something stuck in my throat, I couldn't manage to swallow. "Do they know who cast at Tracy's house?"

"No." Eric folded blunt, square hands on the table. "The

coven did—there was enough left over to identify that. But we don't have signatures for individual coven members, so we don't know who did what. The Alliance could clear it up, of course, but the Alpha is not being particularly cooperative." His face crumpled in something close to a pout. "The paperwork is taking *forever*."

Not surprising, really. Soren would want to handle it, but he would play by the rules and delay the humans with their own bureaucracy. It was witch business, after all, and witch business would be handled by witches. That was fine—if Soren had any witches left.

Eric drummed his fingers on the table, eyebrow arched. "How did you know the witch from the Skein didn't cast at the house? What does the Alliance know?"

I weighed my options as I studied him and the shifting glamours. Stefan wanted to arrest me for dark magic and being nonaligned with the wrong ring. They would have, if not for the lapis lazuli ring hanging heavy around my neck. I didn't understand why it saved me, but it couldn't have been a coincidence that Stefan saw the ring and let me go. Eric could make his career by handing me over. And yet he hadn't.

Of course, I could take him down with me, but obviously he was willing to risk that.

So I took a deep breath. "Because I was the witch who cast at the Skein."

He sat back, hands braced on the table. His face—and the glamours—turned inscrutable, and for the first time I caught a glimpse of a serious investigator, instead of the caricature he played. He waited for me to continue, unblinking.

In for a penny, in for a pound. I concentrated on shredding my napkin into tiny snowflakes. "Tracy asked me for help and I thought I saw what they were trying, so I interrupted it a little. I left some magic behind, I guess."

"You contaminated a crime scene."

"Maybe," I said. I ran out of napkin and cupped my hands around the coffee mug, trying to leech warmth from it. Cold permeated every part of me. "I didn't realize they considered the Skein a crime scene."

"Unauthorized magic conducted the night before demons are loosed on the city? Yeah, it's a crime scene." He frowned at me, then pasted a smile on his face as the waitress arrived with my pancakes and a disapproving glare at the fluffy pile of my napkin. Eric waited until we were alone and the din from the rest of the customers nearly drowned his words out. "It was a summoning. A demon summoning."

The pancakes didn't clear the bitter taste of adrenaline and grief from my mouth. "That's ridiculous."

"If you have a better theory, by all means let me know. I could use a promotion."

Dark magic had permeated the spell in the Skein, but the goal of the Calling hadn't been the demon itself. They used too much power over three nights to try to seal something to them, and that wasn't necessary even for the most dangerous demons. That kind of magic had to be focused against the Ancient Anne Marie highlighted in her book, the same one still waiting in the Remnant where I'd forgotten it on the kitchen table. I wanted to smack my forehead, but instead only considered the possibilities in the patterns of syrup on the cracked plastic plate.

The Ancient, the Barbary lion they'd tried to Call, was not my secret to tell, especially to the Externals. I didn't like the grim look on Eric's face, nor the certainty in his tone. If Eric believed they summoned a demon at the Skein, Stefan probably thought them guilty of far worse crimes, and there was no way I, or the Alliance, could protect them. But once Stefan learned I worked magic at the Skein, doubtless he'd pin the demon summoning on me as well.

Eric glanced around before leaning close and dropping his voice. "After we found the mess at your apartment and the witch's house, Stefan believes their demon summoning went wrong and now the demon is on the loose."

As theories went, it wasn't the worst. Demons had to go somewhere, after all. I studied his unlined face, and the expressionless second face underneath, searching for a hint of his motivation in either. "Who do they think trashed my place?"

"Oh, Stefan thinks you did it yourself, you tricky witch. To divert attention from the other dark magic, and to hide your participation in the coven."

Also not a terrible theory. I put the fork down as swallowing became more difficult. Saints preserve me. "And they're looking for me."

"Bet your ass, sweetheart." His tone was cheerful, at odds with the gravity of the news. "Ostensibly to protect you from whatever destroyed your apartment, but really all they want is a baseline magical signature to pin everything on you. The Bureau is using the attacks as a convenient excuse to round up witches of basher class and above."

"And once they're separated from their covens..." I trailed off, the queasiness growing in my stomach. Pancakes hadn't been a good idea after all.

"The Bureau will collect signature and biographic information. Work up full dossiers on all powerful witches. This is a prime opportunity to identify the Morrigan and her captains." Eric glanced at his watch, tone turning bored. "So if you have any friends left, they should find a dark hole to hide in until this blows over."

I sat back, pushing away the plate before I accidentally ate more. "Why do you want to help me?"

"We're alike, you and I."

"You keep saying that," I said, leaning forward across the table. "What the hell does that mean?"

"We're loki," he said, as if it was the most obvious thing in the world.

A loud rushing noise filled my ears as I stared at him. Loki. "That's b-bullshit," I managed to say, shaking my head. I tried to get out of the sticky booth, wanting to get as far as possible from that lunatic. Loki were dangerous. Outlawed. More reviled even than the Morrigan.

"Wait." Eric caught my arm and kept me in the booth, expression on both his male and female faces hardening. "You didn't know?"

"What the fuck are you talking about?" I tugged at his grip, cursing the weakness of the magical hangover and wishing I could have just hexed him in the middle of the human diner. "You're going to get me killed, you psychopath. Don't joke about shit like that."

"It's not a joke." Apparently assured I wasn't going anywhere, Eric drummed his fingers on the table and talked faster, voice low and blurring into a whisper of insanity. "There aren't many of us left, so I was surprised to find you. I'm astounded you survived this long."

I couldn't breathe. Panic compressed my chest and the diner blacked out around me until all I could see was his face. His fake face and the real one underneath. Loki. Unrestrained shapeshifter. The only thing you could never trust, when it could be anything it wanted. And she thought I was one of them.

It wasn't possible. I shook my head and tried to shove back from the table, even trapped in the cramped booth and stuck to the plastic bench. "You're insane. It's not possible. It's not fucking possible and how *dare* you accuse me of—"

"It's not an accusation, tutz. It's reality." Eric leaned forward and the pudgy male face faded away until the young woman's face took over entirely, though oil rainbow swirls still floated around him. Her. It. *Evil.* "You can see me, can't you? You knew something wasn't right with my face, but I'm guessing you assumed it was regular old witch magic. It isn't."

Someone passed near the table and her face returned to Eric's doughy, unassuming countenance. She waited until we were alone again to go on. "You got away with it for a long time because of the witch stuff, but there's always been unexplained things about you, right? Stuff normal witches didn't do or have or survive."

My brain refused to consider the possibility. Magic had rules, but sometimes those rules were only internally consistent. Some things remained difficult to explain or understand. I shook my head and yanked the necklace she'd given me over my head, slapping it on the table. "I don't need this. I have enough problems already."

"You're about to have a lot more," she said, unruffled. "More than you can handle alone. The Bureau is working on a way to find loki. If you survive this dark magic shit, it's only a matter of time until they get you anyway. The only way we can survive is to work together."

My legs didn't work, and I hovered, half-in and half-out of the booth, as I stared at her and clutched the lapis lazuli ring in my fist. The diner tilted around me. It was too much. Tracy missing, Rosa and Joanne dead, the Externals on my heels, and this guy—girl—telling me I was something terrible.

Eric sighed as she sat back, then pulled a wallet from her back pocket. "Think about it. Sit with it. Call me when you're ready to talk. But don't wait too long, because shit's about to get real. Stefan's going to arrest you for the dark magic, regardless of whether you're guilty. He's got a divireader rigged to show opal when he wants. Leif embarrassed him, so Stefan is going after you to make a point. Imagine the Chief Investigator having a demon-handler as a friend of his pack. Scandal for the Alliance, promotion for Stefan. Death for Lily."

I couldn't swallow around the knot in my throat. It just... couldn't be true. It couldn't be true. I stared at the pancakes, turning to mush in the syrup, and wondered if more coffee would help sort out the mush in my head.

She tossed money on the table, more than enough to cover my pancakes and her coffee as well as a generous tip, and eased to her feet, still wearing Eric's stocky form. She pointed at the ring. "Keep it close, by the way. Think of it as a get-out-of-jail-free card, at least for the time being. Don't wait too long to call, Lily. Be careful."

Then she winked, tossed another business card on the table with a different phone number, and bounced away through the diner, all purpose and drive with a swing in her step. I slouched in the booth and signaled the waitress for more coffee as I waited for the world to return to sanity and stability. Saints save me from morning people.

# CHAPTER 20

*I* hadn't moved from the booth even after half a dozen more cups of coffee. The waitress finally just left a fresh pot on the table next to me. Luckily the stack of cash from Eric convinced her to just leave me be, so I struggled with my thoughts in solitude. Everything Eric said and did over the past few days ran through my mind over and over. None of it made sense. If she was loki, how the hell did she end up masquerading as an External? The Bureau of External Affairs was one of the organizations charged with identifying and destroying loki. She'd walked into the lion's den and made herself one of the pride, all the while waiting for them to find her. She had to be crazy. Stark raving mad.

And she thought I was like her. She thought I was one of them, one of the reviled and hated. Hated more even than the War Witch. I rubbed my forehead and covered my face, wondering where the hell I could go from the diner. I couldn't sit there all day, regardless of how well I tipped the waitress with Eric's money. Getting back to the Remnant would take more energy than I had to spare, and the cost of holding onto the glamour just to sit in the diner grew until it made me queasy to consider. If I didn't have

175

some place safe to land when I released the magic, it would be over before I had a chance to tell Eric she was full of shit.

I forced myself to move to the edge of the booth, gathering the strength to stand, but paused as my phone rang. Moriah. I picked up and leaned against the table, my forehead resting against the stained Formica top. "Hey."

"You sound awful. What's going on?"

"It was a rough night." I squeezed my eyes shut as another headache brewed behind my eyes, even through the cold magic.

"Mick admitted what he said to you," Moriah said, the irritation in her voice well-concealed but still there. "He's an ass. Don't listen to him. You're a friend of our pack as long as you need and want to be, and probably after that as well."

It took a long moment to remember what she referenced—the conversation with Mick in the car after I left the restaurant. So much else had happened that it seemed laughably petty. "It's fine, Mo. Barely a blip."

"Then fill me in on what else is going on. Leif called half a dozen times looking for you. His guys are all over the city. Something big is going on."

I let the silence stretch as I debated what to tell her, how much to get her involved in what would no doubt be an ugly mess, and when I said nothing, Moriah sighed. "So it's that kind of problem."

"Sorry." I rubbed the back of my neck. "There's—"

"Get your ass over here," she said.

"What?"

"Get over here. I don't know where you're at, but it's not safe out in the city. You can come hang out with me and I...I won't tell Mick. Or Leif."

I sat up, squinting as I pinched the bridge of my nose. "Mo, that's—"

"I know what it is." Moriah wouldn't say she'd break pack law outright, but that was what she promised. Not telling the Chief Investigator or her alpha my whereabouts, when they wanted to know, meant betraying her pack. "We'll sort it out once things are a little clearer. So get over here, witch."

I wanted to refuse. I wanted to shelter her from the dark magic and demons and even the craziness that Eric promised to bring into my life. But I had nowhere else to go. I'd pay her back somehow. I'd protect her from the danger brewing in the city, and I'd make it up to her before she even knew I owed her. "Okay. I'll be there in a bit."

She was a better friend than I deserved. It took me an eternity to make my way across the city to the neat suburb where she lived, and by the time I reached her doorstep, I felt myself fraying at the seams. Sleeping in the old clothes I'd borrowed from the wardrobe in the Remnant left me rumpled and uncomfortable, and just as my phone started ringing, the front door swung open and Moriah eyed me up and down. "You're kidding, right?"

I shoved the phone away. "What's that?"

"What the hell did you do to your hair?"

"It's been a long night. You going to let me in?"

She surveyed behind me for potential threats before standing aside. "Park your broomstick on the tile before you get dirt on my floor. Did you walk through a barnyard on your way over?"

"The buses aren't running," I said. I leaned back against the door, my eyes drooping already. The glamour faded away along with my hold on the magic as I stood in her foyer, and the buzz of reality ran through me like pins and needles. Everything hurt. "Sorry. I'll leave the shoes here."

"And the pants." She gestured at my knees and handed me a pair of sweatpants, taken from the basket of fresh, folded laundry right near the basement door. "You've got shit up to your calves."

I grumbled but did as she asked, kicking off the muddy shoes and stripping off the equally dirty jeans, and put on the sweatpants. Even the soft cotton grated against my unbearably sensitive skin.

"You don't look good, Lil," she said, voice quiet. There wasn't any judgment in her, but that didn't make it easy to come up with a response. "Like five years ago."

I concentrated instead on using one of the clean towels to wipe up the muddy footprints I'd left on the clean tile. Moriah pointed at my jeans, crumpled on the floor, as the pocket started to ring. "I'm guessing that's Leif. He's looking for you, but he won't say why. Mick asked me a bunch of questions about where you'd hide and who you're friends with and if you ever used dark magic. If you were slipping again, back to... before. Ending with strict orders to call Leif the second I see or hear from you. Start talking, witch."

I silenced the phone and shuffled toward her living room. If I didn't sit down in the next few minutes, I'd fall flat on my face and never get up. "Some witch business went sideways. Mick didn't say anything about last night?"

Mo couldn't know about the mess at my apartment or she would have tackled me in relief the moment I knocked on her door. That Leif kept the incidents a secret from one of the most trusted wolves in the Alliance did not bode well for either of us.

"Not a peep." She followed me into the living room and folded her arms over her chest as she flopped onto the cushy overstuffed chair across from the couch where I collapsed. "Just...where's Lily? Have you seen Lily? Call her, did she answer?"

I winced. "Sorry."

Moriah put her feet up. "Is this about the bar the other

night? The bet? Or did you do something else to get Leif all worked up? I haven't seen him like this in a while."

"I hexed him yesterday." I frowned, trying to remember through the fog of memory and magic. "Day before that, maybe."

She sat forward, eyebrows arched almost to her hairline. "Wait, what?"

"He broke my wards and almost got himself killed, so I hexed him to save his life. Sort of." I covered my face and flopped sideways. My chest ached with grief. It seemed so ridiculous compared to what happened to the coven. I shouldn't have been hanging out on Moriah's couch. I should have been tracking down the perpetrators that killed Rosa and Joanne. I should have been searching for Tracy. But nothing worked and I couldn't explain that to Moriah. I couldn't explain the coven to Moriah.

"You destroyed his house, didn't you? That's why they're looking for you. We can fix this if you didn't draw blood, we—"

I forced a smile and begged the coven's forgiveness. "I appreciate that you think I'm that strong, but no, I didn't destroy anything. We had a spirited conversation and agreed to disagree on a few things. That's it."

She eyed me, still debating in her head, and eventually got up to wander toward the kitchen. "Well, you look like shit. Go upstairs and take a nap. Maybe take a shower first. Then we can figure out what the hell to do about all this when you're feeling better. I've got Mimi's party tonight, but you can hang for dinner with the girls when they get here."

"Thanks." I rubbed my eyes and staggered to my feet. I'd forgotten about Mimi's bachelorette party. Maybe that would be enough of a distraction for the Alliance that I could get to Tracy's house or the Skein and start tracking down the next link in the chain to the people who killed Rosa and Joanne. Not even the pot of coffee I'd drunk was enough to keep me awake once I sprawled on the bed in the spare room, and some of the agony faded from my joints as the magic retreated further. I'd search for Tracy as soon as night fell. It was safer for us both.

# CHAPTER 21

*I* woke after full dark with the same magical hangover, though it didn't feel like my skin would peel itself off my body if I moved too fast. For a long moment, I peered around the dim room, trying to remember where I was, and the realization of Rosa and Joanne's deaths hit my chest like a lead pipe. I curled up around a pillow and buried my face against the smooth fabric, muffling the scream I'd wanted to loose in the diner but hadn't dared. Rosa. Joanne. Tracy.

And at the heart of it all, Anne Marie.

Tears burned as they escaped and tracked down my cheeks, disappearing into the pillow, and it wasn't enough. It would never be enough.

The weight of their loss pinned me down even as voices rose elsewhere in the house. I couldn't afford to grieve. Just like in the war, that had to wait. Emotions had to wait until the luxury of time and safety allowed it. I said a prayer for them to the saints and rolled out of bed. Rosa and Joanne would have understood. They knew.

I reached for a thread of magic, a bare whisper of power, to fend off the urge to crawl back into bed. At some point Moriah left my laundered jeans in the room with me, so I got dressed and ran a brush through my hair before I dared the landing outside and the stairs. I paused, though, as Moriah's voice echoed through the otherwise quiet house.

"Goddamn it, just tell me what's going on."

"I can't," her brother said. I froze where I was. Mick. He undoubtedly knew why Leif searched for me. But Mick didn't blurt it out. "Leif's orders. But you should cancel the party, Moriah. It's not a good idea, and even in that part of the city, it's not safe."

"Mimi will be crushed," Moriah said. Her tone gained an edge as she went into protective big-sister mode. "We've already rescheduled it four times based on bullshit warnings like this. Is Soren ordering me to cancel this party?"

"No, but—"

"Then we're not changing it." Moriah growled in irritation. "Have you received any threats?"

"No," he said, and he wasn't happy about it. "But there are other things going on in the city, Moriah, and—"

"Tell me what they are and why I should give a fuck, then we can have a conversation. You're the alpha, I get it—but don't you fucking forget you wouldn't be without me. You can't do any of this shit without me. So if there's something *so* dire going on, tell me. Otherwise get out of my way. I have our sister's bachelorette party to manage."

Silence raced through the house and I debated escaping out the window before things got bloody. But Mick only growled at her, said something I couldn't quite hear, then stormed out. The door slammed behind him, and the force of it shook the house. I eased down the stairs and peeked into the living room. Mo sat on the couch, face in her hands, and didn't move as I walked in. I knew she knew I was there, but I didn't press. Just folded myself into the love seat and waited.

She didn't move. "How much did you hear?"

"Not all of it, but enough." I picked at a loose thread on my jeans. "And thanks for washing my clothes."

"You're welcome, witch." Mo took a deep breath and sat up, stress making lines around her eyes. She looked older, and tired. Very tired. "There are rumors in the Alliance that the wolves are starting to turn on each other. Pack against pack. And the felines will take advantage. We can already see the witches turning on us. It's just a matter of time before the entire thing falls apart and we're completely fucked."

I didn't bother with platitudes or cheap reassurances that the worst wouldn't happen. We'd both lived through ten years of the worst-case scenario. "Rumors are just rumors. Until they're truth, anyway."

She scowled up at the ceiling, running her hands through her long hair. "It feels like it did right after the Breaking. That pressure-cooker feeling when the dominoes start falling and you keep hoping something will stop them, but..."

"But nothing does." I took a deep breath. "Maybe you should delay Mimi's party. It doesn't sound like you're in the mood to celebrate anything anyway."

"That kid is going to have a normal life," Moriah said, leaning forward with a hint of the wolf in her eyes. "She's engaged. She's getting married in a month, and she's already had to cancel this freaking party half a dozen times. I'm not doing that to her again. Whatever happens, we'll deal with it."

She pushed to her feet and headed for the kitchen, anger in every line of her body, but I didn't blame her. I'd envied Mimi's normal life for the past several years, and though Moriah loved her sister fiercely, I knew part of Mo mourned that she'd lost her own twenties to the war. Mimi's charmed life was just a reminder of what we'd lost.

I covered my eyes and hoped I was doing something noble and kind rather than self-destructive. A smart witch would have heeded Eric's warning and lain low until the storm blew over. A smart witch wouldn't go running into an Other bar with the goddaughter of the Peacemaker and the entire Bureau of External Affairs on her tail for practicing dark magic.

But history had proven I wasn't a particularly smart witch. "It's dark magic. That's what they're worried about."

She froze in her tracks, still facing away from me, and waited.

"Dark magic, dark witches. There's something bigger going on. If that's what Mick's worried about, I'm not sure you and the pack will be enough to protect everyone."

Mo turned on her heel, arms already folded over her chest. "I'm not worried about witches, Lily. I'm worried about other packs trying to steal my sister."

"I'll go with you, then. I can protect her from both."

She laughed, shaking her head. "You look like you're on death's door, and if I don't feel like celebrating anything, you look like you're ready for a wake."

"I owe you," I said. "Plus I got some rest, so I'll be fine. Seriously, Moriah. I'm sure the party will be great for Mimi, but you'll never forgive yourself if something happens."

Moriah took a deep breath and headed for the fridge. "Okay, witch. But I think we're both going to need a beer before this gets much further."

I wanted to laugh, but she was right. The beer filed the edge off my grief. I couldn't help Tracy until I had more information, and Moriah needed my help in the meantime. I owed Mo my life, and she seldom asked anything in return. She faced a serious challenge that night: preventing another pack from abducting the bride-to-be or the bachelorettes while avoiding the blood feud that would ignite if she fought any would-be abductors.

Snatching remained a popular way for young male shifters to demonstrate hunting prowess to a prospective mate and her family. The girl usually agreed to it beforehand, with only the timing and method of abduction unstated—it was up to the male to get his mate from a well-protected home without getting caught. I found the whole idea rather Neanderthal in execution, but the wolves in particular thought it necessary for a young man to prove his worth, particularly the young men who had not fought in the war. They called it culture and made excuses when the women who objected raised issues of compulsion and choice. Moriah hated it. But even her standing in one of the most powerful packs, and her reputation from the war, wasn't enough to change the practice or protect her sister. There had even been threats from a few packs that they'd steal Moriah herself, just to make a point. The only man who tried didn't survive the attempt.

Some Old World packs allowed, even encouraged, males to pillage as they wanted. No women were off-limits, and the packs generally refused to return even reluctant brides to their families. Appeals to Soren and the Alliance usually resulted in a negotiated settlement, at least for those Old World packs in the States, but in the five years since the Truce, half a dozen full-scale pack wars erupted and threatened to tear the Alliance apart. Grabbing Mimi, the sister and fiancée of alphas and goddaughter of the Peacemaker himself, could divide the packs permanently and remake the face of the Alliance—if it survived. The kidnapping would be the type of escapade that made a young shifter a legend forever.

Of course, knowing Moriah's family—and Mimi herself—forcing Mimi to do anything she did not want to do would make that particular shifter a dead legend. But young males rarely thought with their brains.

Moriah handed me another beer on her way to answering the door and allowing in the bridesmaids and maids of honor and other attendants that would support Mimi on her wedding day, and I covered my eyes so I didn't have to see their excitement and giddy joy. If Moriah killed anyone, she'd embroil their pack in another blood feud. As a nonaligned witch, I could spill as much blood as I wanted without endangering anyone but myself. The Truce didn't apply to me, but at least in that particular situation, neither did the consequences. It left me open to retribution from the other packs, but we both knew I could take care of myself.

Of course, after last night, maybe I couldn't.

I borrowed lipstick and a pair of comfortable boots from Moriah, leaving my hair down instead of in my usual ponytail to try and change my appearance a little. Using a full glamour around Moriah required more of an explanation than I was prepared to give, so I went as myself. I hoped I didn't have to use any magic, but if there was anyone in the entire city that deserved the full force of the War Witch's protection, it was Mimi.

* * *

MIMI ENTERED KINDERGARTEN three months before the Breaking. She spent the war high in the mountains, sheltered with other shifter and witch kids in a place called Sanctuary. Even they didn't escape the horrors of war—Mimi lost both her parents before she got to know them, and an older brother as well.

I met her seven years into the war, just after her twelfth birthday. She should have been in school with ribbons in her hair and a pink backpack, worrying about spelling tests and who she would play with at recess. Instead, she guarded a nursery of toddlers with a lead pipe almost too heavy for her to carry.

The humans threatened Sanctuary to split the Alliance's focus, even as trouble brewed in the War Coven at the front. Sam and I bickered frequently, the coven walking on eggshells around us. Soren Warbringer was not unsympathetic, but he was pragmatic enough to know we needed a break from each other before things got ugly. So he ordered Lilith to reinforce the wards around Sanctuary and search for talent among the children, not knowing he sent the Morrigan away during the darkest days of the war. And because I desperately needed a break from Sam, I agreed to trek to the mountain stronghold in what used to be Colorado.

It took four nights of traveling via Jeep and motorbike and hiking, hiding in glamours and darkness, with Leif and another shifter as guards. Even then there were too few war witches to risk one dying outside of battle. Of course, Soren also ordered the wolves to kill me if capture looked imminent: I knew too much about the Alliance to risk me being captured alive by the humans. It did not make for enjoyable travel, regardless of how fetching Leif looked when he first woke up and crawled out of his sleeping bag.

Despite the secret nature of the mission, word got out among the fighters at the front that I headed west. Many asked that I carry messages to loved ones at Sanctuary. Though the journey left me filthy and on edge, wishing only for a shower and bed, I'd exhausted the satchel of letters by the time I found Mimi. She was the last stop before I could rest.

I'd seen their eldest brother Martin die a year or two earlier, and knew their parents died in battle in the second year of war. Since someone who probably looked a lot like me delivered the news of their deaths both times, her reaction should not have surprised me.

She hefted her pipe, crystal blue eyes narrowed as she evaluated my bedraggled clothes. Her voice was child-high but steady as a rock. "Are they alive?"

Taken aback, I frowned at her. She met my gaze, fearless, though terror lurked in her eyes. She would walk alone in the world, if she lost Mick and Moriah, and she stared into that abyss every time messengers came from the front. I crouched before her and nodded. "Yes. They wanted to say happy birthday."

She exhaled her terror, and I caught the pipe as it slipped from her fingers, pretending not to notice as she widened glassy eyes. Mimi composed herself and put her shoulders back, offering her small hand to shake. "I'm Miri—"

"Mimi," I said, squeezing her fingers despite the dirt crusting my skin. "Your sister told me. You shouldn't give your name to someone you just met, kiddo."

She nodded, weighing this advice, then made a face as she eyed me. "You need a *bath*."

It nearly made me laugh, but she held herself with such dignity I couldn't. "Yes, I do. My name is Lilith. It was nice to meet you, Mimi. And happy birthday."

"Did they send anything?" She managed to sound both very adult and very wistful as she studied her hands, a toddler tugging on her sleeve.

Every kid deserved a present on her birthday. Except Moriah and Mick were very far from any place where appropriate presents could be found, and hadn't sent one anyway. I chewed my lip, then reached into my pocket. I could protect myself; Mimi needed the help more than I did. The coin, covered in Chinese characters, had a small hole punched in the middle, and had been spelled for protection by my mother a few weeks before she died. I put it in Mimi's palm and shifted my feet as she just stared at it. "This. They couldn't find a ribbon or chain for it, but it's for luck."

Her eyes grew shiny again, and she bolted forward to hug me, nearly dropping the coin. "Thank you, Leelee."

I untangled myself and patted her head gingerly, uneasy with the affection. "Okay. Be good," I said, and walked away to find a hot shower.

During the week at Sanctuary, I slowly forgot about Sam's clinginess and tested the older kids for basher or warder strength gifts, not daring to hope I'd find a summoner. And I watched Leif, saw the promise in him despite his grim focus on the war. But the blonde kid with her pipe constantly intruded on my thoughts. She and I were not so different.

She was one bad day away from being entirely alone. I made a quiet promise to the saints and the universe itself that it wouldn't happen. I re-spelled the coin for additional protection before I left, and when I returned to the front, I paid more attention to Mick and Moriah, determined that at least one of them would return to Mimi.

I couldn't save Martin, but I saw Moriah and Mick through the war. Mimi flourished, became an outgoing teenager and a beautiful young woman, living a charmed life as the peace took hold. She finished school, fell in love, and took her place in a pack. Charmed.

I remembered it all in a flash as the front door flew open and Mimi tumbled into the foyer. Reconciling the doe-eyed Mimi I remembered with the young woman in a miniskirt whooping it up with her friends took some effort. As Moriah herded the unruly girls toward the stretch limo parked outside, Mimi leaned on my shoulder, giggling.

"Meems," I said, steadying her. "You doing okay?"

She straightened and her smile fell away as she held out her hand, radiating the same solemnity I remembered from Sanctuary. "It's my 'something old.'"

I blinked several times at the old coin on a faded pink ribbon resting in her palm, and struggled for words.

"This protected me," she whispered, wide-eyed and serious despite being totally smashed already. She nearly strangled me in a hug. "Whatever luck I have, Leelee, I owe to you. Thank you for making sure they...at least they came back, even if Marty couldn't."

I swallowed a sudden knot in my throat, pretending to

cough so I could hide the break in my voice. "It wasn't anything special."

"It was to me." She winked at me, once more a party girl, and dove into the limo as she bellowed for someone to pass the vodka. I wiped under my eyes as Moriah gave directions to the driver, then ducked into the backseat. I stared out the window, my stomach clenching as we drove out of the city and toward one of the open parks where the packs held their mysterious ceremonies.

At least it wasn't anywhere near the witching hour yet.

The girls hopped out of the limo and headed into the field, even with their high heels and party gear, and Moriah paused near the door to give me a regretful look. "You've gotta stay here, babe. It'll just be a second."

"Not a problem," I said, and pretended to put my feet up. "I'll just take a nap."

Mo winked at me, "I'll bring you back some rabbit blood," and shut the limo door to jog after Mimi and her crew.

Twenty minutes later, I still wondered if she meant it.

# CHAPTER 22

*I* waited until the driver stepped out of the limo to smoke a cigarette, then fished out my cell phone and called the number on the new business card Eric had given me. When she answered, I floundered for a response—the voice was female, bright and chipper and a little too much like Mimi. Clearing my throat didn't help, but I managed to force the words out. "I don't want to talk about that thing you said. It's a lie and I don't believe you."

"Whatever you say, sug." Eric chewed on something crunchy, apparently unperturbed by my opening. "Then what do you want to talk about? Get arrested already?"

"No, and I'm not going to be arrested." I meant every word. I'd go out fighting rather than let them put a collar on me. "But I need to get to the Skein tomorrow night. Can you clear the Externals away from there? They've got it blocked off and I can't risk being seen."

"I might be able to create a little distraction," she said. "Although the Skein is Stefan's territory, so he won't be pleased if he catches me out there."

"He mentioned that," I said under my breath, sitting up as

the driver got back into the front of the limo. "Said you should stay the hell away or we'd both end up dead."

"What do I get out of it?"

My heart started to pound as Moriah and the girls reappeared in the distance, making their way carefully across the field. Despite their hair being in disarray and a few carrying their shoes, they didn't look like they'd held a wild revel in the middle of a field under the moon. I cleared my throat and scooted out of the way of the door, just in case. "The credit, if I can figure out what the hell happened."

She made a thoughtful noise, then chuckled. "Sure. Why the hell not. I'll call you tomorrow to confirm. Be careful."

I hung up just as the door opened and Moriah stuck her head in. "Still with us?"

"Bracing for the storm," I said.

"Good luck," she said, and held the door open so the girls could pile back into the limo.

I ended up stuck in the back corner between one of Mimi's dearest friends and her future sister-in-law, a sour-faced girl who oozed jealousy every time she spoke. I stared out the window as we drove back into the city. My stomach clenched as we pulled up to the Pug: even for a Friday night, it burst at the seams, a crowd lining up down the block. I glanced at Moriah as she opened the door, and managed to say over the shrieking bachelorettes, "Are you sure?"

The girls finished attaching veils and streamers and cardboard penises to Mimi, screaming with laughter until my ears rang. Moriah shouted over their noise as the girls tumbled out of the limo. "Soren issued a no-blood truce for this block when we scheduled the party. I guess he didn't cancel it."

I groaned, hustling to get out the door so I could scan for threats. No wonder every shifter in the city stood in line to get into the bar—the Peacemaker himself guaranteed no harm would come to Others there. Which meant feuding packs could break bread without requiring combat to defend their blood feud, and they would be tempted to mend fences during the truce to avoid the exorbitant fees the Alliance lawyers charged to resolve the same. Not that it ever went as planned.

So every lunatic shifter in the city with a grudge would be in the bar, within reach of Mimi. Maybe hiding the half dozen lunatics who really wanted to cause trouble for her. I stood back as the girls extracted themselves from the limo in a tangle of arms and legs, and the waiting males roared in approval. The girls giggled and preened at the attention as they sauntered to the door, and I cursed Soren a little as I looked around. He'd made the promise, but provided no additional security. Just the Pug's regular bouncers manned the door and kept things under control, but things could quickly get out of control based on the number of men waiting to get inside.

A cloud of smoke escaped as the door opened, Moriah waving us onward, and I jostled the stragglers as I warned the hungry-eyed men away with a shower of sparks. I gathered a little power, my nose twitching. Trouble could come from those men, or the ones already inside the bar, or from something unnamed in the night that hunted me instead of Mimi.

Mimi swayed to the throbbing beat as she flung her arms up and twirled, and I envied her with a sudden sharp pain in my chest. To be so sheltered, so cared for and protected. To love a man, and marry him, and look forward to a real future together. To be young and beautiful and free. Unscarred. My breath hitched in my throat.

Inside, the bar heaved with bodies packed tight in front of the stage where the band played. I caught sight of Moriah in the lounge area across the bar, roped off and decorated with bridal-themed tchotchkes. I fought through the sweaty masses, barely emerging on the other side, and perched next to her on a long sofa.

She put her feet up and waved at a waitress. "So much for being loki."

"What?" I froze, heart jumping to my throat.

Moriah leaned closer and yelled over the music. "I said, so much for being low-key. Blending in."

I exhaled through my teeth and managed a weak nod, thinking of Eric.

\* \* \*

I DIDN'T SIT STILL for long, though it was less about adrenaline and more that I was out of practice at casting long-range. Bad aim could fricassee half the bar if I tried to take someone out and missed. I nudged Moriah and shouted over the shrill of the electric guitars. "Going to circulate. I'll send up red sparks if there's trouble."

She nodded, making eyes at a tall dark wolf hanging at the bar, and sipped her drink. "I'll be here, trying to forget that my brother is an ungrateful asshole."

"Good luck with that."

I plunged into the crowd, skirting the dance floor as I sensed who surrounded us in the crowd. I breathed a little easier after discovering no other witches hid in the bar, though I paused with my back to a wall as I scanned the dance floor. Or maybe there weren't any witches left to cause trouble. I squinted at the dancers, but saw only the bloody wreck of my apartment. Maybe demons attacked all of the witches in the city, not just Tracy and me and the coven. Maybe Anne Marie wanted to remove all of her competition at once.

For a mad minute, I considered calling a witch—any witch —just to make sure someone survived. My chest tightened and sweat gathered between my shoulders, chilling me even in the oppressive heat of the bar. The urge to flee passed as Mimi gyrated closer and reached for my hand. "Dance, Leelee!"

"I don't dance." I gestured behind her at all the people desperate to fall within the sphere of her charmed life. "Dance with them."

Alcohol and excitement brightened her eyes, and she nearly crushed the bones in my fingers as she dragged me toward the dance floor. "But you can't come to my wedding and dance with me then. Dance now!"

"For cryin' out loud..." I craned my neck to catch Moriah's eye, but she was fully occupied flirting with the tall wolf. I couldn't tell who was in more trouble—her or the male. But either way, she wouldn't rescue me from Mimi.

Mimi dragged me into her crowd of friends, shrieking until the girls cheered. Being nonaligned might save me from blood feuds on a truce night, but it kept me from attending Mimi's wedding. The Alliance only allowed pack and the aligned to attend official ceremonies, including weddings and funerals. I pretended I didn't resent the restriction because there was no way around it—when the Peacemaker himself would attend the ceremony, Mick couldn't even bend the rules.

Mimi was a force of nature on the dance floor, despite my best efforts to remain dignified, and so I was laughing and whirling around her as three men infiltrated the crowd around us. A bridesmaid beckoned to one of them, drawing him closer as the chiseled jaw and perfect cheekbones distracted the rest of the girls. I circled closer to Mimi, the music beating in my brain as my instincts screamed a warning. The hard edge to those men was not a calculated facade, like so many others in the bar. The ones eyeing the bridesmaids moved with dangerous intensity, and I started looking for the bouncers, just in case.

Then Mimi squeaked, "Hey, don't—" and I left the bridesmaid to her fate.

Mimi grappled with a fourth man, his bulk nearly overwhelming her as she fought in her stiletto heels and mini skirt.

My brain clicked slowly through the disorientation of smoke and music and heat. He touched her. Touched Mimi.

My Mimi. Sweet child with wide eyes and my magic coin.

He pulled her away, toward the rear exit and undoubtedly a waiting car. A waiting life of servitude and exploitation, a pampered doll for some Old World asshole. I bared my teeth.

The truce did not apply to me.

He looked at me and smiled. Recognition twisted that smile, an anticipation of conflict, and the rush of memories almost distracted me. Another ghost risen from the ashes of war: Brandr, an Old World alpha and son of an Ancient, one of the shifters closely related to Lord Fenrir. He'd been scary when the war started; a decade of killing made him terrifying. And even five years of peace hadn't dulled that edge.

Brandr shoved Mimi into the waiting arms of a younger wolf as she tried to reach me. Her arms flailed and she screamed. "Leelee?"

I moved before I knew I moved—slapping my hands together and stripping every ounce of magic from the room in one giant drag. Dancers stumbled toward us with the force of it, and the band jangled to a halt as the bass player fell. I threw a ward around Mimi and me, protecting the bystanders if things got ugly, and isolated Brandr from the rest of his pack.

He might have been a hero from the war. He might have been a direct descendant from Fenrir Varg Himself. He might have come for all the girls, or maybe he'd decided to challenge the Peacemaker by kidnapping Soren's goddaughter. It didn't matter. Brandr signed his death warrant the moment he touched Mimi.

Magic curdled as I hexed the wolf restraining Mimi, blowing him off his feet and through my ward into the mirror over the bar. I sent a cascade of red sparks into the air as silence followed the shattering glass, all before Brandr even stepped in my direction.

I may have grown complacent in retirement, but I could still fight.

And the magic. The blessed magic removed any hint of guilt or grief or emotion at all. Just rage. Only rage survived as a muted burn in my chest, a pressure where I clenched my jaw. Finally.

Brandr snarled, "Witch," and I whipped a killing hex at him. Mimi squealed as he raised his arm and a charmed metal bracelet deflected the hex.

I ducked the magical shrapnel and started to rethink my strategy. He had a strong witch in his pack. Fine. Whoever she was, the bitch wasn't stronger than me. I dragged Mimi behind me. "Keep your back to mine. Shout if they come at us."

The bouncers and other wolves shouted about the truce, but Brandr and I never looked away from each other.

Power swelled around me and I smiled. It had been too long.

Battle.

My heartbeat slowed and steadied, I stacked hexes in preparation, and everything—the noise, the lights, the cold clamminess of Mimi pressed against me—faded away. I tossed hexes at his feet to make him dance, and when any normal witch would have needed to pause and Brandr lurched forward in anticipation, I winged a stunning spell and caught him full in the chest.

He crashed backward into my ward, and I jumped forward to finish him off. Never turn away from the enemy until he was dead. True-dead. I gathered blue death spells in my right hand, prepared to finish him off, when Mimi choked and said, "Lily," and I turned.

I swept her behind me, keeping her protected as I faced the new threat.

Protect the children in Sanctuary. Keep them safe. They're the future. Safeguard them.

The three males from Brandr's pack circled my ward, all

business as they tried to reach their alpha and Mimi. One flung a handful of coins at the power glowing in a blue dome around us, but the coins bounced off as they cracked the wards. Burning sparks of magic fizzled through the bar, and the crowd stampeded for the exits.

The coins broke apart, too weak to really damage my spells, but it only increased my certainty that the Cold River pack had a powerful witch working with them. Saints help me if Brandr kept a basher, because even a war witch could have trouble with a basher's work. I sucked in a breath and glanced back to check on Brandr, still trying to stand.

One of the three betas pulled a metal hoop from the small of his back, and I gritted my teeth as I backed Mimi into the center of the wards. "This might get a little...loud."

He threw the rending hoop, as the ring was officially known, and it sliced through the air; edged in steel and charged by a powerful basher, it collided with my wards and whipped around us.

Mimi blinked at me. "What will—" she started, just as my magic gave in under the hoop's relentless assault.

The wards should have exploded inward, stunning me and probably killing Mimi, but I flexed and released the spell out just before they broke. The magic boomed like thunder, leveling everyone else in the bar.

Enough of that. I tossed my hair back as I brought my hands together at my chest and faced the three wolves, prone on the dirty dance floor. "Is that all you've got?"

One pushed up on his elbow as blood drained from his ear. His eyes glinted gold in the flashed strobes lights of the bar as he bared pointy teeth. "No."

The magic buoyed up inside me, and I reveled in it, turning as clinking echoed behind me.

Brandr regained his feet, unwinding a heavy gauge steel chain, loop after loop coiling at his feet as he hefted a powerful breaking charm in his other hand. A red-orange glow leaked through his fingers.

Cold adrenaline sharpened my vision as magic built like lightning in my chest. I felt powerful and dangerous and alive for the first time in years. In forever. Finally. *Finally*. I could fight. I could feel again. Could release all that anger and fear that built up, and finally feel nothing at all.

I spread my hands in front of me, daring him to use the charm. Fool.

My laughter rang out in the silent bar. Brandr's scarred face creased as he watched me, but he raised the charm, drawing his arm back to throw. I pointed my right hand at him, covered in a soft blue glow from elbow to index finger, and everyone who'd fought alongside witches in the war took a collective breath. Blue. Blue to bring death. I smiled. I relished the power and fury rolling through the blue death in the palm of my head. No one survived blue death. "Don't do it. Because I will."

But mutually assured destruction only deterred relatively sane combatants. I wasn't sure either of us actually was.

Brandr snapped the end of the chain at my legs, making me jump as the iron in the chain raised a tickle in my sinuses. At least it wasn't cold iron. I sent a blue orb out and he barely dodged in time. Mimi squeaked behind me, and whispered, "Get him, Leelee."

"Blue death will destroy your soul," I said, unfeeling through the cold clarity of the magic, though I edged Mimi away from the splintering magic.

His teeth shone white and long, sharpened by rage and battle and the moon. He flexed his shoulders and played with the breaking charm. Whatever reply he prepared disappeared in the roar that emanated from the door. Everyone in the bar froze. Pack magic flooded the room, sending every shifter to their knees and threatening to end my fight.

No. *My* fight. I snarled and sent power crashing against the pack magic in a tide; no one would steal that from me. I'd been so bored for so very long. They wouldn't take it from me.

Another roar and the door exploded in; pack magic raged against mine until the rational part of me reasoned it would behoove me to let it go, regardless of how much I wanted to finish it and raze the bar to the ground. I bared my teeth at Brandr. "You do not go after the pups." I arced blue lightning at him in a final message.

He didn't even try to block with the shielding charm, bracing for death instead, but a red mist rose up and deflected my hex. Protecting him. He had a moment to look surprised, then the timbre of the roar changed and a crushing gravity settled on the room.

I grabbed Mimi's arm so I could run with her if I needed to, but I didn't take my eyes off Brandr. He still had that charm.

The crowd of shifters parted to let someone through. Even with the haughty indifference of magic, my heart climbed into my throat as I recognized the set of his shoulders. I would know him anywhere in the world, even in the dark of night: Warbringer and Peacemaker. Leader of the Alliance. Alpha of alphas.

Soren.

Pack magic surged as he loomed over Brandr, and my hands fell. Soren protected Brandr in order to make his own point. *That* was irritating. I could have killed Brandr myself. He probably would have preferred it to the Peacemaker's justice, by the look on his face as the chain fell from his hands.

Mimi, better schooled in shifter etiquette than me, pulled free of my grip and bowed to the Peacemaker as his gaze swept the crowd. I didn't budge. It took every ounce of willpower I possessed, boosted by magical arrogance, to keep my knees locked as Soren's rage suffocated the bar.

I was nonaligned. I would not bow. I might not stand for long, but I would stand. I edged back a step.

But no one would blame a witch for leaving. Clearly it was a pack matter to be resolved among the Alliance.

A hand slid around my elbow and pulled me back when I took a step. I clenched my right hand, preparing the blue death. Just in case one of Brandr's guys decided to go out in a blaze of glory right in front of the Peacemaker.

"Imagine finding you here," a low voice said, close behind me.

My heart sank. Leif.

# CHAPTER 23

*I* kept my eyes on Soren despite Leif's touch. The Peacemaker loomed over Brandr, shoulders so tense the muscles rippled under his shirt, and his goons spread out to guard the rest of the Cold River pack. Soren's voice was deceptively mild for someone on the verge of an uncontrolled shift, a scary trick I'd heard only one other time during the war. Right before he went straight fucking berserk. "Brandr. The moon must have stolen your reason, for you to break a truce I guaranteed."

The kneeling wolf didn't look away. "I can't say I knew there was a truce to break."

Leif's voice stirred the hair at my temple. "You didn't answer your phone."

"I've been a little busy."

A growl lent an edge of Soren's voice that sent the nearest shifters stumbling to retreat. "And you touched my goddaughter. Why shouldn't I rip your throat out right here?"

Brandr's gaze slid to me and I couldn't breathe. Would he blame me for this mess? Would he offer some excuse for trying to steal Mimi? After a long, long silence in which no one moved or spoke, Brandr said, "I offer no defense," and waited, making no move to placate the agitated Peacemaker.

Soren followed Brandr's gaze to me, and his golden eyes narrowed. I clenched my jaw to stop my teeth from chattering under the weight of his scrutiny and the pressure of Leif's presence. The Peacemaker's personal power hit me like a punch in the gut, though he didn't immediately order me collared. That was a good sign, at least.

The Peacemaker gestured and a dozen Styrma, his most experienced and loyal fighters, seized Brandr and dragged him away. The Old World alpha tracked me even as he disappeared out the door and into the night.

I hoped Soren would just turn and leave, but luck had long since abandoned me. Moriah finally elbowed through the motionless crowd to the small gap around us, her face flushed, as Soren surveyed the crowd. The Peacemaker's attention shifted to where Leif gripped my arm, though he spoke to Moriah. "You brought a witch."

"Lily," Moriah said, bobbing her head in deference to the alpha of alphas. "Our friend. From the war."

"Lily," Soren repeated, as his gaze went to Leif and something passed between them—something unique to shifters or maybe just to men. I wondered what Leif told him about me, but the Peacemaker still did not accuse me of any crimes. "From the war."

He recognized me—he had to. My heart thudded a little faster against my ribs.

A hidden threat lurked behind Soren's mask of civility. "You didn't bring assistance, witch?"

"No," I said, and tensed. Leif's grip tightened as he shifted his balance, preparing to take me down if I threatened his boss. But I'd played these games before, and let my teeth show in the smallest of smiles, a socially acceptable statement of independence. "I'm dangerous enough on my own."

"So I see." He glanced around the silent bar, canines glinting in the strobe light as he smiled back. "And which of my covens is lucky enough to call you sister, Lilith?"

He knew. He had to know the answer to that. But for some reason he wanted me to say it. I hesitated and considered a lie. Lying to the Peacemaker about belonging to one of his covens, even a fictional one, would certainly haunt me. And declaring myself nonaligned meant I became a free witch for him to pursue—or censure. I pinched the bridge of my nose and I hemmed and hawed, until Mimi stumbled back to hug me, jostling Leif's hand loose.

She grinned at her godfather and winked as if she told a dirty joke. "Leelee's nonaligned," she said, and burped so loudly she startled herself.

I swallowed a groan as murmurs spread through the crowd, but I met Soren's gaze without blinking. I would not cower.

Moriah caught her sister's shoulder and propelled her to the side, trying to catch Soren's attention as the Peacemaker's focus sharpened on me. "Sir. Lily is a friend of our pack, and—"

"I'm sure she is." The Peacemaker studied me for an eternity before he looked at Leif and nodded. Soren turned to where Mimi swayed on her sky-high heels, and his demeanor went from homicidal alpha to doting uncle in a blink. "Are you having a good time at your party?"

"Oh yeah, lots of fun." Mimi peeked around Moriah, apparently having forgotten the last thirty minutes. "You should stay, Uncle Soren. Let your hair down," and she dissolved into a mix of giggles and hiccups.

Soren smiled indulgently. "I would love to stay and celebrate, honey, but I have other business." His gaze swept the crowd, creating a wave of bobbing heads and audible gulps. His smile turned self-mocking. "And I would kill the buzz if I stayed. Enjoy your party. Leif will make sure no one else misbehaves."

Mimi flung her arms around his neck and smacked a kiss on his cheek, and half the crowd gasped as her audacity. One simply did not hug the Peacemaker. But Soren only hugged her back, studying me over her shoulder before untangling himself and redirecting her back to Moriah. Soren murmured to Leif, though their words disappeared in the rustle of the crowd, and he strode out without another word. The entire room exhaled as the door closed behind the Peacemaker and most of his entourage.

I spun on my heel to face Moriah the moment he was out of sight. "So, I should go. If—"

"Not a chance," Leif said with a laugh, catching my shoulder. He ignored Moriah's grim look and instead directed me back to the roped-off VIP lounge where empty seats waited.

Making a break for the exit felt like the best idea I'd had all day, but three of Leif's lieutenants remained in the bar, eyeing me askance. The Warder flapped his free hand at them and they dispersed through the crowd, and he pulled me to sit on one of the small couches.

The lead singer, oblivious to the continuing drama, staggered to his feet with the microphone in hand. The drummer flipped his sticks and crashed the cymbals, and the music roared back to life. A heartbeat later, the dance floor erupted and the cheers nearly boosted the room from the rafters. Nothing like a good fight to get the blood pumping.

But even in the seething chaos in front of the band, a three-foot bubble of space protected Mimi and her friends from the nearest male. I didn't know if fear of Soren or my blue arm convinced others to stay away from her, but I wouldn't complain. No one would even bump into her now, for fear of meeting Brandr's fate.

Whatever grief I had to put up with would be worth it. Mimi could enjoy her party. It was a good night, all things considered.

\* \* \*

DESPITE MORIAH'S efforts to sit with Leif and me, she took one look at his expression and kept moving to the couch behind us, inclining her head as she retreated. Leif poured drinks from the bottles that remained, handing me one without a word. I drowned my sorrow with gin as I offered a silent toast to the witches who'd been killed. The saints would carry them home, and we would remember them always. My throat burned—from grief or gin, I couldn't tell.

Magic burned my fingers as I made myself another drink, almost dropping the bottle of gin. The rumor of my nonaligned status would spread as quickly as my humiliating arrest at the restaurant. Wonderful. No use regretting what couldn't be undone. I drained the drink. But I could sure as hell give forgetting a try.

After staring out at the gyrating band as the music reverberated through us, Leif spoke. "Ten minutes after I dropped you off, I stood over the remains of our most powerful witches."

I concentrated on my empty glass, counting the ice cubes over and over. Grieving could wait. It had to wait. I couldn't let it be real yet.

"I called you," he said. "Since you knew them. I called you and you didn't answer. So I went back to your apartment."

"About that..."

"What did I find, Lily?" His voice cut through the pounding drums. "Your front door open, the wards destroyed, blood everywhere. Your belongings burned or in pieces. And your handprint on the wall—in blood—but no trace of you. No hint. Nothing but blood."

I hardened my heart. So he'd been worried. Too bad. I was the one who was homeless. "I couldn't stay there."

"I thought they'd killed you too." Leif remained expressionless, though his eyes flashed gold. "I thought you'd been taken, and if I'd only walked you to your door, you'd be alive."

For a moment I thought of all the people who haunted us, who would be alive if we'd done one thing differently. It wasn't me he regretted not being able to save. I knew that much.

The room blurred as I tried focusing on Mimi and they switched on red and yellow and blue lights. In the eerie lights, I caught his goons watching me from across the bar, faces hard. No more giggling like Adam at the restaurant. I studied the ice in my glass once more, illuminated by my blue hand. "What did you find at Tracy's house?"

"How did you know it was Tracy's house?"

Magic flickered as I leveled a blank look at him. The War Witch suffered no fools.

Half his mouth quirked up in a familiar smile, though there was no humor in it. "You don't want to know."

"She was my friend."

"That's why you don't want to know."

"You wanted to know what happened to Max."

He went rigid and the air around us froze. Bringing up his murdered best friend probably wasn't the best way of deescalating the situation. His goons edged closer and I made a blue fist, keeping a wary eye on them. "So your little buddies don't think you can take care of yourself, huh? Protecting you from the mean ol' witch. How sweet."

"Don't think you can goad me into getting rid of them." I snorted, about to mock him, but Leif leaned his elbows on his knees, staring into the crowd. "You just brought down four of the top males—including the alpha—of the strongest Old World pack in the Alliance. By yourself." He raised his glass to toast me. "Which makes you one hell of a threat."

There wasn't anything to say to that. I wondered if he would tell me anything useful about the scene at Tracy's house, or if I'd have to break into her house in order to learn the truth.

Leif concentrated on the half-empty bottles as he poured me another drink. "Where did you train?"

More of his damnable questions, and no easy escape in sight. "My parents taught me. Are you going to tell me what you found at Tracy's?"

"No. It's an active investigation and I can't share details until we've identified and questioned all the suspects." He leaned back against the couch, half-turned to face me. "You were fully trained before the Breaking?"

"Yes." It wasn't entirely true—I'd been twelve when the Breaking happened, and only halfway trained by my parents. I learned the rest during the war, and made up what I needed to survive. All post-Truce witches trained at regulated academies, the curriculum approved by the Alliance and the humans. They conspired to regulate something that by its very nature was chaotic. My mouth twisted and I reached for the fresh drink. Any witch who couldn't show a diploma from one of the academies was either a pre-Breaking witch or a rogue. Worse still was that all official instruction in destructive magic ceased with the Truce. An entire generation of witches knew nothing of dark magic and could not begin to understand how to defend against it. A generation of helpless charmers. I gulped the gin.

Leif's elbow nudged my side. "What discipline?"

I laughed. Only wolves asked about disciplines. But it was a mistake. The power of his attention shifted once more, and the primordial human in me wanted to flee. Leif was the Alpha's second for a reason, and it was not because he let people laugh at him. He held my gaze long enough to remind me he could kill me without consequence, then flicked my glass. "Drink."

"You forget I don't have your tolerance."

"I didn't forget." His smile turned half-flirtatious, half-predatory. "Like I didn't forget I asked you a question."

"Is Leif asking, or is the Chief Investigator?"

"Chief Investigator Leif."

I cleared my throat, careful not to look at him. They couldn't smell lies, of course—that was nonsense. But they could hear an elevated heartrate, smell increased sweat, see pupils dilate with stress, interpret all those biological reactions. Deception was a messy business. "I never specialized."

"I don't believe you."

He shouldn't have, not with blue running up my arm. Spells and hexes for destruction had always come easiest, even from my earliest memories. There were many reasons I didn't keep mirrors in my house. "I didn't specialize."

"So what kind of witch are you?" And he already knew the answer.

*War witch* hovered on the tip of my tongue. That's what I was during the war, but during the peace... Maybe he had a point. What kind of witch had I become after the Truce? The kind of witch who abandoned her coven and skulked around in dark alleys at night, maybe.

Saints be damned. I drained my drink and reached for the gin, missing the bottle on my first grab. Leif sat forward and solicitously refilled my glass, easing closer on the couch as his arm looped over the back, near my shoulders. The gin fell like a rock in my stomach, oozing blessed numbness down my arms and up to my nose until I couldn't even feel my teeth. Holding the blue death wore at me, draining my energy.

His words were barely a breath as he repeated the question, a whisper between lovers as he touched my arm and sent shivers all through me until my nerves misfired. He wove a spell as easily as a basher, sent a fog of desire through my brain like a practiced charmer.

I cleared my throat and fought for sanity. "Just a witch."

If I were a better witch, I would have had a defense. Something to fend him off and preserve my dignity. It was a clinical observation as I swayed toward him, leaning into the way he stroked my arm. My skin rippled under his fingers, a small wave along the tide of his touch. I turned toward him until my feet tangled with his. It had been forever since anyone touched me with kindness.

He leaned closer until his lips brushed my ear. "Just a witch?"

"Sometimes not even that."

He nuzzled behind my ear, inhaling deeply, and his touch stole away all reason and logic. "Such a dangerous witch."

I wanted to tell him everything, about the war and Anne Marie and Tracy and Eric. About the dark years. I sighed, leaning closer and resting my palm on his flat stomach, and closed my eyes as I inhaled from his collar and got lost in the scent of him, all male and wild.

Leif brushed the hair over my shoulder, kissing my temple. His hand settled on my thigh and I melted into his touch, sighing again as he drew me into his lap. I could have stayed there forever, the music fading away until there was only the gin haze and the magic in Leif's touch, red pack magic swirling with blue witch magic. A contented growl rumbled in his chest, vibrating through me as I clung to him. "What discipline do you practice?"

My hand slid up the back of his neck and into his short hair, and I hid my face against his neck as I murmured, "Everything."

"Everything?"

Part of me knew it was dangerous. The rest of me didn't care. If I told him what he wanted to know, he'd hold me, play with my hair, kiss my neck. "Everything," I told his collar. I took another deep breath, the soft whiskey scent tangling in my thoughts. "White, gray, black. All of it."

"Oh, Lily." He sighed, and real regret colored his voice, slow and slurred with magic and scotch. "Are you the dark witch I'm looking for?"

The gin gave me enough bravery to say, "I'm the witch you're looking for, but I'm not a dark witch."

"Then why do you know dark magic?"

"You remember," I whispered, bracing a hand on his chest as I looked up, needing him to understand. He was the only one who understood. "You remember why. Know thy enemy."

His gray eyes turned amber, his lips parted and revealed a wolf's canines. Saints preserve me. All was lost.

"I remember," he said. Leif nuzzled my nose, drifting a ghost of a kiss over my lips as his hand trailed down to the small of my back. "And I know you. You're a dream I can almost remember. Where have you been, Lilith?"

The memories rose too close to the surface and I didn't think—I let the magic take the words it wanted. "In the last year of war, we asked the Warbringer for help and he denied us."

"So you walked away." His hands cradled my face and forced me to look at him. His eyes turned brilliant gold but glazed, an addict deep in the ecstasy of his drug. He remembered everything, more than I wanted. "Lilith, who went to Sanctuary in the seventh year of war and saved us all, walked away."

I shivered. He knew too much and assumed the rest. But his touch was gentle and warm, his arms pleasantly firm around me, and if I tilted my head just so, he could...

I felt his smile against my cheek along with the tickle of his beard, felt the pack magic slide around me like fleece on a freezing morning. I sank down into madness, into the firm brush of his mouth against the corner of mine, and his teeth tested my lip.

Lost.

# CHAPTER 24

he kiss lasted forever and yet not long enough. I
thought I heard someone speak behind us, thought
maybe there was an effort to change the magic that swirled up
around the couch, but it all faded away as Leif's fingers slid
along my jaw.

My brain shut down completely, the heat from his body as
overwhelming as his proximity. He squeezed my shoulder until
I relaxed, despite the adrenaline still flooding my veins. I loved
him. I'd always loved him, even before I really knew him, and I
desperately wanted him to love me. I wanted to draw him close
and run my hands through his hair, I wanted to mark him until
everyone knew he was mine and I was his.

"Tell me everything," he said, and my heart beat faster.

Tell him everything? Everything about the years when I
followed him like a puppy, when he rendered me speechless
with just a look, when I would have killed to make him laugh.
When I'd been a lost kid, adrift and grieving, and he appeared
like a buoy to keep me afloat. I couldn't explain that, even as the
pack magic tried to drag it all out.

"I don't remember," I whispered, closing my eyes as his lips drifted over my forehead. I ached to tell him. He wouldn't judge me for my crimes. He alone could understand. He'd handed me a medal, eight years ago, for those crimes.

"Liar." I felt his smile against my cheek, through the scratch of his beard, and I bit my lip. He smelled like wood smoke and the wild, like full moon nights in old forests. And the husky grumble of his voice, cutting through the strange underwater throb of the music, reminded me of quiet nights by the campfire. Alone. His hand slid down my back to play with the waist of my jeans. "You've been avoiding me."

My cheeks caught fire and he chuckled, leaning back to study me with those honey-gold eyes. "And what, dare I ask, are you thinking to make you turn so red?"

I gurgled something—a furious denial as I envisioned it—and he smiled more. "It can't be *that* exciting—we didn't sleep together. I'd remember that."

An undignified squeak was all the response I could manage. Saints preserve me. I was the damn War Witch. I braced my hands on his shoulders, intending to push him away so I could untangle myself, but I should have known better as a connection completed and the floodgates opened. Heat rushed through me in a heady mix of magic and memory, and his pack magic rolled through me in a typhoon. My magic rose to meet it, twining around him as it drew me in and stole what little control I had left.

I managed to say, "Oh no," as our eyes locked and everything opened and closed at the same time. His magic tugged and the floodgates to my carefully contained memories cracked. Scenes and people best forgotten rolled out of my head and into his like a bad movie, and too late I tried to turn aside the worst of them before he learned enough to hate me forever.

Leif's eyes sparked gold, and his teeth looked too long for a human mouth as he murmured once more, "Tell me everything, witch."

I struggled to control the memories, though I couldn't stop them. They were all bad: standing on battlefields littered with bodies, knowing I'd killed many of them. Watching friends disappear in funeral pyres. Standing over the wounded, desperate to heal them despite my own exhaustion. Panic as a cast failed and left colleagues vulnerable. Guilt over the ones I couldn't save. Almost getting captured, almost getting raped, almost getting killed.

His hands gripped my waist as grief kindled in his gaze. Only one memory of him slipped by, after his best friend was tortured and executed. One of his other friends betrayed us all, but Max and his partner, Kate, paid the price. When the humans dropped Max's body at the gates, Leif went berserk. Not even Soren, with all his pack magic and alpha dominance, could stop Scary Leif in a full rage.

I'd been a little frightened, but not paralyzed like the other witches, as I stepped in front of him to protect the others. The arrogance of youth protected me: very little frightened me then. I assumed I would die any day and had nothing left to lose.

Leif's expression twisted as he watched my memory of everyone viewing Max's broken body, of Leif mad with grief as Soren restrained him and tried to comfort him as the first contortions of rage and grief twisted the Warder. Watched as he raged free and the shifters tackled Leif, as he tossed them aside like dirty rags. He inhaled sharply as the memory-Leif launched at me, roaring in a heart-stopping moment as inhuman eyes tracked me and said: *prey*.

Even from the safety of eight years later, the memory chilled my blood. Just before his memory-jaws snicked shut on my throat, his hands disappeared from my waist and the connection snapped.

He blinked, looking dazed. "I attacked you."

For once, it wasn't even a small lie. It was the unvarnished truth. "No. I got in your way."

"Soren said I ran someone down. He never said who."

"No need for you to know," I said. I touched his cheek, not liking the way his forehead wrinkled in concern. "There was no debt. You were grieving."

"I don't have the monopoly on pain." He studied my face, and I felt like he truly saw me again. He knew almost everything. The dark stuff, the painful stuff, when I was at my worst. His lips parted and I thought about kissing him again, just to change the conversation.

I tried to smile. "You've had more than your fair share. Besides, no one expected you to sit under a willow tree writing bad poetry. You grieved your own way."

"I'm sorry," he said. Leif took a deep breath and his arms linked around me, drawing me once more to his chest, and the pack magic swirled up again.

All might have been lost except for Mimi. She stumbled up and tripped into the couch, knocking Leif's arms and pack magic aside. Reality snapped back to cold focus as Mimi landed in my lap.

I blinked as the fog lifted and the music roared back and I really heard what I'd said, what I'd shown him through my memories. What I admitted. I slid off Leif's lap as my cheeks burned, and Mimi giggled as she waved a perfectly-manicured finger at the Warder. "You're going to be in trouuuuuuble."

Leif untangled himself, face a little red as he straightened his clothes. "Mimi, Lily and I were talking."

She tried to stand and instead ended up sitting on the floor. "*So* much trouble. Uncle Soren will be maaaaad."

I struggled to compose myself, looking wildly for an exit. Saints protect me. I'd admitted knowing dark magic, crawled in his lap. *Kissed* him. In front of everyone.

Humiliation flashed through me and everything went

numb with shock. Moriah and all of Leif's friends and goons had seen. Half the Alliance witnessed me sitting in his lap and nuzzling into his throat and... I almost choked on embarrassment. They'd seen me lose control and give in.

I turned away and covered my eyes, desperate to just disappear. I'd always wished my magic could let me zap myself out of embarrassing circumstances, but I'd never found the right spell.

Leif took a deep breath and massaged his temples before leaning over me to help Mimi, though she seemed content on the floor. "Honey, go back to your party."

She rested her chin on my knee and grinned at him. "You're so bad."

I tried to drag her to her feet, wobbling myself as the gin tilted the world and her weight pulled me off balance. Leif reached to steady us both, but I pulled away before he could touch me. My heart pounded. I couldn't risk our magic interacting again. I'd lost my damn mind the moment it did.

I kept Mimi between us, trying to back away so I could get to a door and the quiet sanity of the night air. I might reach the back exit if I moved fast. Mimi balanced on her high heels as she beamed at me. "Lucky Aunt Leelee. Leif wants you and—" she said, but she slurred to a stop as one of Leif's men appeared next to us.

He was hard-eyed but mouth-wateringly handsome. Beautiful and rugged and with such delicious shoulders that I was distracted for a heartbeat myself. Wide-eyed Mimi didn't stand a chance as he bowed over her hand. "I know you're engaged, gorgeous, but how about a dance anyway?"

Mimi blinked, dazzled by his dimples, and trailed after him out of the VIP lounge and toward the dance floor. Leif waited until she tottered out of earshot to reach for me, even as I backed away. I didn't know what to say or do or where to look, only that fleeing was the better part of valor that time around.

"What are you hiding, Lily?" Sadness gathered around his eyes as all the promise of our flirting fell apart in the cold reality of the strobe lights.

"I'm not—" I struggled to resurrect the anger that sustained me in the fight with Brandr. Seeing that look on Leif's face, knowing I'd moved from an interesting witch to a murder suspect, hurt my heart.

"You studied dark magic," he said. He caught my non-blue arm, and echoes of pack magic trembled through me, a fog once more drifting up around us. "And there was dark magic at your apartment. Where were you yesterday?"

"You made me say those things," I said. "You influenced me. I would never—"

"Two problems with that, Lil." His jaw clenched and the Chief Investigator entirely replaced Leif. "First, it's impossible to lie under pack magic. So all of that was true, whether you meant to admit it or not."

I filed that information away for later; we'd never talk under pack magic again, saints as my witnesses. I backed up and he followed, tall and broad and competent. "And the second?"

He glanced at someone behind me, making a small gesture with his free hand. "Witches are immune to pack magic. So what does that make you?"

My mouth opened and closed as I floundered for a response, and the first thought that flashed to mind was Eric and her impossible allegations. Witches were immune to pack magic—were loki? I cleared my throat, shaking my head. "I'm a witch. Just a witch."

Saints save me, I hoped it was true. Just a witch. No more, no less. Definitely not loki.

His men circled closer, fighting the raucous crowd, and Leif squeezed my wrist to distract me. His tone gentled, grew cajoling instead of demanding. "If what happened at Tracy's house was an accident, Lilith, just tell me. An experiment gone wrong? If something unexpected happened, it's okay. I just need to know the truth."

"I didn't do it," I said, heart drumming faster as the trap closed around me. No way out. The door was too far, and too many people created roadblocks to freedom. "I'm not in contact with them, and I'm—"

"You were with three of the witches just two nights ago," he murmured, and touched my jaw. Played with my hair with a distant regret. "And you know all of them. What happened?"

Pack magic swirled up again and my heart jumped, my blue magic shivering. I summoned courage and more magic and walled myself off from his influence. With more witch magic came the War Witch, and with her came a distant, cold rage. He'd made a fool of me. A fool. Of *me*.

I wanted to destroy something. I wanted something to disappear in a cloud of smoke and fire. Someone should *bleed* for the humiliation coloring my cheeks. I wanted to turn the tables, make him dance like a puppet on strings. He would pay for manipulating me.

I stepped back and he didn't follow. "I didn't have anything to do with it."

The distance grew between us as he nodded. The Chief Investigator faced Lilith; Lily and Leif faded away. "I need you to come with me to the pack-house to answer a few questions."

A muscle in my jaw jumped as I ground my teeth. I couldn't guarantee I was clean after walking through my apartment, and I hadn't run a cleansing spell on myself. The humans couldn't detect the dark magic, but Leif's gadgets would. If he had any witches left, they would see it, too. "No. I'm nonaligned, and I will not—"

"Lily," he said quietly, holding out a pair of weak but symbolic steel bracelets. "Don't make this any more difficult than it already is."

I laughed.

If he had challenged me like that during the war, I probably would have killed him. But this was a consequence of the peace. And in my heart I knew he told the truth. I felt stupid, and I hated feeling stupid.

"You shouldn't be wasting time in a bar," I said. "Go look for whoever destroyed Tracy's house."

He shook his head, eyes gray once more. "I'm looking at our only suspect."

The cuffs glinted under the strobe lights, moved like metal snakes with each beat of the drums. There were always options, Dad reminded me. You might not like any of them, but there were always options.

I could magic open a loophole to another plane and take my chances with what waited on the other side. I could level the building or the entire block, leave some or none of them alive. I could hex him and run. I could stay and submit to the test, maybe be found guilty and eventually executed for a crime I didn't commit.

Or I could start being a better friend to Tracy.

If I was the only suspect, they would never find Tracy or the ones who killed Rosa and Joanne. I couldn't afford to let Leif lock me up for an hour or—saints help me—longer. I was Tracy's best hope for being saved.

I bit my lip. "I had nothing to do with Tracy's house, but maybe I'm the only one who can figure it out. Are you going to tell me what you found?"

"I can't discuss pack business with nonaligned, and certainly not with a suspect." He reached for his radio, looking around at all of his guys. More waited outside, no doubt.

"It's witch business," I said, and put steel in my voice. He wasn't the only one who'd quelled mobs with a single look. The Warder could learn a few things from even a retired War Witch. "And it's my business because she was my friend, and I owe it to her to find out who did this."

I tried to quell the shaking in my fingers from holding blue death for too long. I was out of practice, and those muscles fatigued too quickly.

"Why are you using past tense, Lily?"

A knot in my throat made it difficult to speak, but it was time to demonstrate how much he needed my help. "Because I scried for her and she wasn't there. She wasn't anywhere I could find her."

His expression froze. "Does that mean they're dead?"

I spun a floating orb with the magic I still held, shaking my head. Blue was good for more than death—it made a hex with a hell of a punch. "Tell me what you found at her house."

Leif opened the cuffs and reached for my wrist. "Lilith witch, I am officially detaining you in the name of the Alliance, for questioning in—"

I shook my head. "You're not arresting me tonight."

He scowled but froze as I flicked the orb at his stomach and bolted.

The goons threw people out of their way as Leif shouted and I ran, kicking open the back door and slamming it shut behind me. The night air grew dense with cold and promise as I melted the steel door into the frame. I turned to flee and stumbled chest-first into a burly shifter.

His eyebrows rose. "Not so fast."

The roadblock's name was Nate, and I remembered him as a watermark from the war. A boy smelted into a man by time and trauma. He tried to catch my non-blue arm. "You're not—"

"Not going quietly," I said, and flicked my blue fingers against his chest.

# CHAPTER 25

$\mathcal{N}$ate flew across the alley and landed against the dumpster in the corner, and I looked to the mouth of the alley for an escape. I had to move fast. There would be other guards waiting outside the bar, and it wouldn't take them long to get around the block to trap me in the dead-end. Already something slammed against the steel door from inside, and a horrible snarling echoed through the walls. Leif.

I bolted for the opening, nearly tripping on an empty box as the security lights flickered. I didn't get far. A wolf bounded into the alley and nearly slammed into me, and I jumped back. A man appeared, silhouetted by the watery streetlight, and I held my hands up, ready to hex him, too. "I'm leaving. Get out of my way."

He eased into the light until I could see his face, and my blood ran cold. He wasn't one of Leif's goons. He was a Cold River wolf, and he carried a long chain in his hands. "We're all leaving. Cooperate and it'll go easier."

They didn't know me very well, and they certainly hadn't learned their lesson from inside the bar. I clenched my jaw to silence chattering teeth, and flinched as the steel door squealed and started to bend outward. I didn't have much time to debate my options.

So I hexed him, knocking the guy back into the street, and the wolf launched forward in a flash of gray and white and teeth and the stale musk of wild animal, and then—

*Teeth.*

It seized my shoulder and white-hot pain erupted. With a mighty jerk, the wolf dragged me toward the street, snarling so loudly my bones vibrated even as they collapsed and splintered in its jaws. Blood soaked my shirt in a warm rush. I dredged up magic and struck out, hitting the damn thing on the head and sides as my thoughts scattered. Shit.

My shirt tore. My skin tore, peeled away. I screamed, trying to crawl so it wouldn't tear me apart completely.

Magic bubbled beneath the panic as the Morrigan took over and I sobbed hexes with all my power. No telling what kind of death waited for me with Cold River, but I would pay the price for their alpha being arrested and humiliated by the Peacemaker.

The wolf collapsed on boneless legs as its heart exploded, and I stumbled to the wall in a spray of blood. I needed something solid at my back so I could gather my thoughts and try to heal myself before things got worse.

It didn't last long. Another wolf leapt into the mouth of the alley, only a few short feet away. I snapped a hex at it and scrambled away, slipping in blood as I tried to hold my shoulder together. They'd cornered me and I'd sealed off my only escape. I hunkered down and tried to breathe evenly as my clavicle grated under my skin, trying not to see the yellow-white bone through torn muscle.

Stronger magic provided refuge as wolves flooded the alley on silent paws. They fought as a pack, some distracting me from one side as others edged close. I hexed and warded at the same time, but they were too nimble and I couldn't think fast enough to kill them all.

The snarling faded into eerie silence, and I tried to scramble to the street as the wolves disappeared. A simple probing spell revealed them backing off, regrouping, and more wolves approaching from the front of the bar. I braced against the cold cinder block wall and forced myself upright. There wasn't much time until I passed out. The shifter virus would have already contaminated me from the bites, and though I'd been bitten before, this time the bites were deep enough the change might take me and steal my magic forever.

My eyes burned and I struggled to breathe. Dying in an alley was not how I'd envisioned my night ending. Even if I remained immune to the bites, the wound itself would kill me before the change came. It was a small consolation.

Shouting rose up and radios crackled, more growling followed the snick-snick of wolf nails on the concrete. At least a dozen more approached, and a couple of witches as well. I closed my eyes to try and gather my strength. Someone really wanted me dead—Cold River or the Alliance, it didn't really matter. The wolves hunted to kill.

Maybe I'd miscalculated how angry Leif would be over the hex.

I put a bloody hand over my eyes, listening for their approach, and my vision grew splotchy as my skin turned cold and clammy. I barely felt the pain in my shoulder anymore. It all faded away to a distant irritation. Once again there were no good options. I could die trying to kill them all, or I could paralyze them and escape to fight another day. It was a difficult spell, and one that would take all of my remaining strength. Getting it wrong meant certain death. Not trying it at all meant certain death.

I concentrated on building power with each inhalation, until magic billowed up in a great column around me. I'd dreamt up the spell in the last days of the war, when I resented the Peacemaker's wolves and envisioned a way to humiliate them if I wanted to leave in a blaze of glory. I'd seen enough pack magic to mimic it.

Three new wolves circled closer as I staggered almost to the sidewalk and the spell coalesced in my mind. I still held onto the wall and unrolled the magic into the street and covered all the shifters who gathered to see me die. It locked them in an alpha's hold, and I commanded, "Kneel."

The three wolves dropped to their bellies, snarling viciously, and a fourth struggled to stand as it inched closer to me. I bared my teeth at it. "*Kneel.*"

Cursing and threats roared through the steel door, and it dented halfway open until I could hear Leif clearly. "Lily. Stop. *Now.*"

Leif. The world grayed around the edges as I held onto the wall. I tried twice before my voice worked, cracked and broken. "Good effort, Warder, but I'm not dead yet."

I gathered myself for the last burst of power, even as my body failed and the feeling left my limbs. The cowering wolves watched me with yellow eyes, and I couldn't risk loosening my hold on the magic.

"You can't hold this forever," he said. "They'll tear you apart."

My eyelids drooped. I was so cold. So tired.

Leif nearly climbed through the bent door, expression fierce as he caught sight of my tattered shoulder. "You're hurt, Lily. That bite is infected. We have the antidote. Just say you'll come quietly and I can help."

I started to tell him what I really thought when some trash rustled behind me. My mind clicked too slowly as I turned my head and saw a skinny kid with floppy hair and just a hint of magic staring at me with wide eyes. A witch?

I inhaled to give him a piece of my mind when he reached

out and his fingers brushed my arm, and a beginner's hex adhered to my shoulder and froze me in place. I couldn't even move my mouth to warn him as he edged close enough to lock an iron collar around my throat.

My magic evaporated like morning fog.

I stared at him as the hexes restraining the Cold River wolves disappeared with my magic.

"You *idiot*," I said weakly, as the witch blinked and the wolves exploded into motion, knocking him aside and trampling over him to reach me.

I crumpled under their paws, barely managing to cover my neck as the kid's elementary school hex faded, and the jolt of broken bones grinding between the wolf paws and the ground ripped a scream from my throat. Its breath reeked of old blood. Far away, Leif shouted.

The witch remained open-mouthed and motionless as another wolf seized my leg, teeth buried in my ankle.

I stared up at the night and concentrated on the stars. Of all the ways my life could have ended, I'd never envisioned being torn apart by wolves. Torn apart by Externals, by humans, by Anne Marie and Jacques maybe, but not by wolves.

Lightning flashes of pain flared from head to toe, deep water closed over my head and distorted everything around me. I opened my mouth to scream or curse or just sigh, and the entire side of the bar exploded.

Brick and steel and splinters sprayed into the alley and a long-legged timber wolf, massive across the shoulders and with an auburn sheen to its fur, joined the fray. The Cold River wolf standing on me disappeared in a burst of blood and fur. A snarl vibrated through my bones as the timber wolf leapt over me.

The teeth in my ankle tore free and I cried out again, trying to crawl away as bodies, wolf and human alike, filled the alley. I focused on a bright spot from a street light. I didn't want to die in the dark.

The timber wolf growled as it stood over me, nudging my shoulder until I flopped onto my back. It looked down at me, amber eyes liquid over the blood-flecked muzzle, and I knew him. Knew him in a heartbeat.

Leif.

His tongue rasped my cheek in a quick kiss, to taste my blood or provide comfort, it didn't matter. He stepped back and then a red surge of pack magic surrounded him. My vision swam as he contorted, curled into himself and then unfolded into a man, the auburn fur receding to a smattering of chest hair.

The young witch's wide eyes appeared over me and his moon face blocked naked Leif from my view. "Holy shit."

I groaned and closed my eyes.

# CHAPTER 26

*I* surfaced through deep water to the glare of floodlights in the alley. A weight on my chest made it difficult to breathe, each gasp a gift from the saints. The young witched argued with someone near my feet, gesticulating wildly. My head rolled to the side despite the burn of the iron collar, searching for a way out. Leif stood nearby as well, buttoning his jeans and still barefoot from the shift. He spoke to Jake, the clownish shifter frowning as he pointed at me, and Leif shook his head.

Leif bent to retrieve a clean T-shirt and the stretch and slide of muscle under his skin mesmerized me. A cross-hatch of stripes covered his back, along with round weals from bullets and a few patches slick and smooth from burns. The shifters healed quickly, but ten years of war tended to mark the body and the soul. And the humans had been ruthless in their pursuit of him, the most feared general in Soren's Alliance, the wolf who infiltrated the humans' command center and rampaged through their leadership. He left behind bodies and dinner plate-sized paw prints in their blood.

A month later, the humans signed the Truce.

Leif carried burdens from before the war as well, some as heavy as the weight that kept me from breathing, but despite the scars and ridges across his back and chest, he moved like a fighter—all grace and controlled violence as he drew on his shirt.

I shivered, staring up at the stars, and sucked in air. His face appeared over me, gray eyes more like blue in the eerie light of the SUVs and streetlights. But he spoke to someone else. "You have to heal her, Kyle. Otherwise the change will take her."

Jake, standing nearby with his arms folded over his chest, scowled. "Let her change. Damn witch made me kneel."

I smiled, imagining them on their knees. Served them right for challenging the War Witch.

"We can't afford to lose another war witch," Leif said, his voice sharp. "Kyle, do it."

"I can't unless we remove the collar," the young witch whispered. "And without the collar... She'll be *angry*. I don't think I can—"

Leif's eyes narrowed. "Do it."

When the witch hesitated, Jake rolled his eyes and stepped forward, dropping more cold iron near me. "Here, you coward." Jake fixed cold iron shackles around my wrists. "Now she can't cast."

I watched Leif through a gray-violet haze of fatigue and blood loss, and a little bit of smoke from inside the bar. The lines deepened around his eyes as he watched me. "You have to cooperate, Lily. Kyle will heal you and we'll give you the antidote."

"Because you can't lose a war witch," I said, choking on the weight of the collar. Not because he cared what happened to me, but because of my utility to the Alliance. My ability to serve was all that mattered. It reminded me of the day he almost killed me at Sanctuary. The bites burned with a deep unhealthy fire, eating at my skin and muscle and bone until fire raced through me. Too late. It was already too late.

Kyle's hands trembled as he whispered the spell to unlock the collar, moving his hands through the air like a conductor.

Leif crouched next to me and leaned down until his beard tickled my cheek. "My life would be far easier if you turned and joined the pack, witch."

I wanted to know why, but the world swam around his face and my mouth didn't work. I'd definitely lost too much blood. My skin crawled as Kyle lifted away the collar, taking chunks of my skin with it, and Leif recoiled. "What the hell?"

The mender dropped it on the broken asphalt and wiped his hands off, and the heaviness of the iron coiling next to my arm tested my control. Kyle didn't look at Leif. Disciplining witches was witch business; seldom did the shifters see the results of witch justice. "Iron is more dangerous the more powerful the witch. Leaving the collar on for more than an hour will permanently scar any witch above charmer."

The wolves exchanged looks, and Jake toed the collar with the bits of my skin, pondering the mass of metal. I wanted to make a joke, but Kyle's magic gathered in a slow crawl next to me and I knew I'd only have one chance.

He still looked frightened, leaning away from me, though his magic brought a measure of self-assurance. Leif pinned my upper arms when I tensed, and pieces of my collarbone ground together under the pressure. I moaned through the crepitation, blinded by tears, and pain shorted out my brain and whatever plan I'd had to steal Kyle's magic.

Leif's expression turned grim. "You have to hold still, Lily."

It would be easier if he hadn't jostled my broken bones.

Kyle's magic was clean and new, unsullied by dark or even gray magic, haunted by no memories of war or demon dreams. It was like drinking cold spring water on a blazing summer day in the desert. I shivered as it flushed through me, and started to fill a bottomless pit in my center. Kyle froze, staring at me as his magic disappeared.

The power cycled through me, from Kyle's right hand and through me to his left, until the bones and flesh in my shoulders and ankle knit. The poison in the bites burned as the magic tried—and failed—to eradicate it.

"It's so strange," Kyle whispered, peering down at me as his magic slowly disappeared. It always happened when other witches healed me, as if my magic hungered for more power. Even through the haze of pain and drunkenness of pure magic, I wondered what he felt as he healed me.

But I didn't want to see his face, and focused instead on Leif. At first I thought my eyes played tricks on me, or the blood loss made me see shadows in the night. Then a laugh wheezed out between my clenched teeth.

His cheek pressed against mine. "What could possibly be funny about this?"

"Purple under your collar," I whispered, choking. I thought maybe my hex missed him, but apparently I'd struck the Warder at least a little.

He hid a smile in a frown, though he tried to look stern. "About that. I—"

I squeezed my eyes shut as Kyle's magic receded, leaving pain behind. Leif stroked my forehead but I ignored him to focus on the retreating magic. I only had one chance. Kyle struggled to engage as I touched his right hand and drew away a few strands of magic. I couldn't truly absorb it, not with the iron around my wrists, but I twined it through my fingers to keep it safe. Once I had enough to free myself, I released Kyle and he flopped backward into a pile of garbage.

I examined my shoulder and the tender new skin; it looked like it would hold. It wasn't as good as Rosa could manage. The thought of Rosa made my throat close, and it grew hard to breathe once more.

Leif took a breath as he touched my throat, a hint of concern in his eyes, but a cleared throat drew his attention to Jake's disapproving frown, and Leif's demeanor stiffened to the Chief Investigator. As his hand fell away, I felt his distance as strongly as the absence of my magic. When Leif spoke, his tone was formal and reserved, as if we'd never kissed on that damn couch. "By my authority as Chief Investigator of the Alliance, you are under arrest for attacking Alliance representatives in the course of their official duties. You are required to present yourself to the Alpha for judgment."

I concentrated on the magic in my hand: the ticket to freedom. "I do not recognize Soren's authority to judge me."

Kyle picked up the collar and the iron descended once more around my throat, and as Kyle fumbled to secure it, I forced myself to wait passively. Let them think me cowed. I cringed as it snapped closed around the wounds in my neck, and Jake exerted a little more pressure on the wrist chains as I tensed again. I wanted to lash out as panic rose up. Collared and chained, my very worst nightmare.

But I focused on Joanne's mantra. I needed patience. The magic remained in my hand. I could free myself at any time. I just needed to wait for the correct time. The iron grew weightier with each empty heartbeat.

Jake and another grim shifter grasped my arms and hauled me up, securing the collar to a chain around my waist as they walked me toward one of the giant SUVs on the street. I took measured breaths to combat the growing panic of not feeling magic, of knowing I was defenseless against any demons that might spring up in the night. I didn't trust any of them to protect me when it came to demons.

I set my heels as they lifted me into a dark SUV, Jake shoving me in despite my struggles. He pinned me against the center bench as the second shifter dug through a medic bag and produced a giant syringe.

"What the hell is that?" I kicked at the man with the needle, trying to dislodge Jake as well.

Jake easily put me in a full nelson, assisted by the chains. "It's the antidote. Unless you want to join the pack, hold still."

I thrashed, my panic boiling over as the shifter dodged a wild kick and seized my leg. "No," I said, voice breaking. "Please, no. I'll risk it. I've already had the antidote once. Please don't—"

"It doesn't hurt," he said, adjusting his grip as the new skin near my throat began to tear. "Don't be such a baby."

A cry escaped as the needle plunged into my hip and the antidote raged into my muscle, scorching and destroying everything until it ignited a thousand times the pain of the earlier attack and the collar combined. Tears burned my cheeks as I writhed, almost losing the magic I held onto like a lifeline.

Jake fought to restrain me as I convulsed, and looked at the other shifter. "You sure you gave her the right stuff?"

"Yeah," the medic said, and glanced back at Leif. "I've never seen this reaction before, boss. What do you want to do?"

Leif gestured for Jake to get out of the SUV, then Leif climbed in as I curled around the festering pain in my middle. "I'll take care of it. Aaron, drive. Kyle, up front in case something happens. The rest of the team can handle Cold River. Let's get back to the pack-house."

A flurry of motion set off outside the SUV, and as Leif squeezed into the bench next to me, Jake cleared his throat. "Boss, should—"

"Do you really want to finish that sentence?" Leif snapped, pinning my shoulder to the seat as I seized, trapping my legs with his body as my nerves misfired and convulsions raced through me. "No? Then shut the hell up and do your job."

In the silence that followed, Leif's pack magic rolled over me in a warm blanket. He leaned over me, murmuring a few soft words against my temple. "Explain to me, Lily, how you can control a dozen wolves with pack magic, but your blood tastes nothing like a shifter."

I squeezed my eyes shut and sank into darkness. It was easier than dealing with the pain coursing through my body and his questions. At least in my dreams, it didn't hurt nearly as much.

# CHAPTER 27

When I was eight, I cast a spell that knocked me unconscious for over an hour. The world was black when I woke. I tried desperately to undo what was done, despite Mother's advice to be patient. In the end, my sight came back after a week without any intercession from me or her, but the damage was done: I loathed the darkness.

After I forced my eyes open, I was back there, waking up in permanent night with no hope of ever seeing the sun again. I inhaled sharply, reaching out for magic, and nothing was there. A different kind of pain socked me in the stomach, and the weight of iron around my throat dragged me back to reality.

Mimi's party. Cold River. And... Leif.

Something moved and a shadow moved away, and I could at least see the glowing dashboard of the car where we sat. Leif sat, motionless, beside me. I'd listed into his side during the drive, dozing off in the warm car and the comfort of his presence once the antidote ceased playing rugby with my guts. Heat bloomed in my cheeks.

The SUV idled in a driveway in front of one of the castle mansions outside the city, a crowd of armed men and women blocking any escape. Jake opened the door of the SUV and eyed me with a hint of grudging respect. "Hati's balls—you're arrested, collared, and brought to face the Alpha himself, and you fall asleep. Are you so powerful, or just that arrogant?"

I rubbed my chin on my shoulder, despite the collar, and wondered if I'd drooled on Leif. That wasn't exactly the way to endear myself to him. "Neither. I'm just that tired. Where are we?"

"Soren's," Leif said, then gestured for Jake to move so he could get out. The Warder kept the chains taut so I had to scramble after him, biting back a yawn. I would have paid the driver everything in my anemic bank account to circle the block a few more times so I could get another few minutes of shut-eye. With the collar blocking all my magic, I couldn't even muster a pretense of energy. I felt eighty years old.

Jake maneuvered a sawed-off shotgun as he stepped back, giving me as well as himself room. "This is your only warning, witch—you're in the Alpha's den. You try to run or cast, and I shoot."

I didn't bother hiding another yawn. "So I kill you first. Got it."

For a moment he watched me with a grim, lifeless expression as he calculated the risk. Then the semi-familiar grin returned. "Fair enough. But you'd better be fast."

An answering smile tugged at my mouth, and I let my teeth show perhaps more than was wise around so many shifters. "Don't worry, I'll try not to make it hurt. Too much."

As Jake geared up for another threat, Leif tugged me toward the house. "Cut it out, both of you. And don't do anything stupid, Lily. He's not kidding—there are wards on the house to make sure no aggressive magic occurs inside."

I snorted, shaking my head despite the burning iron of the collar. "That's bullshit. Wards don't work like that."

He didn't respond and instead headed for the door to the

enormous mansion. We'd drawn considerable attention in the driveway; a circle of armed shifters surrounded us, eyes on me. The circle constricted and I sighed. I may have grown complacent, but there was an entire Styrma team that had forgotten war witches were more dangerous the closer one got to them.

We moved en masse into Soren's mansion. Gold-threaded marble covered almost every surface, with statuettes placed in recesses in the walls and gold-framed paintings reminiscent of Versailles. Well, Versailles before the Breaking. I craned my neck to look up, trying to relieve the pressure of the collar, and laughed in spite of myself at the enormous crystal chandelier dangling over us like a sword of Damocles. I caught Leif watching and shook my head. "He has the worst taste."

The Warder grunted noncommittally, but I knew he felt as out of place as I did in the nouveau riche monstrosity. Kyle chanted quietly behind me, making my skin crawl, and I set my jaw to keep from correcting his pronunciation. I turned my attention to Leif instead, wondering about the shifter I'd launched into the dumpster in the alley behind the Pug. "How is Nate?"

"Fine. No permanent damage that we can find."

"Of course not," I said, scuffing my foot on the marble. "I only knocked him out because he got in my way."

"Maybe instead of running away from your problems, you should face the consequences of your actions."

"Oh really." Irritation boiled up as we stood there in the damn foyer, waiting for the Peacemaker to appear, and half the Alliance gathered around us. I didn't care that they could overhear what should have been a more private discussion with the Warder. "Maybe instead of using pack magic on a girl while she's drunk in a bar, you should have a normal conversation. Or —saints forbid—ask her out on a real date."

He stared straight ahead as his ears turned red. Jake beamed like a kid who'd gotten an unexpected and noisy

Christmas present. I imagined he didn't get many opportunities to tease the Chief Investigator.

The mender stumbled on his spell and I winced. Kyle flushed as Leif shot him a warning look, and I pitied the kid just the smallest bit. From what I'd sensed when he healed me, Kyle could be powerful, a truly dangerous witch, with the right training and an appropriate mentor. Anne Marie would ruin him.

One of the Styrma returned from inside the house, a curious tension in his demeanor for someone so heavily armed. "There's a complication."

Leif shifted his grip on my arm so his weapon hand was free. "What—"

"You *chained* her?" The shriek set my teeth on edge even as it made me smile. Moriah.

Jake muttered, "Fuck," as Leif shoved me behind himself. "Mo—"

She threw a shifter out of her way, and the two-hundred-pound man went airborne before crashing into the wall and rattling one of the fancy portraits loose from its hook. I blinked. Her sights zeroed in on Leif. "How *dare* you collar her! I'll—"

"*Stop.*" A ribbon of pack magic got through her red-eyed fury.

As the silence stretched and the tension grew, I leaned around Leif to say, "Hey Moriah."

"I'm pissed at you too," she said, though her gaze never left the bristling Warder. "You're lucky I didn't find you first."

Leif tensed, elbowing me behind him once more. "Moriah, you will not interfere. This is an official Alliance investigation, and she is a suspect in several crimes."

"She goes nowhere without me," Moriah said, folding her arms and staring at challenge at his chest. "You cannot question her without pack representation, and the fact that you dragged her here without someone from my pack just speaks to how fucked up this investigation already—"

A growl rumbled in Leif's chest, and I wondered if Jake would still shoot me for running if I tried to get out of the way if they brawled. Leif advanced a step, posture aggressive enough that I edge sideways. "Is that a challenge, wolf? Strong opinions for someone who hasn't seen the evidence."

They faced off and the tension in the foyer escalated until I hoped almost anything would break it and release us from the showdown.

* * *

I STOOD in the foyer and concentrated on that thread of magic in my hand, all that remained from the contortions as the antidote burned through my muscles. Blessed saints, it hadn't hurt that much the first time I was bitten. Maybe it got worse each time. I shivered to think of it, and drew breath to distract Leif and Moriah from fighting, maybe ask Leif to remove the collar. There was no need for it, not really.

As I turned, the world slowed around me and my heart beat slow and steady. Threat. I looked for the trouble, breathing deep and even as I clenched my hands into fists. Then... appearing from an adjoining hall, three witches, all wearing the symbolic but ineffective steel bracelets the Alliance used when they detained witches but didn't feel the need to block them from their magic. The tallest one's face twisted, teeth bared, and her right hand snapped out to point at me. "*You.*"

Another, with long dark hair that reminded me of Joanne, pointed at me with both hands. She spat curses with enough vehemence and magic that they could have stuck, flaring out from her palms like green smoke.

Chaos erupted as Kyle stumbled back over his own feet, and I reached for the collar as I curled my body in and down, making a smaller target as I got my hands on the iron. Felt the deep burn as it scored my palms. The thread of magic was enough, weak but pure, and all I really needed was intent. The collar came loose, peeling out of the furrow it burned in my neck, and I threw it at the witches as I raised my hands and drew a shield up like a curtain.

Their shifter guards swore, grabbing one to contain her, but were repelled with a wave of magic. More curses spilled out, hateful and dark, and the tall one picked up a nearby vase to chuck at me when the hexes didn't seem to do the trick. "You *murdered* my coven mate, you *bitch* I will kill—"

"They had it coming," I snapped, raising my left arm to block another hex and then swung it back, knocking Moriah and Leif and Kyle behind my shield and into my sphere of protection despite Jake's snarls. My right hand called down a stream of blue magic and turned it into spikes, ice and hate, and drove into their clothes and shoulders to pin them to the wall. At least with the magic I didn't feel exhausted and resigned. I could fight as long as it took. "And I'd do it again in a heartbeat, except maybe I'd do it more slowly."

The witches howled in rage, struggling against the magic icicles that trapped them like drab moths against a pin board, and pitched wild spells that bounced off my shield and pinged into the walls like magical shrapnel.

Soren roared inside the house, and Leif cursed under his breath as a cloud of red magic rose up and tangled around our knees. "*Stop.*"

Too bad pack magic didn't work on witches. Except, apparently, me—because his command made it a bit harder to send spells at the witches, despite how they threatened me. That wasn't fair at all.

The tall witch's eyes flashed dark, and I wondered if they were all demon handlers, if maybe she were about to call a demon in the middle of the Peacemaker's home. She threw instead a regular old death hex. "I will see you dead for your crimes, witch, you *murderer*."

I ducked the hex, sent it crashing into the chandelier that hung over us until crystals shattered on the marble floor all around. "They were dark witches, doing dark magic on an innocent kid in a back alley. You defend them, you defend the darkness they bring down to stain *all* of us. They are the reason none of us are safe. They're the reason the humans hunt us like before the war."

Her eyes narrowed, and she looked to her other colleagues and then to someone standing behind me. "You sided with Anne Marie; you defended her home and killed Wendy. What the hell are you talking about, 'they'?"

Oops. I straightened, hands loose at my sides though I didn't release the magic I held. "She attacked me first and I defended myself. That wasn't my fault."

"Did you—did you kill Cara and Danielle?"

"No." It was the truth, through and through, with the saints as my witness. "The demons they were summoning did. I just arranged the meeting."

Her jaw went slack, then red flushed across her face. "Lies. Damn lies, and spoken in front of the Peacemaker, how *dare* you accuse two witches in good standing—"

"They weren't." I felt tired all of a sudden, and desperately wanted to sit down and rest my eyes even with the coldly calm magic. Underneath it waited the crippling fatigue and grief of everything that happened in the previous few days. "They tied that kid up in the alley and—"

"Don't say another word," Moriah said, grabbing my right arm despite the blue glow. She dragged me back, attention on Leif. "She admits nothing. Admissions spoken during confrontation carry no weight, she—"

He took a breath, expression unreadable, but Soren loomed over Kyle and clapped Jake on the shoulder as he watched me.

"Yes, but we all know Lilith's accusations are slightly different than everyone else's. Don't we?"

He didn't wait for a response, turning his attention to the guards who tried to chain the witches as they struggled to free them from the wall. His expression soured as he studied the trapped witches. "You attacked a guest in my home, unprovoked. A grievous crime. You'll be placed in detention until I decide what to do with you. If you so much as touch an iota of magic, I'll have you collared, and not with that weak shit we use. With the real stuff," and he toed the iron collar that still carried flecks of my skin.

Then he pointed at Kyle, canting his head at the witches. "Go with them. Make sure it happens." The Peacemaker raised his eyebrows at me. "Couldn't just play along, could we?"

I pointed at my neck, furious beyond words. "Does this look like playtime to you? This will scar. I'm going to look like a goddamned criminal the rest of my life because your people can't listen to reason."

"We'll have someone fix it." He looked at Leif. "I told you a collar wouldn't hold her."

"It did what it was supposed to." The Chief Investigator didn't look happy.

Moriah's teeth ground loudly enough to make me wince as I imagined them cracking to pieces in her skull. "Can we discuss this somewhere else? Preferably somewhere without the witches who just attacked a friend of my pack?"

Soren glanced up as Kyle muttered and yanked at the blue spikes still securing the witches to the wall. The Peacemaker leveled a look at me. "Lilith. If you would?"

Irritated beyond measure and tempted to just leave them up there, I folded my arms over my chest. "And in exchange?"

"In exchange I won't have you executed for killing three aligned witches."

I scowled, maintaining eye contact as I raised my left hand, palm up. I curled my fingers in one at a time, starting with the pinky, and with each finger, the magic holding the witches to the wall dissipated, disappearing with soft puffs of smoke. They fell, slid to the floor, lurched back to their feet. I curled my left hand around and then opened it, and all the magic dissipated as gray smoke across the floor. It was all for show, of course, but at least Kyle looked impressed.

The dark-haired witch got a step closer to me, despite the restraining hands of the shifters and Leif's scowl, but stopped in her tracks when I turned to face her. Whatever she saw in me, in my expression, was enough. But her face went bloodless as she confronted me. "Are they gone? Beyond where we can get them back?"

"Bring me a mirror and I can show you where they are. But they are not coming back."

"You murdered two witches to save a human?"

Despite Moriah's tightening grip on my arm, I didn't turn away from the witch. Clearly my stance perplexed her as much as hers befuddled me. So I enunciated, to make sure everyone in that foyer understood what I said, and slowed the words to the type of cadence the humans used with foreigners. "They tied a human girl down and used her for blood sacrifice. They opened a rift to a demon realm in an alley less than half a mile from *our memorial*. Where we honor our dead. They summoned demons where we go to pray. And it wasn't the first time—Cara was already demonsick. Red around the eyes. Your entire coven is infected. Or just as guilty as they were."

The tall one shook her head, kept shaking it. "My sisters would not—"

"That's enough," Leif said, and shared a look with Mo. She started dragging me down the hall, though I didn't resist. Whatever else Leif said to the witches was lost as the rest of the chandelier crashed to the ground, scattering the shifters and Soren alike.

# CHAPTER 28

*L*uckily we didn't go far. A few turns down more gaudily-decorated halls led us to an office on the first floor, a pretentious setup with an enormous oak desk and bookshelves all around and leather chairs. Leif leaned back against the desk as he watched me, and Moriah prowled near the door as she growled and snapped. I wandered along the perimeter, searching the bookshelves for anything useful, and gingerly patted at my neck. Maybe I could break into Anne Marie's store and liberate some of the healing creams she made. She used Rosa's formulas, so they'd be almost as good as getting some of Rosa's work.

My heart stumbled as I thought of Rosa, and I sent a prayer to the saints to keep her safe, wherever she was.

"Tell me everything you know about the girl in the alley." Leif's expression was difficult to read as he watched me, and asked me for the fourth or fifth time about the same crime. "Every Skoll-damned detail, do you hear me? No more pretending you don't remember and don't know. This is your last chance, Lily, and even Moriah knows it."

I glanced at my friend, who gave me a dark look, and I

sighed. I hobbled over to sit in the most comfortable-looking chair in the office, exhaling in relief as I could finally put my feet up on a cushy ottoman. But I didn't quite look at him. I still felt guilty for what I'd done, and I didn't need him seeing that when I spoke.

"Some of the witches gathered at the memorial to ward the trees and remember the dead. As I was on my way to the Pug for Moriah's party, the bus broke down and I had to walk. Before I got more than a block, I saw demon magic coming out of an alley. I should have kept going."

"No shit," Mo said under her breath.

"Go on." Leif was not amused.

"Two witches stood over a human girl, tied to an altar. They had a book, a chalice, a knife, and had opened a rift to a demon realm. They were in the middle of a spell and didn't notice me at first. I interrupted them, they attacked me, and then they tripped and fell into the demon realm they'd opened."

"Tripped and fell. Both of them. Right into a demon realm."

I held my hands up, the very picture of innocence. "Bad balance. It's killer."

Moriah snorted, shaking her head, and scrubbed her hands through her hair until it stood up in a snarled mess. "The Varg Himself couldn't keep you out of trouble, witch."

Leif didn't move from where he leaned on the Peacemaker's desk, his eyes mysteries to me. "The girl's name."

"Indira Modi." I held off the queasiness of memory, the warm wet squish of fresh blood between my fingers and the reek of human insides. "She told me to find her parents if she didn't make it, and tell them she was sorry. I tried to heal her but I couldn't do much, and left my scarf tied against her wounds after I called the ambulance. I stayed with her until the sirens were too close. I did what I could, Leif, but I couldn't wait around for the Externals to show up and arrest me for dark matter."

"They would have called—"

"They wouldn't have paused to call you, and you know it. I'd have been in iron with a bullet in my head before they cleaned the blood off the ground." I shook my head. "And even if they'd called you, you would have sent Anne Marie, and she would never have listened to my side. I'm already guilty in her eyes."

Leif rubbed his jaw. "The victim's name was never published, but that's her. So you resurrected Darkwing to buy you some time?"

"I always liked Ivan. And better him get in trouble with the Externals than me. Being nonaligned and all." I wondered if the Chechen heard us say his name, wherever he was.

"And it didn't occur to you to just tell me these details that night, when Stefan and Eric wanted to question you, or later when I was at your house, or maybe even the three times after that?"

I felt like a kid sitting in the principal's office, getting lectured about bad choices. "When I figure out how to turn back time and rectify my mistakes, this is at the top of my list. With Anne Marie calling me a murderer and threatening to kill me if she saw me again, I was a little hesitant to admit knowing two of her aligned witches were demonsick."

Soren strode in, his expression sour, and threw a bunch of papers on the desk before throwing himself in the massive chair behind the wooden monstrosity. "Only two?"

"Probably three or more," I said slowly, glancing at Moriah as my friend paced closer to stand behind my chair. "The two in the alley should have had a third with them. But if they've been in the coven while working dark magic, they might have infected all of them. You should probably get someone to run an impartial cleansing spell on them, just to be sure."

The Peacemaker grunted, watching me with a dangerous glint in his eyes. "Well, you killed one more, so that's a start."

"She attacked me. I'm allowed to defend myself, Soren."

"Funny how so many of my people who cross your path end up dead or hexed. Including my second-in-command." Soren glanced at Leif, who adjusted his collar to hide the purple hex, and frowned more.

I folded my hands over my stomach and watched him, waiting for him to go on. I'd already said my piece on those accusations, and I couldn't keep denying and defending something I knew was my right.

Soren sat back in his chair as the silence stretched, then flicked his fingers at the stack of papers he'd brought in. "We have a few problems I wish to resolve as quickly as possible, Lilith."

"You meant the warrant for my arrest?" I pretended only a polite interest, even though it made my blood boil. I didn't recognize his authority to judge me, that was for damn sure.

"Yes," he said, tone bland. He'd always been good at sounding like he discussed the weather even when he handed down death sentences. "Before we address the charges, though, we will address your status. You stand alone as nonaligned, despite our efforts to bring you into the Alliance, but I have been reminded—several times—that you are a friend of the Stone Hills pack." He raised an ironic eyebrow at Moriah, who didn't look at all embarrassed that she'd badgered him into recognizing her support.

I inclined my head to the Peacemaker. "I accept the friendship of Stone Hills pack."

Soren grunted, rubbing his jaw as his gaze drifted to where Leif took up a casual lean against the wall. "And you have other supporters in this. So. You stand before the Alliance nonaligned, but certainly not alone."

My throat clogged at the unexpected kindness. Not alone. I pulled myself together; it was just an elaborate charade to get me to lower my guard and admit things they could pin on me later. I set my jaw. "I am always happy to answer the Alliance's summons."

Soren tossed one of the papers across the desk so I could pick it up and study the long list of items on it. "You are accused of practicing dark magic, falsely identifying yourself as a basher and a mender, falsely aligning yourself with a nonexistent coven, attacking Alliance representatives in the conduct of official duties, fleeing the scene of a crime, killing one Alliance wolf, and killing three Alliance witches. Possibly more, if we are to consider the attack on the First Coven."

"That's all?" I said weakly, studying the warrant. It wasn't funny in the least, but it was an impressive list for just three days' work.

"Actually, no," he said. "But the Chief Investigator determined the charges from the Externals were baseless, and chose not to press charges on your lack of cooperation during his investigation, as well as the lies you told you hide your involvement in other crimes."

I slouched a little lower in the chair. Damn. The list swam in front of my eyes. I almost couldn't remember which of them I'd actually done.

"Let's start with the easy ones." Soren held up his right hand to show off the massive alignment ring he wore. "Rings. Failure to accurately identify one's nature and strength when in public is punishable by branding and parole for the first offense if you are within two classes of your actual ability. Jail for no less than six months is required on the second offense or in the case you have pretended to be more than two classes weaker than your natural class. This is required by the Truce. What is your explanation for being caught marauding as a basher and mender?"

My mouth went dry. The jail he mentioned wasn't the run of the mill prison the humans thought of—no, it was a hellish place made of iron and steel, designed just for witches who couldn't be controlled. One month there would drive me crazy; six months might just kill me outright.

I rubbed the back of my neck as the wounds itched, wishing they could bring the cream immediately so it didn't hurt quite as much. "I wore a charmer's ring for work. Anything more than that and the humans get nervous."

He didn't blink, those hard blue eyes unyielding. He loved his power, all right. And he'd do anything to keep it. Tracy's warning drifted through my mind, that there was trouble brewing among the shifters, but I pushed it away. I couldn't afford to be distracted. I reluctantly pulled the necklace from under my tattered shirt, and flashed the lapis blue stone at him. "I read as a summoner on most devices. Given what's been going on the past week, I thought it safer not to openly identify as a war witch."

"Have you an accurate ring?"

"Yes." My onyx war witch ring remained safely in the Remnant. It was a gift from my parents and had survived ten years of war. I couldn't risk losing it to some External's pocket or one of Anne Marie's minions.

Soren scratched a note on the paper, then glanced at me. "Resolved. You are hereby reprimanded, in the company of two witnesses, for wearing the wrong rings. If you are caught again, you will be sentenced to three months at the Reserve."

His dark look made the threat clear—don't get caught again.

I gripped the arms of my chair, wishing I could take a shower. I smelled like a damn abattoir.

"Next charge. Killing an Alliance wolf. What is your explanation?"

I hesitated, then cleared my throat. "When, uh, was this supposed to have happened?"

"The alley behind the Pug," Leif said quietly from my right.

He didn't look at me, but instead studied the floor near Soren's desk. "Cold River."

"One of them died?" I shook my head and sighed. "They attacked me in beast form. I defended myself when they bit me. You and the Chief Investigator witnessed their attack earlier in the night, and when I... departed the Pug through the back door, Cold River attacked me again."

"You mean when you fled the Chief Investigator when he intended to arrest you?" Soren didn't wait for an answer, his expression sour, and scratched something else off his paper. "Fine. You are entitled to self-defense, and Cold River admitted to attacking you in the alley. This alleviates you of further criminal charges, but understand the pack can still levy blood debt against you."

"Stone Hills will deal with that," Moriah said. "They owe us blood debt for attacking Mimi during the blood truce."

Soren arched an eyebrow at her and said, "I'm sure you will."

I wondered if he still respected her as much as he apparently had during the war. His patience seemed to have disappeared when it came to Moriah, although Soren never grew impatient with Mick. Maybe the equality we'd earned in combat faded in the peace.

"Next charges. Killing three Alliance witches."

"Just three?"

"Those are the ones we can prove are connected to you, thank Fenrir," he said. "Whether you killed the First Coven witches remains to be seen."

"I didn't," I said. "My apartment was destroyed, too."

"It what?" Moriah leaned forward and smacked my shoulder. "What the hell has been going on with you, Lily?"

"We can talk about that later," I said, and sat up to ease the pain in my lower back. The chair wasn't as comfortable as it appeared, or maybe I'd aged thirty years in the last hour.

"Soren, two of the witches practiced dark magic on a human girl. I did not kill them. Demons did."

"And the third?"

"She and the rest of her coven broke into Anne Marie's home. I happened to be there looking for a book the Morrigan stole from me, and the witches attacked me, thinking I was her. I defended myself." Fatigue slowed me down and snarled all the thoughts in my head. I couldn't remember what was real and what had only been a dream. "Their coven attacked me again in your foyer."

"I bear witness to these facts," Leif said.

The Peacemaker sighed, rubbing his forehead. "We don't have enough strong witches for you to just go around killing whomever attacks you. Stop pissing so many people off, for Hati's sake. Seriously. Stop killing witches."

"Stop letting your witches attack me."

He wrote more on the paper. "Against my better judgment, you're absolved of legal consequences for the deaths of three aligned witches."

His gaze went to Leif as he went on. "The next issue. Attacking Alliance representatives in the course of an official investigation, including hexing the Chief Investigator, misleading efforts to identify the perpetrator of other crimes, fleeing the scene of a crime, and resisting arrest. Leif, do you wish to comment?"

"I provoked the witch," Leif said, no emotion in his face or voice. "I intended to get a reaction out of her, but did not antici-pate the degree of that reaction. I recommend the charges be dropped."

My heart stuttered as hope took hold. Saints preserve me.

Soren drummed his fingers on the desk, irritation in the thin slash of his lips. He finally crumpled up that paper and threw it into the basket next to his desk. "Great. Upon further testimony from the Chief Investigator, these charges are dropped. But don't think you'll get that lucky again, Lilith."

Moriah exhaled, and I glanced back to study her face. Relief etched across her expression. Those must have been the charges she worried about.

The Peacemaker leaned back in his chair and watched me, face impassive. "Which leaves us with dark magic. You fled Externals as they attempted to identify the source of dark magic on two occasions. Dark magic contaminated your apartment, as well as Anne Marie's after you'd been there. You admitted knowing dark magic to Leif. The dark magic from your apartment was linked to a horrific crime in another witch's home. Explain yourself."

I took a deep breath and marshaled my thoughts through the fog of memory and fatigue. Explain myself. Right. Saints save me from myself.

# CHAPTER 29

y head ached and I braced my hands on my knees so I wouldn't keep rubbing my shoulder and irritate the wounds on my neck. "I know dark spells and hexes because my parents believed the only way to defend against evil was to understand how it works. As you remember from the war."

"Fine." Soren tapped his desk. "But you are nonaligned. No one can verify your intent now. And knowing what you did in the war, that concerns me. You are a dangerous weapon to have roaming the city, uncontrolled."

My pride rankled as I scowled at him. Uncontrolled. I'd almost forgotten what an asshole he was. "I follow my own code of conduct, and I've got remarkable self-control, dick."

"Clearly," he said under his breath, though his eyes glinted gold with irritation. "Watch your mouth, witch. Does your code of honor allow breaking and entering, as well as theft?"

"I'm sure I don't know what you're talking about."

"You broke into Anne Marie's house and stole a book from her, possibly more."

Damn. I tried to remember if I'd already admitted to that,

but as I formulated a response, Leif started to smile. Expecting a pack of lies, no doubt. So I threw caution to the winds. If they'd forgiven me for killing a couple of witches and a wolf, how could stealing a book that Anne Marie shouldn't have had in the first place put me in jail?

"In certain circumstances, yes. She stole the book from me in the first place, and it's a dangerous book for just anyone to have around. She didn't even have it warded. Anyone could have taken it."

"And did you leave something behind?" He dropped a scrap of parchment on the desk in front of me, and I immediately recoiled as a hint of sulfur curled through the room.

"Why is *that* here?"

"What is it?" Soren traded a look with Leif, and Moriah leaned over my shoulder to sniff at the little scrap.

"Dark." I shivered, and the bile rose in my throat as I caught a reflection in a decorative mirror on the wall. At least it wasn't set in silver and a perfect circle, otherwise we might have already been overrun. "It's a focus for summoning demons."

Soren pressed his fingertips together near his mouth, frowned at me. "How do we render it safe?"

"A bowl of salt water," I said, drawing my feet up on the chair. "Don't burn it. Some activate in fire."

Leif went to the door and spoke to someone outside, but Soren's attention never left me. "Did you make it, Lily?"

"Of course not. *That* is demon magic—not light gray, not dark gray—just dark. Worse than dark."

"And yet you recognized it easily." He grunted and waved a hand. "I do not absolve you of the charges related to dark magic —that will stand until we determine what happened to the coven and I am convinced of your innocence. You'll remain in the custody of the Alliance until you are either released or sent to the Reserve."

I didn't like it, particularly that custody part. I didn't want to hang out with Soren a second longer than I had to. But I breathed easier as Jake returned with a shallow bowl of water, cloudy with salt, and submerged the parchment. Soren watched him before going on. "So why were you at Anne Marie's house, if not to leave dark magic behind for her?"

"I thought there might be information about what happened at Tracy's house."

"It is not your place to—"

"The investigators were following the wrong leads," I said, not daring to look at Leif as he resumed his casual stance near the wall. "And you have no one else with the magic to find them. It is witch business."

The Peacemaker opened a desk drawer and brought out a velvet ring box, tossing it to me. It fell with a thump in my lap. I picked up the heavy thing—lined with lead, no doubt, so the silver wouldn't make him sick.

I cracked open the box and sighed: a beautiful princess-cut black diamond ring, set in silver, with the Peacemaker's crest engraved on one panel and the Alliance crest on the other. The box clicked shut in my hand, the snap loud in the still room.

Soren pointed to the box, eyes hard. "You want to be part of the investigation? Wear that and consider yourself acting Morrigan."

The silence quaked around me. Interesting, to go from accusations of dark magic and horrible crimes to an offer of alignment. Something wasn't right.

I turned the box over in my fingers, imagining all the benefits that came with it: guaranteed paycheck, a place to stay, carte blanche for research and spell testing, insincere but obligatory respect from lower-ranked witches. I shook my head and placed the ring box back on his desk. "The first time a man gives me a diamond, I have to give it back. Not fair, Peacemaker."

He grimaced and retrieved the box. "Then consider the

information you provide tonight your contribution to figuring out what happened at Tracy's house."

"I will answer what I can." But he was a bigger fool than I thought if he assumed I wouldn't keep looking on my own. Witch business was witch business, and no pack would get in the middle of me finding my friends. I folded my hands in my lap.

"Has anyone threatened you recently, Lily?"

"Only Leif."

The Peacemaker snorted. "Anyone else?"

"Maybe Jake," I said, nodded my head in the clownish shifter's direction. "And Anne Marie called me a murderer not too long ago, but that's pretty routine."

Another hint of a smile touched his face, though it disappeared quickly. "When did you notice Cold River at the bar?"

"Three of them started dancing with the girls. They stood out from the crowd due to... intensity. Mimi said something and when I turned, I saw Brandr touching her. Everything got...a little red after that."

"Had you seen them before tonight?"

"Not since the war." Uneasiness bubbled up in my stomach, since I thought we would be talking about the investigation into what happened to the coven—not the relatively minor crimes of an Old World pack.

He and Leif traded one of their laden man looks, and Soren braced his hands on the desk, frowning down at them. "After extensive interrogation, they still insist Mimi was not the pack's target. She was collateral damage."

I rolled my eyes and prayed the saints would protect me from the wolf's single-mindedness. "Of course he wouldn't admit trying to kidnap your goddaughter, Soren, be serious—"

"Brandr says they were after you."

It was my turn to laugh. "I'm a little old for bride-snatching, Soren."

"No kidding," Jake muttered, and I shot him a dirty look.

Soren said, "I know."

No one else laughed, though. Any hope that he was joking faded as Soren continued to look at me. I shook my head. "That's preposterous. I certainly haven't done anything to Cold Water that would have warranted an attack like that."

"Apparently you did something," Leif said. I looked at him despite the creak in my shoulder and the breaking scabs on my neck. Just seeing him made me feel a little steadier. "Someone paid the entire pack to bite you, so you'd turn."

A fate worse than death, after having that collar on. I took a deep breath, trying to focus despite a curious blurring of my vision. I really hadn't done anything to deserve that, for someone to take away my magic. "Someone wants me dead."

"Turned," Leif corrected.

"Same thing," I said. "For a witch."

Soren got up to pace the length of the room behind his desk. "Why would anyone pay a pack to break a blood truce to bite you?"

"The truce didn't apply to me," I said. I watched Leif and his curious stillness from beneath my eyelashes, trying to account for all the reasons someone might want me dead. Maybe Chompers had a few favors to cash in with the packs? "I really don't know. We ran into a little problem with a witch neighbor of mine, but that's it."

Soren faced me, eyes narrowed, but Leif stepped forward. "The witch who was beating his girlfriend. We took care of it. He wasn't powerful—or rich—enough to employ a pack like Cold River. It wasn't him."

"How's Amber?" I asked, wishing I knew where she ended up or what happened. I'd always liked her.

"She's okay," Leif said, nodding. "She's in one of the sanctuary houses, getting treatment."

"Good." That helped me breathe a little easier.

Soren grunted, then held something up and tossed it at me. "What can you tell me about this?"

I caught it out of the air and winced as I recognized it: the powerful breaking charm Brandr carried in the bar. I cradled it in my right palm and instinctively fed a little magic into it, just to test how much potency remained.

A light flashed red above us as a siren whooped in the silence, and Jake lurched forward with a sidearm ready. Soren waved a hand to forestall him, still watching me. I sighed and crumbled the charm to dust between my fingers. Damn Anne Marie to the coldest of hells. What the hell was she doing working with Cold River? She hated them in the war, and feared them in the peace.

Soren's expression darkened as he watched the mess the dust made on his floor. "And now I can charge you with destroying evidence."

"It was too dangerous to leave active," I said, wiping my hand on my tattered jeans. "Particularly with you winging it around like a fucking Frisbee."

"And how are we supposed to find out who made it?" Irritation gathered in deep lines around his eyes.

"I know who made it." Another burden settled on my aching shoulders. Saints damn it. The only question that remained was whether Anne Marie gave the charm to Brandr for a specific purpose, or if he'd purchased it from her store under different pretenses. "I'll deal with it."

Soren picked up the ring box again and waved it at me. "Not your responsibility unless you take this. Still no? Okay then— tell me who the hell made it and I will deal with it."

"You seem to be missing all of your witches," I said, not quite looking at him. "So who do you expect to handle it? I'll take care of it for you. Pro bono."

"Why?" Leif straightened from his casual slouch so he could see my face.

Because it was time I acted like a good witch. Something haunted the witches, not just Tracy. It might be too late to save the coven, but I could maybe spare others their fate. "Who else will do it?"

"I will guarantee you're protected until the Morrigan is found," Soren said. "Then *she* will deal with whomever aided Brandr. I cannot have a nonaligned witch doing Alliance work."

"So you will wait for Anne Marie," I said, pinching the bridge of my nose. I'd forgotten how infuriating the wolves could be. "When she is either dead or a dark witch, to arrest the witch who helped Cold River?"

He nodded along, then stopped and gave me his hard stare. "And how do you know Anne Marie is the Morrigan? She has not made that public knowledge."

"She can tell you, when you find her." I thought of my scrying bowl, the clouded water when I searched for Tracy, and I corrected myself. "*If* you find her. And you can't expect her to punish herself, Soren. She's the one who made that charm."

"You think she made that charm?"

"I don't think, I know. It was hers."

"Why would the Morrigan want you dead?"

I smiled, resisting the urge to close my eyes and doze. At least his office was warm and comfortable. "Would you like the list alphabetically or chronologically?"

"The Morrigan would not do this," Soren said, perhaps to convince himself more than me. If he remembered the war at all, the Morrigan he knew most certainly would do something like that, and worse besides. "You're the center of a lot of trouble, Lily. There has to be a list of people who want you out of the way."

"Instead of guessing and keeping me up all hours of the night, why don't you just ask Cold River?"

His expression, though I thought it impossible, turned

grimmer still. "Someone erased their memories. They have no recollection of who hired them."

I studied the knockoff Klimt on the far wall as I considered all the possible implications of such a thing. Memories burned out with precision. Only a powerful pre-Breaking witch would possess those skills, or someone trained by dark witches. None of their snooty academies taught that kind of magic. "Not many witches left with that kind of skill, not without turning the subject into a total zombie."

"Who's on the short list?"

When I hesitated, not wanting to reveal witch business, Leif's expression darkened. "The time for playing games is over, Lily. Someone wants you dead or out of the way, and they used one of our packs to do it. Fill us in."

I stared at the wall behind Soren's desk. Leif was right, of course—the conflict went well beyond witch business. "The only witches I remember being capable of that are in Anne Marie's coven now. The ones who still live—Anne Marie, Jacques, Tracy. Maybe Dana or Beth, although Dana retired out west and I don't know where Beth is now. R-Rosa could have." I cleared my throat against the burn of tears at saying her name. "It might be possible to tell from the hex itself. There's usually very specific handiwork in something like that."

"Changing memory comes close to influencing free will," Soren said, gripping the edge of his desk. "And that's against the witch code of conduct."

Code of conduct? Like they signed a chastity pledge or something. "It depends on personal ethics. I would never change memory, but Anne Marie did not think it any great crime, so I assume the rest of her coven followed her lead."

"Why wouldn't you do it?" Leif remained on the perimeter of the room, somewhere behind me.

"Because someone did it to me," I said. Everyone went still. I stared at the leg of Soren's desk, seeing only Sam's face as he pleaded for understanding. For forgiveness. "And he wasn't very good at it, so I know what it is to have fog in my memory. I wouldn't wish that on anyone."

Even Anne Marie.

"Who did it?" Leif's tone was casual. Too casual. I didn't dare look at him.

I wished I could have played with the jade ring. "He's dead. Died in the war."

Died in the war because I killed him.

Soren leaned his fists on the desk, frowning at me. "Is there a way to reconstitute the memories?"

The bunching muscles in his forearms distracted me from thoughts of Sam. "It depends on how they took the memory. Occasionally it is possible to identify a scrap or two."

"Okay," Soren said, and shoved upright, all controlled violence as he strode to the door.

I glanced back at him, raising an eyebrow. "Okay?"

The Peacemaker gestured for me to get up and precede him into the hallway. Moriah looked nervous. "We'll find some scraps and figure out who wants you dead."

Except I already knew who wanted me dead. "But—"

"You don't seem too concerned that someone wants to kill you."

I sighed and rested my head against the chair, closing my eyes. This night just kept getting worse. I gathered my strength and slowly forced myself to stand. "Guess I'm used to it."

He snorted and started walking, leaving Moriah and Leif and me to catch up.

# CHAPTER 30

$\mathcal{W}$e walked in silence through the halls and down several sets of mysterious stairs in Soren's mansion, the route so twisted I could barely tell which way was up. My magic faded and I felt older with each step, gravity weighing me down until I slowed enough that Soren practically disappeared ahead of us. Moriah linked her arm with mine and half-carried me, and Leif brought up the rear, muttering into a radio.

My tension grew as the number of armed men in the halls increased, and a suspicion that maybe this was just a ruse to get me trapped in the bowels of the Peacemaker's home surfaced. I wouldn't put it past him to have secret jails below his house, incarcerating those who crossed him or might have presented a political challenge. I put my faith in Moriah, that she at least would have warned me or stood up to Soren to save me.

And then the Peacemaker stopped in front of a reinforced steel door, guarded by four armed men and two wolves. When he nodded two of the guards inserted keys into hidden spots on the door, and the whole contraption creaked as they dragged it open, muscles standing out in their shoulders and arms. So chances were I wouldn't even be able to budge the damn thing.

I stood back as Soren walked into the room without hesitation, questioning my decision to help them, but Moriah nudged me forward with a whispered, "Don't be a coward, witch."

"Caution is not cowardice," I said. "Crazy-ass wolf."

She winked and dragged me into the tiny room, though I stopped short just inside the door. A metal table took up the center of the claustrophobic room, and the walls were reinforced and padded to prevent the occupants from hurting themselves or creating weapons. A man sat behind the table, and an empty chair faced him. The only light came from a few bulbs recessed in the ceiling and covered with cages, casting eerie uneven light as the door swung shut behind us. Nothing else cluttered the grim room—no evidence of an interrogation, no chains, no water or food or any hint of comfort for the man at the table.

Brandr waited, blank-faced, as I lingered near the door. Leif leaned back against the heavy steel, and the tiny space became even more an airless coffin. I gazed at the orb of Soren's pack magic keeping Brandr motionless in his chair, and cleared my throat. "Maybe we should try this on a younger one first. They recover better after these sorts of hexes."

They were also a hell of a lot less intimidating.

Soren took up a broad stance behind Brandr. "He's the leader and the one whose memory was least affected. Start with him."

The Old World alpha exuded tightly-coiled danger, as if he only waited for an opportune moment of his choosing to break free. And the smirk on his face convinced me he knew perfectly well why I wanted to start with someone else.

I eased into the empty chair and studied his hardened, weather-beaten face. It was lined with work and worry, the miles of his life's journey. He was ageless but still old, especially with ten years of war factored in. Cold River had been the vanguard at nearly all major battles during the war, and Brandr led every charge. I would get nowhere with threats or bluster. He wouldn't believe me, to start, and more importantly, he did not fear death. He'd already faced it and survived. He was proud, like all Old World wolves, and already the Peacemaker brought him low.

So I would ask permission where normally I demanded obedience.

I bowed from my chair, hands palm-up in front of me, and used the Old World greeting I remembered from the war. "Brandr, son of Skoll, son of Fenrir. May the night be long and the hunt plentiful."

He blinked. For a heart-stopping moment, I wondered if his family descended from Hati, not Skoll, and I'd insulted him by mistake. Then Brandr fought Soren's iron control to incline his head. "Lilith witch, daughter of witches, descended from the saints. May the saints guide your cast."

The weight of Soren's gaze dried my throat and chilled my blood. Maybe he hadn't realized I knew those particular greetings or spent any time around the Old World packs. I'd avoided them as much as possible, but they'd saved my life at least once.

I cleared my throat and focused on Brandr. It was foolishness and arrogance to take my attention off him, when he was the most dangerous thing in the room and I sat within his reach.

"I knew of your heroism, the blood-letting you did for our people," I said, burying my unease in formality. For someone to have given Brandr the name Lilith could not have been an accident. "It would have been an honor to die at your hands."

The ghost of a smile crossed his face. "And yet you couldn't go quietly."

"I never do," I said. Leif paced to stand near the long end of the table, his expression grim, and I took a deep breath. "I do not know what they told you, Brandr son of Skoll, to convince you I deserved death, but—"

"Not death." Brandr inclined his head to me, a perfect gentleman despite the circumstances and having tried to kill me only a few hours before. "I would have given you the change, taken you into my pack." The chivalry burned up in a long appraisal, his eyes sparking with gold. "As my mate."

"And I would have been honored to be found worthy," I said, raising my voice over Leif's growling. But still dead, since the bite would have killed me eventually.

Leif staggered back with marionette-doll awkwardness to brace against the wall, followed by Soren's hard stare, as pack magic forced the Warder away. I marveled at the control the Peacemaker wielded over his magic, the influence he exercised on subordinates. It put my little spell to shame.

A smile crept over Brandr's face as he watched someone else on the receiving end of Soren's irritation. "The Warder guards you well, Lilith witch."

I flattened my hands on the table and tried not to think about why Leif got so protective. "Brandr son of Skoll, for the witch who hired you, the change would have been a death for me."

"It is a gift," he said, implacable. Stubborn wolves. "Trade herbs and chanting for the freedom of a new form, howling at the moon in new snow." He paused to study me, then shook his head. "It's too bad. You would have made a beautiful wolf."

Leif snarled, lurching forward, though he silenced with a grunt as Soren's expression darkened. "If you cannot control yourself, Second, find something else to do."

I resisted the urge to agitate them all a little further, just to buy myself time, but the longer we screwed around in the interrogation room, the longer it was before I could get some sleep. "As I said, I would have been honored. But whatever crimes the witch listed to convince you, those crimes were not mine."

"She said—" His face compressed, the lines deepening as he struggled against the darkness in his memory. "You brought the seven plagues to the humans in the seventh year of war because... the saints appreciate symmetry."

I took a deep breath; he must have had as much mental fortitude as Soren to exert such mastery over his own mind even after a hex. And what he said was technically true, as much as I hated to hear the plagues discussed in the light of day, but there had been better reasons for doing it than symmetry. "Well, it sounds worse than—"

"She said you killed your mate."

My breath caught. Sam. His smiling face replaced Brandr's in front of me, and I clenched my hand around where I'd worn his ring. Sam hadn't been my mate, not as the shifters used the term, but there was no real word for what he'd been.

Tears burned my throat, closer to the surface than I'd expected. I couldn't look at Leif or even Soren, though I tried a joke when I dared glance at Brandr. "Now I know you're crazy. Even thinking I killed my mate, you would have made me yours?"

"I like dangerous women," he said, with not a hint of jest.

I waited for Leif to fly across the room to rip out his throat, but nothing happened. I refused to look at anyone but Brandr. Killing a mate was one of the unforgivable crimes with the shifters. I stored that grief away for later, frowning at my hands. I'd had beautiful, graceful hands before the war. A cellist's hands, Mom used to say. Now they were scarred and stained and crooked, a testament to hard work and deep hurts. It was okay for a man to show the world his history through his hands, but I wanted pretty fingers, graceful wrists, delicate nails. My vanity seldom surfaced, but I wanted a lady's hands.

I rubbed a ridge of scar tissue along the back of my wrist. "Despite that, I—"

"You hurt for him," the wolf interrupted. "This mate you killed."

"We are not here to talk about me."

"Are we not?" Brandr smiled, deceptively congenial, the ruthless killer buried deeply. I had no doubt he would still bite me, if Soren's control faltered. They didn't believe in abandoning a mission, in Brandr's pack. They always finished the job. "This is about you at least as much as it is me."

I managed a tight smile. He was right, after all. "Yes, I regret how things ended."

"Did he deserve to die?"

The pain built in my chest as memories flooded back. Sam, begging for mercy, desperate to explain. Tracy, standing between us, screaming that it took two war witches to condemn him. Black holes in my memory, making me crazy and convincing me I'd done things I would never remember. I shook myself and straightened in the uncomfortable chair. Had he deserved it? Should I have waited, like Tracy begged? "I don't know. I thought so. But it haunts me. All those I killed haunt me. I'm sure you know what that's like."

He shrugged. "If I killed them, they deserved to die."

His expression tensed as he leaned forward, one hand rising an inch at a time to settle his battered fingers over mine, fighting Soren's control the whole way. His gruff words were meant to reassure, no doubt, even as it sent chills down my spine. "If you killed him, Lilith daughter of the saints, he deserved to die."

I blinked several times as his face swam in front of me. The cold calculation of the Old World packs had once been a comfort—we could sleep, knowing they guarded the borders and passes and would die before falling back, knowing they would do the grim work with no hesitation and no regret. But on a clear night five years after the Truce, his calm assessment of the value of life, and the ease with which he dismissed Sam's, chilled me to my core.

I pulled my hand away. "The witch who hired you did you a grave disservice. She used your pack to further her own ends."

"I know what I did, witch," he said. "She did not trick me. It was a calculated risk and it did not go our way. We will pay the price." He clenched his fist until his knuckles cracked. "You are not the only one who did not go willingly into captivity."

An ache built in my temples, and even massaging them didn't help much. He had to know something, the stubborn ass. "She changed your memory, Brandr Two-natured. You may have said or done or sworn a dozen things you can't recall."

His expression darkened. "She said she would only take her name and face."

I held my breath, the air growing tense as he pondered. It would work so much better if he volunteered...

Sweat broke out on his forehead as Brandr raised his other hand to the table despite Soren amplifying the pack magic. Brandr gritted his teeth, eyes already gold. "Find out, witch. Find out what she took."

I slid my hands over his and Brandr turned his palms up, fingertips resting against the pulse points in my wrists. I did my best to ignore Leif's prowling behind me. After a moment, I shook my head and looked at the Peacemaker. "You'll have to get rid of the pack magic, Soren. It's hiding everything I need to see."

His attention landed on Brandr like a ton of bricks. "If I release you, I want your oath you will protect Lilith as if she were your mate. And because I know how much you value your oaths to me, swear on your life, your pack, and Lord Fenrir Himself."

The sarcasm didn't seem to affect Brandr as he tilted his head, studying me. His thumb stroked across the back of my hand, and his words sealed a quiet contract with me, as if there were no one else in the world but us. "By my honor, by my pack, and by our Lord Fenrir of the Northern Reaches, I swear: my blood before yours, my life before yours."

I shivered, unable to look away, as Moriah made a disbelieving noise behind me. The calm delivery of such a binding oath made my stomach clench, particularly as pack magic rippled around him in a violet and magenta fog. Rage cracked the air from Leif's corner, and the Peacemaker watched him more than the Old World alpha in front of me.

Soren released the pack magic and Brandr exhaled in a rush, rotating his head until vertebrae crunched. He stretched massive shoulders before returning his elbows to the table and reaching for my hands. "Let's get this over with, witch."

I pressed my palms to his, creating a circuit as I drew power from my limited store. My view of him illuminated into sparks of red and tangled webs of magic. There was indeed a hex on him, suppressing parts of his memory. I shifted in my chair as I squinted at the mess, frowning. "That's different."

Brandr arched an eyebrow. "Good or bad?"

"No spell is good or bad," I said, intensely aware that the Chief Investigator listened to every word. "How you choose to use something is good or bad. This hex is just different. I can't tell if it was placed with ill intent."

I brushed my left hand against the hex's stands, fingers working into the mess to try and pry it apart for a better look. "Spells are tools, son of Skoll, just like knives or hammers. It is the wielder who determines the intent."

The hex snarled around his thoughts, crude in its design. Maybe not Anne Marie's work after all. She hadn't improved a lot since the war, I was sure, but I doubted she would have gotten so much worse. The hex hid a few places where his memory was burned away, small dark pits underneath the web of colorful magic. I sighed. "Some of it is gone forever, son of Skoll, I—"

"You may call me Brandr."

The strange timbre of his voice yanked me out of the magical reverie. "What?"

"You may use my name," he repeated. "Since you're playing with my hair."

My fingers indeed twined in the soft hair at the back of his neck, and I flushed. I snapped my hands away, expected a smart remark, but he only sat there, hands loose and easy on the table. Waiting.

I pushed my chair back from the table as the air disappeared from the room. The men breathed it all in, took up all the space. The pressure of their watchfulness, the weight of their judgment, made my stomach rebel and bile creep up my throat, until I feared I would be sick all over the table. I'd definitely lost my touch.

# CHAPTER 31

When my breath hitched and I scrambled to get out of the chair, Moriah caught my arm to help me and gestured for Leif to open the door. He started to protest, but took one look at me and did as she asked, standing back as I staggered for the relative freedom of the narrow hall.

Mo helped me walk, murmuring, "Keep it together," as we maneuvered around the guards and wolves, and she didn't let me go until we were in a broom closet of a bathroom away from the interrogation cells.

She ran the water in the tap and handed me a dampened hand towel. "You okay? You turned white as a sheet."

I scrubbed the dried blood from my face and examined the damage to my throat from that awful collar. It looked like it had started healing under the scabs and blood, so maybe Kyle's magic did more than I anticipated. "I don't know."

As the towel turned rust-red, she folded her arms over her chest. "Are you afraid of finding out the Morrigan did it, or that she didn't?"

I met her gaze in the mirror, and imagined all the things lurking on the other side of the glass. "I don't know."

She opened the door once I'd splashed more water on my face and dried my neck, trying to arrange my tattered clothes to keep myself decent. She even patted my back as we walked toward Brandr's cell. "Fifty bucks says it was the Morrigan."

I smiled half-heartedly as we edged through the massive door once more and it clanged shut behind us, though I hesitated as soon as we were inside. The tension had noticeably increased. Neither Brandr nor Leif looked happy. Soren remained expressionless as Brandr placed his hands on the table once more. "Whenever you're ready, krigen-heks."

My eyebrows arched at the jump in formality. Soren's doing, most likely. I stood next to Brandr and rubbed my hands together, building power through my fatigue. I'd used too much defending myself in the alley; burnout was a real possibility at this rate. I needed a good long sleep and a few slow weeks to recover—which seemed about as likely as winning the lottery and finding Tracy at the same time. As static gathered around me, snapping and popping in the dry air, I squinted at Brandr's aura and reached into the hex. "This might hurt a little."

As I looked for the right place to begin unraveling, it became clear two witches had been at work. One, more subtle, burned out half a dozen specific memories. The second had unrolled a magical carpet over the burned patches, hiding the other's work but not doing permanent damage as other memories were hidden as well.

Brandr tensed, and I frowned as part of the hex slipped away. "Don't move or you could spend the rest of your days reliving one memory, over and over. I haven't lived many days that would make that a pleasant end, and I know you haven't either. So quit moving."

He went still; everyone else held their breath.

My hands shook and my back ached by the time I thought I had it figured out. Pain gathered in the lines around his eyes, and his hands gripped the table in a white-knuckled vise.

I dragged the weakest point of the hex away from him, untangling strands as I did so. A growl started in his chest, building as the tension around his mind stretched, tearing apart his memories and awareness and control. The table creaked, then bent with a sharp crack, and the metal crumpled to the floor. Brandr's growl turned desperate as he searched for an anchor.

He grabbed my waist, fingers bruising. I concentrated on breathing and ignoring the heated strength of his grip as another crash echoed in the room. Brandr's grip created the connection I'd dreaded, and his pain flooded through me.

Feeling drained from my legs as he crushed my hips, and I bit my lip to keep from crying out. I worked feverishly on the hex. It had to end. It had to come apart or he would go mad and tear me to pieces. I pulled at the magic faster, desperation replacing caution as his growl turned into a howl.

Veins stood out in his throat and forehead, his cheekbones sharpening. Nails dug into my jeans until the fabric ripped. I gritted my teeth. "Don't you dare shift."

And then—as my bones creaked in his grip, as he lost control and another howl emerged from his clenched teeth, as the door crashed open and more bodies crowded the room— there it was.

There it was, small and inconsequential. The path to undoing.

"Saints be praised," I whispered as I seized the thread of magic, just as Brandr bared wolf's teeth at me.

The whole mess came free with the bang of a car crash. Brandr shouted, lifting me off the ground as he seized and shook, and then collapsed in the chair, his head resting against my stomach.

I blinked sparks from my vision, resting my hands on the back of his head when I couldn't hold my arms up anymore. "I think I got it."

Moriah, face bloodless, helped Soren pin Leif against the wall, all three of them staring at me in silence. Half of the guards from the hall stood frozen in the doorway. I swallowed hard under the collective weight of their gazes. Despite so many shifters in the room, the only sound was Brandr's labored breathing, at least until Leif spoke. "Are you okay?"

It took effort to even breathe, much less speak. "Yes."

My legs wouldn't hold me, though, and I leaned into Brandr just to stay upright.

Soren released his death grip on Leif, though Moriah didn't budge. The Peacemaker straightened his clothes and smoothed his hair, moving with deliberate care around the crumpled table. "Do you need assistance?"

I shook my head, still fighting a fog in my head that made responding difficult, but Brandr chose that moment to force himself upright. As his hands fell away from my hips, my knees buckled and I hit the floor.

Two guards leapt at Brandr, a third knocking Soren out of danger with a well-placed elbow, and Leif hurled Moriah out of his way before scooping me up, arms like steel bands.

It happened too quickly for my fatigue-muddled brain, even more so as the magic faded from my grip. We were nearly in the hall by the time Soren snapped, "Stop."

Leif froze, grim as he watched the Old World shifter on the floor, buried under the guards as they struggled to restrain him. Brandr's eyes found me, though, and he smiled.

I took a deep breath. I really didn't need this complication.

"Put me down," I said to Leif, since he just stood there in the doorway and scowled.

He didn't notice, glaring at Brandr and growling when Moriah took a step in our direction. I resisted the urge to put my head on Leif's shoulder and let him carry me away to a bed, where I could sleep and he could sleep and we could sleep together. Leif went rigid, as if he'd heard my thoughts, and pack magic swirled in a red rush around us.

"Leif," Soren barked, but his voice was tinny and far away. The Peacemaker's fury was insignificant. Inconsequential.

I closed my eyes and let the pack magic diminish all the worries of the past few days. I didn't have to think about Anne Marie or Tracy of my apartment or people wanting me dead. Someone else could worry about that. I exhaled, Leif's arms drawing me closer as—

"You're out of your fucking mind," Soren said, growling, and the world crashed back into place as everything tore apart.

Moriah dropped me in the chair as Soren propelled Leif into the hall. My cheeks caught fire under Brandr's scrutiny and the raised eyebrows of the guards. Mo wasn't having it, though —she snapped her fingers at them and jerked her chin at the hall. "Get out. You didn't see a Skoll-damned thing, understood?"

It was a testament to her fierceness that they tripped over each other to get out of there.

Then her ire turned on me. "Why do you let him do that?"

I shook my head. "It just happens."

"Please," she said under her breath as Soren stomped back in, alone. "I haven't accidentally influenced someone since I was four."

Soren returned to his post behind where Brandr clambered into the remaining chair, his voice deceptively mild. "Witch, are you well?"

"Fine," I said. I ignored the heat in my cheeks and the ache in my collarbone from getting jostled around. Imagine, behaving like a love-struck teenager when Leif picked me up. I concentrated on Brandr, leaning my elbows on my knees. "What do you remember?"

"Nothing," he said. "Everything is cloudy—worse than before."

"It might take a while for your mind to recover. There was a great deal of trauma from the hex, as well as the removal."

"And the witch who hexed him?" Soren folded his arms over his chest.

"It looked like Anne Marie's work."

"That's just not—"

"Two witches worked on him," I interrupted, too tired for tact. "She was one of them. There wasn't enough for me to recognize the other; that damage was hidden under her hex."

The Peacemaker frowned, and I wondered if he was irate because of my interruption or because of what I'd found. A muscle in his jaw jumped, then he announced, "We'll discuss this in my office," and he strode out, throwing the door open like it weighed no more than a handful of spaghetti.

Moriah helped me stand and shuffle to the doorway; we were almost outside before Brandr spoke. "Krigen-heks."

I turned, holding my breath. He pushed to his feet and Moriah tensed, propping me up against the wall so she could tackle him if necessary. Using the chair for balance, Brandr of Cold River bowed to me—a real bow, not a trifling nod. A lopsided smile gave him a boyish look, though it was not as easy a smile as when we started our little conversation. "Perhaps you are too dangerous a woman for me after all."

Moriah snorted, tugging on my arm, and as Leif swung the door shut, I put the remark out of my head and focused on putting one foot in front of the other. Rest seemed so very close, yet so far away.

# CHAPTER 32

$S$oren paced behind his desk as I hobbled into the office, my cheeks heated from the very long walk back from the interrogation cells. Shifters crowded the halls between the dungeon and his office; apparently rumors got around fast and the entire Alliance wanted a look at the witch who'd made an Old World alpha scream.

The Peacemaker drew out his chair, sat, and squared himself at his desk. He straightened some papers before aligning his keyboard and address book and ledgers. When everything was at right angles and appropriately spaced, Soren pressed his hands together at his chin. "I find myself, witch, with a magical crime scene and no one to interpret the evidence."

My heart sank.

As the silence stretched, he smiled a very small smile. "Going to make me ask, hmm?"

"Asked and answered is a very different thing from volunteered," I said, the response automatic. It was the first rule of magic: never volunteer for anything. Volunteering put the cosmic debt on your shoulders, instead of the requestor's. I hoped Brandr learned that lesson well after our little encounter.

The Peacemaker cleared his throat. "Examine Tracy's house for evidence and assist us in determining the perpetrators, and I'll rescind the charges against you."

"I can't."

At length, he sat forward. "I'll request the Externals drop their investigation. Will that suffice?"

"I can't." My gaze slid away. I wasn't a coward. Just because he asked didn't mean I had to face the gruesome scene at Tracy's and the deaths of close friends. "I'm too weak to do anything until I recharge a bit. Can't it wait until later? It's still the middle of the night."

"It's almost dawn, actually, and no, it can't wait. The Externals want to examine the scene before noon, and we don't know what they'll fuck up. Our best chance to figure out what happened is now, before they show up. So what do you need? Caffeine? Food?"

Typical shifter, thinking food fixed everything. "I need a few days of no magic, or to borrow power from another witch. You can see how that's a problem."

Soren picked up the phone on his desk, said, "Send Kyle in," and hung up.

"No, that's—"

"He's happy to help," Soren said. "And even if he's not, he will do what he's told."

My lip curled, disgust making me unwise as I caught Moriah's gaze. "You asked me before why I would not align. That—right there, what he just said—is why." I shook my head as I concentrated on the desk, unconcerned with the Peacemaker's irritation. He hadn't changed much after all. "To take power from an unwilling witch is crossing the line into dark magic."

No one spoke until the mender, the floppy-haired kid with

big eyes, opened the door, dry-washing his hands as he gazed around the office. "You wanted to see me, sir?"

Bile rose in my throat and I looked away as Soren gestured for the mender to approach the desk. "We need Lily's help but she's too weak. Let her borrow some of your magic."

Kyle recoiled, not looking at me. "Sir, I'm not sure that's a good idea."

"I don't see the problem."

Of course he didn't. The mender stammered and I shook my head, unable to raise my eyes from the floor. "You just told Kyle to let me rape him magically."

Soren's expression soured. "I certainly did not."

I forced myself to sit upright despite the exhaustion, and inclined my head to Kyle. He was just a kid, but his instincts were good. Sharing magic created debts and bonds that could not lightly be put aside. "It was asked and answered, witch. Go your way in peace."

Kyle retreated, relief in every line of his body, but froze as Soren's voice cracked into the silence. "She might be the only way to find the Morrigan and the rest of the First Coven."

The mender paled, glancing between us. The wheels turned in his head, and it was Anne Marie's lucky day that the kid wasn't as power-hungry as she was. His voice shook as much as his hands as he held them out. "Freely offered, summoner. Take what you need."

I shoved to my feet, muscles aching, to face him. "We will be connected, mender, for the rest of your natural life. Are you prepared for the consequences?"

New resolve built in his expression. "If it helps the Morrigan, yes. I knowingly offer my power."

Soren's growing impatience echoed in his fingers, drumming on the desk, but I would not rush. The only witch I'd taken power from was Sam, and part of me feared I might form a similar attachment to this scared kid. Which would be downright embarrassing. He had *cojones*, that was true enough, since he marched into a fight between a war witch and some wolves to hex me, so at least he had the power of convictions in his corner.

I exhaled the trepidation; nothing could be changed until we finished. "You are thrice-named?"

He shook his head and I pinched the bridge of my nose. By his age and demeanor, he'd probably come from human parents, and attended one of those fly-by-night academies before joining the Alliance. I held my hands over his. "Then that is the first thing we will remedy."

His magic waited in a puddle compared to the river of Sam's power. My palms rested on Kyle's and the floodgates opened. He went rigid, making a surprised noise as his eyes widened, and I shut mine so I wouldn't see him as the ecstasy of free magic rolled through me. With Sam, trading power had been better than the best sex.

In the maelstrom of magic, they were Sam's hands I held, Sam's magic I drew like air to breathe. I held on in desperation —I wasn't ready for it to end. I felt so weak and alone, and finally someone else was there to help me stand. And I couldn't lose Sam a second time. Even as the power disappeared and only static remained, I couldn't let go.

From far away, another man—someone else who wanted more from me than I was prepared to give—shouted my name. Something grabbed my wrists, yanked—tried to steal Sam from me again.

I held on, and didn't open my eyes as a different set of hands, large and callused, grasped mine and the static disappeared. Something wild and strange but powerful replaced it.

Powerful.

The wild magic cascaded through me in red sparks and electric snowflakes, building into the sound and scent of an old forest. A wild urge to run and hunt, to chase prey under a new moon, sang in my blood. I dragged at the wild magic, inhaling the unfamiliar strength, and it snapped through me like pure adrenaline. Too much. It was too much.

My heart raced, blood pounding in my ears, as something hungry inside me rejoiced. My skin stretched to contain all that energy, threatening to split apart unless I did something. Anything. Cast or shifted or just broke into a million pieces.

"Stop," I said, the words slurring as I fumbled to free my hands and break the connection. "Too much."

I trembled like a leaf in the wind as I looked up and found Soren with his paws around my wrists. Pack magic roiled up, the wild hunt strangling me with blood and lust and hunger. I flailed at the end of his grip, terrified he might somehow push me to shift as well as his features turned predatory and hair sprouted along his arms. "Moriah. *Help.*"

But she was across the room, supporting the unconscious mender, her face pale as she stared at the Peacemaker and me. Mo dropped the witch as another wave of magic went through Soren and sparked, zinging around until his bones started breaking. She couldn't beat Leif, though, as he threw his shoulder into the Peacemaker and knocked me back to freedom.

Soren and Leif flew across the room, tripping over the mender as Soren snarled and snapped. Moriah dragged me out of the way and propped me up against the wall. "What the hell happened?"

"I don't know." I trembled, dazed from the wild magic. Soren paced, animal gaze fixed on Moriah and me, as Leif tried to corral him near the desk while he talked him back to humanity. The words stuck in my throat as I looked at her. "Why Soren?"

"Kyle froze," she said, grim. "Soren stepped in. I tried to get there first but he beat me."

My heart thundered against my ribs and my hands shook as

I covered my face. I'd never heard of witches using pack magic or even being able to feel it, and I wondered if somehow Soren's wild magic broke something in my head. I couldn't concentrate on anything, and it still felt like my muscles spasmed and popped unpredictably, just sitting there.

Kyle groaned as he rolled to his side. "Did you get enough?"

Shame whittled at my soul. I'd almost killed the kid, draining his magic, and he wanted to make sure I got enough. I nodded. "Yes, and thank you."

I couldn't sit still, not with all the pack magic zipping through me. I got out of the way as Moriah lifted Kyle into a chair and Soren limped back to his desk, mostly human. I glanced at the rumpled Peacemaker, wondering if I looked half as crazy as he did. "That was not pleasant."

"Not pleasant doesn't do it justice," he muttered. "Are you prepared to evaluate the scene at Tracy's house?"

"Maybe." Part of me still didn't want to go, but after taking Kyle's magic, I felt obligated to at least use it for the purpose he'd intended. "Something feels really... off."

"Leif will go with you to the scene."

I glanced between them, searching for some clue to the lingering tension as Leif inclined his head stiffly to the Peace-maker. I picked at my jeans as he made a beeline for the door without a backward glance, though he froze as Soren added, "And for Skoll's sake, get that purple shit off him."

I tried to walk calmly over to Leif, but the wild energy made it a skip despite my best efforts. An echo of pack magic, like what caused so much trouble at the bar, rose up when I reached for his arm, and I hesitated. Neither of us could afford that kind of distraction. I laced my hands together behind my back instead, and looking back at the droopy mender. "Kyle?"

He swayed, half-conscious, as I used our fledgling connection to pull him upright. I urged a little power back to him despite the way he shivered, and nodded at Leif. "It's time you learned something useful."

A little life—and irritation—flooded his expression. "I attended one of the most prestigious—"

"Sure, whatever you say. But knowing *this* makes you invaluable. You're the only other person in the city who knows how to undo this. So pay attention."

He grumbled but focused on Leif, and I fed more power into the hex as the wild magic bubbled in my veins. The muscles in Leif's jaw jumped as the purple glitter covered him from head to toe once more. "You *said*—"

"Oh, calm down. He has to see what he's working with. Keep complaining and I'll leave it like that." I ignored Leif's sour expression as I glanced at Kyle. "Look at the hex. Someone snarled it up quite a bit, but a *good* spell can always be undone. It's only when witches get sloppy or lazy that real damage is done. And cannot be undone."

For a moment I thought of Sam.

"It's really complex." Kyle leaned close and peered at Leif's shoulder while the Warder grumbled about being a "blasted science project."

"That design makes it spread. I could show you a contagious variant, so anyone he touched becomes contaminated."

"Neat," the mender said, nodding eagerly, and Leif pulled away, his eyes dark.

"Damn it, would you *just*—"

"Hush," I said, and absently stroked the back of his forearm. For a giddy heartbeat, my magic tangled with his, cascading through his aura in a swirl of sparks.

I folded my hands together so I wouldn't do it again, and focused on the witch. "Look here, toward the top. Where those two knots are formed, there is a trailing end. Do you see it?"

Leif tensed as I guided the witch's hand. "Right here."

The kid beamed as he twined part of the hex around his

fingers, oblivious to the Warder's grimace. I chewed my lip to keep from laughing at him. "Take the end you have and pull gently to his elbow, no less than ten counts."

Both Leif and Kyle held their breath; the witch even leaned back, as if the hex would transfer when it popped loose. Kyle pulled a face and Leif scowled at both of us as the tension grew, then an audible *crack* caught Soren's attention.

Leif looked down at his glitter-free body, said, "Flippin' miraculous," and stormed out, flinging the door open with such force it slammed shut in my face.

Kyle blinked, dazzled as he studied the fading hex, tangled in his fingers. "Can you show me how to build that?"

"Maybe." I edged toward the door, uncomfortable with the hero-worship in his eyes—between that and the magic sharing, I was in trouble.

# CHAPTER 33

$\mathscr{L}$eif waited at the passenger door of another black SUV outside the mansion. Tracing his path through the halls had not been difficult: he left behind a wake of cowering shifters and air blued with cursing. I eyed him as he jerked the door open, aware of the tension rippling through him but uncertain of the cause.

"Get in," he said.

I hesitated, but did as he said. Leif slammed the door and stalked to the driver's side. I studied his profile as he got in and started the car, waiting until the rumble of the engine concealed our words from outsiders to say, "What's wrong? I got rid of the hex."

"I have no reason to be angry." But he gripped the steering wheel until his knuckles went white, then exhaled and pried his hands free.

As the tension simmered and he pulled out of the long driveway, past a few groups of guards, I debated reaching for the door handle and freedom. I could run or even fly, I had so much nervous energy. I could get to Tracy's house on my own.

My hand twitched closer to the handle once we passed the gates.

Leif didn't seem to notice until a soul-deep sigh made his shoulders slump. "If you run, I'll chase you. I won't be able to stop myself. Please wait."

I leaned back, forcing my hands to relax in my lap. "Okay."

He grimaced and fiddled with the heater controls, warm air blasting into the car, then abruptly swung the car to the side of the road and shoved it into park.

But still the silence stretched, so I took a gamble. "Was it Brandr? Something he said?"

Leif scowled at the distant hint of dawn beyond the city. "I'm not the wolf. I'm not the guy who can't control himself."

"Spit it out, Leif. Help me understand."

"He looked at you and I wanted to kill him. He said he planned to turn you and make you his, and I almost tore his throat out. If Soren hadn't held me back, I would have. He swore that *oath*, and..." Leif growled, nails tearing into the leather-wrapped steering wheel.

He hit the steering wheel and the blare of the horn made me jump. I raised an eyebrow. "Leif, maybe—"

"And he *touched* you. He held onto you, he—" Leif stopped, gathered himself, and took a deep breath, scrubbing his hands over his face. "I have no justification to feel this way, you have given me no indication that you'd welcome these feelings from me. And you're still a suspect, or at least a witness, and this is the kind of unprofessional behavior I'd fire someone for. I just...I ask your tolerance. Sometimes our animal nature is not entirely flexible when it comes to something it wants."

*Something it wants.* He wanted me. At least some part of him did. And admitting such a thing must have cost him a great deal. I nodded as I studied the car's spotless interior. It was insanity to broach the subject as we headed to a house where witches died, but my stomach squirmed in anticipation at the possibility that he might like me. Might really, honestly, like *me*. My voice came out so low I thought he might not even hear it. "What would be an indication?"

Leif stilled, halfway to switching off the heat again. "An indication of what?"

My heart pounded against my ribs and I could hardly breathe. "An indication that I might not be entirely opposed to maybe one day eventually welcoming that. From you."

For a dozen heartbeats he only breathed, hands braced on the steering wheel, then he seized my hands in his, crushing my fingers. "Break into my house and leave something. To mark your territory."

I swallowed a laugh despite the thrum of magic through my muscles, his touch sparking a connection. "You've got to be kidding. The Chief Investigator encouraging me to break more laws?"

"You didn't seem to mind before."

The familiar fog tugged at me, and I pulled free. Succumbing to pack magic while alone in a car with him was not a good idea. We'd never make it to Tracy's. "Okay. But you could just ask me to dinner. That's how people normally do it, I think."

"Maybe." He sported a rather goofy smile as he pulled the car onto the street and navigated through the early morning traffic. He caught my hand as he drove, and it felt natural. Easy.

My thoughts drifted to what we'd face at Tracy's, and I tried to prepare myself by rehearsing useful spells. It had to be done right. For all of them. But the easy slide of his palm and the pressure of his fingers distracted me.

The spells distracted me, or maybe I just dozed off, because the next thing I knew, the SUV rolled to a stop in a middle-class neighborhood and Leif sad, "We're here."

Tracy's house. No Externals lurked outside with ominous

black vans, no crime scene tape marked the door. The house looked normal.

Except for a patch of dead grass shaped like a body, the head and heart singed black. *That* was never a good sign.

He tapped the dash but didn't move, scanning the empty street. "We should get moving, the Externals are probably on their way, or at least watching the place."

I fumbled with my seatbelt. "What?"

He leaned to unlatch it for me, smiling, then walked around to open my door. "They drive by to check on what we're doing. But I'm here, and we have Styrma nearby just in case. Soren is prepared to call the Judge if anything happens. We'll be fine."

I slid out of the SUV, a little flustered to find myself chest-to-chest with him. "Easy for you to say—they don't have a warrant out for your arrest."

He snorted. "They have a bounty on me instead—if they thought they could kill me and get away with it, I'd be a dead wolf with my head over someone's mantle."

I surveyed the surroundings, wondering whose body left the mark on the lawn. I dreaded what waited behind the solid oak door. "This isn't a good idea."

His mouth quirked in a smile as he flipped the car keys around his finger. "What other choice do we have, if we want to figure out what happened? And if you want to clear your name once and for all?"

"You're right." I took a deep breath and forced my feet to move up the driveway to the front porch. "Then let's get this over with."

Leif and I both gagged on the stench of old blood spilled in anger the moment he opened the door. I tried to be thankful no one had cleaned up, since it preserved the distinct signatures of the participants and an echo of their actions. But that didn't make it easy to step inside onto the stained tile and squishy carpet.

Her place wasn't fancy—at least, it hadn't been even before demonspawn redecorated. But it had been a home, and it retained memories of Tracy. I hesitated in the foyer. A few clean patches of carpet revealed the original beige fibers, but the majority of it was black and still with blood. Leif waited, silent, at my elbow as I struggled to breathe.

I dragged my gaze from the gory scene. "The rest of the house?"

He pointed through the living room to an open doorway. "The kitchen...it's not this bad. We found Rosa in the bedroom to the left."

I nodded, rubbing my hands together so I could summon power—more power than I really needed, wrapping it around myself as magical insulation. Smell barely registered, but the lingering magical signatures in the house became a heightened bouquet of old friends and new mysteries. I trod on the stiff but soggy carpet, fingers drifting over a clean end table. "Let's see what we can find, shall we?"

Leif remained near the door, his mouth twisted. "I'll wait here."

"I need you to be a witness." I paused to study Tracy's bookshelf, frowning as I noted a few gaps in the otherwise packed shelves. Perhaps someone stole her books, too. "To remember what happens."

"No one doubts—"

"The testimony of one nonaligned witch is insufficient to convict an aligned witch of any major crime," I said, considering the pristine carpet on the stairs before continuing my tour of the living room. I avoided the path to the bedroom where Rosa died. I wasn't ready to see it yet. "Your testimony is necessary, if there is someone to answer for these crimes."

I peered into the kitchen, wrapping the magic tighter around me so I wouldn't care about the blood on my shoes or a bloody handprint on the wall, like someone tried to drag themselves up but failed.

No defensive wards clung to the walls in the kitchen or anywhere else in the house that I'd found. Whoever caused the mess entered without a fight. Been invited, maybe. Expected and welcomed. Part of the coven.

"What do you expect to find?"

"Salt," I said. "I need salt to clean up."

"Lily," he said, exasperation making his voice rough. "An entire crew couldn't—"

"Not the blood," I said, shivering as my name rippled through what remained of the spells. "The magic. It's dangerous to leave it like this."

I climbed on the counter and began searching the tops of the cupboards. My shoes slid, slick with blood on the stained granite, but Leif stood behind me to catch me if I fell. I sidestepped down the counter, and came up empty at the end of it. Dishes, spices, a few cans of soup—but no salt. I studied the neat breakfast nook and cafe table, the baker's shelf with copper pots and pans, and braced my hands on my hips as I balanced. Nothing out of place, but nothing where I expected.

Leif stepped back to look up at me. "What do you need?"

I needed my life back. I needed to get away from that house, and those memories. I needed the Externals and Eric to disappear forever. I needed Rosa and Joanne back, and Anne Marie gone. "Sea salt. She has to have a bag around here somewhere."

His head tilted back and he breathed in, mouth open to taste the air, and I arched an eyebrow—smelling anything through the reek of blood and death was quite a trick. But he held out his hand and said, "Hop down," then led me to the far end of the kitchen. He didn't release my hand, and our fingers laced together easily. Naturally.

Soren's pack magic surged through the duller layer of Kyle's, reaching out when it felt the connection to Leif. I braced for the inevitable fog of lust. But instead of reacting, Leif dropped my hand.

His shoulders tensed as he stared at a framed painting of the sea hanging on the wall. "You feel like Soren. Like you're his."

"So it was not just about Brandr, hmm?"

Leif stared at the wall as if he could set it on fire with his eyes alone. "I tried to take Kyle's place when the witch fell. But I cannot defy Soren, so he helped you."

I made a thoughtful noise as magic shimmered across the wall. Leif gestured at the painting, ignoring the issue of Soren's interference and the fact that his magic marked me. "It smells like salt over here."

I lifted the painting down to examine the wall, running my fingers over the stiff paper and probing what turned out to be elaborate wards, and I sighed. "But if it had been you, Leif, would either of us have survived? We don't have the best track record under magical influence, you and I."

"I never said this was logical."

My touch triggered the ward and it started glowing. It was well-done, a sophisticated thing. I would not have noticed it without Leif's nose. Tracy had gotten a lot better.

I took a deep breath, glancing over at Leif as I pressed my left hand into the ward. "You didn't see me do this."

A tingle built as the ward resisted for five heartbeats, then ten, and the fizz in my fingers built into a burn. Leif's expectant expression faded. "What's supposed to—"

The pressure wave of the breaking ward knocked him into the table, collapsing it into a pile of kindling, and the released power rolled through me as a sneeze built in my nose. The cleaner magic from Tracy's spell boosted what remained of Kyle's magic, and felt almost refreshing after the cloying darkness of the spells in the living room.

Leif clambered to his feet, brushing himself off, as I studied the wall. A small recessed panel hid behind the ward; I stroked the edge until a latch caught. The panel slid back to reveal a cupboard about a foot deep and two feet high. I retrieved a cheesecloth sack of sea salt, handing it to Leif so I could poke through the rest of what hid in the cupboard.

More than just salt and sage and copper spoons and parchment, more than ink and talcum and all the normal trappings that the experienced witch needed. I stepped back and put my hands in my pockets, as Mother always made me do when I was tempted to touch something I shouldn't.

I felt like a naughty kid all over again, even if I wasn't the one keeping secrets in my wall.

Leif leaned around me to peer into the recess. "What's in there?"

"Some things I did not expect," I said under my breath, not taking my eyes off the cupboards. Sometimes things disappeared if you looked away from them. "We need a bag."

"A bag?" Leif retrieved a large canvas tote from the pantry. One of her grocery bags, most likely—it had *Recycle* printed on the side in cheerful rainbow letters.

He held it out so I could transfer the contents out of the wall and into the bag, holding my breath as I took a mental inventory. A glass jar of grave-dirt. Half a dozen finger bones. Three ivory combs. Several rocks—smooth volcanic glass, rosered sandstone, crystals, a piece of meteor. Three circular mirrors, set in tarnished silver, made Leif's hands recoil as I set them in the bag, until I tucked a cloud of aged white fabric—a christening gown—around them.

"What the hell is that?"

The christening gown's removal revealed a deeper shelf with three books. I paused as I peered at them. Dark leather bindings, stiff with age and hate, titles stenciled on with talcum and sealed with minor wards. "You remember what kind of magic I said I did?"

"All of it," he said. "Black, white, gray."

I reached for one of the books, keeping my voice low so I wouldn't disturb the spirits of the grimoires. "This is where the road turns gray."

The second book was heavy with knowledge, but it was only a copy of the real book, which sat in my parents' house. I handled the third book with more caution: it was a darker book, an original primer for dark witches from before the Inquisition. I couldn't judge Tracy for owning it, since my own shelves held far worse.

I wiped my hands on a towel as I closed the cupboard up again, and Leif held the bag at arm's length as he grimaced. "This is not good stuff. Fenrir protect us."

"It depends on how you use it." There were certainly legitimate reasons for owning those things, or so I tried to convince myself. The fingerbones were a bit odd. But knowing your enemy, as I'd so often said, meant knowing your enemy's capabilities and weapons. "But we should cover it with something innocuous."

He pulled open a couple of drawers until he found some dish towels to stuff on top of the books, hiding even the delicate, yellowed lace of the christening gown. Leif frowned at the doorway. "Is it possible the coven did this to themselves, by accident?"

I very much doubted it. But I hefted the bag of sea salt and strode past him to the living room. "Only one way to find out."

"Find out what?"

I tripped in the doorway as Stefan, bundled up in a dark trench coat, raised an imperious eyebrow. A smirk made him even uglier. "Bureau of External Affairs, witch. You're under arrest for compromising a crime scene, resisting arrest, and interfering in an official investigation. Release the magic immediately or I will shoot you."

I believed him, despite the dubious protection of the lapis

ring on my necklace, and I believed the gun aimed at my chest despite the way his hand trembled. A low growl from the kitchen told me the Warder believed him, too.

# CHAPTER 34

$\mathcal{L}$eif shoved the recycle bag at me as he pushed between me and the External, so at least the bullets had to go through him before they killed me. "Stefan. Normally I'd be surprised to find you lurking in a bloody room, but this is becoming a habit of yours."

The External didn't lower his weapon, but instead shuffled to the side to try and get a better shot at me. My heart beat faster in anticipation, and I tried not to let the wild magic take over as Stefan's eyes narrowed. "The witch is violating at least four laws as we speak, and she is wanted for questioning related to two murders, the use of dark magic, and a handful of other crimes. As you well know. So perhaps I ought to call the Judge. He would want to know the Alliance is harboring felons."

"Nice try," Leif said. He took a step, his posture more aggressive than I expected. "Soren requested the witch's assistance with this crime scene."

"She is a *suspect* in this crime!" Stefan gripped the pistol harder, knuckles white.

"Threaten her, and you threaten the Alpha."

"She's a criminal." The External shook his head. "We've worked together for several years, Leif. I am disappointed that you'd choose some *female* over the work we've done to make this city safer for humans and Others alike."

My heart sank. He sounded sincerely disappointed, something almost like betrayal in his eyes. Like somehow the brotherhood of law enforcement would supersede Leif's loyalty to the Alliance. Maybe it did. Maybe he doubted.

"Why are you here, Stefan? The Alliance still owns this crime scene. We need to check a few more things, then we can arrange for your investigators to have access." Leif's shoulders flexed and his hands clenched into fists.

The whole time, the canvas bag weighed heavier and heavier in my arms with the weight of the grimoires and fingerbones and all the other dark stuff. I shifted my feet, prepared to run or hex if things went sideways.

Leif's arm swung out to keep me behind him as Stefan tensed, and the Warder tapped a small metallic device affixed to his belt. A small light flashed on it, and I frowned more as I pondered its meaning. It definitely wasn't magic.

Stefan adjusted his grip on the weapon as his arm started to droop. "We received an anonymous tip about some dark magic here. The Bureau will investigate any allegations of that kind without hesitation. And here we are, a dark witch on the premises."

"Why didn't you alert my office that a tip of that nature was submitted? You're in no position to investigate magical leads." Leif folded his arms over his chest, a hint of a growl starting in his chest.

"The tip indicated the Alliance might be complicit in the activities here," Stefan said. "You can imagine our concern with alerting you to our suspicions."

"Yet you just did, and I'm not in any mood to listen to that bullshit." Leif shook his head and pointed at the door. "Get out,

Stefan. The Bureau is no longer going to have access to this crime scene based on your continuous lack of disclosure and openness. Soren will take this up with the Judge."

"I'm not leaving without that witch in chains." The External's lips thinned as he stared at me, sweat breaking out on his forehead as his eyes flashed with some kind of murderous zeal. "And you have to declare when you use nonaligned witches for official business, so it seems we are both remiss."

"Go write up the complaint. Standard Form 76A, if I remember correctly. But get the fuck out of my crime scene." All semblance of professional courtesy evaporated as Leif advanced another step.

Stefan retreated, though his weapon swung to aim at Leif instead of me. Which was an even bigger mistake than threatening me. The Warder growled more, his muscles tensing, and some dark hair sprouted along the backs of his arms.

"She's coming with me," Stefan said. His tone remained utterly convinced of his own rightness. "She's nonaligned and guilty of murder, and she's holding magic, threatening me, and—"

"She's holding magic because I instructed her to," Leif said. "I can't stand the smell. If you want to try and arrest her, come back with a full team."

"The Bureau is requiring all nonaligned witches to register in order to protect them—"

"The Alpha extended his protection to all nonaligned witches until this issue with disappearances is resolved. I would be surprised if any witches reached out to the Bureau for your...hospitality."

Stefan's expression hardened. "You son of a bitch."

Not such a damning insult with the wolves, really. My head tilted as I calculated the possible repercussions if I just hexed Stefan, maybe killed him. It would be easy enough—I already held more than enough magic, and the hex to stop his heart waited on the tip of my tongue. I doubted Leif would turn me in, but bodies—particularly human ones—were difficult to get rid of quietly.

I kept my war witch face impassive as Dad murmured in my memory, *Never let them see you sweat, kiddo*. I glared at Stefan as I eased around Leif's side, no longer so worried about the weapon the External carried. A ward would be an easy thing as well, to at least slow the bullets. They didn't know we could do that. Seeing the look on his face might have been worth revealing the trick.

Stefan's cold gaze landed on me as he reached a stalemate with the Warder. "Got something to say, witch? Cat got your tongue?" His gaze slid to Leif, and the External's expression turned ugly. "Or should that be wolf?"

That was it. I dropped the bag and brought my hands up, a hex already forming as I shoved past Leif and covered us both behind a ward. I knew the magic might disturb what remained from the night the witches were attacked, but I'd had enough of Stefan's accusations and lies. The moment I approached him, magical alarms went off and he stumbled back, swinging the gun as he squeezed the trigger once, twice, three times.

Even behind the wards, it was deafening. Leif roared and grabbed me around the waist, but I didn't budge. I winged Stefan as Leif threw off my aim and the External fired more, and I gritted my teeth as magical shrapnel threatened to destroy the scene.

The front door swung open and a semi-familiar figure skidded into the house, pulling a face as they stepped on the sticky carpet. I recognized the oil rainbow aura and the blurry face as Eric held her hands up, still wearing her male face, and shouted over the gunfire. "What the hell is going on?"

She didn't seem even moderately concerned that Stefan felt threatened enough to shoot at us, which appeared to piss him off even more. I kept the ward up but stopped trying to kill him.

"He entered the house unannounced and surprised us, then threatened us. I defended us."

Leif snarled and once more pushed me behind him, looming larger as he faced two Externals instead of one. "I have a reaction team on the way. One more move and you're both dead, understood?"

Eric fidgeted with the collar of her trench coat, grimacing as she looked around, then her gaze slid to Leif and a hungry smile spread across her real face. The fake face betrayed only polite surprise as she nodded to him. "Let's try to sort this out without anyone going to the hospital."

Leif's knuckles cracked as he clenched his fists more. "Get out. File whatever complaints you want. We have work to do and you're impeding our investigations."

The scent of blood and death wouldn't help Leif's control over the beast. Any extra bloodshed would definitely change what we could learn from the spell over the coven's demise, but... A berserk rampage to kill both Externals would solve a couple of my more pressing personal problems.

"Sure, sure." Eric tapped her chin. "We can assist with the investigation, if—"

"We're not here to investigate," Leif said. "The Alliance is focused right now on giving our dead a proper pyre."

Lies, all of it, but with the way Stefan still glared at me, I didn't mind. I should have killed him. Leaving him alive just meant another threat in the night, waiting for vengeance.

Eric offered a tight, conciliatory smile as she retreated. "Then we leave you to your work, with my sincere condolences."

Stefan didn't budge, his teeth practically cracking as he clenched his jaw. His hand shook with the weapon, and he started to move it just as what seemed like an entire hockey team of chaos rolled through the front door.

Leif's Styrma, a little late to the party as usual.

The stormtroopers spread out around the perimeter of the room, weapons and attention trained on Stefan—who at least knew when he was outnumbered and mostly beaten. He uncocked the pistol and shoved it into his holster under the wary gaze of the Styrma. "This isn't over, wolf."

"Bet your ass." Leif's teeth flashed white and even in another threat.

Stefan grudgingly stomped through the scene, ignoring the bloody mess, and shoved past Eric on his way out the door. Eric nodded to everyone and turned, about to follow his colleague, but Leif cleared his throat. "Agent."

"It's Agent Smith. Eric Smith." Her pudgy fake face barely blinked.

Leif eased closer, a hint of a predator in his posture. "Have we met?"

"I was there at the bar, but we weren't formally introduced. I don't believe we've worked together."

The Warder shook his head. "It's something else. You're... familiar."

My throat closed as panic set in. Could shifters recognize loki?

Eric shrugged, still a slightly dumb semblance of a cop. "Well, I hope we can work together in the future."

"Maybe." Leif didn't sound particularly hopeful. "And a word of advice. If Stefan tries to detain any witches—aligned or not—they will have approval from Soren to defend themselves with any means necessary. Unofficially, of course."

"Of course." Eric nodded once more, then disappeared out the door.

Leif grunted, uninterested in her departure, then faced me. He studied his hands. "Do you know him, Lily?"

"Why would you think that?"

"Just curious. You know him?"

I shook my head, cognizant of all the stormtroopers

watching us, and released the wards so I could retrieve the recycle bag with all the dark shit and move it out of the way. "No, I've never met him."

It was only a small lie. A very small lie.

# CHAPTER 35

Once the Styrma at the door confirmed the Externals departed, Leif looked at me. "Now what?"

"Now's the exciting stuff." I handed him the tote bag and studied the room's layout. Sustaining a large circle would be dicey with borrowed magic, but there was no telling where the battle started and ended.

Leif and the stormtroopers watched as I paced a slow circle through the room. "What are you doing?"

I concentrated on weaving my intent for our safety and the purpose of the spell into each step, and shooed one of the younger shifters out of the circle before I completed the first circuit. After I'd finished the third and locked in the ward, I paused near the front door. "I set the circle to contain the spell. No one break it."

"Or what?"

I didn't bother to look at Jake; he was the only one impertinent enough to question a war witch. "Or you'll die a horrible death and ruin any chance we have of finding out who killed the witches."

Leif cleared his throat as I gathered more power in a steady build, letting the remnants of Kyle's magic and the wild pack magic smooth and disperse into the spell. "What exactly are you going to do, Lily, to figure out who did what?"

I winced, pausing until I cleared the sound of my name from my mind. "No names until I say so," I said, and squinted at the bloody living room. Even through the cold unconcern of magic, I hesitated to invoke the spell. I didn't want to see any more friends die.

Static crackled in my veins as the magic seethed. "I'm going to see if the house will show what happened."

"But it's...a house." The Warder peered at the bloody mess of the carpet, then around at the ceiling and walls. "It's not sentient. It doesn't have memory."

Maybe I was a coward. I should have invoked the spell and let them see what I meant, but I welcomed the delay. "The ancient Maya believed consecrated ground absorbed the energy of the faithful, stored it, and built upon it. This house had a coven working in it for years, casting powerful spells, convening as friends. Those connections are powerful magic. The house absorbed that."

"And this helps us?"

"We should see the replay of everything that happened that night—if I get the spell right and have enough magic to sustain it to the end."

"And if you get it wrong?" Jake, the cheeky bastard, had stalked closer, eyes dark with anticipation as he prowled.

I waved my hands to distribute the magic into a dome over the living room, invisible until I squinted and everything faded except the blue-silver sheen. "You all die horrible deaths. I'll be fine."

It wasn't entirely true, regardless of what I hoped. They'd die in the backlash of the magic, or the magical overload would force them into uncontrolled shifts and they'd go mad in wolf form. The magic would destroy the crime scene, and the wolves would do the rest. And odds were I would be too weak to defend myself against rampaging werewolves. So it would be a horrible death for me as well.

At least it wasn't dark.

"No more talking." I held up my hands for silence and waited until they all nodded and Jake even mimed zipping his lips, then I pressed my right hand into the dome as I invoked the spell.

It didn't require a fancy Latin poem or dramatic gestures. A powerful witch could invoke spells by intent alone. All I needed was power and the desired outcome, and the spell unfurled. In comparison, Anne Marie looked like no more than a crude illusionist.

The air inside the dome sparked as lightning zinged within the circle. Ghostly figures appeared and I manipulated the spell through time until Tracy stood frozen in mid-step, an eerie avatar with a question on her face.

I shifted my feet, though I kept my hands steady for fear of losing the connection. "When I release this, the evening will unfold. I don't have the power to do it over, so pay attention. Bear witness. And by all the saints, don't break the circle."

Silence answered. I took that as acquiescence and released the spell. The image wavered and I held my breath, then Tracy completed her step and moved through the living room. Sounds filtered to us, as tinny as the pre-Breaking records my parents loved.

The Styrma jumped at a faint knocking, looking around to see whether any more Externals dared interrupt us. I sucked in a deep breath as Tracy headed for the door and walked into where I stood, disappearing out of view of the dome of magic. Leif, next to me, tripped over the tote bag as he dodged out of the way, but I remained rooted to the spot. My heart flinched at the cool breeze of a ghost's passing.

I pushed any thoughts of ghosts away as Tracy reappeared,

and the rest of the coven, except for Anne Marie, followed her into the living room. They dispersed throughout the house, comfortable enough in her space to meander into the kitchen for drinks or down the hall to the bathroom. For a moment the easy comfort of a coven—even a dysfunctional one—lured me in and sparked jealousy in my stomach. I missed that, maybe more than I knew.

I shook myself out of the reverie and cleared my throat. "Warder, please name the participants."

"Names or nicknames?" At least he remembered that much.

"Names are okay. Except for...the dead. Do not name them." We didn't need to summon them back as ghosts, not so soon after their passing. As much as I loved and missed Joanne and Rosa, I didn't want them tied to Tracy's home for eternity, unable to find their own rest.

His rough voice drowned out the banal small talk of the witches. "Tracy, in red. Beside her, Betty in the skirt and Lauren in the green sweater. Andre by the television, and Jacques near the window. And—one more I don't know. The woman who came out of the back room."

The magic trembled when he said Andre's name, and my heart sank. He had also passed, then. His body was the one yet to be identified. My stomach turned over to think of what had happened that the Alliance couldn't identify him. I sucked back the grief and focused on the mystery woman.

"Desiree," I breathed, and the image hiccupped.

Another ghostly knock drew Tracy to the door, through me, and Jake blanched as he retreated another step. "Creepy."

The Warder stepped back as the Morrigan entered the circle. "Her too?"

"No," I said, a vindictive anger goading me to flick Anne Marie's ear one more time. My lip curled as Desiree and Jacques fawned over Anne Marie and the warding box she carried. I used the language she spoke in her youth, a guttural

Quebecois dialect. "Anne Anastasia Annette Marie de Sousse. *La sorciere.*"

Static overrode the image and darkness collapsed the dome as thunder rolled from the center and out. Anne Marie stood alone in the living room, her figure frozen as the rest of the ghosts wisped away.

The darkness dissipated until the witches came back into focus, and the coven once more filled the living room. Leif cleared his throat. "What the hell was that?"

"Just wanted to wake her up a bit," I said. "In case she was sleeping."

"That was immature," Leif muttered, though something like a smile quirked the corner of his mouth.

Jake, however, eyed me with reproach. "You could wake the dead like that."

"No," I said, not looking at him as Anne Marie gathered the witches in a half-circle. "That requires a spell with a little more... oomph."

Anne Marie raised her hands to the witches. "I'm glad you all could make it."

A frown twisted Joanne's kewpie doll mouth. "The Externals are everywhere, Anne Marie. I don't think this—"

"I have my reasons," Anne Marie said, hands resting on the warding box. "Something went badly wrong on Tuesday. I reviewed the spells and went back to the Skein, and I found something disturbing."

I bit my lip. This could get a little awkward.

Tracy hovered at the edge of the group, almost outside my spell. "You went back? Alone?"

"Yes." Anne Marie's mouth thinned in irritation. "Before I went to the Skein, someone showed up at my store. Turns out she was the same witch who mucked with our work."

Saints protect me.

One of the younger witches I didn't know—maybe Betty—gaped at the Morrigan. "Another witch?"

She was young, immature; I would not have had the patience to keep her in my cover even if she were powerful enough, but Anne Marie had a great deal of tolerance for lemmings. She would ruin Kyle, but this vapid little wretch would probably inherit an impressive career.

Anne Marie nodded. "One of our... colleagues from the war interfered. Lilith. Lily, as she is known now."

I held my breath as Leif's scrutiny hit me like a ton of bricks. We hadn't talked about that part of the week. I refused to look at him; those questions could wait.

Tracy leaned over the back of the love seat, between Andre and Rosa. "Lily went to the Skein?"

"And she knew we'd cast there. Someone in this room told her, because no one outside the coven knew we were working that night. Not even Soren."

The audible gulp from the coven—and Jake—would have been comical were it not for the gravity of the transgression. I shook my head. Nice, Anne Marie. Summoning an Ancient without informing the Peacemaker. And he wanted to arrest *me*.

Silence stretched in the room, growing weighty with tension even though we all knew how the night ended. I wanted to yell at Anne Marie to get on with it so I could get started finding Tracy and whoever else survived. But I could only wait and hope she didn't spill too many of my secrets.

The young witch tugged on her ponytail. "Why did she go to your store?"

Anne Marie paused for dramatic effect before taking a deep breath. "To attack me."

More disbelief from the witches in the coven, and Jake's hard gaze joined Leif's on me. I snorted and shook my head.

Ridiculous. I'd gone there to help her. She was just too hateful to hear it.

Tracy shook her head. "Come on, Anne Marie. Lily doesn't like you, but she would never just attack you. It's been years. Why waste the time and energy?"

"Are you suggesting I provoked her?" the older witch asked.

She met Anne Marie's gaze unflinchingly. "We knew you both during the war, and you two together are like matches and kerosene. Bad news."

"That's true," Joanne said, perched on the arm of the love seat next to Rosa. My chest tightened to hear her voice. "Come on—you really expect us to believe Lilith just walked into your store and attacked you? She's way sneakier than that. If she wanted you gone, she wouldn't just start swinging."

The Morrigan's mouth twisted. "She's desperate and unhinged, saying she's still...responsible for the covenant with the Peacemaker. That she's protecting the witches from something else going on."

"She's not desperate," Tracy said, shaking her head. "And she's no more unhinged than she was eight years ago, when you two were friends."

"How would you know, Tracy?"

"Because I spoke with her yesterday," Tracy said, no hint of remorse in her tone. "Before the circle. I asked her to help."

"Traitor," Jacques breathed, lurching to his feet as his fists balled at his sides.

I held my breath. Anne Marie folded her arms over her chest with an air of grim triumph. "I knew it. I knew you told her about the Skein and our project. What did you ask her for that you couldn't get from us? Something dark? Or just gray, as she was always so fond of saying?"

The weight of the shifters' gazes dragged at me, and I hoped they waited to attack me until after I'd seen enough to find Tracy.

Rosa stood. "That's not fair, Anne Marie, and you know it. We all edged into gray magic when we had to. All of us—even you. It was just easier for Lilith."

Anne Marie and Tracy ignored her, focused on each other like prize fighters. I doubted they even heard Rosa.

"I asked her to join the circle."

Anne Marie's ghostly face drained of color, and she drew herself up. "You *what?*"

"I invited her back to the coven." Tracy's defiance surrounded her like armor. "I'd much rather have a proven war witch standing beside me for the shit you've got planned than some random charmer Jacques picked up in the street. Even you have to admit Lilith is more powerful alone than most of us combined. I asked you to think of what was best for the coven, but no—you were too stubborn and jealous to ask her, and for something as dangerous as summoning a rogue Ancient."

Deeply-inhaled breath all around stole air, and Leif took a step back. I raised an eyebrow—a rogue Ancient was dangerous business even with a well-trained coven, far more so than the average Ancient, if there was such a thing.

"She's not welcome. You *know* that," Anne Marie snapped. "She's unpredictable and cruel and a saints-damned demon junkie."

"No, she isn't, AM," Rosa said, a frown wrinkling her forehead.

"Don't *call* me that." Anne Marie ran a hand through her hair, wild-eyed as she looked around—her new witches stunned into silence, and the old witches verging on mutiny.

It warmed my heart a little, even through the magic, to see her suffer.

Anne Marie gathered herself, took some cleansing breaths, and held up a hand to cut off whatever Joanne was about to say. "Tracy, we'll discuss your questionable decisions later. For now —she was at the Skein, she interfered with our spell and cast a serious spell of her own, then showed up at my store and blew apart my wards."

Joanne fumed at being shushed, dark eyes flashing, and Rosa patted her knee as she asked, "But what did Lilith cast? While we were there?"

"Someone cast a redirection without our spell," Jacques said, nose in the air. "And if she was the only rogue signature, obviously Lilith did it."

"Don't be an idiot," Joanne said, studying her inch-long nails. She sounded bored with the entire argument, and over the coven meeting. She probably had a date or three lined up. "The extra cast could have come from inside the circle."

Anne Marie nodded reluctantly, even as Tracy leaned to flick Joanne's ear. "Don't be ridiculous, Jojo."

Joanne tossed her dark hair over her shoulder to frown at the other witch. "Cut it out, you know I just got that pierced. And one of us could have cast within the circle and redirected the spell. We didn't see the outcome we wanted, maybe it happened at the Skein. It would have taken a hell of a lot of control, so we know Jacques didn't do it, but it could have been done by one of us."

Anne Marie shook her head, waving her hands to dismiss any other argument. "It had to be Lilith. It *was* Lilith, hiding in the woods while we cast."

"But why?" Andre sat forward, weather-beaten face wrinkled further in a frown. He came from a family of fishermen; I'd always imagined the craggy skin and rich voice were inherited, that he'd been born with crow's feet and a deep tan. "She's got her own life, what does she care what we do? And what, exactly, did she cast?"

"It was a redirection, attempting to Call something else instead of the Ancient." Anne Marie bit off each word as if it had wronged her. "Which is too dangerous to leave there—we need to go back, do a regressive cast to reconstruct what happened, and we'll see what she summoned instead of the Ancient."

I winced; I never would have admitted such a failure to a coven I led. Anne Marie revealed she hadn't known what happened as it happened, and still didn't understand the point of the spell cast within hers. She showed the same weakness she would have exploited were she on the other side. Losing her touch, as well as her control.

Tracy shook her head. "No way. It's too dangerous. There are Externals all over the city arresting people, and witches are disappearing. And you haven't told Soren. If the Styrma catch wind of this, we'll all end up in the Reserve. We should wait at least a day or two."

"We go tonight," Anne Marie said.

Tracy got up and started pacing the perimeter. "We're going to get arrested or killed by the Externals, and Soren won't protect us. The dogs are already trying to consolidate power and knock us down further. Don't give him more justification to dismantle the coven and send us all into exile. You're going to get us killed."

It was my turn to frown at Leif, who just shook his head.

But Anne Marie's gaze chilled as she watched Tracy, and a familiar cruelty surfaced as she sensed a challenge to her power. "We go tonight. Deal with it, witch, or get out."

Tracy's eyes narrowed as she glared at the Morrigan, and I held my breath. Maybe this was where it started. Maybe Anne Marie really caused the disaster and got my friends killed. I clenched my fists and leaned forward, hatred making the magic strengthen.

# CHAPTER 36

Tracy had never been easily intimidated, and a hint of magic gathered around her. Her mouth twisted in an ugly grimace as she made another full circuit of the room and kept going. "This is my house, AM. I'm not leaving."

"I meant out of the coven."

The witches stilled. I stepped closer still, holding my breath as Tracy's eyes narrowed and she gathered herself. Her voice remained deceptively quiet as she folded her arms over her chest and her lip curled in disgust. "Good luck explaining to Soren how you lost yet another war witch. Tell them why you can't keep anyone in the First Coven, how you're driving away everyone with experience. How your mismanagement is destroying the aligned witches. You haven't even bothered to look for Cara and Danielle, or talk to the Warder about how to protect the rest of us from being targeted by the Externals. Go ahead and explain that, *witch*, when the rest of us break off and form our own coven. Good luck."

My attention zeroed in on Anne Marie's trembling fingers as she patted her hair. She put her hair behind her back and I tensed: an aggressive move, for a witch. She was scared.

But she pretended haughty indifference, taking refuge in her pride. "Your call, witch. Abandon this coven and your colleagues, just like Lilith did. Take your bullshit threats and walk away. No one else is going with you."

Tracy looked at the others, but Rosa and Joanne didn't meet her gaze. No one else moved, waiting for the storm to pass, and Tracy's face flushed. Clearly she'd been expecting overwhelming support from the older witches, and when none came, Anne Marie started to look triumphant.

The Morrigan raised an eyebrow, suddenly cocksure. "Or you can cast with us tonight, finish our business, and make your decision tomorrow."

Eternity ticked by, one heartbeat at a time, as Tracy stared down Anne Marie. Her face grew redder and redder with each passing moment. I bit my lip—I remembered that expression. Tracy was one snide comment from going straight berserk.

Rosa recognized it, too, as Tracy paced the room like a caged tiger, about to strike. "Come on, Tracy. Let's just do the cast while it's still viable, and find out who screwed up. If it was one of us, well... You remember how that story ends. Stick around until we know more, then we can go get dessert and talk about the rest of this stuff."

Joanne smiled with false cheer, showing all of her teeth as she smacked Tracy's hip. "Look on the bright side—Jacques probably fucked up again and put all of us on the Externals' radar. We can burn him at the stake for betraying the coven through stupidity."

The male witch hopped to his feet. "You *bitch*—"

He silenced as Joanna stood and held her right hand out, magic flaring, and Anne Marie shouted for all of them to stop fucking around and get it together before they ran out of time.

Tracy's grim expression and the fury on Joanne's face didn't bode well for Anne Marie's plans. But the Morrigan was nothing if not overconfident in her power and ability to get the unruly coven to follow orders. She didn't know Tracy well enough. "So what's your choice, witch? We're wasting time."

Tracy surveyed the room, gaze sliding over the witches as she measured her options. After a long pause, she turned back to Anne Marie, her face curiously blank. "Fine. I'll stand in your circle for this farce, but we'll have a long talk tomorrow."

The way she said "talk" made it sound like "fight" instead.

"Count on it," Anne Marie said, then pointed at the door and right at me. "Let's go."

The coven got to their feet, though Tracy cleared her throat. "We should start here. So there's less time for the Externals to catch up. Or Soren, for that matter—unless he's in on that one?"

Anne Marie ignored the last jab, clearly over the whole argument and just wanting to be done with the cast as soon as possible. "Fine. We set up here."

She stroked the top of the warding box, disabling the magic, and lifted a book bound in old, cracked calfskin out of the recess. My nose twitched as I peered at it; I hadn't seen that one before. Maybe I'd stolen the wrong book.

Anne Marie flipped pages as the coven formed a circle around Tracy's furniture. They gathered power, weaving their individual magic into a fiery mass, more powerful than the sum of its parts. It was familiar enough to me, but the shifters stared, slack-jawed, at the inner workings of coven magic. They were not supposed to see how the coven worked, but in the long list of rules I'd broken, this was a minor one. The saints would forgive me.

Anne Marie walked a circle with her book, muttering— another of her bad habits. As she drew the coven magic in her wake like spidery blue and gold webs, I squinted to study the spell. Regressions were tough casts to initiate and maintain, and... I stepped forward, as if to warn her, as another circle flared to life, set outside her circle and intersecting with mine.

Something held me back. I concentrated on the construction, the signature in the ward. Tracy. Tracy set a circle? I stared at her image, my stomach knotting. If she didn't trust Anne Marie, maybe Tracy meant to protect herself and the coven. I might have done the same, regardless of the risks.

I tensed as Anne Marie hesitated, then fumbled through another manipulation of the spell. She hadn't done a regression in a while, it seemed. She should have prepared more, should have studied as long as it took to memorize the spell, so she wasn't lost in a book when things started going wrong.

Desiree's magic flashed, brighter than the rest, and upset the delicate balance. Tracy scowled at the younger witch. "Control yourself."

"That wasn't me," the girl snapped, her strained expression betraying the effort of maintaining her part in the powerful circle.

"Shut up and focus." Anne Marie finished her circle and glanced once more at her book before intoning the rest of the spell. Apparently she still needed the pretty Latin poems.

A low buzzing made me twitch, brushing my ear. It grew louder, more insistent. I glanced over at Leif. "Do you hear that?"

"Just chanting," he said. "Do you need to stop? What is it?"

"No." If I stopped—*when* I stopped—I would collapse and not move for days. I shook my head, straining to hear Anne Marie's clumsy repetitions over the obnoxious sound. "I don't know what it is."

The buzzing intensified and Rosa tossed her head as if a mosquito whined in her ear. My heart sank. Good for me, bad for them. It reminded me, suddenly, of the interference when demon magic interacted with witch magic. I drew breath to warn her, tell her to run. Break the circle and save herself before it got worse.

"No," I whispered, but it wasn't enough. They couldn't hear me.

It began quietly, as those things usually did. Like watching a car crash from afar—in slow motion, unable to help, unable to warn them of the impending disaster. But I couldn't look away, even as my heart broke.

The magic surged in Anne Marie's spell and again Desiree's magic spiked. A halo flared behind her; I focused on it but it was gone too quickly to identify.

Andre frowned as he said, "What the hell—" as a sunspot flickered to life in the center of the living room.

Betty wavered, her voice thin. "Anne Marie?"

The circle convulsed as the name unbalanced the delicate magic ballet, and the sunspot shivered. "No," I said, repeating it again and again as the ripple spread, and I took a step forward.

If I could just—

Something yanked me back. I put my hands over my mouth, wanting to run. Saints shelter them. Saints and stars above, bless and keep them. I rocked back and forth, unable to look away as I hoped—I prayed—they felt no pain.

The sunspot grew as it rotated, creating coronas of light flaring from the center. Anne Marie should have recognized the danger and ended it. She could have saved everyone. But she just stood there, peering at her stupid book.

"Stop it," I said, panic building into fury until I stomped my foot. "Damn it, they can't—that's a *demon*. Break the circle, Anne Marie."

My spell shivered at the name, but Anne Marie didn't do anything. She just focused on her book as the coven fell apart.

"Who's doing that?" Rosa demanded, rubbing her ear. Her magic vibrated green and soothing—she was a natural healer, a mender who brought together oceans of magic. *She* would have healed my collarbone with a wink and a lollipop. "TT, is that you?"

"No," Tracy said. "Jojo?"

"Not me," Joanne said. The dead witch gritted her teeth with the effort of keeping the spell from shattering. "But that looks like a... Hey AM? We should probably—"

The buzzing exploded into a shriek and Rosa clapped her hands over her ears. The sunspot coalesced in a blinding white flash and with a *pop!* turned itself inside out.

In its place was a form of pure darkness. Malevolence incarnate.

Demon.

Jacques cursed and blasted power at the thing. His panic echoed in the shifters around me as the demon swirled into something resembling a half-snake, half-cat. It fed on his desperation, absorbing his magic easily. It had been too long since they practiced fighting demons, and it showed. I wanted to shut my eyes as the demon launched at the wide-eyed Lauren.

*Turn away.* I couldn't look away. I couldn't even cover my ears to block the sound of their panic. If I didn't see it, maybe it wouldn't be real.

Rosa sucked in power and knocked the younger witch out of the way. Lauren stumbled back, safe, but the demon wasn't picky. It bit Rosa instead.

She screamed.

I pressed my lips together as the first spray of blood coated the ghostly furniture.

Rosa flailed and hexed, battling as a true war witch did even when she was down and hurt and a demon clawed her guts. The demon turned for Betty, and Rosa caught it, dragging it back. It turned her green, healing magic into daggers.

Anne Marie startled out of her trance and clapped her hands together, dropping the book as she tried to regain control of the circle. "What the—"

Joanne shoved Betty out of her way and flung a staying

ward at the demon to keep it from hurting anyone else. "Andre, Tracy! *Here.*"

The true names agitated the magic, and the demon squalled as it struggled against the ward. Andre cleared the couch like an Olympic hurdler, seizing Joanne's hand to combine their power as they lifted the demon off Rosa. Desiree stumbled, spattered with Rosa's blood. "Is that a—"

Joanne's face froze in a snarl as she kicked the girl toward Rosa. "Help her, you idiot."

She clutched Tracy's hand and said, "Stay strong, Rosita. We're here. We'll—"

She and Tracy and Andre dodged the demon and slowly calmed as they slid into their war witch personas, flashing back to real battle. The demon changed and expanded as they struggled to contain it. It absorbed some of their magic and wallowed in Rosa's blood as she tried to drag herself to safety.

"You can't kill it like that," I whispered, reaching out as Joanne argued with Andre and their power diffused, not strong enough to finish it off. "You're just—you're *feeding* it."

Bile rose in my throat and swamped my mouth as Desiree crouched by Rosa and tried to staunch the blood pouring from her side and legs. Betty sat in the middle of the room, clapped her hands over her ears, and sobbed as she rocked back and forth.

The demon scrambled around the circle and away from Andre's efforts to contain it. It found Joanne before she could ward or jump out of the way, and grabbed her leg. Tore it away. She screamed and fell, and Andre blasted the demon as Tracy dove out of the way and fell onto the couch. The demon rampaged as it consumed Joanne's flesh, and Desiree dragged Rosa's limp body toward the back bedroom, leaving a river of red behind.

Rosa wasn't moving.

"No," I said, gasping for breath. I struggled against something constricting my chest. It couldn't get worse. It just couldn't get worse. "You'll break the—"

The coven circle disintegrated as Desiree fell through, Rosa's blood destroying the spell, and the magic snapped through all of the witches, knocking them off balance still more. Anne Marie fumbled for the emergency alert ward glowing on the wall, but her hand stopped short with a crack as she hit the second circle, a cascade of sparks flowing out. Tracy's circle.

I shook my head, chewing my lip ragged.

Anne Marie cried out, cradling her hand. "What the hell?"

The demon rolled and tumbled, carrying Joanne's bones, and Jacques and Anne Marie battled to protect Desiree and Betty. Andre comforted Joanne, slowing the bleeding with all his power as Betty reverted to screaming and clinging to Lauren. The demon oozed around, tired of attacking the Morrigan, and found Andre.

I tried to look away. I desperately tried to look away. Even Anne Marie started screaming, hexing randomly as the demon slid through the blood and she couldn't escape. Lauren crumpled to the ground in a dead faint.

Andre cradled Joanne as she shivered, pale and bruised as her blood drained away. He tried to protect her. He sheltered her from the demon's claws. They curled into each other for comfort. They were scared, and watched death coming for them. Their power deserted them when they most needed it, and no one saved them.

No one helped them.

No one even tried.

They died. The light in their eyes went out and their hearts stilled and their magic faded and they were dead. Gone.

*Gone.*

I stopped breathing, felt my own heart slow. Felt life fading to a dull echo.

Not again.

Betty shoved Tracy out of her way and through the remaining circle, breaking it, and the younger witch bolted out the front door. The demon, finished with Andre, flowed after her, running and tumbling in boneless acrobatics. Betty raced through me and the demon followed. I didn't flinch as it ghosted through, forcing myself to watch the living room. To witness what followed.

"Shit," Tracy said as the demon reached open air.

Anne Marie, Jacques, and Tracy chased it. Rosa lay limp and silent near the bedroom. Desiree stood in the middle of the room over the unconscious Lauren, face streaked with tears and splattered with blood, and turned in a slow circle. She saw Rosa but only stared, didn't seem to register her predicament, leaving her guts on the carpet.

"Help her," I said, voice catching. "*Help her.*"

Desiree's hands shook as she gathered residual power. Rosa sighed and her soul faded away, her helpful green magic evaporating away to nothingness.

Desiree raised trembling hands as she faced the door—faced me—and her expression hardened. "You."

Power crackled, even through time. She blasted the door, the spell, whoever stood behind me. Me.

I inhaled when the power should have hit, looking down as a fireball shot through me from behind and collided with Desiree as whoever stood outside attacked. Desiree absorbed the blow but flew into the wall with a wet thump, collapsing in an unmoving heap. And then...

Silence. Only silence and blood.

# CHAPTER 37

Steel bands compressed my chest, making it impossible to breathe. I wondered if Desiree's hex somehow paralyzed me through time, though I'd never heard of such a thing. I looked down, expected a burn or worse, and saw arms.

Arms?

I turned my head and came nose-to-chin with Leif. His red beard scratched my cheek, and his chest made a wall at my back. "Are you here? You're still with me?"

"Of course I'm—" I stopped short. My voice broke, unrecognizable and hoarse, and my throat burned as I tried to swallow. I looked around and caught the Styrma watching me with varying degrees of horror and sympathy.

Leif's hold trapped my arms. I couldn't pat my cheeks, but something was wrong. All the muscles in my face hurt. "You have to let me go."

"Why?"

He wasn't teasing, not even a hint of a joke in his tone. Exasperated, I tried to step away. My legs didn't respond. I looked down again, past his arms, and saw my knees bent, lifeless and numb. I couldn't even wiggle my toes. "Are you holding me up? Why are you holding me up?"

Another shifter crept close and set an unstained chair next to Leif, then retreated in silence.

The Warder didn't budge. "Tell me where we are and why we're here."

"I have to dissipate the magic, we can't just leave—"

"Tell me, *kjaereste*."

His voice was soft, even sympathetic, but still unyielding. Stubborn wolf. I coughed to get rid of the hoarseness, but my voice still broke twice as I said, "Tracy's house. We had to reconstruct what...what killed the witches."

My heart ached.

"Good." Leif's grip eased as he sat in the chair, though he still held me against his chest and dragged my legs across his thighs.

I was too tired for embarrassment, particularly with what remained of my magical dispassion, but still—I sat in the man's lap in front of his friends. It was at least as embarrassing as kissing him in public. I still had a few shreds of dignity to preserve. "You have to let me up, I—"

"Nope." Leif tilted his head at Jake, who skirted the edge of the room to take up a ready stance at the Warder's elbow. "*Kjaereste*, tell me what you need and we'll do it. But you stay here."

I fought the urge to rest my head on his shoulder and sleep. "I'm fine. Just..."

"You're not fine," he said, squeezing me. "*Kjaereste*, you're nowhere near fine."

I wished I knew what he called me, that rough music in the whisper of a nickname. Instead I tried laughing, ignoring the choking sound I made. "Really, I'm fine. This is silly."

My gaze drifted to the center of the living room, where the magic remains of Joanne and Andre flickered. A strange keening sound filled the room and I looked around for the source, but as Leif's arms tightened around me, it cut off and he kissed my shoulder. "It's okay. It will be okay."

So maybe I made that horrible noise. I shook my head woodenly. "I can finish the spell."

"You started screaming when that fireball thing hurt Rosa," he said, rocking me slightly as that sad whine started again. I couldn't control it. I couldn't choke it back. "And you didn't stop until that woman hit the wall."

"That's ridiculous," I said. "I did not."

"There are two reasons I'm holding you," he said, talking over my objections. "I grabbed you when you tried to run in after the fighting started. And you didn't stop. You fought me; you kept trying to get to them."

I blinked as the living room went out of focus, and I cleared my throat a couple of times, laugh a little watery. "That's preposterous. I couldn't help them. I couldn't—"

My voice went high and I stopped. I hated the pity on their faces, hated that Leif's arms tightened around me once more, an attempt at comfort, and he rested his forehead against my temple. Red pack magic tried to nudge through the frozen disdain of witch magic, but failed. I felt nothing but empty, only an echo of grief. I swallowed the knot in my throat. "The second reason?"

"You collapsed, when that thing ran through the door. You just—fell."

I nodded, and kept nodding mechanically until I feared I might not ever stop. I couldn't look away from Andre and Joanne, though I regretted that Rosa lay alone near the bedroom, that I couldn't see more than her legs. I stared at them, crumpled like a child's dolls thrown aside.

I blinked, self-conscious as I realized Leif rocked me gently, pressing my head to his shoulder as he shushed me. I tried to straighten and pull away. "What is—"

Leif turned so Andre and Joanne disappeared from my view, tucking my forehead against his throat so I couldn't see anything but the broad expanse of his chest. "Tell me how to make it go away."

"I'll do it." I wanted to push free, but my arms didn't cooperate.

"No, *kjaereste*. I'll do it. Just tell me how."

His gentle tone only made it more difficult to breathe. I closed my eyes and leaned into him, even though I meant to shake my head in defiance. My voice wouldn't stay in one octave—it kept breaking, going higher, until I sounded like a prepubescent boy. "No. I ha-have to do it."

"Lily." He said my name like a secret, and it shivered deep into me as it glided through my magic and settled around my heart. He leaned his head against mine. "Baby, you haven't stopped crying since that monster hurt Rosa."

I blinked, felt the weight of my eyelashes and knew he was right. My eyes felt too big for my skull, and my head pounded, and even magic couldn't really dull the pain and grief. I closed my eyes and hoped I sounded like myself. "I have to do it."

"You can't—"

I took a deep breath and pulled away. I couldn't muster even pretend fierceness, only resigned exhaustion. I owed them this. "I have to. Witch business."

Leif didn't ease his grip. Nothing moved in the silent room. "What do you need?"

"Salt." I sighed. Nothing would ever be the same. "To break the circle and banish the rest of the magic."

"Okay." Leif stood, taking me to the edge of the circle. Andre and Joanne wavered like we had bad reception. The spell weakened without my magic to sustain it, and only the Warder kept me upright.

Jake brought the bag of salt and set it in my hands, supported by Leif's. The clownish shifter hesitated as he looked at me, and after a long moment, he said, "I'm sorry," before retreating to the periphery.

Leif balanced the open bag on my palms, his other arm around my waist to keep me tight against his side. "How far do we throw it?"

"The whole circle. I'll tell you when."

He squeezed me closer, murmuring, "Soon, *kjaereste*."

"And—" I hesitated, closing my eyes so I wouldn't be weak in front of Andre and Joanne, after all they'd sacrificed. And poor Rosa, there by herself. "After it's done, I'll probably pass out. Just don't...don't leave me where—"

His arm exerted gentle pressure against my ribs. "Don't worry. I've got you."

I nodded, blinking rapidly as I clutched the salt. My breath came faster and faster until I teetered on the verge of hyperventilation, hiccuping with guilt as I stared at the broken bodies on the floor. Hoping they would start breathing, sit up, and call it a great prank on Anne Marie.

Leif's lips brushed my temple. "Do it, Lil."

I closed my eyes until tears burned my cheeks, reaching for power Mother warned me never to use—the deep well of life force. Expending that risked a half-life or death. But I couldn't use borrowed magic for this. I only needed enough for a simple blanket spell, and I owed them that. I rolled it out so the illusion covered Joanne's broken body and what remained of Andre, until I could almost believe they rested peacefully.

I cleared my throat. "I'm sorry I wasn't...wasn't there."

I should have been. I should have put away my differences with Anne Marie years ago and remained with the coven so I could have protected them.

My voice went high and I paused. I felt Leif willing me to dismiss the spell, but it was my last chance to speak to my old friends, face-to-face.

I took a deep breath. "I will find who was responsible, and

they will answer for what they did. You will be three times avenged."

Squaring my shoulders took monumental effort but I did my best, tilting my head back to call up the War Witch, so at least I could play the part. The Morrigan felt only rage, until my voice crackled with fury instead of fear. "The coven is broken. Three witches are fallen. Rosa Rosemary Rosario Marquez. Joanne Joan Ju-yeon Park. Andre Andrew Alastair MacFadden. These witches are fallen. The coven is broken."

The words hung in the still air.

I shook my head and whispered, "I'm so sorry," one final time. I rolled the blanket spell over them completely so I wouldn't see their faces fade away.

"Okay," I said, and we flung the salt as I released the rest of the power.

The reconstruction spell disintegrated with a hiss. The salt flew everywhere, scattering through my circle and bouncing off grim shifters, and everything collapsed until only the blood-soaked living room remained, not a trace of magic left.

I went limp as my muscles failed, and sank into darkness.

\* \* \*

WAKING FELT like swimming in the murky lake where we'd vacationed before the Breaking. Light and sound distorted, becoming clearer as I struggled to the surface.

It was an annoying ring that dragged me out of the dark, and I scrabbled around for the phone on the bedside table and the sheets around me. I nearly knocked over the lamp, blinking and cursing as my muscles betrayed me, and rolled until I half-fell out of the enormous bed.

It was a long drop to the floor—apparently Soren's guestrooms had beds on stilts. But the jolt woke me up enough

I could squint into the dim room and figure out where the hell the phone hid. I managed to wheeze as I answered it, "Yeah?"

Noise filled the background until I held the phone away, wincing. Sirens and alarms and shouting, all of it reminiscent of the kind of panic happening when someone breached the walls. The clamor faded and then Eric's voice, just a thread of sound, cut through everything else. "Lily. What happened?"

I balanced on the edge of the bed, touching my forehead. I didn't really know, so I wasn't in much shape to explain to her. "I'm still figuring that out."

"Something big is going on," she said, an unfamiliar urgency in her tone. The lackadaisical federal schlub was replaced with a nervous, maybe panicking, young woman. "We're getting reports across the city of demons and bad spells and shit going wrong. But we can't trace it to any witches we've got in the files. So that means rogue witches, maybe an Ancient. What do you know about this?"

"Nothing," I said, though bile rose in my throat. Demons and rogue witches. Maybe Anne Marie's Ancient arrived just in time to make everything worse. "I've been unconscious for... I don't know how long."

Eric cursed and then shouted at something, returning to her gruff persona. She returned to a whisper, and I imagined her crouching in her unmarked cop car like a criminal hiding from the law. Despite that, she managed to sound gleeful. "Look, we have to meet at the Skein tonight, like you asked. Whatever you need to do, we can do without any other Externals around. The Bureau is gearing up for raids across the city, so no one is bothering to guard an empty park. They're even going to target—"

"Lily?"

I froze, heart in my throat, and looked at the door. A dark silhouette stood in the doorway, and Moriah flipped on the

335

light as she edged into the room. "Are you awake? Who are you talking to?"

"Got a call," I said weakly, holding up the phone. I hung up before more of the sirens could blare through the tinny speaker and alert Moriah to some of the other shenanigans I was involved with. I put it aside and slid back under the sheets on the bed, acutely aware that I wore someone else's T-shirt and no pants.

I wondered who undressed me.

She retrieved a cup of water from the attached bathroom. "How do you feel?"

It took several gulps to clear the fuzz from my throat, and several deep breaths to gather the nerves to ask, "What happened?"

"Well," she said, taking a deep breath. "Leif brought you back here and wouldn't let anyone touch you. Kyle checked you over and said the only remedy was rest."

I wanted to throw back the sheets and stride forth in triumph, to show the mender how a real witch recovered from powerful magic. But I doubted I could have even lifted my head as I'd spent all my energy in answering the phone, and I counted my heartbeats as I tried to keep my eyes open.

Moriah leaned forward, a curious intensity in her wolf-like gaze. "Leif wouldn't leave. He sat here for three hours, watching you breathe. Soren finally sent him on an errand so I could get in here. You tell me what happened while you were at Tracy's, babe, and I can help translate."

I studied the pale blue stitching on the sheet folded across my middle, debating how long I could occupy the Peacemaker's guest room before I incurred a debt—particularly if there were demons popping up around the city. "We talked in the car on the way to her house. He was angry about what Brandr said, and how Soren stepped in during the magic exchange."

She frowned, slouching a little before propping her boots

up on the mattress near my feet. "I figured that might be part of it."

"Fill me in, Mo."

Moriah's head tilted as she watched me, a hint of the wolf still in her eyes. "After that night at the Pug, and the restaurant, and everything else, it's obvious Leif likes you. By our rules, even with the investigation and trying to be professional, he's made it clear that he's interested in the chase. Even though we were all betting on what happened, no one was really sure how things would go, with you being... nonaligned and a witch and everything. With him being the Chief Investigator and all... It's a little unprecedented."

I rubbed my forehead. "We talked about it. Briefly."

"Right. So if you and Leif were officially together, or he'd made his interest in you known—which he did—then some of the things Brandr said would have required a fight to the death. Especially the part about him turning you. And you hexing him could be interpreted as you marking him back—staking your claim. With all of that, he's a little off-balance and kind of a dick lately. What did you talk about, exactly? He called you *kjaereste* at least twice."

"What does that mean?" I couldn't face the conversation Leif and I had before and during the chaos at Tracy's. It still felt like a red, raw wound.

"Technically, it means 'sweetheart' in one of the old languages."

"Tell me what it really means," I said. I couldn't meet her gaze. Saints preserve me. *Sweetheart.*

A laugh bubbled up in her words, and a mischievous twinkle made her blue eyes brighter. "It implies a long-term relationship, a deep commitment. Soul-mate kind of love. So spill, girl—don't keep me in suspense."

Soul-mate kind of love. Heat crept up my cheeks and I sank lower in the bed, wanting to pull the sheets up to cover my face.

It felt good, at least, to think about something other than demons and dark magic, even if talking about Leif made me want to squirm. "We agreed on something I could do when—*if* I change my mind about dating him."

The smile spread until her white teeth flashed. "If it's serious, or getting that way, give me a heads-up. The pool is huge and we could make a killing if I get the date right."

I just shook my head, wanting to curl up on my side and sleep for another twelve years. Maybe Leif would come back and lie next to me...

Moriah's smile faded as she watched me, and the deep breath signaled something I probably didn't want to hear. "Leif told me a little of what happened at Tracy's. What you had to watch. I'm sorry, Lil. Really, really sorry. That blows."

That was the last thing I wanted to talk about. Rosie and Joanne and Andre, uneasy ghosts waiting for someone to avenge their deaths. I sent an arrow of magic into the universe once more, to reassure them I hadn't forgotten and I would do whatever it took to bring the guilty to justice.

But I picked at a loose thread on the sheet to distract myself. "It's difficult to watch people fight for their lives and lose."

Her lips compressed in a thin line and her gaze went far away, a hint of red in her eyes. We'd all done our fair share of witnessing violent deaths. Before she could go on, the door swung open and we both jumped.

Soren filled the doorway and stole all the air from the room, his expression dark. Pack magic and red tension propelled Moriah to her feet and out the door, though she called, "I'll check on you later," before Soren shut the door behind her.

I clenched double handfuls of the sheets. If Moriah's questions were unpleasant, at least I knew she wouldn't push me. Soren, on the other hand, would get his answers, come hell or high water, and there wouldn't be any way to distract him.

# CHAPTER 38

Soren took her seat and watched me with half-closed eyes as I dragged another blanket up to better conceal me.

His deep voice rumbled through the still air. "Are we connected, witch?"

"What?"

"I felt them die in your heart."

I opened my mouth to ask for more detail, but Soren didn't pause long enough for me to do more than take a breath. "Yes, I felt them leave the pack bonds that night—one downside of being alpha. The witches were connected to me. They all blinked out at once that night." His gaze cut straight to my soul. "So I ask again—are we now connected?"

"Maybe." I tugged on that loose thread. "Normally the exchange of magic once, in a one-sided fashion, would not create a lasting connection, but... Your magic is different. I've never seen it with pack magic, so I don't know how it works."

"Your Varg-damned witch magic..." he grumbled, scowl deepening.

"Nice try," I said. I wouldn't let him get away with sloppy

thinking. That kind of behavior around magic meant bad news and unpredictable results. "You reap the consequences of jumping in to be a hero, ace."

"Do not," he said. "Call me *ace*."

Mocking him took too much energy, as appealing as it was. I closed my eyes. "Soren, magic doesn't have a lot of rules, and the ones it does have are only internally consistent. The rules for how witch magic works bend when you throw pack magic into the mix. I don't know why you felt a connection."

"You didn't know I was there?"

"No." My cheeks heated to think he might have overheard that awkward hopeful conversation with Leif in the car. The idea of the Peacemaker riding around in my head was too disturbing to even consider. "Although Leif touched my hand as I used magic and said it felt like I belonged to you."

"Not a good sign."

"No shit," I muttered, managing to open my right eye.

He grimaced but didn't respond. Silence filled the room, and I focused on breathing. In and out. The Peacemaker folded his hands over his flat stomach and watched my feet move under the sheets. His gruff voice might have been comforting were it not for the subject he chose. "From what I saw and felt, and what Leif told me—you tried to help the coven."

"Too little, too late."

"But it says a great deal that you tried." Soren continued his study of my feet, and I stopped moving them so maybe he'd look somewhere else. "And how much you valued them."

Again I begged their forgiveness. "No more than any witch."

"No," he said, shaking his head. His gray-green eyes locked on mine, and I couldn't look away or even blink. "What I felt from you was personal. You want to save *Rosa*, not just another witch. Memories—good memories—of Rosa and Joanne and Tracy and Andre came up. Shared battles, shared losses. Good times and bad. And real grief, real outrage at their deaths, locked up in your heart. It was suffocating, Lilith."

My eyes burned and I made a fist under the sheet. "Why does it matter? What difference could it possibly make?"

"The time for secrets is passed, if we're connected like this."

"The connection will fade," I said, hoping it was true. Maybe intent would be enough to carry the day once more. "And we all carry secrets, Peacemaker—I certainly don't want to know where *your* skeletons are buried."

His voice gained an edge as his eyes narrowed. "I do not like when people—*my people*—lie to me."

I remembered well what happened to people who willfully deceived the Warbringer. Not many witnessed their fates, but I had been executioner once or twice. "What your people tell you is not my concern. You should address that with your Morrigan."

"Explain this," he said, lifting the cheerful *Recycle* bag, with its grim contents, into view.

"I don't know why Tracy had those things." I didn't take my eyes off the bag. "Maybe research, maybe she didn't like what Anne Marie was up to. I thought all copies of that book were destroyed, but there's no telling where it all came from."

It wasn't entirely true. I could examine the grimoires and get a sense of the witch who'd copied them, but that was a slippery slope. It would be easy to get sucked into the Alliance once again.

He put the bag down and watched me in silence. He wasn't usually one to think before he spoke, and the consideration on his face made me very, very nervous.

"I want your professional opinion, witch. Who was responsible for this?"

"I do not know." Admitting it hurt. I stared at the ceiling and prayed someone would interrupt us. "Something went wrong during their first cast at the Skein, and introduced dark magic

into what they were doing. When they did the regression at
Tracy's house, it was there again. The whole cast turned into a
demon summoning, and everything unbalanced. Maybe one of
the young witches lost focus, or maybe someone inside the
coven was out to get them."

"About the Skein," he said. He pressed his hands together in
front of his face, hiding most of his expression from me.
"Enlighten me as to what happened."

My eyes drifted shut as fatigue welled up. "I'm tired, Soren,
maybe—"

Pack magic surged and I sat up with the force of it. Soren's
expression turned grim behind his fingers. "You are trying my
patience."

The wild magic sang in my veins, and my fingers trembled
as I tucked hair behind my ears. I rested my hands on my
thighs, marshaling my thoughts. "They held a full circle at the
Skein on Tuesday. The circle had eight witches when Tracy
asked me to join them."

He waited, silent.

I rubbed my temples. "I assume, from what we learned at
Tracy's, that Anne Marie intended to summon an Ancient."

A long pause answered me, then Soren asked in a low voice,
"Which one?"

"They didn't say." Which was true enough—they hadn't.
Anne Marie's notes filled in the gaps, but he didn't ask me that.
"I don't think it matters."

The Peacemaker sat forward, tension coiled in every
muscle. "It matters to me."

"He hasn't shown up yet, has he?" His lip curled and
reminded me I skated on thin ice. "I went to clean things up
after them, and there was no evidence they'd succeeded in
Calling him. They left a hell of a mess, but it wasn't a proper
Calling."

"Then what was it?"

"Something darker." The wild pack magic fizzled in my blood, my muscles still twitching with the extra energy even though my head ached. "It felt like demon magic, but not by the whole circle."

"You're suggesting one of my witches dabbled in demon magic."

"You already know some of them are," I said. "Cara and Danielle, and more from their coven. But yes, I'm suggesting your Morrigan was also getting her hands dirty."

He shook his head in immediate denial. "Not her. I refuse—"

"She controlled the circle both times something dark happened," I said. "She had a demon focus in her workroom. And Anne Marie was always ambitious. What she had was never enough. She always wanted more power, and...demon magic is powerful. Seductive and addictive and not something you can walk away from easily."

"She would *never*—"

"She told the coven you didn't know about the Ancient or any of the spells the coven cast this week. So did she lie to you, or to them?"

His upper lip curled as he gritted the words out. "To me, apparently."

"Then can you really say, Peacemaker, what she would never do?"

Soren stared at the wall, fist clenching and relaxing. "The rest?"

"The Calling didn't go as planned, and they stopped in the middle of it—tied it off and left it to come back to. The Externals could have followed it straight to your coven, and then to you. There was enough dark magic in that spell to have gotten you all arrested. So I hid it. I meant to go back and deal with it, but the Externals have been all over the Skein."

Tonight, though. Eric wanted to meet there, and I would be

able to clean everything up and wipe away any evidence. And maybe learn something useful, like who I needed to kill to avenge my friends.

"How is it bound?"

Explaining myself to the shifters over and over grew so damn tedious. I missed the days when I could have said, "I'm the fucking Morrigan, I don't have to tell you anything." If I'd wanted to teach magic theory, working at one of their ridiculous academies would have been a better use of my time. "I covered it up so no one could see it."

"Why?" When I just stared at him, trying to parse what the hell he meant, Soren started ticking reasons off, one finger at a time. "You don't like Anne Marie. You don't like that coven, or aligned witches, or the Alliance. They did something illegal, or at least ill-advised, and they didn't bother to tell me about it. And they left a mess, enough to draw attention and punishment—something I assume you wouldn't shed any tears over. I'm having a difficult time understanding why you covered for Anne Marie."

"I didn't do it for her. I did it for Tracy, Rosa, Joanne, and Andre. They sure as hell weren't mixing with demon magic, and if the Externals found out, they *all* would have been executed."

"So you let them get away with it instead? How magnanimous for a war witch."

"No," I said, sensing a trap. "I went to Anne Marie's store for an explanation, and to offer my help. She tried to hex me and kicked me out of her store, right after she called me a murderer. So I figured she deserved what she had coming."

"Did you."

My jaw clenched until bright sparks of pain flared in my temples. "I would find the symmetry pleasing—that the demon she summoned killed her—if the damn thing had killed her instead of three good witches. So yes, she deserves whatever hell she's going to."

"Do you think she's dead?"

"If she isn't," I said, eyes narrowing, "she'll wish she were by the time I'm done."

Soren leaned forward. "I don't understand why *your* apartment was ransacked and covered in blood. Why were you a target, and why didn't they catch you?"

"Anne Marie knew I had useful books, and she's never had a problem with stealing. Or maybe she wanted to kill me, steal my magic, and use my blood for rituals."

"That's ridiculous."

I studied the ceiling, waiting for him to come to his senses.

Soren growled in irritation. "I don't believe it."

"Why not?" I actually wanted to know, curious about his ability to deny the obvious.

"Because I have been in her head, too, Lily, and it is not nearly as scary as yours."

That made me smile.

Before I could do more than sit forward to tease him a little more, a low boom rolled through the house, rattling the frames on the walls and making the lights flicker.

We both froze. An eerie silence followed the noise, and my heart raced. It sounded too much like artillery landing too close. It could have been thunder. I really hoped it was thunder.

But two-tone alarms sounded throughout the house, and running feet raced up and down the halls. Soren launched out of the chair and wrenched open the door, bellowing for a status report.

Questioning shouts competed with the clangor. I started searching for pants. Nothing magical caused the acrid smoke that rolled across the expansive lawn and into the house, so there was nothing for me to do. I couldn't defend the Peacemaker's house.

Luckily Moriah left a duffel bag of clothes in the bathroom, so I was at least dressed as I went to the window and peered out. A dozen armored vans, the chariots of the Externals, arrayed in the long drive up to the Peacemaker's mansion, and the wrought-iron gates crumpled inward as men in black clambered into the open, guns ready.

Growling rose as shifters converged from every direction, and Styrma teams moved into position as wolves snarled and snapped to keep the Externals at bay. I held my forehead as I stared at the chaos. The Bureau had lost its fucking mind, raiding the Peacemaker...

My blood ran cold. No wonder Eric sounded so damn gleeful when she mentioned raids—she had to have known the Bureau was on its way to break down Soren's gates. I just hoped she hadn't arranged the raids to give us time to search the Skein. I couldn't afford to replace those wrought-iron gates, damn it.

The Externals shouted warnings at the approaching shifters, weapons clicking and popping, and flares and smoke grenades made it impossible to see who was where. Tensions skyrocketed as they traded accusations and more people shouted. The Alliance prepared for battle inside the house, and when I dared to peek into the hallway, I took a sharp breath.

Everyone carried weapons and radios, moving efficiently and calmly through the house, and I wondered what the hell I was supposed to do. I couldn't just stay in the room, not with that damn bag full of dark magic implements and a creepy grimoire—if the Externals got inside and caught me, I'd be executed for sure.

And if the Externals found it in Soren's house, they'd hold him responsible for it. He could be executed or the Alliance dismantled. It was just enough evidence of wrongdoing to place all the recent attacks, demons, and strange activity on the

Alliance. The humans would finally have their justification to depose Soren, to prosecute the witches they hadn't killed yet.

Shit and double shit. Saints keep us.

I shoved the grimoire, a bag of salt, and a mirror into my large shoulder bag, then put the rest of the bag in the closet. At least Soren's ostentatious mansion had walk-in closets in every room, because that left plenty of room for me to walk a circle around the bag and cast a very small look-away spell. The Externals wouldn't be able to tell the bag and its dirty contents were right under their noses.

I shouldered the bag and headed for the door.

More sirens wailed. It was definitely time for me to go.

# CHAPTER 39

*I* made my way through the halls, head down, and focused on getting to the first floor and a back window. A simple spell would conceal me once I got outside; I didn't dare cast inside Soren's house in the middle of an emergency.

As much as I wanted Moriah or Leif to go with me, I couldn't risk them. A coven of powerful witches couldn't stop the demon at Tracy's house, and even if I was there to face it, Moriah and Leif could be torn apart before they even had the chance to shift. And if either of them suspected I was heading into the night on other business, they'd insist on going with me.

But this was witch business. It was *my* business. I might have done my fair share for the Alliance in my lifetime, but I hadn't done enough for Andre, or Rosa, or Joanne. They deserved more.

I ducked around a corner and ran into someone, muttering, "Sorry," under my breath as I redirected and hoped they didn't recognize me.

But a familiar voice said, "Lily?"

I blinked. "Amber? What are you doing here?"

My former neighbor, looking far healthier and happier than I could remember seeing her, hugged herself and offered a tentative smile. "They're letting me stay here for a while. It's very kind of Soren to offer to—"

"He's not usually kind," I said, reaching out to squeeze her hand. "So be careful of debts. I know you're not a witch or a shifter, but the Peacemaker rarely does anything without a couple of reasons."

She smiled more, and I forgot some of the chaos around us. Thank the saints we got her away from Chompers. My head tilted as I studied her, sorting through the glamour around her, and Amber went still, her eyes wide. "You can see it, can't you?"

"The glamour?" I squinted. "A little bit. It's better than the last one."

"You knew?"

The sirens abruptly cut off, and my ears rang in the sudden silence. That was either a good sign, or a really, really bad one. I didn't want to be around for either. "I'm sorry, Amber, I can't stick around. It's good to see you."

But she followed as I waded back into the busy halls, sticking close to my side. "Please don't tell anyone. Not until I get my operation."

"Tell them what? That you use a glamour? I don't think anyone will care, but—"

"That I was born male," she whispered.

I stopped dead in my tracks, facing her despite the Styrma running back and forth and huge cases of ammunition and flares rumbling over the marble floors. "What?"

"I was born male," she repeated, flushing, and gulped for air. "Please don't tell anyone. That's the only reason I stayed with Kurt, because he cast the glamour so I could look like a girl. I can't afford the insurance for the medical operation or the magical one, so I thought... I thought it was worth it."

Her eyes went glassy with tears and she looked away, flicking the moisture off her cheeks.

"Damn, girl." I hugged her, taking a deep breath. That explained a lot. And it pissed me off even more, that Chompers exploited her so cruelly and no doubt beat down her self-esteem into nothingness. I straightened and locked eyes with her. "I'm sorry. I should have dragged you out of there sooner. I'll help however I can."

"Thank you," she said, and it looked as if a burden lifted off her shoulders. "Do you know where Rosa is? I wanted to thank her for throwing him down the stairs."

And just like that, reality crashed back around me like a punch to the gut.

She saw it in my face, slowly covering her mouth before I even said a word.

I stopped giving a shit about Soren's rules, and drew enough magic that it numbed away the pain. Just that one time, just to take the edge off. It was too soon, after what I saw at Tracy's house. I could deal with it later, after all of this was over with.

I'd said the same thing during the war, as Moriah would no doubt remind me, and "later" never came.

"She died," I said, forcing the words out and hoping I sounded almost normal. "Killed by a demon."

Amber swayed and put a hand out to steady herself on the wall. "A d-demon?"

"Yeah." I looked around, noting new flashing lights—blue and silver, special indicators for active magic on the premises. "Their pyre will be in a few days, maybe. Soren will tell you. You can go, to show...show your respects. If you want."

For some reason, the sympathy in her eyes nearly unnerved me. For a human who had suffered a great deal at the hands of a witch to feel so deeply over Rosa's death... It was too much, even through the magic. I cleared my throat. "And I still have to go, so—"

I turned away as my vision blurred and I dragged more magic to me in a slow build to cover it over. I got about three feet before I knocked into someone, and Leif grabbed my arms. "There you are."

He cursed and dropped them immediately, shaking his hands to dispel whatever charge from the magic hit him, and frowned at me as he held up a radio. "Got her. Get the trucks ready to move."

"I beg your pardon?" I raised my eyebrows, then pointed at the hall behind him. "I'm going that way, and I'm getting the hell out of here before whatever is going on out front becomes my problem. I'll be in touch when I know more about the demons."

"Nope." Leif nodded to Amber but tried to take my arm again. "We're getting you out of here. The Externals broke through the gates and are trying to enter the house—they said something about Soren harboring dark witches, and that certainly sounds like you."

"Stefan," I said, sighing. "Just like he said."

"You pissed him off at Tracy's. Made him look foolish. So now we pay for it." The radio squawked and Leif muttered something into it.

I frowned, not wanting to take a ride with any of his people. I'd never get to the Skein in time. "I would have just killed him. It was your stupid laws that left him alive to make trouble, so this is firmly on your doorstep, bucko."

The Chief Investigator was not amused. "Let's go, witch. I'll arrest you if I have to."

"Amber comes with us," I said, reaching for her, and the other woman cleared her throat. "What?"

"She needs to get out of here too." I hefted my bag and dragged her along with me as I started walking. "The Externals might accuse Soren of keeping humans hostage in his evil den. Can't have that."

Leif hustled us along. "Fine. But Amber, not a word to anyone about what you hear, okay?"

She nodded and mimed zipping her lips with shaking fingers. I felt a little bad that she got caught up in any of it, even briefly, but I wouldn't put it past Stefan—or even Eric—to use her as a pawn if they found her in Soren's house. And I wanted a friend along for the ride, too.

With Leif behind us, the crowds parted and the halls cleared to get out of his way. We ended up in some kind of a sub-basement under the house, away from the prison cells, and I wondered what happened with Brandr. Maybe he languished in the cells, waiting for his memory to come back. An armored sedan with darkly tinted windows idled near the ramp, and a grim Nate waited by the driver's side, while a shifter I didn't know stood at the passenger side, heavily armed.

I glanced at Leif. "You can just give us a car and I'll drive, I can take—"

"You're still weak from earlier today," he said, shaking his head. The set of his mouth and the twitching muscle in his jaw left very little room to argue. Maybe that was where being his *kjaereste* turned from adorable to irritating as hell.

"Nothing is going to—"

"*Lilith*," he said, and the old name chilled my blood. His eyes shone gold, the wolf barely controlled, and he caught my shoulders so I had to face him. "By the Varg Himself, go to the pack-houses south of the city. We can defend them, and if we need to evacuate to Sanctuary, we own the airspace out there."

I couldn't breathe, staring at his face until my vision blurred again. "You can't mean... The Truce is over? It's broken? Are we at war?"

"No one knows," he said. He didn't look away even as Amber started praying. Leif's lips thinned as he watched me, and my heart nearly choked me as all the terrible possibilities battered against me like stormy waves.

Impossible.

We couldn't be back at war. We couldn't. Everything we'd worked for, everything we'd built... gone in a blink. More deaths. Losing friends and family and everyone. Mimi would never get her big wedding, and Moriah wouldn't survive this time. I wouldn't be that lucky.

My breath came faster as even the magic couldn't deaden the panic. And Tracy was still missing. The whole War Coven, maybe gone right on the eve of disaster. Maybe it was a bigger plan. Maybe the Externals managed to trap them, or worked with some other faction other than the wolves, elevating that shifter power struggle into a fucking catastrophe for all Others.

I shook my head, trying to back out of his grip. "It can't be. Not again. Not again. I can't do that again."

Leif grabbed my face and his lips crushed to mine. A shock raced through me, deeper even than the magic, and I closed my eyes.

He broke away, his own breathing a little ragged, but he rested his forehead against mine as he whispered, "We don't know what's going on. We can't risk losing you, Lilith. You're the last war witch we have right now."

Of course. Cold water drenched me and washed away whatever shock I'd struggled under. They had to protect the fucking war witch, so they stood a chance of surviving the next war.

I tried to pull away, and Leif growled, his fingers working into my hair. "And I will lose my mind if I don't know that you're safe, do you hear me? I have battles to fight and I can't afford to worry about whether you're in danger. Lilith, please."

I met his gaze, still not believing him. It could have been a ruse to keep me on their side, to keep me hidden away as Soren consolidated power and got rid of his enemies.

Another thought struck me and my stomach dropped to my feet. Maybe Soren had known about the Ancient and Anne Marie's unsanctioned magic, and feared she helped some of his opponents. Maybe they set the witches up to get rid of the threat, and Leif was just there to string me along until they broke me down and I gave in and joined the Alliance.

I couldn't breathe. All the pieces fit. Everything.

Leif's thumbs stroked my cheeks. "Please. Go with Nate and Scotty. They'll get you to the pack-house safely, and as soon as I know what's going on, I'll give you an update."

I couldn't formulate a single thought that didn't spark another betrayal. So I nodded, woodenly, and let him guide me into the back seat of the car. Amber jumped in the other side, holding my hand on the leather seat, and Leif closed the door gently next to me.

And then proceeded to growl a riot act to his guys on the seven levels of hell they would experience if anything happened to me.

It might have made me feel better, even an hour earlier, to hear that kind of protective fury from the Warder. The Wardog. The Ghosthound himself. But every word rang hollow as I tried to reason through the rice pudding in my head. Someone betrayed the witches, and someone betrayed me. I just didn't know who was who anymore.

CHAPTER 40

*N*ate and Scotty got in the car and shut their doors, locking everything and checking the windows, then started driving up a long ramp. It felt like we spent forever in the darkness, with only eerie emergency lights to show the way. My heart pounded against my ribs and the magic wisped away as my control frayed.

I couldn't fight another ten years. I didn't have it in me anymore. I barely survived the first time.

Amber's hand tightened on mine. "He can't be serious, right? The Truce will hold. There can't be another war."

"The Externals attacked the Alliance," I said, and each word sounded foreign as I forced it out. Like this was just a nightmare and I could wake myself up if I tried hard enough. "If the Judge approved the raid... That could be the end of it."

Nate shook his head as he drove, guiding the car off of the ramp and into the night. We popped up somewhere well away from the house and onto a normal road. I looked back and could only see a faint glow from the flashing lights around the mansion. "It has to be a misunderstanding. Soren will figure it all out, and Leif will enforce it. We'll be fine."

"That's what they said after the Breaking," I said. Numbness, maybe shock, settled around my heart. "And they said it every day as it got worse. It can't get worse. It won't get worse. We'll be fine. Don't worry. It won't get that bad. That's how we ended up with attempted genocide and ten years of war."

"I don't need a history lecture," he said, muscles tense in his shoulders and neck. "I was there for it, too."

"People forget," I said. The hair curled at the back of his neck, like a little boy who hadn't gone to the barber in too long. I remembered him being very young in the war, and carrying a chip on his shoulder because of it. "Grow complacent."

"Not like you, right, Lily?"

I wondered where his anger came from, whether I was the cause of it. I'd hexed him, sure, but there wasn't any permanent damage. He still deserved the truth. "No. I'm worse than all of them. I forgot to be afraid."

Scotty, the guard, cleared his throat. "If it is war, then we fight. And when we can't fight, we find the young ones who can. We survived before, we will survive again."

The silence stretched until Amber whispered, "There's always Canada."

Nate snorted, and I caught a glimpse of a smile in the rearview mirror. "Right. There's always Canada."

We drove through the city, cruising slowly to avoid some of the patrol cars haunting the twisting streets. I touched the window as I imagined what life would be like in the middle of another war, alone. The last war witch. It sounded like a bad movie.

"I need to stop at the Skein," I said, not thinking. Eric might know something. She could fill me in on the raid. I could start putting together the pieces, maybe find the rest of the War Coven so I wouldn't be alone.

It was my second chance, maybe. As awful as it would be, I would have my coven back.

The thoughts burst through my head too quickly to catch, a staccato barrage that overwhelmed everything else. Betrayals and possibilities and dread and despair so deep I wanted to sink into a hole...

My dad's voice drifted through my thoughts, reminding me of his smile, and he quoted Napoleon for the millionth time. *Nothing is lost as long as courage remains.*

"I need to go to the Skein." I repeated it, because the wolves acted like they couldn't hear me.

Scotty didn't turn. "We have orders to take you to the pack-house south of the city. No detours."

"I can't go there yet. I have to get to the Skein before midnight. It's important."

Nate snorted. "We're on the verge of war and you want to go to the memorial for the last one?"

"This might prevent the next war," I said, leaning forward to slap the console between their seats. "Hati curse you, we have to stop."

I checked my watch. I could still make it. Eric would be there, and we could figure everything out. I just needed to get out of the car.

"Bring it up with Leif," Nate said. "At the pack-house."

Stubborn wolves. No wonder the rest of the shifters rebelled. The wolf way was the only way.

Not tonight.

I squeezed Amber's hand to warn her, and she took a deep breath. She'd had too much trouble at a witch's hands. I hoped she could forgive me for putting her through more.

I grabbed the door handle and sent a thread of magic through the frame, hoping the metal didn't warp too much when I killed the engine.

And nothing happened except a bunch of lights flashed on the dashboard.

Nate shook his head. "We're not amateurs, Lilith. The car has cold iron in the frame."

Saints damn them.

Scotty picked up his radio, clicked it a few times, and Leif's voice reached me through the static. "What?"

"The witch wants to stop at the Skein," he said. "Tried to juice the car."

"Go to the pack-house." He growled, even through the radio, and his voice hardened. "Lilith Lucy Lavender, just go to the pack-house."

"Those aren't my names," I said, irritated that he thought I'd be called Lavender. Ridiculous.

Scotty's eyebrows rose as he glanced at me, and I scowled at the back of Nate's seat. I probably shouldn't have told him Lilith wasn't really my name. I pinched the bridge of my nose.

Something crackled and then exploded in the background as Leif said something else, but his words were lost in the chaos. Scotty waited for a reply, but nothing came back over. He put the radio down. "We're going to the pack-house."

"I'm sorry." I really was. Poor Nate would hate me forever. I fished the pepper spray from inside my bag, shrugged at Amber, and sprayed both of the men.

A noxious cloud of foam and peppers and other magical shit from the special formula filled the car, and Nate slammed on the brakes. "You're fucking *kidding me.*"

He reached into the back seat, trying to grab me, but I wormed out of the way and yanked on the door handle as we all coughed and spluttered. Next time I definitely needed to ward myself before doing something like that.

As I struggled to stay free of Nate, Amber leaned forward and managed to hit the locks on Scotty's side, and the soft *click* echoed in my ears. Freedom. I kicked my door open and bolted, running as fast as I could through the dark streets as doors slammed behind me and at least one of them turned into a wolf.

Stupid, to think I could outrun a shifter. I cast confusion spells and smoke screens as I ran, out of breath with the heavy bag and grimoire bouncing against my side, but I had to get to the Skein. I just needed a little time to figure things out, and then we could avert the war. I could get the witches back.

I focused on that as my lungs burned and my legs grew heavy and not even magic could give me energy to keep going. But the streets grew quiet and still behind me, the only sound my panting and coughing, and I slowed to a halt still several blocks from the Skein. They'd given up awfully easy for two guys under threat of death by the Chief Investigator.

I didn't bother to celebrate or question my good luck, and started a limping jog to make it the rest of the way to the memorial. If they stalked me from a distance, so be it. At least I had a cleansing spell to get the pepper spray off me.

# CHAPTER 41

*I* welcomed the darkness as I limped into the Skein. The trip through the Slough's overgrown paths to reach the memorial left me covered in sap-laden leaves and scratches. And I still couldn't catch my breath, though I couldn't tell if that was because of exertion or the periodic tsunami of panic that rolled through me every time I thought about not having anyone to trust in the world.

In contrast, Eric looked unruffled and impeccably dressed in a man's suit and trench coat, not unlike the one I'd left in the Remnant. Maybe she had a closet full. She eyed me askance, rubbing the five o'clock shadow that was an elegant touch to her disguise. "I didn't think you'd make it."

"It's been a rough night," I said. I picked another twig out of my hair. "What the hell is going on? Did you guys just throw the Truce out the window? Why the fuck would you attack Soren's house?"

"You needed everyone away from here to do your thing," she said, slowly and deliberately like I'd forgotten something obvious. "After this morning at the crime scene, Stefan figured you found some kind of dark magic. We saw the War-dog carry you out of there, so we assumed that you brought the bad stuff to the Peacemaker's house. Done and done."

I clutched at my head, staring at her. "You just started another war. Don't you understand?"

Eric shrugged and picked something out of her teeth. "I think it'll settle down again, but it won't matter to us. While the humans and animals fight each other, we can finally be free to do what we want. To get lokis to the top of the food chain."

"This isn't an opportunity, you psychopath!" I shoved past her into the clearing and tried to focus. Finding the witches had to be my first priority. Once I had Tracy back with me, and maybe some of the younger witches, we could figure out what the hell happened and what we could do about it.

Eric followed, though her eyes narrowed and darkened as she watched me. "I'm not crazy, Lily. You are, if you think for a second that the animals would allow you to live, if they knew what you are. Those animals are crazy, thinking they can remain in control a single day longer, and the humans are the worst of all."

I strained to hear the sounds of pursuit or ambush, but nothing reached me but the rustle of leaves and Eric's stomping feet. Under the moonlight, she looked almost human. "I appreciate the warning, but I'm not about to stand by while another decade of war destroys everyone I love."

"Who, exactly, is that?" Eric folded her arms over her chest. "Because you looked pretty damn alone over the last month."

I set my bag down and got out the salt, wishing she would leave so I could finish my work in peace. It would be hard enough to dredge up magic to complete the spell without her distracting me and draining my energy with wild claims. "The last month? What, you followed me around all month?"

"To a degree, yes." Her fake face lost all expression and her real face, shimmering in an oil rainbow, chilled me to my core. "I found you during a routine survey of nonaligned, at the market on Fifth. You stood out, sparkled. I knew what you were, so I decided to find out how much you knew about us. Whether you would be an ally or an enemy to our cause."

I stopped in my tracks to face her. "I don't even know you, Eric. I'm not your enemy, and I don't think I'm your ally. Not yet. We can talk about this later."

I may have added, "If I survive the night," but I hoped she didn't hear. Gathering loki together was the fast-track to consolidating cooperation between the humans and the Alliance once they caught a whiff of the plot. The only thing they agreed on completely was the danger posed by uncontrolled shapeshifters.

Although that would be one way of averting war and shoring up the Truce...

The External shoved her hands in her coat pockets, still distressingly calculating as she watched me. "Soon, though. You'll learn the truth about Loki's Children."

"Fine, soon." I centered myself and hefted the bag of salt.

The clearing lay dark and still, burdened with the dark magic festering under my binding. Containing it there for so long had not been kind to the forest. The trees and grass and even the dirt faded to a pale watermark of the rest of the forest. I paced a circle around the clearing, wide enough to encompass the bound magic and everything left over.

But my curiosity got the better of me. "What is that, some kind of loki self-help group?"

She didn't smile. "It's evolution. We're the next step up the ladder. We're beyond them, above them. They outnumber us now, but they won't forever." Her eyes narrowed, grew cold and distant. "And all those years of running and hiding will end."

I watched her from beneath my eyelashes as I weighed the salt against the mirror from my bag. The salt would wipe it all away and leave nothing to point me to Tracy. Or I could balance on the slippery slope once more and invite something out of

LAYLA NASH

the mirror's silvery surface. The mirror glimmered, so innocuous, in the moonlight.

Eric sidled a little closer. "And you're pausing to check your hair?"

"This mirror," I said, studying the imperfections in the bubbled glass. "Is set in silver. Probably with bone and blood mixed in, maybe some gravedirt."

"Why?" Her coat moved and the badge at her belt gleamed in the moonlight. I wondered how much I could really trust her. She could kill me for what I was about to do, and get twice the promotion she coveted.

I crouched outside the circle to sift dirt through my fingers, seeking an anchor in the earth as I debated. "It's a focus to call demons."

"Holy shit." Her eyebrows arched.

No other paths revealed themselves. I straightened. If Anne Marie summoned a demon, it should have been bound along with the rest of their magic. If it answered my call, I would have my answers. "Not holy. But close."

Her features melted and reformed into a similar face with subtle differences. "Why do you have it? I thought you were a Glinda."

"Do you really want to know?" I slung the bag across my chest once more, settling it against my back as I tucked the salt away. I cut my ring finger and squeezed three drops of blood onto the mirror, stomach clenching as the glass instantly absorbed it. I tossed the mirror into the center of the circle and side-stepped to complete the circuit.

I pressed my palms together at my chest as the bound magic rose through me. I could almost see them standing with me in the circle: Anne Marie, Jacques, Desiree, Tracy, Rosa, Joanne, Andre, Lauren, and Betty. No strangers, no unknown signatures. The only anomaly was a thread of demon magic.

As the dark magic wheeled and brushed against me, the

366

magic's hunger to be used buffeted the dispassion I found with my own magic. Worries over a new war and the damage I'd done to whatever relationship I might have had with Leif by attacking his friends faded. Finding the witches meant fixing everything else.

The demon magic, cold and foreign, swept through me and set my teeth on edge until I hated Eric for her powerlessness. Useless. I focused on the mirror as she paced behind me.

The spell waited in the back of my head, learned so long ago I didn't really remember the first time I'd heard it. I'd even used it a handful of times, in circumstances that still left me wondering if I'd been an instrument of good or evil.

As a last resort to save the Alliance, loosing demons on a human army seemed the best choice, when we were backed into a corner and facing certain death and the fall of Sanctuary. No one looked at me for weeks afterward, but Soren marveled at the efficiency. He asked me straight-faced why we didn't use demons sooner as we stood in the mire created by the effluence of twenty thousand human corpses.

Yet another reason I swore no oaths to him.

I shook myself out of the blood-soaked memories. I was a coward for delaying the inevitable. At least using a demon to find Tracy, to save her life, fell in the "good" category. No one would fault me. The remains of their spell fueled the summoning, so I didn't technically call the demon. Anne Marie did.

Even through the War Witch's disdain, my hands shook as I reinforced the spells to contain the demon. Opening a door without knowing what had been invited from the other side was a stupid, dangerous thing to do.

Smoke curled from the mirror in graceful strands, collecting at the top of the magic dome. A disembodied voice oozed into the night. "Who disturbs my rest?"

Bloody demons and their flare for the dramatic. My jaw

locked as my skin crawled under the slime of its voice. "I have no name to give you, demon."

"Only a witch would tell that lie," it said with a calculated sigh. "Always you witches, asking favors. Offering no payment but a few measly drops of blood."

"Demon, did you answer a summons here?"

It made a noise like a pleased cat. "Mmm. That delicious coven." A chuckle rolled from the mirror as the smoke grew dark and viscous like old blood.

"You," it murmured. "Were not one of them. Your magic is... controlled. Seasoned and aged."

I tried to force my jaw to work, but nothing moved. Rosa's screams echoed in my ears. Was it the same demon that killed them? Or had it been lying in wait for them all this time?

"What do you want of me, witch? To know the future? To change the past? Choose your fate? Perhaps three wishes."

I closed my eyes and focused. I could have just asked for Tracy's location, but that would have required payment. One did not want to be indebted to a demon. It was worse than being indebted to the Peacemaker. "Tell me why you were summoned."

"You ask much and offer nothing. A poor bargain for me."

"I have nothing to offer you, demon. I do not make deals with your kind."

"Three more lies," it murmured. "True artistry. You should own your past, witch, and your blood."

Magic shielded my uncertainty, at least. I only counted two lies. "Tell me why you were summoned."

"Such iron control." It nearly purred, and the smoke thickened and pushed at the boundary between our worlds. "Hiding your dark deeds. You called me too clearly, and bound me too well, for this to be your first time playing in a mirror."

"If you will not answer, I will banish you."

It heaved a sigh, reluctant to return beyond the mirror. "I

will have to teach you patience, I see. It is a gift. Here is another, then: I was summoned to retrieve something lost."

My back slicked with sweat, clammy and cold as my shirt clung in a sudden breeze that smelled of sulfur. "Something lost."

"Yes." The sibilance sent a frisson of fear down my spine, called up memories of crinkle-dry snakeskin gliding through dead leaves.

I tried to swallow the knot in my throat. "Who summoned you?"

A dark chuckle made my skin prickle. "You did."

A lie. It was definitely a lie. The hair stood up on my arms all the same. I hated demons. I truly did. "What was lost?"

"I was."

I looked up, across the clearing, to where a ghost stood. Made real, in the flesh. Solid. Wearing a dead man's face and speaking with a dead man's voice.

Sam smiled at me. "Hello, lover."

# CHAPTER 42

*I*t had been seven years since his death. Seven years since he betrayed the Alliance and the coven and everyone who needed him. Seven years since he crushed me, heart and soul, rampaged through what remained of my faith in humanity. Seven years since he stole memories from me, until I couldn't trust the accuracy of my own thoughts. Until I imagined myself guilty of such heinous crimes they haunted my dreams. Seven years since I killed him.

He still had the power to take my breath away.

The world tilted on its axis; the universe reoriented itself. My ears rang as I stared at him.

My traitorous heart leapt to see him alive. I still missed him —the man who held my hand through the war. The first man I really loved with the whole of my heart. The person who stood by me when life was at its very worst. I missed the man he was, the witch he'd been.

Sam.

He lingered on the farthest edge of my circle, neither inside nor outside. Existing in the border—trapped. He remained shrouded in darkness and a veil of gravedirt and smoke. His eyes glowed red and black, deep-set like embers hidden in ash.

The demon reveled in the tension, lightning sparking out of the mirror's surface as it purred. "I am called Berith, witch— remember. We will meet again."

Its magic melted away until the smoke dissipated, and I faced only Sam.

"Nothing to say, Lilibet?"

A chill slid through me as he used the old pet-name, some- thing I hadn't heard in seven years, and the clammy touch of the dead dragged down the back of my neck. Him saying the name was only half of it. I swallowed the sudden taste of bile as panic rose through me. "You're dead."

His smile didn't slip.

"I killed you."

A grunt of disbelief behind me reminded me Eric witnessed all of this. Sam's attention sharpened on the External for a tense eter- nity before he looked back at me. He wagged his finger at me like I'd been a naughty child. "And I have not forgiven you for that yet."

I shook my head, trying to gather my thoughts. It was impossible. I'd killed him, then burned his body. "How are you here?"

Sam brushed dirt from his clothes—the same clothes he'd worn when I killed him. The clothes we burned him in, but untouched by flames or soot. His hand glided over the boundary of my circle, testing it until cracks ran through the magic. "I have so many things to tell you."

"Are they things I already knew and you stole from me?" Finally—*finally*—a spark of rage surfaced through the disbelief and panic. I'd killed him for a reason, after all.

His creepy red gaze looked away. Maybe some part of the real Sam survived, deeply buried under all the demon madness and dark magic. I almost hoped he would apologize, beg forgiveness. But when he faced me, the sickening smile returned. "I've learned many things since we parted. Perhaps I can rectify some of my mistakes."

"Stop," I said, hands clenched at my sides. "How did they raise you, Sam?"

The circle trembled and his head tilted back, body convulsing, when I said his name. He straightened, eyes dreamy through the red glow. "I missed hearing you say my name. You have not spoken it since you killed me."

Sickness burned in my gut. Our bond ended with his death. I'd felt the connection sever in a second heart-rending loss. He had no hold on me. I hoped. My voice came out in a croak. "Only to curse you."

His smiled deepened, dug ditches in his cheeks. "I would have heard that, too."

Swallowing revulsion and fear at the same time nearly choked me. This was not my Sam. This was an ugly revenant. An abomination. Demonspawn.

He edged around the circle, caressing the surface. I felt every drift of his fingers through my magic, and hated myself for getting lost in the memories of what it had been like to share magic with him.

Sam's voice deepened and darkened, like the demon smoke. "Such elegant magic. I'd forgotten how naturally you summoned demons. I am so pleased it was you who finished Calling me."

Air rushed out of my lungs. *Finished Calling.*

His smile stretched. "You didn't realize? Clever girl like you? Such a pity. And here I'd hoped you did it out of love."

I wobbled back a step. Not possible. It just wasn't possible. I was the War Witch. I should have seen it.

"That worthless coven tried to raise me," he murmured, sharing the secret with a wink. "They failed—not enough power, the wrong spell, no conviction. But I knew you wouldn't fail. You were worth the wait."

I steadied myself, forcing the War Witch to stand and defend herself. Intent mattered, was all that mattered, and I had not intended to raise him. It was not my crime. He made vulgar allegations in front of an External, cowering in the trees. "I did no such—"

"You did," he crooned. That spawn of hell with my lover's face smiled. "Their summoning froze when you bound it. You pulled me from purgatory. Thank you for my second life. My second chance."

I couldn't breathe. It had to be a nightmare. I struggled to form a coherent thought, a real denial or a hex or anything so I wouldn't die in silence.

But Mother chided me—*never open a door unless you know what waits on the other side.*

It seemed I was as sloppy a witch as Anne Marie after all.

Sam's gaze slid to the tree line behind me. "Other men have no place in your life, Lilibet. Now that we are together again, we will rule the world together—this world and the others. But I will not tolerate dalliances."

"That's rich, coming from you." I clenched my fists and let that anger boil up. "Since you were fucking practically every witch in the Alliance before you came home to me. And we're not together, witch. Never. You're dead and evil, and the only future we have together is where I kill you again. True-dead."

"It's too late," he said, shaking his head. Sam moved closer through the circle, until I could see the gravedirt under his fingernails. "Darling, we're connected again. You raised me. We will be together. Forever."

Suddenly he was too close, getting closer, and the darkness closed in around me. I could smell the gravedirt crusting his skin, the sulfur curling off his body as well. A knot rose in my throat. If he touched me...

"I banish you," I said. I struggled to raise more magic, enough to send him back to hell. But fatigue caught up with me and the energy required to sustain the binding drained away whatever strength I'd regained at Soren's house.

There wasn't enough to send him away forever. I grabbed the bag of salt as I retreated, terrified he might manage to touch me and drag me into the circle. I whipped a hex at him to send him back, and hurled the bag of salt over the circle. Power sizzled through me as the circle imploded, and lifted me up until my eyebrows caught fire, but Sam still waited, demon eyes laughing at me.

I retreated and shoved Eric toward the path. "*Run.*"

I fled into the trees, not caring if she followed, and left the thrice-damned mirror behind. I didn't look back. Maybe the Morrigan would have died on her feet, but I didn't feel like her anymore.

I was scared and alone and a demon with Sam's face wanted me for himself.

I'd raised a demon with my blood. Brought Sam back to life. Suspended their cast and bound the demon to their magic, so it waited until they cast at Tracy's house. I let the demon into their spell. Rosa's blood, Joanne's, Andre's... It was all on my hands.

# CHAPTER 43

*I* ran through the Slough, branches lashing my face and tearing at my clothes. Sam's laughter chased me until I reached the street. The pounding of my heart and the ragged draw of my breathing drowned out everything except my panicked thoughts.

Not just war, but demons loose in the world. Raising the dead and opening the door to the saints only knew what. And if I was the last war witch...

I shivered and stared into the darkness, not seeing anything but Sam's dead coal eyes.

He wasn't dead. Or maybe he was dead, and reanimated. Or he sold his soul to a demon, and the demon rose instead.

I gripped my head, bending over as I gritted my teeth and tried to stop the maelstrom of thoughts. I stumbled to a halt in the weak puddle of a streetlight as my legs wobbled and my lungs burned. Memories of Sam flooded through me as my dinner splattered across the sidewalk, and my vision swam. Tears finally broke free.

Anne Marie hadn't succeeded in raising Sam, but I'd blundered in and done it. No wonder the Ancient never showed up

—they called Sam to shore up the coven, to take the ninth's place. And I'd stopped them, made a mess, and turned it into my own catastrophe.

My parents would have been so disappointed in me.

Tires screeched nearby and I froze. A slamming door and running feet made me turn, prepared to fight or flee though my feet remained glued to the pavement.

"Thank Skoll," Leif said, and I closed my eyes. Not Sam. Leif was welcome warmth and sun-soaked life after Sam's gravedirt cologne. "Lily, what the hell happened?"

"I couldn't go," I said, staring at him. He could anchor me in the present as everything else went wrong. All the noise in my head... It would go away if I could just get Leif to understand. "There's too much going wrong. I can't do it on my own, Leif."

"Do what on your own?" He looked around, scenting the air, and sneezed. "What did you do, Lily?"

I blinked and instead it was Sam standing before me in a jolt as everything changed and we were back in the war. Sam shouted at me, angry, demanding to know what I'd done. I'd missed a spell he planned when humans attacked my patrol and we barely fought free. I was too muddled and exhausted to fend him off as he insisted I help with delicate spells. Demon spells. He claimed they were just harmless practice. Said he loved me and trusted only me. That he needed me. And I'd believed him because I didn't want to see otherwise. I clutched my head and whirled away.

It wasn't real. Sam was dead but coming out of the forest behind me somewhere.

"Lily," he said. Leif's voice held a hint of a growl, but I could see the struggle to communicate on his face. At least he still wanted to listen. He still tried to understand. "Take a deep breath. Tell me why you hexed Nate and Scotty and ran out of the car."

"Hexed? I didn't. It was pepper spray. A special kind of

pepper spray." I backed away from him, not wanting my back to the Skein. Just in case Sam showed up, I would see him coming. Or Eric.

What if the External bolted out of the forest? What would Leif think?

"Why did you pepper spray them? I told you to go to the pack-house. We're in the middle of fighting the Externals, and the last thing I need is to worry about whether you're safe." Another bit of growl escaped, and Leif ran his hands over his hair as his eyes went wild. "And yet here I am, wanting to help you, while Soren and the rest of my pack battle alone. Soren is right. I've lost my mind."

He shook his head in disbelief.

Again my brain sparked and he became Sam, looming over me after I met with Soren and Sam decided I cheated on him with the Warbringer. Things had been rocky; I suspected Sam used a spell on me but I didn't know what or why. I had headaches all the time and couldn't concentrate, and everything from the previous few days was covered in a gray haze of uncertainty. Something in him had changed; his magic pulled at me constantly, hungrily. Jealousy boiled over as he wrenched my arm, trying to drag me to his quarters. "What did you do? Why did you talk to him for *three hours*?"

"I feel like I'm losing my mind," I whispered. I hadn't released my magic in weeks. Maybe months. I couldn't remember what it felt like to feel something other than fear and anger. "I can't do this anymore, Sam. I can't."

Time skipped and it was Leif staring at me. "Sam? Who the hell do you think I am, Lilith?"

"Are you doing this?" I couldn't breathe. Something rustled in the trees and I backed up more, though Leif followed. "Is this part of your plot to get rid of the witches? Make me crazy and arrest me and throw me in the Reserve?"

He stopped in his tracks. Something changed in his expression, in his posture. Part of him returned to the Chief Investigator, instead of Leif who wanted to protect me. "Lilith. What day is it? Where are we?"

Stupid questions. I didn't have time for that. He didn't deny the plot. The Alliance finally wanted to clean house. Tracy had been right.

Before I could come up with a response or another accusation, the trees parted and Eric stumbled out, brushing leaves and dirt off her coat. Leif turned to scowl at him. "What the fuck are you doing here, Smith?"

"Assisting the witch in a small inquiry," she said, not missing a beat. "I'll be on my way. I've heard there are a few other issues to address in the city tonight."

She started to walk away but Leif blocked her, his features sharper and more dangerous as he stared down the External. "Stay right there. Is this part of the Bureau's attacks? Turning our witches against us?"

"She's not yours, friend." Eric checked her watch and pulled out an odd-looking device. "And you're not going to stop me."

I retreated as the past and present melded, separated, blurred. It took six years but I was finally losing my mind. The world tilted. I smelled wood smoke and cordite from the guns and a hint of metallic panic on my tongue.

"What have you been telling him, Lilith?" Leif remained still but I felt stalked, pursued.

I clutched my forehead in a panic and bent over in pain. "No. No."

He wasn't Sam. Leif wasn't Sam. This was a different time, a different argument. The rat-a-tat-tat of gunfire echoed, made me flinch, stole my breath. I couldn't breathe. Couldn't run. Magic didn't come and it didn't leave, until I teetered in an unbalanced in-between place, out of control.

Leif turned his attention to me, and Eric started edging away. The Chief Investigator watched me warily, that alert button flashing at his belt. No doubt calling in more backup. Diverting more troops away from fighting the humans. Maybe we'd lose this war in the first day. He held up his hands. "Help me understand, Lilith. Tell me what's going on in your head."

"I don't know, Leif." I said his name to remember who I was talking to, and because it made me feel better to hear it. I turned around, searching the darkness. Nothing made sense. Magic raced through me in static and lightning, taking away whatever control I thought I had. Demons and Sam. War or not. Missing witches. External raids. The whole world lost its fucking mind and dragged me with it. "I just can't—nothing makes sense. I don't know what to believe."

"What to believe? Hati's balls, Lily, believe the truth. The facts. Believe *me*."

He said it like it was just that easy. That facts presented themselves without any gray areas. Like there was one single truth that stood out in a shining beacon above all the chaos and confusion.

But it wasn't like that. Not in the real world. Not in my world.

And he wanted me to leave Tracy and the coven to their fate. I couldn't live with myself if I did that.

"I have to get them back," I said. He had to understand. A demon waited in the woods and would hunt down the witches.

"We will," Leif said. He held out his hand. "We'll find them. Come with me, Lilith. We can sort this out back at my house."

The slow, careful words set off alarm bells in my head. He thought I was crazy and wanted to get me somewhere with a containment cell.

Or maybe those sirens were real. I looked around as something else crashed through the trees, and girded myself for battle.

Leif snapped his fingers until my attention returned to him, and he reached for my arm. "Come on, Lily. Get in the car with me. We can drive together."

He had cold iron on him, I could feel it. He meant to collar me. Send me away. I backed up. "No."

He drew breath, shaking his head as sadness gathered around his eyes. "Lily—"

"Uh, guys?" I blinked, surprised Eric was still there. She backed up closer to us and held that odd device toward the trees. "I think we've got a problem."

"Get the fuck out of here," Leif growled, yanking me behind him.

"I would love to," she said. "But first—"

Before she could finish, I looked at the Skein and my heart seized up. A small opalescent figure popped out of the trees, rolling through the dirt and leaves, and reared up in a cloud of sulfur.

Demon.

# CHAPTER 44

*L*eif shouted a warning, barking orders to the saints only knew who, and tossed a charm from his pocket at the demon as it circled closer. The charm didn't do much to slow it down, but it gave me enough time to focus and inhale more magic. I dipped into the source of my magic, the personal well of power Mother warned me never to use.

It would be worth it, if I could save our lives.

There wasn't much left, but I formed a weak ward and called to Eric, "Get over here. I can't cover you right now."

The External aimed that weird device at the demon and hit a few buttons, looking like a fumbling bureaucrat more than any sort of cop. "If this works…"

Leif growled and caught the back of my shirt, dragging me back toward his car one step at a time. The demon charged at us, slamming into the ward and cracking it. Saints blast it. If it managed to break the wards, the backlash of magic would do me in. I'd be useless to defend any of us, and then we'd be dead.

I gritted my teeth and dredged up more magic, spinning a hex at it as the demon whirled and raced toward Eric. She slapped the side of the device, muttering under her breath, then hit another button and it blazed to life.

A golden net, made of no magic that I could see, shot out of the device and covered the demon, connected by a thin thread to the gun and Eric. The demon squalled and fought as the net tightened, and the smell of burning oil and sulfur wafted on a sudden wind.

Eric squinted and moved the device, dragging the demon away as it clawed the pavement, and glanced over at us. "This should hold for a bit. Why don't you two take off? I'll be in touch."

Leif stared at her. "What the fuck is that?"

"Don't worry about it. I don't know how long it will hold, so get moving."

The Warder growled in irritation, then abruptly grabbed me around the waist and carried me to his running car. I stared at Eric and the odd net that restrained the demon. The humans found a technology that worked against demons? My heart sank and soared at the same time—finally, we could protect people without having a war witch on guard all the time to hold back the demons. But it also meant that the humans could defend themselves against one of the Alliance's best, last resort weapons. Saints preserve us.

Leif put me in the passenger seat and slammed the door, leaping over the hood to jump into the driver's seat. He didn't hesitate—he hit the gas and started driving, picking up the radio to direct more Styrma to the Skein to deal with the demon and Eric. I concentrated on breathing.

The car sped away from the Skein and the demon, and I looked back to see whether Eric's device had failed yet. It still glowed, at least until we turned a corner and the darkness returned. I gripped my knees until my fingers ached, staring through the windshield at what lay ahead. What if Sam and the demons had the coven? I wouldn't wish that fate on anyone, even Anne Marie.

But I didn't know how to find them. All the evidence of where they'd gone was bound up with Sam at the clearing, and I'd destroyed most of it with the salt. Maybe I'd just killed them all, if they'd survived.

My chest constricted and I struggled to breathe, tears burning my cheeks once more. Damn it.

Leif's jaw jumped as he ground his teeth, and eventually he glanced over at me. "What's going on, Lily? You're all over the place."

"I have to find the coven," I said. That was all I could think about. "It can't be war, Leif, but if it is, I can't fight alone. And if...if this is just part of Soren cleaning house, you have to tell me. Please. You have to tell me if this is the Alliance getting rid of troublemakers."

"That's insane, Lily." He shook his head. "Soren isn't going to kill witches if they disagree with him. This isn't about the Alliance. This is something else. The humans, maybe. I don't know."

I remembered the first time I sat in his car, as he drove Moriah and me home from the Pug, and we talked about the memorial and the anniversary. How the witches fought alone for months on end because the shifters put themselves first. Whether Soren meant it or not, this was another time when the shifters would put their Alliance ahead of witches. Ahead of my coven, my friends. We'd never find the witches alive if the entire Alliance fled to the pack-houses south of the city.

"It's something bigger," I said. I whispered it, just in case Sam heard and laughed along in his demon realm. "Leif, I have to go. I can't run away."

I'd done enough running in the last six years. I'd fled my problems, and the coven's problems, and witch problems, and it went sideways. People got hurt. People I loved died. Because I didn't stand up for them. And now Tracy was somewhere dark, alone and afraid, and the safety of the pack-houses and the Alliance tempted me. Lured me away. Made me forget who I was.

Leif gripped the steering wheel until the leather creaked. "We're not running away. It's a tactical retreat so we can refit and figure out what the hell is going on."

"This is witch business," I said. I reached for the door handle. "I'm sorry. I have to go. The coven needs me."

"The coven is dead," he said, voice flat. No emotion, not even anger, colored his words. To him, it was just a fact. "With everything we saw at Tracy's, and everything else going on, there's no way they survived. We have to get you to safety and figure out how to screen and train more war witches. That's our next step, Lily. *That* is your witch business."

"They're not gone," I said. I gripped the strap of my bag, still heavy and sticky with the grimoire. "They're not. And I will find them."

The car turned south. Leif didn't look at me. "You won't. You're officially in Alliance custody, for your own safety. You'll be released when this emergency ends."

Alliance custody? Saints above.

"Stop the car." I gripped the door handle and braced my feet. "Leif, stop the car and let me out. I'm not going with you."

"This isn't a choice, Lilith." Leif's mouth compressed in what could have been regret. "I'm sorry."

I wondered if he really was, or if he said it just to keep me from fighting being arrested and detained.

"Then I am, too," I said. And I meant it. I really did.

His car wasn't made of cold iron, and the engine died when I jammed a very small hex into the dash. Leif snarled in rage, and turned to catch my arm. "Damn it, Lily, you can't—"

I hexed him and shoved my door open. Leif swore as he froze in the seat, unable to move as I reached for the radio. I didn't want him to die; I couldn't just leave him there, in case the demon got loose and chased us down after it killed Eric.

The radio crackled and Jake's voice reached us. "What the hell just happened? Why did you stop?"

Of course they had a tracker on the car. So I wouldn't even be able to steal it to get to the Remnant faster. I clicked the buttons on the radio and didn't bother to disguise my voice. They already knew. "I killed the engine. Leif is hexed and can't move. It'll wear off in twenty minutes. You should get here faster. There are demons in the area."

Howling responded, and in the distance, sirens wailed. Maybe they were closer than I planned.

Leif rolled his eyes to glare at me. "Lilith, do not do this. This cannot be undone, do you hear me?"

"I have to find the coven," I said. Some residual numbness from the magic helped. I placed the radio in one of his frozen hands, so he could call for help as the hex faded. "I won't let you stop me."

He growled something else, his face reddening as he strained to break the hex, and I got out of the car. He was right. This couldn't be undone.

# CHAPTER 45

t took forever to get to the Remnant. Almost nothing stirred in the city, though police cars and SWAT vans periodically broke the silence with sirens and horns and loud-speakers shouting orders to any citizen who dared the empty streets. By the time I made it to Remnant Park, I didn't care that I walked through the shantytown with no concern for whether anyone witnessed my passage. It wouldn't matter much in a few hours, whether Sam or the Alliance found me.

Instead I walked through the front door of my parents' house, locking it after I stood in the wards for a few moments, absorbing the warm familiarity of my mother's magic. I would be safe in the house. Demons couldn't get through those wards. She'd buried them deep and made them well, with sticks and bones.

I stumbled into the kitchen and leaned against the butcher-block island, staring at the first glimmer of dawn illuminating the eastern sky. Daylight always made me feel safer, even knowing nightmares walked as easily in the day as in the night.

I turned away from the window and slid to the floor, hugging my knees to my chest as I leaned back against the cabinets. Hiding my face against my knees didn't help much, though it did block out the light. My mind raced even as my body begged for rest. Sam. A line of sunlight appeared on the cracked linoleum, creeping toward my feet. How did they raise him? If I boosted the spell and finished it, someone had to have started it. But how?

Anne Marie would not beat me. I smacked my fist into the floor, pain blossoming in my bruised knuckles. It helped focus my thoughts. I supervised the destruction of his body myself—cremation with no rites, no washing or prayers or words spoken over him, the pyre made from unholy wood, his ashes mixed with sea water. No one saw him before the cremation. Only Tracy stood with me as he died. The Morrigan could pass judgment without a second opinion. I hadn't waited for Tracy to declare him guilty.

I knew he was guilty.

No one got close enough to touch him. I'd never raised the dead, but I knew a witch needed a blood-and-bone focus to stand even a minute chance of success. Blood and bone, and a hell of a spell done with powerful witches.

I pushed to my feet, resolute as panic faded in the dawn. It was witch business, and since I was the only witch left, it seemed, it was my business. Mother lectured in my ear: we cannot change the past. We can change memories and perceptions and sometimes reality, but what is done cannot be undone.

The memory of Leif's warning made me pause, but not enough.

Sam was back. Instead of sitting in my parents' kitchen, hiding from what I'd done and hoping it would go away, I needed to fix it.

The knot binding him to this world couldn't be loosened until I knew how they tied it.

Small salt circles contained Tracy's book and the one I'd

stolen from Anne Marie in different parts of the living room, so their magic and history didn't interact and start wreaking havoc. I paged through Anne Marie's first, a little unimpressed. Despite the outside appearance of being an important book, in reality it was a glamour covering rather amateurish work, copying much greater witches without the skill and finesse. A non-magical human probably copied the original, but didn't have the knowledge of what needed to be highlighted and preserved.

It was meant for security, so that dark grimoires were easier to trace, but in practice it meant kettles of dark witches hired humans to copy their books. I'd spent the last five years cleaning up after witches who experimented with bad books— something their expensive academies could not protect them from. I tapped the cover as I concealed the book in its circle. No help at all. Much like Anne Marie herself.

I sat back on my heels as I hefted Tracy's book; it felt heavier despite the similar size, as if its gravity were stronger than everything else in the room. It felt sticky, the book's soul hungry and seeking.

On the surface, the only real difference was that a powerful witch copied Tracy's book; the power of the spells rolled off each page and clung to my fingertips. But as I flipped through it, serious ideological and practical differences became obvious. Potions required dark ingredients, spells needed death energy for activation, and many only worked during specific phases of the moon.

But that wasn't all. It took longer to figure out, and I retrieved the original grimoire from where Mother kept the dangerous books just to be sure. The differences were so incon-sequential that a lay witch wouldn't notice the changes. Spells for summoning demons and the dead were copied incorrectly. They weren't careless omissions—they were deliberate alter-ations. The witch copied steps out of order, changed words around, altered the rituals—right hand instead of left, yew twigs instead of oak. Deasil instead of widdershins.

Unease burbled in my stomach. This was a horrible land-mine of magic, buried deeply and just waiting for an unwitting witch to pick it up and try a spell. Nearly all of them would kill the practitioner, or at least required a hapless victim to pay the price. I shivered and wiped my hands on my jeans, wanting to be rid of the cloying feel of the pages. I wondered if maybe the pages weren't made of vellum at all, but of something... darker. Maybe human.

I forced myself to page through the book until I found the spell I would use to raise the dead, if I'd been inclined to consign my soul to the deepest pits of hell. I studied Mother's grimoire on the other side of the room, memorizing the spell so I could compare as I crouched next to Tracy's.

The setup was the same in both books, though they diverged after using a blood focus. Tracy's book included a bone focus and detailed chanting. More pretty Latin poems for inferior witches. I read it three times, and double-checked against the original, before I was sure. That spell alone justified the evil of the book, the way it longed for power.

With the spell in Tracy's book, the coven summoning the deceased would end up dead themselves, their magic and life force drained at the price for fueling the spell. Only the witch who invoked the circle would survive to control the revenant.

But why did Tracy have the book? The entire coven couldn't be involved; there was no way Joanne and Rosa supported it, or Tracy herself. She'd witnessed Sam's crimes. She knew what he was capable of. For Anne Marie to sacrifice an entire coven of war witches just to get Sam back didn't make sense. Unless she had a new coven on standby to replace them. A dark coven, one of the kettles she protected after the Truce, that would obey her every command without question.

I got up to pace as nervous energy flooded through me,

though I kept a wary eye on the vicious book. Too many coincidences and lies tangled up over the last few days, and Sam sat in the middle of it all like a malevolent spider, taunting me with the past. I had to find the simple truths, and start from there.

Sam had been reincarnated. Somehow, some way, someone brought him back from the dead. I'd completed the spell, but someone else started it. They used a modified version of the spell in Tracy's book, since what I'd seen at the Skein didn't match anything in my book or Anne Marie's.

The entire First Coven participated in the summoning, all of their magic intertwined at the Skein, at Tracy's, and around Sam. The coven was involved, knowingly or unknowingly.

Afterward, the coven regrouped at Tracy's house. Something went wrong in the circle, or maybe the original spell culminated, and summoned a demon into the circle. The demon killed three witches before it escaped, and Anne Marie, Tracy, or Jacques killed it on the lawn. Then someone attacked Desiree through the door.

That was the last time I knew the coven lived. The same night something attacked my apartment, and at least three other summoners across the city.

I massaged my temples, banishing the thought, and I started to pace again. My steps were uneven and I almost veered into the piano, but I needed to keep moving so I didn't pass out.

Anne Marie plotted to raise Sam, whatever her reason.

Or...another plot among the witches, maybe, that went back much further. In the last days of the war, I suspected Sam of casting with another coven as we grew apart and the coven fragmented. A dark coven, a kettle. My heart sank with the possibility of a full kettle operating in the city. Maybe it was Rook, Sam's mentor, after all those years.

Eradicating his kettle and as many others as I could find became my obsession after Sam's death. I refused to spare any of them, but Anne Marie tattled to Soren that I killed strong witches who were willing to repent and support the Alliance. The Peacemaker insisted on rehabilitating as many as possible. Too many survived for my liking, and aligned to join standard covens.

They'd had five years to regain their strength and reorganize. Maybe Sam's kettle survived, somewhere in the world. Maybe Rook wanted him back more than Anne Marie did.

I slid into the recliner, my brain pudding. Something caught in my shirt, and I looked down. The jade ring. I pulled it off the chain to study it. Jade for a mender. Because even though we all knew my talent was destruction, Sam believed I could bring things together. Keep them together. I shook my head as I clutched the ring.

The Sam I fell in love with was not the Sam I killed. The dark magic changed him, warped his magic and his personality. It turned him into someone else. He'd loved me, before the dark magic. He'd love me and been worthy of my love.

I replaced the counterfeit books on the warded shelf. Once they were safely away, I searched my parents' library for spells to banish the dead permanently. I thought I'd done it right the first time, but apparently someone sneaked off with a finger-bone or two.

I held my eyes open as I pored over the books, fighting fatigue and hunger and a desperate urgency that made my leg bounce even though I had no energy. The answer had to be there somewhere. I just had to find it.

* * *

IN THE END, there weren't a lot of options. With the degree of uncertainty around how they raised him, the only spells to guarantee his true-death took more power than I had. Unless I used up my life-force in its entirety, and even that wasn't a sure thing. Killing Sam again, maybe saving the witches—it meant my death.

I covered my face and wished for a few days of rest, more time to plan and research. Any other alternative than a noble sacrifice. I'd never been particularly noble. That moment seemed a curious time to start putting the world ahead of my own needs.

At least Mom and Dad would be proud. I hoped.

I'd almost talked myself into getting up and heading for the Skein to end it all when my phone buzzed. Moriah. I hesitated before I answered; hearing her voice might destroy whatever resolve I'd pulled together.

But I wanted her to know the truth, at least. Whatever stories and lies they made up later to explain my death and the coven's disappearance and Sam's resurrection, I wanted her to know the truth. "Hey, Mo."

"Lily, I don't know what the hell's going on or where you're at, but you've got to get out of the city." She sounded like she was running, and people shouted in the background. "There are demons popping up all over the place, and we can't find the source. We can't contain them. We can't fight them. The Alliance is evacuating. You've got to run."

"I can't run," I said. "Like I told Leif. This is witch business. And I...I had a hand in it."

"It's not your business," she said, desperation making her shout. "Skoll curse you, Lilith witch, this is *not* your business. You don't have to do this. You can't fight them all on your own."

I could barely whisper. "I have to try."

She didn't speak for a long stretch, then took a deep breath. "Where are you going? How do you know where to fight them?"

"It's the Skein," I said. "Keep everyone away from the Skein. If things go wrong... I don't know. I won't be able to control it. You might have to firebomb the whole Slough, maybe sow the earth with salt. It will be another Remnant."

"Lilith," she said quietly. "As your friend, I'm begging you. Let me bring you more witches. We have strong ones. They're not trained like you, but they can at least help you."

"I'm not going to endanger any more witches." I looked around the familiar living room as my heart stuttered and my vision blurred. "You'll need them for cleanup, Moriah. Just keep everyone away from the Skein. The Externals have something that will hold the demons at least temporarily. Maybe that will help."

"They've denied having anything like that, and no one can find your pal Smith." Moriah cursed and growled at someone else. "You can't do anything until dark. Just wait a bit and we'll get reinforcements to you. Let us fight with you."

I took a deep breath, afraid I'd have to hang up on her before she changed my mind. "It's too dangerous, Mo. Believe me. Please. Don't come to the Skein. Keep everyone away."

Her voice reached me in a whisper. "You're not coming back from where you're going, are you?"

"I don't think so." I was too tired to grieve yet. "I wish I could, but this looks like... This doesn't look like something I can stop without a major sacrifice, and the only thing I have to give up now is me."

"Damn it, witch." Moriah growled at someone in the background, and kept the same tone when she went on. "Don't do some ride-off-into-the-sunset bullshit now. You fought for ten years, and for another six, to live. Keep fighting. Keep fucking fighting, do you hear me? And when you need to, ask for help. We'll be there. I'll be there. Don't forget you're not alone. *Keep fighting.*"

"I'll try, Moriah. And—just in case. Thank you. Love you." It was all I could get out before my voice cracked.

"This isn't goodbye, witch," she said. "It isn't. I love your stupid, stubborn ass too, and I'm going to kick your ass up and down this city the second I see you. Which will be soon. Got me?"

"I got you." I couldn't hang up, and neither could she. I stared at the phone, listening to her breathing on the other end, and tried to swallow the knot in my throat. There wasn't anything else to say, but I didn't want to end the call. I didn't want that to be the last thing I said to her.

I covered my eyes and turned off the phone.

Tears still blurred my vision as I stumbled across the room, tripping over my shoes, and shoved the phone in my pocket. Getting back to the Skein early would allow me to set a few circles and maybe even create some traps. I still couldn't see well as I opened the front door, hopping on one foot as I struggled with the shoe.

A shadow detached from the wall of the house and I froze. Brandr.

# CHAPTER 46

*I* stared at him, seeing the Old World alpha in the light of day for the first time since the war. His wild eyes scanned the house behind me and the surroundings, and his nostrils flared as he searched for threats.

"Are you safe?"

I eased behind the door, and peered at him from around the heavy oak. "Why are you here?"

"Where is here?"

The shantytown behind him didn't stir, and no Styrma burst out of the ratty buildings to chase him down and arrest me too. If they'd followed him, they would find me as well. I dropped the shoe so I could hex with both hands—not that I had any power to spare. "Here is the Remnant, Brandr. Why are you here?"

He frowned as he looked around. "Something bad happened. I needed to find you."

"Something bad?"

"You're okay?" He put his back to the wall and studied me from head to toe. "You don't look okay."

"Yeah. And thanks." I eased forward; he couldn't mean to

kill me, not when he looked a heartbeat away from offering me aspirin and a hug. "I escaped the house when the Externals attacked."

His lip curled as he tilted his head at the wasteland behind him. "Trust you to find sanctuary in the creepiest neighborhood in the city."

I scowled.

A smile softened the scarred granite planes of his features. "Why do you feel safe here?"

"Why did you come for me?"

"I swore," he said, and held his hands out in a gesture as if it were obvious. "I swore to Lord Fenrir to protect you. So...I am here."

I took a calming breath. Saints shield me from overprotective men. A handful decided to shelter me, but more things tried to kill me in the last few days than in the previous five years. "I appreciate you *think* you need to—"

"I have no idea how I got here." He shoved his hands in the pockets of his tattered clothes. "The house was attacked, alarms went off, crazy shit happened, and all I thought of was you. You weren't in the house, so the wolf thought... run. Find her. Lord Fenrir guided me to you."

I ground the heels of my hands into my eyes. I doubted Lord Fenrir cared whether I lived or died, and the longer I stalled, the harder it would become to walk to my death in the Skein. "There's a lot going wrong, Brandr, and I've got a mission to complete. I'm not really in the mood for company."

"Too bad." He jerked his chin at the house behind me. "Invite me in. Standing out here gives me the creeps."

I hesitated. No one else had been in the house in sixteen years, since the morning strangers flooded our kitchen and killed my parents. As I waffled, Brandr arched an eyebrow. "I take it you're not interested in what I remembered?"

The bastard. I stepped back and let the door swing in

enough to admit him. We stood in the foyer after I closed the door, staring at each other until Brandr tilted his head at the interior of the house and said gently, "Ask me in and offer me something to drink, girl. Were you raised in a barn?"

Flustered, I turned on my heel and stalked into the kitchen. I didn't have time for hospitality. I thumped a mostly-clean glass of water onto the kitchen table and folded my arms over my chest. "Start talking."

He wandered through the kitchen like a king surveying his domain. "Well. Aren't we domestic?"

"This is the Remnant," I said, irritated that my lousy welcome amused him. "What did you remember?"

"Yes. That." He tested the table for shaky legs with a frown, peering at the floor and the cracked linoleum. "When I broke out, there were some bodies around the mansion and wounded as well, and this animal thing rolling in their blood. It grew with each attack. They were still trying to contain it when I left."

My forehead thudded into the table. I really hoped that bag I'd hidden in the closet wasn't the source of the demon. Maybe they forgot to destroy the demon focus I'd found at Anne Marie's. "Great. Demons attacking the Peacemaker."

"He wasn't the Peacemaker for everyone."

"Just because you two—"

"Not just me," he interrupted. The bluster and bravado faded. Instead, a proud man worn down by years of servitude sat before me. "Most shifters fought for the Alliance because the humans wronged them, or because everyone had to pick a side, or because they just liked fighting. Not everyone signed up for a lifetime of cowering in front of that man. Not everyone is meant to take orders."

"I don't think—"

"Why haven't you aligned?" Brandr spun his heavy Alliance ring across the table until it bumped my hand. "Soren's anxious to get his paws on you, yet you've avoided it like an iron neck-lace. No goody two-shoes Glinda would walk away from that opportunity. So what does that make you?"

I concentrated on the soft gold of his ring and the blood-red stone glinting in the lingering sunlight. His question didn't have an answer, or at least not one that I wanted to share. "Did the demons escape?"

"I don't know. I left." His head tilted as he watched me. "Why did you run?"

I nudged the ring back toward him. "Because I don't belong to the Alliance."

"And neither do I." He smiled, tight-lipped, as ghosts gathered in his eyes. "I'm done living by another man's rules." Brandr picked up the ring, studying it in the half-light. "I wore this for too long. Here," he said, offering me the warm gold. "You keep it."

"I can't." I shook my head, but he caught my hand and pressed the ring into it, folding my fingers around the heavy ruby. "Brandr, I—"

"Keep it, sell it," he said, holding my hands. "I don't want it."

Magic tingled where he touched me, a sense of greater connection, and I held my breath. The red haze of pack magic around him faded as his connection to Soren and the Alliance disappeared.

"Welcome to the dark side," I said weakly. A terrible joke.

He studied me, eyes narrowed just a hair. "I could swear you're two-natured. When you did that voodoo on my head, there was something very familiar about you."

I pulled my hands away, still holding his ring. "What did you remember?"

"I don't care who you were or what you did. I don't care why you insist on helping Soren. It doesn't matter."

"I'm glad, but—"

His eyes remained impassive, dark but steady. "I'm leaving.

Come with me. There's nothing for you here. Leif will always put Soren ahead of you, and you deserve more than being his second thought."

My heart sank. I feared he was right. Leif even admitted as much—he thought he'd lost his mind for coming after me instead of obeying Soren's orders. It wouldn't be fair to him either, to stress his relationship with Soren at every turn. And not much else held me there, only Moriah. Once Leif told everyone what happened and the Alliance blamed me for the demons, I wouldn't have any friends left.

But I couldn't ignore demon summonings. I repeated my question, concentrating on the ring.

Brandr took a deep breath. "She hired me to turn you, not kill you. Just make sure you turned. Then I would take you into the pack and order you to answer their questions and cooperate, regardless of whether you wanted to."

Breathing grew more difficult. "And yet you didn't."

"Oh, I fully intended to capture you." He winked, a smile not entirely covering the lingering threat. "I tracked you until I was sure. By then I had no intention of turning you over."

"Why?" Unbidden, the memory of a wolf in the shadows as I fled my apartment rose in my mind's eyes, and I shivered. I wondered how much he'd seen.

"I watched you break into the witch's house, so I knew you were no friend of the Alliance. I figured I could change you, we could take the money, then disappear."

A solid plan, if it hadn't meant pissing off a witch powerful enough to selectively alter his memory, as well as his pack's, and stealing my magic without my permission. I pressed my palms together as I asked Mother for patience. "When did she hire you?"

He frowned at the ceiling. "Wednesday night, late."

Wednesday night. After I confronted Anne Marie, after the Skein. "Four days is a long time to survive an Old World hit. I don't know if I should be proud of myself or disappointed in you."

Brandr bared his teeth in a smile. "I enjoy the chase more than most men."

I laughed in surprise and a little because of the flirting, the edge of danger in every look. It was a welcome distraction from the looming fight to the death ahead of us. "Did the witch say why they wanted me turned?"

"She said they wanted something from you but you were... uncooperative." He gave me a look, like he commiserated with whoever hired him. "She said it was far safer to get what she wanted if you had no magic, and had no way of getting magic. Which meant turning."

I frowned. If I turned, a collar wouldn't drive me mad, and I wouldn't be able to resist Brandr's orders, not with the pack magic he would wield as alpha. A good plan, all things considered.

"Huh," I said, and slouched in the chair.

"And then the Morrigan warned me about you."

Cold flashed through me at the warning. I shook it off as Brandr grinned. "She knew someone hired me to change you, and said you were unstable. Vindictive. That I should kill you instead because the change would drive you insane. She didn't like you much."

I got up and tossed the glass of water in the sink. I wanted to believe Anne Marie hired Cold River to catch me, but my heart knew she hadn't. Which made all of her other behavior even harder to understand. Maybe that third dark witch working with Cara and Danielle did...

"Did she say who hired you?" I leaned against the counter to get a little distance from him, still distracted by his large, battered hands, resting so easily on the table.

"No names, but she knew her. An Alliance witch."

"Oh, *that's* helpful. Why didn't the Morrigan hand you over to Soren to deal with?"

He snorted, smirking just a hair. "As if I would have let her."

"She's a bitch and a sloppy caster, but she's still a war witch, honey. If she wanted to hand you over, you'd go."

When he smiled, the edges of his teeth glinted. "Honey?"

I made a get-on-with-it gesture as my cheeks flushed. My death waited for me on the other side of the city—I didn't have time for this back-and-forth.

"She was on her way somewhere," he said after a long pause, letting me suffer. "She told me not to follow you, that she'd take care of it—then she did something to my head and everything went cloudy."

I stared at him as if the answers would write themselves across his face or fall out of his ears. I needed a name. Maybe if I shook him a little...

As I said nothing, Brandr sat back and studied the kitchen. "Who died here?"

"What?"

"It smells like lives ended here. A long time ago, sure, but it's unmistakable."

I focused on the doorway to the living room, trying not to see the same ghostly horror show I always did. "Maybe."

"Someone you knew?"

Mom. Dad. "Maybe."

Only the ticking grandfather clock broke the silence. Brandr nodded to himself after a while, tapping his knuckles on the table. "I waited seven lifetimes to find my soulmate. We married a week before the Breaking. She and I—we had plans. Things to do. I thought we had plenty of time, another ten lifetimes maybe. Humans ambushed our pack five months later. They had rifles, shotguns. Silver in everything. We fought, but they were too many. She died."

I studied his face, though it was cast in shadows as he leaned back. He concentrated on his hands on the table, though I didn't think he really saw them. "I didn't think I could survive her death. I didn't want to. It was the need for vengeance that drove me—the desire for blood, to inflict as much pain as I felt. It faded, but... I don't know. I will never love anyone like I loved her. I would rather not try. But I think life could be good if I shared it with you."

"That's sweet." I didn't know what else to say. What was there?

He shrugged, and even in the daylight, it seemed like darkness filled the Remnant.

I wiped my hands on my thighs as I looked away and the world tumbled out. "My parents died here. Were executed here." My mouth went dry and I rasped to a halt, hugging myself. "I was twelve. Two months after the Breaking."

He made a thoughtful noise, and his fingers drummed the table. "And now we are both fighting alone, for ourselves. Now what do we do, Lilith?"

I looked at the piano in the living room, still wary of that damn book. "The Alliance is evacuating everyone south of the city. Immediately."

"Are you going?"

"I don't belong to the Alliance," I said.

"Okay." Brandr knocked his fists against the table once more. "What are we doing first? Who do we need to kill?"

"Brandr," I said. "You should get as far from here as you can before demons come after me, or Soren does."

"Can't." He looked as immovable as a boulder, sitting at my mother's table.

"I fully expect to die doing this," I said, and I didn't even choke when I said it.

"Or maybe not, if I'm there." He folded his arms over his chest and arched his eyebrows at me.

Stubborn damn wolves. A spark of hope ignited in my

chest, though it made me deeply uneasy. Hope was dangerous. "Or you'll die instead, hero."

"Then I've fulfilled my oath," he said. "And if we both win, I'll take you to dinner. I win either way. And I don't have anything waiting on me but a death sentence. So what are we doing first?"

I rubbed my temples. If the saints tormented me with Brandr's attention, there had to be a reason. Some kind of divine plan. "We have to find the coven, destroy some demons, close a rift, and kill a dead man."

He didn't blink. "I take it you know where to start."

"Not yet," I said, pushing away from the counter. I felt rejuvenated, now that I had someone at my side. "But I will."

He followed me into the living room, and as he sat in my dad's lounge chair, I wondered if I would ever show Leif this house where I grew up, where my war started.

In the steamer trunk under the piano, a warded box protected a few silver mirrors. I retrieved the smallest, no larger than my palm, and placed it on the coffee table. Mother enforced strict rules: no demon summoning around the food.

I didn't look at Brandr as I set a circle and cut my finger. "They'll execute me if you tell anyone about this."

"Baby, I have my own death sentence to worry about."

I almost smiled as I dripped blood on the mirror. I wanted to tease him about it, but froze as smoke curled up the instant my blood touched it.

Brandr sat back. "Shit."

The stench of gravedirt followed, blossoming as the smoke unfurled. My stomach dropped. It shouldn't have worked like that.

"Darling, you finally called," Sam murmured, a hideous mockery of caring.

"I'm not your darling." Sam couldn't be in the mirror. Blood and mirrors didn't summon humans. Only demons. I stared at the glass, willing it to crack and trap him in the Betwixt. "How did you find me?"

"We are linked. We belong together."

"I am not—"

"You still wear my ring."

My finger trembled as I touched the ring, barely refraining from ripping off the chain and throwing it across the room. "It is mine. A man I loved—a man who died seven years ago—gave it to me. I don't know what you are, but I'm going to banish you to a hell you deserve."

"Oh, I missed that passion."

"What do you want?"

"You."

Brandr tensed next to me, a growl rumbling in his chest, and he touched my back in a glancing touch. I stared into the smoke until my vision swam. There had to be a sign somewhere to reveal what he was, what animated him. "And the coven?"

"I'll free them, as a gift. But I want something in return."

"Release them." I wasn't about to negotiate with him. At least he confirmed they still lived...maybe.

He chuckled. "We will discuss the terms in person. I want to see your face again."

"Bring the coven."

More laughter. "Meet me at the Skein. The witching hour."

Always the damn witching hour. I hated the dark. "They must be alive."

"You must be there, alone."

"Yes, alone," I snapped. "Who would I bring?"

"The human, perhaps?" Sam sighed. "You are so much better than that, Lilith."

My heart jumped. I consigned Eric to her fate, hoping it had been a quick death at least. But Sam didn't know about Leif. "You set a low standard, witch."

He purred, making my skin crawl. "Be there. You don't want me to find you first."

The smoke thinned, grew sparse, and the mirror went dark.

I broke the circle and covered the mirror in salt, debating as I sat back. I could free the witches. There was no telling what he wanted in return, but at least I could free Tracy. Once the coven was free, maybe they could fight back. We wouldn't be nine, but we'd stand a much better chance of defeating him with seven war witches instead of one.

"What the hell was that?" Brandr sounded remarkably calm.

I wished I shared some of his aplomb. "The dead man I have to kill."

"Ah." He watched as I retrieved another book from the warded shelf. "And how do we kill a dead man?"

"I had an idea," I said, paging through the book. "But things change if you're willing to go with me. I need a different spell."

He folded his hands across his stomach and propped his legs on the coffee table, eyes half-closed. "We'll find a way."

"I hope so," I said under my breath, almost a prayer. The grandfather clock kept ticking away the seconds until witching hour; there weren't nearly enough. "I really do."

## CHAPTER 47

*B*randr crouched next to me, eyes reflecting the moonlight. "It's a good plan."

"No, it's not." I swatted a bug on my arm. We'd slunk through the Slough and up to the Skein, pausing to regroup before the final push. "You're enjoying this too much."

His mouth twitched and the pronounced canines glinted. "This is the most fun I've had in years."

I thought of the rush when we'd faced off at the Pug, the surge of adrenaline as we battled. I didn't look at him. "Me too."

Brandr tilted his head at the clearing. "Ready?"

No. Not at all. I took a deep breath and offered my hand. "It was an honor fighting with you."

"No goodbyes, witch. We will fight again." But he pressed my fingers with his.

I wished I shared his confidence or at least his denial, keeping my eyes wide as I stared into the darkness. "Maybe in Valhalla, wolf. Don't let them take you alive."

He winked, clapped my shoulder, and disappeared into the undergrowth, not even the leaves swaying to betray his path.

I paused to murmur Rosa's mantra for strength of will. The

witching hour approached. A deep breath didn't steady my shaking hands, but I straightened and walked into the clearing anyway. If I waited for confidence, I'd never move. Sometimes bravery meant doing what needed to be done despite being terrified.

I wrapped power around me like an embrace, reveling in the War Witch's indifference as I stood in the open. I'd snuck in a short nap after we got the plan together and before the sun went down. I had enough power to feel overconfident.

When Sam said, "Lilith, my love," from the darkness, only mild disgust ruffled my calm.

Disdain for him and the three witches cowering at his feet filled me up as I faced the first man to break my heart. Two more witches, tainted with dark magic, retreated into the trees. I hoped Brandr killed them. "Sumo."

He grimaced at the old nickname, and I neither celebrated nor cared. His coal-fire eyes flashed as he gestured at the three witches. "Your coven."

"Not mine," I said as I looked at Tracy, AM, and Betty. Disgusted with the young one, Betty. The one who covered her ears and cried while a demon murdered Rosa and Joanne. Murdered *my* coven-mates, and she did nothing to help them. I turned my ire on Sam. "You owe me six witches."

"Half now," he said, smile eerie as he watched me. He knew I judged all three for their failures. "The rest after you free me."

"Free you?" I laughed, strolling closer to the chained and collared witches. Betty stared vacantly at me, long red scratches striating her cheeks. Tracy's brow furrowed as she watched me. I rolled magic into blue death, to remind him to fear me. "From what? I already reanimated you—what more do you want?"

Betty keened as she hugged her knees to her chest, a low whine like an abused dog. I gritted my teeth.

Sam raised his arms and dirty opalescent magic slid around

the clearing, demarcating the border of my first circle. "While I appreciate that, you also managed to bind me here."

I laughed, enjoying his predicament even through the War Witch's indifference. "How sad for you."

He smiled as he seized Betty despite Anne Marie's half-hearted attempt to save her. Sam dug his fingers into the young witch's throat, and her whine escalated to a wail. "Yes, it is. But more sad for your friend here."

I pretended boredom and thought of Brandr, Old World death stalking the forest. When I gave the signal, he'd leap in and rescue the witches. I'd finish off Sam. Easy, in theory.

When I shrugged, Sam's smile twisted and blood bloomed on the girl's throat as he dug in dirty nails. Betty got very quiet and very still, but in her eyes she screamed. Sam licked the delicate curve of her ear, murmuring, "If you do not free me, Lilith, I will tear this sweet little witch to pieces in front of you."

Tracy choked on a plea for her life; Betty's eyes entreated me to save her as her panic reverberated through the clearing. The iron collar dug into her flesh where Sam's wrist pressed against it, and her skin bubbled around the bloody punctures.

Feigned indifference settled around me as I studied the girl, my mind racing to find a way to save her. Even though she hadn't saved Rosa. I had to remain aloof; if he knew I valued her, he'd do his worst. "Sumo, I killed *you*, my partner and coven-mate, and burned you without rites. You think I care what happens to that kid? I don't even know her."

I didn't know her. And what I'd seen, I didn't like.

But Sam knew me. He knew I bluffed. He knew I would never consign a junior witch to a dark death, regardless of the price. He knew I would free him to save her. His smile gave it away.

I turned to Anne Marie to buy time. Lank hair tangled around her face, and blood crusted her shoulder under a tattered sweater. Hard to believe it had only been a few days. "Well? It's your choice—do you want me to save the girl?"

She exhaled, as dull and lifeless as her hair. "Do what you want, Lilith. There is nothing else to tell you. Death comes eventually to us all."

My head tilted as I studied her. Resignation was not normal for Anne Marie, even in the worst circumstances. I faked a yawn as I turned to Sam. "Bring the other witches, Sumo, and I will consider it."

"Oh no," he said, whispering to Betty like a lover. "Half now, half after you free me."

I took a breath, about to agree and then kill him the moment I fulfilled the obligation. The saints did not like oath-breakers. But Tracy whispered, "Don't do it. He's too powerful."

I bristled; I could destroy Sam any time I wanted, whether he walked free or remained trapped. I was the Morrigan, the most powerful witch in the city, and that undead bastard would not beat me. I smiled with all my teeth. "No, Tracy. I clean up my messes. Sometimes I clean up Anne Marie's messes, too."

I jerked my chin at Betty. "Put the kid down. I will free you and then you will bring me to the other witches. Agreed?"

His smile grew, teeth too large for his dark gums, as he threw Betty aside. "Agreed. You will be with your coven soon."

I hoped Brandr was ready, wherever he was.

Power built around me as I focused on Sam. What a disaster. Almost enough to convince a girl to swear off men forever. Part of me really looked forward to killing him. Again.

The spell shivered to the surface of my mind as I slid power into the magic binding Sam to the clearing. His eyes glowed red and his mouth gaped as he inhaled my magic, stealing a hint before I shut him down.

Sam crooned. "Do it."

The delicate web binding him was built from the remains of our bond and locked with what survived of my love. I took pleasure in destroying it. It snapped apart with the crack of dry bones, and Sam shouted in triumph.

The killing hex drifted from my fingers, formed with the deepest of blue death, and rolled along the web as it receded. Like a rubber band snapping a paperclip back into his eye. I smiled to myself, waiting for the moment he recognized his death.

Something slammed into me and I staggered. The blue death fell, scattering in the dirt as my concentration shattered. I looked up just as Anne Marie's fist smashed into my nose. "You *bitch*."

I threw her off me and jumped up, but only Tracy, Betty, and Anne Marie stared at me in the silence.

Sam was gone.

* * *

I LAUNCHED AT ANNE MARIE, breathing fire despite the icy fear running down my spine. "What the hell is wrong with you?"

"How could you kill them?" She shoved to her feet and spat a curse at me, though her eyes reddened and her voice wavered. "Rose and Joanne, you...I never thought you'd—"

"Don't you dare accuse me of *your*—"

Tracy elbowed between us. "Is he gone?"

"Yes," I said, and sprayed green sparks in the air until Brandr rose out of the underbrush like a gray ghost. His cheekbones stood out and fur lay heavy on his forearms, matted with something a little like blood. I strode over to Betty and examined the collar on her, even though she cringed. "Because Anne Marie fucking *let him go*."

"I did not. You brought him back, bitch." Tears streaked her cheeks. "And for what? Some sick game? Sacrifice my coven for your own gain?"

"You're out of your mind," I said. I hauled Betty to her feet and marched her over to Brandr. "Get her out of here. And get the collar off her."

"Don't act like you're the hero, witch," Anne Marie snapped, as Brandr gave Betty a jagged but kind smile, and caught her arm.

I turned away to face Anne Marie, though I searched the trees for any hint of Sam. Tracy saw Brandr for the first time. She fumbled her chains off and yanked at the collar as she stuttered, "W-wolf."

"Yeah," I said, but before I could take a step, magic surged and she raised her hands.

"No," I said, reaching out. "He's with—"

But the hex left her hands before I reached her.

It wasn't blue death—she wasn't strong enough to make it on the fly—but it was close enough. Brandr grunted and dropped like a stone. Betty looked at the bloody handprint on her arm and bolted into the forest, screaming her head off. No one moved to stop her, or even said her name. I knelt by the Old World alpha, trying to reverse the damage. He lived, but barely. I glared at Tracy. "Why did you do that?"

"He was paid to kill you," she said, brusque as she checked Anne Marie's restraints.

My heartbeat slowed and the world got quiet except for my breathing and the weak thud of Brandr's pulse against my fingers. I flicked the hex off of him and anchored his life to mine with a thread of magic, but I focused on Tracy. My oldest friend. The only witch I truly trusted. "How do you know that?"

Anne Marie watched me with narrowed eyes, pointed face more severe under purple-brown bruises. Me knowing about Brandr and the hit surprised her, but Tracy's knowledge did not. My throat went dry as Tracy struggled for words. Two witches worked on Brandr's memory. Anne Marie was one of them. The other...

Tracy cleared her throat, waving her hand toward the new Morrigan. "Anne Marie told me—"

"I didn't tell you anything, witch," Anne Marie said, and time slowed as deep waters rose around us.

Two witches worked on Brandr's memory. Anne Marie was one. I closed my eyes.

"Maybe you should tell Lilith—" Anne Marie started, and I looked over in time to see the hex that flung her across the clearing and into a wide oak.

Dark-cloaked witches rose from the undergrowth and a pearl-white circle flared to life, trapping us in a shrinking noose of fetid magic. I screamed curses and threw myself against the ward, trying to break it before it solidified, but I bounced back and tripped over Brandr's still body.

I fought.

I dragged up as much magic as I could until the War Witch burned bright around me and I found refuge in the cold clarity. I rampaged against the kettle from inside their circle, and leveled the forest in a half-mile radius, setting the trees ablaze to consume the dark witches as they retreated and hid and ducked under their own wards. I Called every predator in a fifty-mile radius to kill them, and used that hybrid magic to Call as many shifters. I screamed every word of power I knew.

And it wasn't enough.

I howled my fury like the wolves as the circle constricted and battered dark witches stood up instead of died. I sent my wrath into the night on a bolt of magic, and watched the stars scatter.

I shielded Brandr as much as I could, kept his heart beating with mine, and Called Soren and Leif and even Kyle, hoping for rescue as a hex sliced through the circle and into my foot.

Another clipped my shoulder, and the circle shrank.

Anne Marie, still collared, tried to help Brandr, but it wasn't enough.

Betrayal burned a cold abyss in my heart. As the kettle of dark witches converged around us, my last words to Brandr mocked me: don't let them take you.

I'd failed him. Failed them all.

Somewhere, Sam laughed at me.

# CHAPTER 48

*D*arkness. And cold. And silence. The sound of breathing mocked me.

Iron—true cold iron—burned my throat and wrists and ankles. Magic was only a distant memory.

I understood Anne Marie's resignation. Death came eventually to us all. But it was an unfortunate truth that sometimes we suffered before we died.

They worked in teams. Always in pairs. One crouched by my head, whispering that I could make it stop if I told them what they wanted to know. The other used iron or magic to hurt me, to draw the pain out in ropey strands. Stretching but never breaking.

It went on for eternity. A thousand times eternity.

They got into my head, dug through my memories. Always promising it could end. "Tell us. Tell us and make it stop."

"It costs nothing. Just let us in."

"We don't want to hurt you, sister."

"Don't make this harder than it needs to be."

They asked about demons, about revenants and ghosts. They wanted spells for resurrection and banishment, for mass destruction. They coveted curses to destroy souls, blue death hexes, true-death words of power.

They wanted the forbidden knowledge. They wanted the slippery slope and the abyss below.

It stayed hidden, locked in a carefully-constructed corner of my mind. I hid with it, huddling around that dangerous knowledge. Mother and Dad guarded me, their whispered instructions balancing the dark witches, regardless of how much the iron burned.

I curled around the dark knowledge as the suffering dragged on, as pain blurred into one long night. I held onto Mom and Dad, and even though the witches whispered that it would be so easy to give in, Mother told me the easy step taken was a mile climb to respectability. Dad held my hand and told me to hang on, to be strong.

Said they were proud of me.

I heard them over my screams, as I begged for it to end, begged the witches to kill me.

Over and over, a soundtrack that blurred in my ears: We're proud of you.

Hang on.

Be strong.

* * *

WHEN THE THREATS and cursing and questions and pain drowned out my parents' encouragement, there was deep water.

Deep water, closing over my head, making it harder to breathe.

A new witch whispered in my ear, breath hot on my cheek. "Look at the vaunted Morrigan, crying like a baby."

The world got very, very quiet.

My lips parted, cracked until blood coated my teeth. I

couldn't feel my face enough to know whether he told the truth about the tears.

He laughed against my temple, tweaking my broken nose. "Your friends will watch me use you for something spectacular. You will fuel a spell to remake the face of the world. We will destroy the Alliance, the Truce, the humans... Everything. With your blood, your bone."

Cuts stung as scabs pulled and broke as I tried to form words.

"This will be your greatest contribution," he whispered, fingers tiptoeing down my throat, pressing the collar deeper into my skin until another seething pain bubbled to the surface. "Despite Samuel's claims, I know you will never join us. So we will use your blood and bones. It is all you are good for."

No. A small part of me, a small spark buried deeply, rebelled. I'd done many good things in my life, whether they made up for the bad or not. And I focused on the small things, like Kyle's wide-eyed hero worship as he studied my hex. Moriah's grin as she filled me with margaritas. Soren's dry respect as he tried to arrest me. And Leif.

Leif, who in the fifth year of war reminded me that men could be strong and kind and everything that Sam was not. Leif, who restored my faith in humanity after Sam destroyed it, and me besides.

"And your wolf. He's already mad." The dark witch chuckled, fingers trailing down my arm. "We healed him up so the young ones could practice on him. It's a beautiful thing."

I kept my eyes shut. Brandr's suffering hurt my heart and eradicated anything positive in my mind. I dragged it back to Leif, who in the fifth year of peace recognized me when I didn't recognize myself, and was glad to see me.

That evil witch kept whispering as he tried to break me.

But there was Leif. Gray eyes and dangerously long

eyelashes, the calluses on his palm as he held my hand. The warm fog of his pack magic. The way he held me in the SUV as the antidote burned through my blood. Soft lips on the couch at the bar, the sting of teeth against skin.

Leif.

I found his image in my mind, his serious face an anchor. Help me, I said to him, and in my heart he answered: Always, *kjaereste.*

"You will cooperate eventually," the dark witch said, fingers cold against the clammy skin of my palm. I barely felt his touch, all the blood run out of my arm, fleeing the cold iron. "Everyone always does."

I told Leif he owed me a real date, a real dinner.

*Anywhere you want in the world.*

It was almost enough to make me smile.

"You will cooperate, witch." Something cold and sharp rested against my pinkie.

Anywhere else, I told Leif, squeezing my eyes shut despite the swelling and the tears. Anywhere but here. Soon. *Please.* Soon.

"If only," the witch said. "Because you will have no fingers left," and pressure seized my pinkie. White fire clipped my flesh.

I screamed as my finger fell to the floor with a dull thump, as heat consumed my hand and blood splattered onto the concrete. The witch laughed. He painted my forehead with my own blood, drawing idly as I screamed and clenched my fist and kicked the table and still the blood poured out.

The witch kept laughing, and it seemed all the blood had not run out of me. Turned out I had plenty left to bleed.

# CHAPTER 49

*I*t was safe in my head. I leaned against Leif, who stroked my hair and promised it would end soon if I told him where I was.

My hand throbbed with every beat of my heart, raw and fierce. I stayed with Leif. It was safer than the unknown. The waiting pain.

Something warm and damp patted at the sunspot of pain where my finger had been, and my whole body twitched.

A soft voice, gentle as the touch on my wrist, cut through the sharp paid. "Hold still, honey."

Everything in me froze.

She hummed the lullaby she always sang when I was sick, and a cool salve smoothed over my hand and extinguished the pain. "I think we can save it."

A damp cloth brushed my face, patting away the fever. My chin wobbled as I took a shaky breath. "Mama?"

Her perfume drifted over me and I squinted into the dim glow of our living room. Her face hovered next to mine, blurred through my clotted eyelashes. I'd dreamed of having her back.

Maybe everything had been a nightmare. A terrible fever dream, and I woke up whole on my mom's couch.

"There's my girl."

I closed my eyes in exhaustion, sinking back against a pillow. "It hurts."

"I know." She wiped my cheeks. "You can rest soon. There's just one thing you need to help me with, honey."

"Anything." My head swam, the room a slow spin around me. My hand faded to a distant ache. Mama would fix it. Even the fever burning through me weakened and retreated.

Her perfume grew stronger. "Walk me through how to summon a fire demon."

"You already know." I frowned; she hated talking about demons. She expected me to memorize the spells the first time through.

She smoothed my wrinkled forehead. "I know. But it's important. I need to hear you repeat it, to make sure you know it. It's a dangerous world, my love."

The deep water called to me, but I desperately wanted her to stay. She left too soon the first time. She knew all the bad things about me and didn't care. I kept the dark at bay, blocked out the deep voice asking where I was. I knew where I was. I was home and Mama was there, and everything would be okay. "A silver mirror, no more than three handspans, set inside a double circle. Three drops of blood and then..."

I drifted within the soft cloud of her perfume as I told her how to summon a fire demon. The scratching of a pen on paper made me pause.

Mother never took notes.

As the silence stretched, she patted my shoulder. "What comes after the invocation?"

My insides contracted. "You said never say it out loud."

"I need you to tell me now."

"I can't." I tried to open my eyes but the blood and tears clotted into a horrific glue on my lashes.

"We need to know." Her fingers touched my wrist near the cold metal she should have removed and thrown out. "You have to tell me, Lilith."

Lilith.

My heart beat faster as I tried to breathe normally. I didn't become Lilith until the third year of war. Four years after she died.

"They will keep hurting you," she said. "They will stop if you tell me."

"*You* can make them stop," I whispered. She was more powerful than a measly kettle.

"Be strong for yourself," she said. The pressure on my wrist increased, the touch turning into a pinch.

"It's too dangerous."

"Think of yourself." Her voice quieted even as it echoed in my skull, rattling through my brain. "Save yourself."

I forced my eyes open until the blur of light revealed the curve of her jaw, the glitter of an earring. "What?"

"You are more important than the others. Better than them. Leave them." She touched my cheek. "Just tell me what I want to know, Lilith, and you will be free. The others can pay the price."

My heart slowed to a lingering drumbeat. Through the haze of magic and grief, one certainty shined bright. Mother would never say that. She had a moral compass, and though mine faltered in the war, I knew she would never bend.

She would never tell me to leave other witches behind.

It wasn't her. She wasn't real.

None of it was real.

I forced my eyes wider, even with the swelling, and fought through the deep water. The soft lighting of my parents' living room faded, replaced by a damp basement. The glamour rippled, and in a dark corner, Anne Marie huddled in chains, eyes huge in her tear-stained face. Our gazes met.

None of it was real.

Bile rose in my throat as the witch who wore my mother's face loomed over me. She demanded I tell her how to finish the spell. I'd already said too much. They could almost complete the spell with enough power and a little intent; I'd given them far too much of the dangerous knowledge. But maybe a little more wouldn't hurt.

My lips cracked as I smiled. A spell to summon ice demons drifted through the dark water, and so I murmured the invocation to that instead. It would cause a massive disruption in the spell at the moment of culmination, and the split focus would unbalance the magic. It might release fire demons on us, or it might burn the house down. Either was preferable to living another day with those sick bastards mining my memory for more ways to hurt me.

She repeated it back, satisfied as she scratched more notes. She even thanked me, said how proud she was, how I'd done the right thing. The bitch used my mother's voice.

She asked about revenants, demanding I tell her as I pretended not to know what she meant. She said she wouldn't love me if I didn't tell her.

But Anne Marie sat in the corner, knees pulled to her chest, and stared at me. Willed me to be strong.

And Mother reminded me: this too shall pass.

I thought of my parents, and let the warmth of their memories surround me. And there was Leif, frantic to find me again, to settle next to. Even as the witch grew irate, said awful things, screamed curses. I curled into Leif as my hand started throbbing once more.

This too shall pass.

# CHAPTER 50

$\mathcal{I}$ lay somewhere cold, ice seeping into my back through my tattered shirt. A collar weighed my head down, and iron burned my wrists. I could lift my arms or shift my legs, but it was too hard. Too painful.

When I opened my eyes, Anne Marie sat only a few feet away, drawn and pale in the eerie half-light. We were in one corner of a large room, empty save for a long table with restraints and a puddle of blood on the floor. It looked like someone's dingy basement, with smooth concrete floors and exposed insulation in the walls.

I closed my eyes so I wouldn't see the blood. "Is it really you, Anne Marie?"

She didn't answer, just stared at me.

Air whistled in my nose. I breathed deeply but stabs of pain in my sides warned me not to try it again. I finally croaked, "Why, Anne Marie? Rosa and Joanne were—"

"Don't you dare," she said. The tears trickling down her cheeks shined in the light. "This is *your*—"

"You think I planned this?"

"I thought it was a trick," she said. "When they tortured

you. They made me watch. I thought you made them do it to prove you weren't with them."

"They're not my people, Annette." Her old name came too easily; the darkness reminded me of painful conversations at the campfire during the war. Back when we were friends. "I'm not a dark witch."

"Tracy saw dark magic at your apartment."

I dragged myself over to my side, wheezing as my ribs creaked and broken scabs ignited fire all over my back. "I killed two dark witches that night. She interrupted the cleansing."

Her gaze didn't waver. "Why raise Sam? Why free him?"

I went up on an elbow and groaned, finally heaving to sit up and lean against the wall. It made breathing easier but ignited a ring of fire across my stomach. "I didn't raise him. Someone cast inside your circle when you tried to Call the Ancient, and directed it to someone else. Something else. Sam. If you hadn't hexed me, I would have killed him."

"How did you—what Ancient?"

I snorted and immediately regretted it as blood poured out of my nose. Lovely. I leaned my head back against the wall. "Tracy told me."

She muttered something under her breath, then cleared her throat. "I don't know what I could possibly have done, Lilith, to deserve what you—"

"I didn't do this." I met her gaze as best I could through my swollen lids. "I went to the Skein to hide your circle, and I bound it. When I went back to get rid of it, Sam rose. I didn't Call the demon."

I didn't mention the demon I *had* Called. She wouldn't have understood.

"How did you know about Rosa and Joanne?"

My heart hurt more than my hand and all of my other wounds combined. "Leif and I went to Tracy's house. I did a reconstruction."

Her eyes closed and more tears traced clear tracks down her grimy cheeks. "I miss them."

So did I. I rested my head against the wall and stared at the ceiling. "How did Tracy know about Brandr?"

"She hired him."

I wished I was surprised. But nothing really mattered anymore, sitting there in the dark and imprisoned by dark witches. "Why?"

She shook her head, eyes half-closed. "She thought you were involved in dark magic. I caught him stalking you and her magic lingered on him, even though he pretended not to know anything. When I asked her why, she said we had to turn you so you lost your magic. That if you kept practicing, you would become invincible."

I squeezed my eyes shut and tears escaped. Tracy. "What proof did she have?"

"She didn't need any proof." Anne Marie sighed. "I remember the war."

Didn't we all. "Tracy asked me to break into your house to steal a grimoire."

"She claimed you set the second circle at her house. On the lawn, when we killed the demon, she said she recognized its magic from your apartment. The witch torturing us wore your face." Anne Marie exhaled. "You tortured us, Lilith, and then at the circle when you spoke to Sam... It was like seven years ago, when you were so far gone..."

I covered my eyes despite the weight of the iron manacles. The tears hurt more than the severed finger. "It was the only way I could do it, Annette. Pretending to be the Morrigan again."

Anne Marie winced as she adjusted how she sat, dragging the chains across the floor in a chilling rattle. "During the reconstruction—did you see what happened?"

"Tracy set the circle outside yours," I said. "There was a very

429

small summoning, but it was enough. She might have set a beacon before any of you showed up. But you couldn't reach the alarm because of her. She...did it."

An ache built in my sinuses. Tracy. It couldn't be. Couldn't be. Impossible. To speak it would mean a treason I couldn't accept.

"Tracy."

"She wouldn't," I whispered. Saints preserve me. Not her. Anyone else.

Anne Marie shook her head, eyes dull. "She did."

The sick feeling spread to my heart. "Tracy."

"I really thought it was you."

"I really hoped it was you," I said, and she cracked an eye open to scowl at me half-heartedly. I sighed. "Not because you're a black witch, because you're a *bad* witch."

The muscles in her jaw jumped, and when she didn't snap back, my heart sank. Our eyes met, and for a moment we only stared at each other. Two old combatants in a new war.

Her gaze drifted to a point high over my head, her voice growing distant. "I, Annette Marie, the Morrigan, find Tracy war witch, daughter of witches, guilty of dark magic and demon-handling. I find her responsible for the deaths of three witches of the War Coven. The sentence for each of these crimes is death."

I couldn't breathe, my eyes too dry to even blink. Memories of Tracy played through my mind like an old film reel, skipping and jumping, and in the end it burned to ash. Lies. All of it or just most of it didn't really matter.

But it took two war witches to condemn a third. Anne Marie didn't see me as aligned, so she wouldn't ask. The Morrigan's word was enough. She could do it all herself.

Her voice went quiet. "How do you find, Lilith war witch?"

Grief burned white hot in my chest, the words bitter on my

tongue. "I, Lilith war witch, find Tracy guilty of the stated crimes. I concur with the sentence of death."

The only sound was the rasp of our breathing, the whistle of air through my broken nose. I tried to concentrate on the pain in my hand, a focus for all the misery surrounding us. Tracy. Tracy betrayed me, offered me up to the kettle. Betrayed her true coven, and killed Rosa and Joanne and Andre.

Anne Marie's chest expanded as she inhaled, letting it out in a rush. "I hereby authorize you, Lilith war witch, to carry out this sentence. I authorize you to execute the traitor."

The tears wouldn't come. The words did, though, stiff and formal. Finding refuge in the ceremony. "I will execute if I am able."

She deflated, and her gaze dropped. I cradled my right hand to my chest and watched the throb of blood against the gory hamburger and the edge of bone. He'd lopped it off with pruning shears. "They have my fingerbones."

"I'm sorry." She sounded like she actually meant it.

I waited until my voice was stronger. "We'll only get one chance."

She nodded, and for the first time in our shared history, Anne Marie and I plotted against Tracy. My heart hardened with every beat of pain in my hand. They had my fingerbones, and they meant to use them.

# CHAPTER 51

The hooded dark witches shoved Tracy through the door with bluster and ineffective hexes splashing around, to prove they tormented her as they did us, and she sank to her knees under the weight of the chains. Her eyes filled with tears.

I felt nothing.

The kettle gathered somewhere above us, their dirty magic intertwined and building toward a major spell. The fire demons, maybe. It felt familiar, with a heated static crackling through the air. I leaned my head against the wall, too tired to care. Too hurt to give a damn. Death comes eventually to us all, but a little quicker for her.

Tracy scrabbled across the cement, trying to reach me. "We have to get out of here."

"And how," Anne Marie said, caustic enough to strip paint from a car, "do you suggest we do that?"

"They want Lilith's spells. She can free us."

I focused on breathing, in and out. In and out. This too shall pass. Somewhere, far away, Leif waited. And somewhere far closer, Brandr suffered. He deserved more than dying for some foolish plan and a witch's betrayal.

"So this is your fault, Lilith." Anne Marie's words stung, cold and hateful, despite our plan. She probably meant it.

Tracy moved closer. "Just tell them."

I shook my head, not bothering to open my eyes.

"Tell *me*," she whispered. "I'll tell Rook."

My eyes opened. Rook. The same bastard who got to Sam and stole him away. The same witch who cut off my finger. I counted a dozen heartbeats before I dared speak, so I wouldn't condemn her and spit hate at Rook at the same time. "Can't."

She edged closer. "It doesn't really matter, Lil. You already told them how to summon fire demons. It can't get worse than that."

She had no idea, bless her heart. If she'd studied Rook's book, she might have thought she knew how dark the world got, but there were levels and levels below whatever hell she deemed the worst.

But the thought that she might have convinced me, once, sickened me. Even a few days ago, I would have sided with her over Anne Marie in a heartbeat. Smiling at her hurt every cell in my body. "Sure. Telling them how to summon fire demons sounds like something I would do."

A long pause, her face lost in darkness, then she spoke, so casual my stomach turned. "You didn't?"

"My mother never called me Lilith."

Movement, sudden and violent, exploded next to me. Anne Marie lurched up and tackled Tracy near the door, and I had to wonder where she found the strength. The new Morrigan spoke through gritted teeth, "Running to tell Sumo?"

"Are you crazy?" Tracy struggled to throw her off. "Lilith, help me!"

I forced my eyes all the way open, so I could see her face

when she lied. "Is that why Rook wanted my fingerbones? Fire demons?"

"No, for—" She paused, and only their ragged breathing broke the silence.

I watched her, unable to summon any emotion stronger than disbelief. I should have hated her for what she'd done and all the lives she'd taken. I should have despised her, for helping Rook. For the demons lurking inside her. But she still wore Tracy's face.

The emotion fell from her expression as she looked between us. A stranger replaced my friend. Tracy lifted her hands and the chains dropped away from some hidden mechanism. She pulled off the fake iron collar and let it clang to the floor, shoving Anne Marie away.

"Why?" It took effort to care, the weight of her betrayal heavier than the chains. "You saw what it did to Sumo."

"We were getting slaughtered," she said, crouching near me. "We were never going to win. You did the complicated stuff, and you were so damn *reckless*. It was only a matter of time until you got killed, and then where would we have been?"

"Don't put this on her," Anne Marie said, forcing herself up. "You chose this. That burden is yours alone."

Tracy concentrated on me, eyes wide. Wide enough that I could see the red ring around her iris. Demon-mad. "And you wouldn't use our best weapons. Demons could have saved us in the third year, could have ended the war and saved thousands of lives, but you were too good for that."

"So Rook went after Sumo. And you." I considered the growing list of reasons I hated Rook. Having nine fingers instead of ten topped the list. "When did he get you?"

"The seventh year," she said.

The desperate urge to cry or curse almost overwhelmed me. Eight years. Eight years she lied to me. To her coven. To everyone. I watched her feet as she started pacing. But a few other mysteries solved themselves. "So you protected Sumo after I killed him."

"Oh yes," she said, eyes shining. "He had protective glyphs in his clothes, to preserve him. They activated when you burned him."

Anger twisted my stomach and a storm of magic waited, hidden by the iron. There wasn't enough magic in the world to destroy what needed to be destroyed, to quiet the rage in my heart. Traitor.

But Anne Marie, at least, remembered the plan. Her voice grated on my frayed nerves, even knowing she was on my side. "So while they summon fire demons upstairs, you're relegated to the basement. Sounds like you're really important, Tracy."

"They need me to distract you."

"Distract two collared witches too tired to fight. Sure," Anne Marie said. "But you stayed in our coven full-time, so obviously you weren't too important. If Rook really needed you, your charade wouldn't have lasted more than a month."

Tracy's mouth puckered. "Rook relies on me to—"

"To do the easy shit?" Anne Marie laughed. "Fetch the salt? Give him power? Are you sleeping with him, too? How could you be so *stupid*?"

A hex caught Anne Marie full in the chest. She grunted before she collapsed, and I turned toward her, patting her. "Anne Marie?"

Tracy laughed.

Anne Marie stared at me as I curled the hex's magic around my fingers, and I attempted a smile. From the look on her face, I failed. I faced Tracy, waiting for the hatred I felt toward Sam to transfer to her. "If she dies, your friends will be disappointed."

"She'll serve her purpose, dead or alive," Tracy said, checking her watch. "We'll get enough out of her either way."

I recoiled, unable to reconcile that callousness with the

friend I'd cherished. "Saints, Tracy—what the hell happened to you?"

She shrugged, though her voice cracked. "You said it yourself, Lil—it's a slippery slope. I started experimenting and then Rook...found me. They appreciated me. Needed me."

I held my breath, acutely aware of Anne Marie's growing tension. I hoped she didn't screw everything up. "They used you. Look what they made you do—hide how powerful you are."

"It's not like that. You don't know them."

"Do *you* know them?" I rolled to my knees, steeled myself to stand. Everything hurt. And her magic waited, slippery and thin, around my fingers. "How much time did you spend in their circle? Or do they keep you away, to protect your status in the Alliance?"

Tracy stared around the room as though she'd never seen it. "They said I know too much."

"Oh, Tracy." In the darkest cockles of my soul, I felt a touch of sympathy for her. She'd been more adrift than I'd ever imagined. Maybe if I'd called her, after the war, I would have seen it. Could have saved her. I pushed to my feet and swayed as I balanced against the heavy collar and the chains dragging down my arms. "He lied to you. You have to see that."

"*No.* Rook gave me a book, he said one day I would lead my own coven and—"

I stepped closer. "That book—I found it at your house, in the kitchen. I looked at it, Tracy, and it's been altered. The spells all backfire if they're used."

"That's a lie." Her hands clenched. "You don't know anything about that book."

"I have the real one, Tracy." I reached out as shock settled over her expression and Anne Marie made an irritated noise. "I can show you the differences. I have all the books you'd ever need. We can start a new coven that will make the world cower in fear."

"I can't—"

"You said," I interrupted. "You would be the first to follow, if I started a coven. So let's do it. I'll lead, if you want me to, or we'll make you a Morrigan to terrify the world."

Seconds ticked by as she considered, the darkness weighing on me as the chanting overhead grew louder and the magic spiraled up in heady waves. Her expression cleared just as I wanted to scream to break the tension. "We have to eliminate some competition."

I forced a smile as I held out my right hand. My conscience flared, but the War Witch knew Tracy was too far gone to save. Madness stained her magic. Red circled her irises. She was a rabid dog, and one with the power to not only summon demons, but the willingness to use them. She would be a pebble in the city's magical pond, sending ripples of insanity into every nook and cranny.

I managed a more genuine smile. "I already have a list."

The opal ring on her hand glimmered as she reached for mine. "Welcome back."

"Guess I'll need a new ring," I said, and reached out, decision made. The hex trembled in my hand. It would be enough.

"Not so fast," a deep voice said, and Tracy went rigid as magic zinged.

I swayed back with the weight of the collar. Sam.

# CHAPTER 52

He walked around the corner and into view, and still looked almost like the man I'd loved. Only his eyes gave him away, with the red ring glowing around the irises. Sam's eyebrows rose as he looked from Tracy to Anne Marie and me. "Having a good time, are we?"

Tracy cleared her throat, remarkably calm for being caught in the middle of her newest treason. "Lilith was just telling me about the fire demon spell."

"I find that hard to believe," Sam said. He didn't remove the hex that froze her. His attention drifted back to me, and my skin crawled with the sense of pure evil staring at me from behind his eerie eyes. "But I have been looking forward to this, Lilith."

"So you enjoyed me killing you the first time around?"

"Even that was exhilarating," he said. He inhaled deeply and stole all the oxygen from the room, wild-eyed. "To feel death take over my body and soul, and then to—*burn*—feeling it all but knowing that immortality awaited. I would give that freedom to you, Lilith. We could remake the world."

"I like the world the way it is." It was one of the biggest lies I'd ever told. He knew it, too.

Sam moved closer, murmuring, "I miss exchanging power with you, Lilith. I miss the rush. We can have that again, you know." The corner of his mouth curled as he eyed me. "The sex wasn't bad, either."

Heat rose in my cheeks, more from rage than embarrassment. "I've had better."

Anne Marie laughed.

But Sam only smiled and shook a finger at me. "So I heard. The Warder, that animal—really? He's a little...proletarian for you, isn't he? Although I suppose you spent enough time lusting after him while we were together. Don't think I didn't notice, dear."

"I meant power," I said, and my cheeks burned still more. Sam wouldn't have to kill me—rage and spontaneous combustion might get the job done first. "I've had power that dwarfs yours."

"Forgive me if I don't believe you," he said. Sam wandered closer and examined the edges of the ward that contained the three of us, peering at where Tracy remained motionless as if he didn't know the cause. "I've been watching you, and you haven't gotten close to any male witches, other than that weakling who follows the animals around."

Poor Kyle. I wondered whether he looked for us. I wouldn't want him to challenge Rook or Sam, not when it meant torture and death. But I had to knock Sam off balance and distract him from the magic that still tangled around my fingers. "Did I say he was a witch, Sumo?"

"You can't take power from humans," Sam said. "And you certainly can't mean—"

"Soren," I said, releasing his name like a talisman on a thread of the stolen magic. I Called the Peacemaker and summoned him like a wandering puppy. Our nascent connection had to work a second time—our lives depended on it.

"That's right. Guess who learned to control and manipulate pack magic?"

Another set of lies, sort of.

His ghastly face went whiter still, and I eased another step closer to Tracy. Sam shook his head. "That's not possible."

"You always underestimated me," I said, taking one long last look at his serene face.

Before he could speak, the spell above us built in a dangerous crescendo as they attempted to summon the fire demons. The kettle's chanting hiccupped, paused—then the cursing started. Magic flared out, seeking, and sulfur curled through the house until everything reeked. Sam glanced up, his concentration broken, as the kettle's spell faltered and the crackle of flames grew louder.

I lunged to reach Tracy, using her magic to rip away the iron around my throat and wrists, and grabbed her shoulder with my left hand. I pulled her back as Sam shouted and the wards climbed around us, Anne Marie trying to hex him before we were sealed off even more.

Power sparked as the fire built and I dragged Sam's hex off Tracy. She smiled in relief and tried to embrace me, demon-mad eyes blazing with excitement. "Thanks, Lil. We should—"

"I'm sorry," I said, and I meant it. I really did.

Her face went blank as her power rushed out, and she stared at me in confusion as I stole everything she had.

# CHAPTER 53

*S*am leapt back instead of attacking as I lowered Tracy's limp body to the floor. She still lived, but she would never cast magic again. I'd done my part. Anne Marie could do the rest.

Wards flared up and shouts built upstairs as a garbled regression spell failed, then the clatter of feet on the stairs alerted us to the kettle's approach. Why they'd run into the basement of a burning house escaped me until they skidded behind Sam and started chanting, trying to redirect the mess from upstairs to our little piece of heaven in the dark.

"Shit," Anne Marie said, and I spun Tracy's magic out into a ward around us, inside the kettle's ward. Just in time, too, as smoke and sulfur coalesced too close.

My lip curled as I looked at Sam, letting the cold magic seep through me. Even with the tinge of demon madness that Tracy carried, the magic was strong enough to lift me up and protect me. I tried to remember the good times, before she changed, and concentrated on the heroics she performed during the war. She'd saved my life. That memory cleansed some of the hate and evil from the magic, until I knew I could do some good on her behalf by killing the dark witches. A small repayment for her role in so much damage. But Sam—hiding behind the black-cloaked witches, had always been a coward. Unwilling to risk himself when survival was not assured and others would take the chance instead of him. Fool.

The dark witches kept up their chant until a sunspot appeared just outside my wards, but I didn't take my eyes off Sam. I'd raised him; he was my responsibility. I rotated my head to the right, then left, my vertebrae cracking. Then I'd get Brandr the hell out of that house, and we could even more scores. It felt like a dream as smoke drifted into the basement and ash and cinders dropped all around us.

Anne Marie tried to keep an eye on all the kettle members as they started to spread out, trying to surround us in the large room. I pulled her collar and chains off, dropping them as they burned my hands, and she muttered curses and hexes that should have fucked up those dark witches as well as three generations of their ancestors. It was just a beat, and then she drew her own power, lighting up like a beacon, and we stood shoulder to shoulder to face death and the small demon that popped to life and started attacking my wards.

The temperature in the basement climbed, and it was another degree of cruelty that sweat dripped into the open wounds and reignited the fire that even magic couldn't dampen. My pinkie throbbed in time with my heartbeat, a distraction from the business of saving ourselves. Anne Marie's breath hissed in her teeth, and I wondered if she experienced the same.

"We can save you. You just have to cooperate," one of the dark witches said, and I took a moment to count them—a full nine. Without Tracy. So Rook always had a spare. Disloyal bastards, all of them.

Most of them hid in deep hoods, but I memorized the strands of their magic and knew I would be able to find them.

As they continued to feed magic to the demon rampaging against my shields to reach Anne Marie and me, I leaned to pull the opal ring off Tracy's finger. I studied it closely, searching for whatever side panel crests they decided to corrupt with their damn dark magic, then held it up for Sam and Rook to see. "You want this back, stud? Give it to your next girlfriend?"

"Keep it," Sam said. He pulled my jade ring out of his pocket and held it up to kiss, closing his eyes as if he could sense me on the silver. His mouth twisted as he played with it, and it might have been my imagination, but his teeth looked black with blood as he smiled. "I've got this, and so many happy memories to go with it. I don't think I can trust you enough to keep you, Lilith. After all this... How could I sleep next to you again?"

"Listen while my heart breaks," I said. "What are you going to do about it? Kill us? Go ahead and try."

"Maybe don't antagonize them just yet," Anne Marie said. "What with the demon right there."

I turned my back to the kettle, though the back of my neck itched in paranoia even with the wards, and faced her. They didn't need to see me winking at her or trying to make her understand. At least none of them managed to get all the way around our ward. "Maybe if you weren't such a coward and a bagwitch, we wouldn't be in this position."

Her eyebrows arched and I winked hard, though having both eyes nearly swollen shut may have precluded the message being passed. They'd used me to trick her, and her to trick me, and it was our turn to completely fuck them over. No more games. No sleight of hand or fancy charms. Just war witches destroying everything around them.

She took a deep breath and folded her arms over her chest. "And if you weren't a complete psychopath, we wouldn't be in this position. So I guess that makes us equal."

"Not by a long shot." I really hoped she kept an eye on that damn demon. I willed her to understand what I intended. If she could hold off the demon, I could break the kettle's circle, the same as I broke the wards on her store. It might kill me, but at least I'd have a chance to get rid of Sam once and for all. Rook could slaughter us, or the house would collapse on top of us, but I needed to know that Sam no longer haunted the world. I wanted him in hell. Forever.

"I've wanted to say this since that day at your store, Anne Marie. Now we're stuck here and it's your fault, and I'm going to walk out of here and make sure the Alliance knows just how badly you failed."

Her eyes narrowed as she watched me. "How dare you—"

"This shit is as low budget as your wards," I said, waving my hand back at the kettle. My wards shot through with lightning as the demon redoubled its attacks, growing larger and hungrier with each moment it was denied blood. I widened my eyes and hoped my concentration alone would make her psychic. "And just as useful at keeping me contained. This is it, Anne Marie. I'm done."

The knowledge broke across her face like clear dawn, but she immediately shook her head. "Lilith, you can't—"

A larger crack appeared in my wards, and it took longer to seal up. The kettle fed the demon more and more power, and mine began to fade. I clenched my hands at my sides. "I will not die here, Annette. *Je vais pas.*"

She dropped into a defensive crouch, like we were about to fight, and her voice shook though her hands held steady. She drew up power, expression resolute, and prepared to go down fighting. I was almost proud of her. "Like hell I will either, Lilith. Prepare yourself."

But something in her eyes pleaded with me, and she shook her head a little as she whispered, "Not like this, Lil."

"You said it yourself—I have much to atone for." I slapped

446

my hands together and walked to the edge of my wards, placing my hands against the magic to reinforce and control the shield, so I would know exactly how to drop it. "This makes up for at least three of the seven plagues, no?"

Some of the kettle retreated as the fire roared overhead and a beam in the ceiling began to smoke. I took a deep breath and braced myself. It was now or never. Remaining frozen would only get us killed faster.

Before Anne Marie could argue with me or try to convince me not to take a run at their wards, I glanced over and nodded to her. "I'll make sure you get a nice pyre."

"Ditto," she said through gritted teeth, and pursed her lips.

As Sam preened and offered us safety if we only cooperated, I centered myself and dropped the wards.

The demon lunged forward and the kettle yelled, some in triumph and some in fear. The snake-like being got close enough to my leg that its sulfur breath singed what remained of my pants, and I wondered if I would die before I even got to the wards. I hexed it and Anne Marie snarled something, then her magic shot out and trapped the thing with only a few millimeters to spare.

I dragged myself past the hungry demon and leaned into the kettle's wards as Rook raised his hands and summoned more power. With as cowardly as he was, the fact he stayed in the basement as the house burned struck me as strange. Maybe it was all an illusion, an effort to make Anne Marie and me act hastily.

It would have been a hell of a glamour.

The power of their wards crackled through my hands, a punch in the chest like grabbing an electrified fence. I braced myself and gritted my teeth, forcing my hands through. I just had to break it. Just had to crack it a bit and the backlash would disable the kettle, we could escape, and I'd save Brandr. Saints protect and keep me. *It had to work.*

LAYLA NASH

The dome around us cracked, from my hands to the ground and back in a spiderweb of potential. The kettle shored it up, reinforcing and patching as fast as it weakened, though more than one looked around at the smoke and ash with flares of concern in their magic. Anne Marie muttered behind me and the kettle faltered, distracted by her spell, and I bit back irritation at the noise they all made.

Sam smiled as he mirrored Rook's raised-arm gesture. "You will not win, Lilith. I've learned many things since I've been gone."

I leaned into the wards more, my brain rattling in my skull with the force of it, and blinked as smoke stung my eyes and blurred my vision. It had to work. The wards had to fail.

But Anne Marie still hadn't killed the demon. I looked back, hesitating, and she snapped, "Don't you dare interfere. I can handle this demon."

"You have to unbalance the elemental connection," I said. I shoved my foot into the wards to create another source of fracture. Almost there. The dark witches' hands shook and their chanting fell out of rhythm.

"I know what I'm doing, *witch*."

I found the weakest link in the kettle's spell, the witch who struggled to maintain his part of the spell. That one. That one was the key to undoing. I clenched Tracy's opal ring in my hand and shouldered my way into the ward. Magic burst through me like lightning and I felt myself coming apart, being consumed by the magic, and the wards flexed around me.

Sam started to sweat. "If you wanted to share power, lover, you should have just asked."

"I'd rather die than let you touch me." My voice shook and I swallowed a cry as pain ripped through me.

"That's not a problem for me," he said, smooth as silk and just as pretty. He slid closer to the wards, magic flaring around

448

him in a greasy black halo as his fingers drifted over the kettle's efforts. "My tastes have... expanded since we parted."

Anne Marie's strangled yell made me tense. "Stop playing around, witch—end it already."

"This isn't *easy*, you stupid cow," I muttered, as the power raged through me and melted my bones into nothingness.

I forced myself to smile at Sam. One last chance. My hands vibrated in the wards and I focused. One last shove. One push. That was all I needed. I leaned into it and hurled myself into the magic, praying the saints would protect me, and then...

My fingers broke through just enough, and I threw the opal ring in his face.

His head snapped back and he fell, tripping over his own feet. Without Sam as the anchor, the young one faltered. I pushed harder. Right there. The dome of magic bowed out, expanding under the pressure of my power.

Someone cried out, fell. A beam broke and crashed to the ground behind them, and everything shattered.

Some of the magical backlash exploded out, searing into the standing kettle members, and Sam flew back in a clap of thunder. But some of it rolled inward, and I staggered back to Anne Marie. "Shield yourse—"

It was too late—I turned in time to see the demon vaporize in a wave of power and Anne Marie collapse in silence. I went to my knees in pain as my whole brain melted and everything blackened around the edges. It was a thousand times worse than when Leif broke the wards on my apartment.

I braced my hands on the floor, unwilling to simply collapse as the fire licked closer, and found myself staring at where Tracy lay, motionless, on the ground. Not even a faint spark of life or magic remained.

My eyes burned, too dry from heat and magic to cry, but my heart ached.

Maybe I'd been her executioner after all.

# CHAPTER 54

*N*othing moved except the smoke.

I concentrated on breathing, telling myself to get up. Get up. *Fight*. Don't just lie here and wait for something to happen. Didn't want to die in the dark, in the fire.

*Get up.*

I crawled to Anne Marie but stopped, staring as Tracy's opal ring spun across the floor with the sweet chime of silver. Sam rolled and tried to stand, and I reached for Anne Marie. We'd only survive if we worked together. I shoved Tracy's ring in my pocket. "Anne Marie. We have to go."

She forced her eyes open and raised shaking hands. "I hate you. What the fuck *was* that?"

"Another bad night," I said. I flinched as something creaked and cracked in the basement, and sprinklers and smoke detector went off in every room above us. "We've gotta move."

"Find the coven," she said, holding her side as she started to sit. "We can't leave them here."

I staggered to my feet and stepped over Tracy's body to the back rooms of the basement. Something exploded upstairs and all the lights went off, plunging us into even more terrible darkness. I blinked and held my breath, an overwhelming anxiety gripping me. I hated the dark. I really hated the dark.

And somewhere, Rook and Sam waited.

But so did Brandr and Anne Marie's coven. I used a tiny thread of power to shine a light into the darkness, moving as fast as I dared through a maze of boxes and the saints only knew what else.

People shouted behind me, in the main room, and I paused, looking back for Anne Marie. But we couldn't leave the witches. I had to find Brandr. He didn't deserve to burn to death somewhere in the basement. My foot disappeared into a hole and I fell, wrenching my knee as my leg caught between the bars of a large grate in the floor.

I stared down into the hole and found Jacques looking back at me.

The cold iron grate burned my leg and I dragged myself away, breathing through the pain. He, Lauren, and Desiree cowered away from me in the bottom of a dank hole. Magic burned through the lock on the grate, and I heaved the grate up and away with a grunt. "Come on. This place is burning. We have to get out of here."

None of them moved, though they braced as if expecting an attack. And I wondered if they believed I'd tortured them, like Anne Marie said, instead of the dark witches. We didn't have time for a detailed explanation. I ground my teeth but tried to understand where they were coming from. "It wasn't me. It was Tracy. Tracy betrayed us. Anne Marie will tell you the rest, she's through that door. We have to go."

Jacques stared at me for a long second, then held his hand up. "I'll trust you this time."

"Great," I said under my breath, and grabbed his hand. He nearly wrenched me into the hole with them, but I grabbed a nearby unused piece of exercise equipment and managed to haul him out.

I zapped the collar off him and pointed behind me in the darkness. "Anne Marie is there. Have you seen the wolf? Have they brought a shifter through here?"

"Not here," he said, grim. "I'll get them out. Go."

So maybe he didn't entirely trust me.

I didn't have time to give a shit. The darkness and smoke closed in until I coughed and hacked and couldn't see, even with my magical flashlight. I got low, trying to crawl under the smoke, and scrambled back to the main room. There had to be a closet or somewhere else to hide Brandr. He couldn't be gone. He couldn't. I still felt him, in my heart.

The stairs opened up to my left, offering an escape, but I passed them without hesitation. Utility space on the other side could have hidden him. I coughed and dragged my tattered shirt up to cover my mouth and nose, wondering if Anne Marie made it upstairs. Nothing else stirred in the hellish darkness.

Something seized my ankle and I cried out. Looking back and seeing Sam, I kicked back as a sludge of magic rolled out and clawed at my insides. Blood streaked his face as he dragged himself after me.

His expression turned even uglier. "You're not getting away from me again."

The greasy power I'd taken from the destroyed wards and Tracy grew slowly as I fought the desperation of getting his hands off me. But he paralyzed me, stealing life from my muscles as he sucked away my magic. He crawled closer with the clammy grip of the dead. "I missed you."

He was cold, his body ice, and his breath reeked of gravedirt and maggots. I struggled against the overwhelming tide of his dark, cloying magic, and strained to throw him off as he crawled up my body. He reached my soul, consuming all of me until I couldn't move or breathe or hope. I swallowed my screams, not wanting him to have the satisfaction, and whispered, "Not like this."

Sam closed his eyes in rapture, lips parted as he inhaled my magic and tried to inhale me too. "Couldn't be any other way, lover."

The world dulled around the edges. Sam dredged my life force, the pool of magic that sustained everything that was me. It whispered away in a drift of smoke, insubstantial.

No more magic. It was worse than being collared—there was simply nothing left. My aura faded. And Sam, dead and evil, lay against me.

As hope drifted away, something stirred deep inside, beyond all the memories and magic and grief.

Life.

I wanted to live. I wanted to fight. I'd struggled for so many years to survive, I couldn't give up. Not in a dark basement at the hands of an evil revenant. I wouldn't surrender myself to him or his dark spells, even in death. If it was my time to go and the saints guided my path to the afterlife, then I would do it on my terms—under the sun or stars, on the earth, breathing fresh air.

My lips parted and breath escaped. "Samuel."

He lifted his head, practically purring. "Yes, my love?"

"I banish you," I said. "Samuel."

"You won't," he murmured.

I closed my eyes as tears gathered in defense against the smoke and a rising tide of panic. The stairs were so close. "I banish you, Salvatore."

Sam looked down at me, coal-fire eyes narrowing as he studied me in the darkness. "You can't do this, Lilith. You don't know my names."

This part was the worst. It was the worst. I dreaded it so much death almost seemed preferable. But I needed magic. I opened myself up to his power and let it crawl over me, through me. I shuddered in revulsion as Sam groaned, reveling in the connection, and bile filled my mouth as I forced myself

454

to remain still and passive. Let him think me defeated. Let him think he won.

"I banish you," I said again, gathering enough of his power to make it matter. "Szemere."

He went rigid. "No."

The power gave me strength. "Szemere, I banish you. *I banish you.*"

Sam screamed as I used his third name, the one with all the power and the one he thought I didn't know, and flew backward as the stolen magic and all of my intent combined in a full spell.

I couldn't breathe. At least the magic helped me scan the surrounding darkness—no shifters. No sign of Brandr.

Sam got to his knees, crawling toward me. "Lilith."

"Coward," I said, pushing backward. I dragged myself upright with the help of the wall, though my concentration broke as Anne Marie and the other three witches appeared out of the smoke.

Sam ran through me, knocking me down, and bolted up the crumbling stairs. I cursed and slid to the floor once more. Anne Marie leaned down and caught my hand, not flinching from the bloody, four-fingered grip. She shoved magic at me and I tensed. "What are you doing?"

"If I'm going to prosecute you for performing magic in front of shifters, you need to be alive." She didn't smile.

Her magic, at least, was clear and cold and crisp, the very opposite of Sam's evil sludge. She gave me the strength to haul myself up and charge after Sam, fighting through the flames and smoke. He disappeared toward what remained of Tracy's living room, and I dodged falling pieces of ceiling as I followed.

Time for Sam to die.

\* \* \*

CLIMBING the stairs felt like trying to scale Everest without any equipment. The boards crumbled in places and broke, burning wood scraped my calves as I hauled myself toward the living room. Somewhere up there, Sam waited. Rook waited. I bared my teeth in a snarl and imagined the air clear and clean.

The bloody carpet in Tracy's living room turned black with soot and fire, dark smoke filling the place until I tripped over an overturned end table. Sam hesitated in the doorway, though all I could see were his glowing eyes.

Anne Marie growled in fury behind me and hexed him. Sam dodged and flung a hex back; it was badly made but well-aimed, and clipped her. Anne Marie went down and Jacques crouched next to her.

I chased Sam and tackled him on the lawn, hatred driving me to cripple him. He tried to crawl away, but I dredged up the power—some of it his own—to cast the spell from Mother's book.

"Bet you haven't seen this one," I said, gritting my teeth. I pinned him down with a beam of magic, trapping him like a butterfly on a board, as I built the spell in my mind. At least the air was clean and I could finally take a good breath. Thunder rolled overhead, and somewhere far away, sirens rose. "This is for death. Final, forever, never-coming-back *death*."

I raised my hands to summon the fountain of magic I needed. He begged. He said he could be rehabilitated, sobbed that he'd only been misled by others. That it wasn't his fault, he'd been tricked. It was an exact repeat of the first time I killed him. I'd almost fallen for it then.

Not anymore.

I thought of Rosa and Joanne and Andre, and even Tracy, as I created the dagger of power to rip his soul from that revenant body and send all of him to an afterlife of suffering. It was for them more than me.

Anne Marie shouted, "Look out," and a figure blurred from the darkness in my peripheral vision.

Something slammed into me and I fell, my hand trailing through the circle. It broke. Sam scrambled away in the wet grass, still alive. Still alive, damn him to the coldest hell.

I screamed in rage and slammed all of my power at the one who saved him, knocking the dark-cloaked witch back as I rolled to my feet.

He chuckled, the same velvet creepy voice as the one who'd taken my pinkie, and said, "We will meet again," before he tilted his face to the sky and sang out a word of power.

I almost saw the flash of lightning before it crashed down on top of me and the world turned to flames again.

Smoke rose from the grass around me as I lay there, conscious only of the stuttering, slow beat of my heart. The dark-voiced witch, who could only have been Rook, jogged into the night with Sam. The other witches were long gone—so there was no honor among dark witches, either. Sirens grew closer, more and more of them gathering. I wondered how the Alliance knew. Maybe they heard me, when I Called.

Anne Marie took a few unsteady steps onto the lawn, holding her dislocated shoulder from the hex, and collapsed. She managed to avoid the scorched earth where the lightning had struck me.

At least I could see the stars.

The house burned behind us, fueled by magic, and made the air gritty and hot. I badly wanted a shower. I released whatever magic I held, not wanting to feel the greasy slime of Sam's magic anymore, and the wave of pain that rolled through me as it receded almost knocked me out completely.

I stared up at the stars, trying to remember which ones Dad and I had moved around. "Anne Marie."

The quiet stretched as the three other witches ran away from the house, huddling together a few yards down to wait for the cavalry to arrive, and left the new Morrigan and the old Morrigan alone. She took a deep breath. "You were right. When you killed him. I didn't want to see it, but with everything... You were right."

"I didn't see it in Tracy." I blinked soot and ashes away, though it might have been tears that blinded me. The full moon revealed more than I wanted. I tried not to think of Tracy, lying still and lifeless and alone in the basement.

"None of us did."

It didn't make me feel any better.

The sirens cut off before they became deafening, and instead voices and shouts and running feet approached. The Alliance, coming to rescue us.

My fingers dug into the earth to anchor myself, despite the pain in my hand, and I searched for Brandr. He had to be close. If he lived, he had to be near. But the darkness revealed nothing.

I cleared my throat, raw from smoke and screaming. "I think I'm going to pass out now."

"Good," she muttered. "I'm tired of listening to you."

"You're welcome," I said, and gave up trying to stay conscious.

# CHAPTER 55

When I woke, I expected to see Moriah or maybe Leif, if I hadn't been abandoned on the lawn. But instead, moon-faced Kyle perched on the edge of a chair next to the bed, hands pressed between his knees as he stared at me.

I blinked, waiting for reality to adjust itself around me, and couldn't speak. My throat felt raw and brittle at the same time, and every inch of me ached.

Kyle still stared at me, wide-eyed.

I took a deep breath, testing my lungs, and wheezed. "What?"

"You're awake," he said, breath exploding out in a rush. He sagged back in the chair as if his bones melted. "Praise the saints, you woke up."

None of my muscles cooperated as I tried to sit, so I settled for raising my head to study where I lay. "Was there suspicion I wouldn't?"

"Anne Marie said—"

"She had my pyre planned, didn't she?" My mouth twisted into something like a smile. Just like she'd promised.

He flushed, flipping the dark hair out of his face. "She said she'd agreed to—"

I snorted, then used my left hand to push myself up and drag the sheets back. I couldn't stand the feel of my skin another moment—and though I didn't think I had enough strength for a cleansing circle, I could take a really, really hot shower. I didn't look at the mitten of bandages around my right hand.

Kyle averted his gaze from my bare legs. "Uh, I'm supposed to tell the Alpha—"

I lurched forward and grabbed the front of his shirt in both hands, yanking him closer until we were nose-to-nose. I kept my voice low, because to speak some truths too loudly meant returning to a very dark place. "A dark witch was *inside* me. He stole all my magic and then I had to take some of his just to survive. They tortured me. Used my dead mother against me. They almost burned me alive. I want to take a shower. The Alpha can join me if he's so desperate to talk, but I'm going to scrub off at least three layers of skin."

He gulped, wide-eyed, as I released him and shoved him back into the chair. I braced myself on it and the mattress until I was certain my knees would hold me up, then began the marathon shuffle to the attached bathroom.

Kyle fidgeted. "Do you...should I tell the Alpha to j-join you, or—?"

"Saints preserve me," I said, leaning against the wall to catch my breath. Four feet from the bed and already dizziness threatened to lay me out. "Can't you wait half an hour before you tell him?"

The mender slid lower in the chair, avoiding my gaze. "He already knows."

I used the sink for balance, though I avoided looking in the mirror. I didn't want to know what I looked like. "I'm still taking a shower."

"Should I tell him to, uh—"

"Get out, Kyle." I shut the door.

Near-boiling water didn't help. Neither did soap or the loofah I used until my skin rubbed raw. The violation seethed inside me, tainting my aura and the little magic that remained. I couldn't forget the feeling of taking in Sam's magic, of voluntarily inviting him into me, despite everything he'd done. Even though it was only to save my own life, it still hurt. I feared he'd contaminated me forever. That my magic would always be dirty and corrupted and... wrong.

I cried until the water ran cold and my eyes swelled so I couldn't see and a headache drove a spike through my ears. I didn't want to leave the protection of the shower curtain; there was no telling what waited outside. I doubted the world had gotten any kinder.

As I stood there with my face in my hands, the door opened. I held my breath, wondering if Soren actually planned to join me in the shower. But the door clicked shut and no one else disturbed the air. When I dared peek around the curtain, a pile of clothes waited beside two towels, still warm from the dryer. Even though a knot formed in my throat at the sight and hiding under the water for another hour seemed like the best idea I'd had in weeks, I climbed out and got dressed.

They were Moriah's clothes—I hoped and dreaded that she waited outside. If I asked, she would sit in silence, but she would have so many questions that I couldn't answer. I wasn't ready to talk about anything that happened. Not about Tracy, not about Sam, not about anything.

I wondered what Anne Marie told them. She probably made herself the hero. I still lived, so she hadn't told them everything.

I pulled my tangled hair back without looking in the mirror, so I wouldn't have to see the scars around my throat from the iron collar. No amount of healing would fix those, and I didn't have the strength for a glamour. I didn't even want to touch magic, for fear Sam's evil still lingered. I took a deep breath to steady myself before I opened the door.

Soren sat in the dim room, hands relaxed on the arms of Kyle's chair. He watched me but didn't speak.

I shivered as I plodded to the bed and curled up under the sheets with my back to him. I squeezed my eyes shut, wanting to block out the world and the building migraine from all the crying. The bond, stronger after my Calling him, rippled. Soren wanted to know what happened. My eyes prickled and my sinuses burned, and I shook my head against the pillow. Couldn't say it. Couldn't speak it or it would be true.

The chair creaked as he shifted, and the smell of his cologne grew stronger. I pressed my face into the pillow and tried to block out the world. He waited.

The bond made it easier. I didn't have to speak. I showed him, instead.

Soren tensed as images of Brandr and me in the Skein filtered to him, as the evening began. As Sam tricked us and the kettle trapped us. As they tortured me using Mother's face. As Rook cut off my finger. Tracy's betrayal.

He saw the fight, the demon, the miscast spell and the burning house, the feeling of Sam overpowering me and stealing my life, and the hopelessness. The emptiness as I watched my life fade away. The dirty contamination of taking Sam's magic. Trading my soul for survival. The lightning bolt on the lawn that drove me into the ground but didn't cleanse any of the past despite the fire and pain. Soren felt, I hoped, the desperation of deep water, the bitterness of Tracy's treachery, and the hope that remained each time I found Leif in the darkness.

When there was nothing left to show, Soren exhaled. The chair creaked as he got up. "I still do not like being in your head, witch."

The door whispered shut behind him.

# CHAPTER 56

*T*he next time I pried my eyes open, Soren occupied the chair once more. I was too tired to care, still too drained and hurt to wonder how long he'd spent watching me breathe. He got up and opened the door, saying something to someone outside, then returned to the chair.

"You should have called us sooner."

Us. Perhaps Kyle and Leif heard me as well. Or maybe he meant that little arrow of power I'd used as a last resort. Either way, it didn't matter. We could not undo what was done.

He folded his arms over his chest and frowned at the bed. "Knowing what happened... The Alliance owes you—*I* owe you —a great debt."

I didn't look at him. My voice still didn't work right, all gruff and intermittently squeaky. "It was witch business. There is no debt."

His head tilted as he studied me. "Anne Marie returned to her coven, or what remains of it. She will officiate the pyre for Rosa, Joanne, and Andre. It will be held in two days. You may attend."

It was an honor I hadn't expected. I'd just assumed my

persona non grata status had been reinstated the moment Anne Marie reappeared. "Thank you."

I didn't want to know, but I had to ask. "What was done with Tracy?"

Someone scratched at the door and Soren rose to retrieve a lap tray from someone outside. He placed it on the bed and helped me sit up, though I flushed as he fluffed the pillows and propped me up, then put it over my legs so I could examine the contents. Soup and pudding, water and hot tea.

Soren cleared his throat after shutting the door and collapsing back into the chair. "The house burned a great deal before we were able to dampen it, including the basement. What we recovered of her remains, Anne Marie supervised. There was no ceremony. She was submerged in salt water and then cremated. The ashes were mixed with more salt and cement, broken up and scattered on a trash heap."

Not even an unmarked grave for Tracy. I still couldn't reconcile the dark witch with the woman I'd known as my friend. It didn't seem possible. I sighed.

I stared at the ceiling, hoping no tears rose to the surface. "And Brandr? Did you give him a good burial?"

"Brandr?"

My throat closed. "You found him, didn't you? He wasn't in the basement, but he had to be there somewhere."

"Not in the house," he said, picking up his phone.

"He helped me," I said, heart pounding. Blessed saints. "He risked his life, and—"

"They probably killed him," he said, and it was a testament to the kettle's cruelty that death seemed the best option. "He's dead, Lily. I can't feel him in the pack bonds."

"He renounced his alignment before we went after the witches," I said. "He gave me his ring."

It still waited, in a warding box in the Remnant.

Soren muttered, "Arrogant ass," then leaned to pat my

ankle. "We'll find him. We can't use pack magic, but there are other ways to track him down."

I lay back, staring at a dim corner of the bedroom. I would find him, once I regained my strength. I wouldn't leave Brandr with them, even in death. I owed him more than that.

My throat ached and I attempted the tea, uncertain how well my stomach would tolerate anything when my guts still felt torn apart from the magic. Everything seemed to float, disconnected, and sometimes hurt with a sharp pain.

Soren put his feet up on the end of the mattress, near mine. "I want you to listen to me, Lily. This is important. I want your word you will consider what I'm going to propose."

"I'm tired." I picked at the soup. "But I'll listen. No other promises made, Peacemaker."

He laced his hands behind his head. "I do not normally offer this unless I am entirely certain of someone's loyalties, but this seems the wisest course of action, given what happened."

My heart sank. If he brought out that diamond ring again, I might not have the strength to refuse. Sheltering behind the Peacemaker as the dark witches hunted me down was just too tempting. Someone else could fight for once, even when it was witch business.

He smiled at his hands before looking back at me. "Don't look so repulsed. My offer is this—align to me."

"I don't—"

"You agreed to hear me out." He waited until I spooned up more soup, then Soren studied his shoes where they rested on the bed. "You would swear only to me. You owe no loyalty to the Alliance, and you are required to obey no one but me. You would have a direct line to me, the same as Leif and my alphas."

Even through my fatigue I could see the obvious flaw. "Anne Marie would kill me before the dark witches got the chance."

"Perhaps," he said. I couldn't guess the cause of his smile.

"Or perhaps we need not tell anyone. There are many ways to approach this, Lily, for us both to benefit."

I wondered if maybe it was part of his cleaning house in the Alliance. But I hesitated, wondering whether I'd only heard that from Tracy and had to question its veracity. So many tangled lies to sort through. It would take me weeks to figure out what to trust again.

I squinted at him, the soup forgotten. A slow swirl of pack magic, complicated and dense with his connection to hundreds of shifters, dominated his aura. "Why, Soren? What do you gain, if no one knows I'm aligned? And why would I want you in my head permanently? The connection we have now is bad enough."

"That connection may have saved your life, Lily."

As if I needed the reminder. I focused on the pudding. "I would have been fine. We got out of the house okay."

Soren shook his head. "You weren't breathing when we got there. But I'm not going to let you distract me, Lily. If you align to me, yes, I would see benefits. First, you're powerful and capable, and I would like reassurance that you're not working for someone else. Second, your knowledge of dark magic exceeds my witches, and it seems like that skill set will be useful in the coming months. We still haven't tracked down all the demons that escaped during the raids. Third, I owe you a debt, and if I'm going to repay you before you get yourself killed, I need to keep you close. And..." His lips twitched in a smile. "You drive Leif nuts, which is always fun to watch."

I refused to be convinced.

"And for you..." Soren took a deep breath before ticking each point off on his fingers. "If you're openly aligned, you get a proper ring with an Alliance crest, and all the protections that offers. A place to live, if you need it. A Styrma team at your beck and call until we kill the dark witches and know you're safe. There would also be a salary and discretionary funds for research and supplies. And—when you are in pain, Lily, I can take it away. It is an alpha's duty to protect his pack, and that includes bearing the burdens of my people when they can no longer shoulder those burdens themselves. I can help you. I can take away some of the darkness."

I swallowed hard as I put the spoon down. Everything tasted like ash. Doing memory surgery on myself seemed like a better idea with every passing moment, so I could be rid of those deep-water days. It was tempting to think he could shield me from the past. But the bad things made us who we were— fire smelted iron into steel and made it stronger. Even when those bad things made me want to crawl out of my own skin.

"There's too much tension with your people, Soren. It wouldn't work."

"You mean Leif?" Soren glanced at his watch. "Whatever argument you had, it can't have been that traumatic. He tore the city apart looking for you. Literally—I have to reconstruct three city blocks. And you reached for him ten times as much as you called me."

My eyes burned as I looked away. There wasn't anything to mourn. Leif had done all that because Soren couldn't afford to lose another war witch. He'd said it before. Hexing him and accusing him of treason only finished off whatever remained of our connection. I'd burned that bridge; it wouldn't get rebuilt before those city blocks. The dark witches still roamed the night, and I couldn't risk Leif sharing Brandr's fate.

Soren made an exasperated noise and nudged my leg with his foot. "I do not make a habit of involving myself in the romantic entanglements of my people, but from what I have seen, you and Leif are surprisingly well-suited. While I won't speak for him, he is...unaccustomed to being out of his element to this extent. I would ask you to take pity on him when you are ready to. Even though it's a great deal of fun watching him self-destruct into a melodramatic fool."

"Moriah told me about the bet. How much do you have riding on this?"

He smiled but didn't take the bait, instead canting his head at the door. "You want to know the only reason he's not here right now?"

A dozen possibilities scrolled through my head: on the prowl for his next conquest, maybe, or out drinking with Jake. Sacked out on his couch, drinking beer and congratulating himself on not having to deal with any more witch business.

Soren's voice dropped as he looked at his hands, shaking his head. "He's been hunting the dark witches since the moment we found you. It's been four days and he won't stop."

My heart hurt. And the tears that had gathered in my throat at the small kindness of clean clothes escaped at this much greater kindness. They burned my cheeks, so hot I feared they would scar and the world would always see the marks.

I wiped at my cheeks, knowing he could hear my sniffles. I tried to compose myself enough to speak in an almost-steady voice. "I didn't realize you gave out relationship advice."

"Yes, well." Soren leaned close and a few tissues fell onto the mattress next to my hand. "I don't make a habit of it, or I'd be knee-deep in lovestruck teenagers every day. So don't go telling anyone."

"Don't tell anyone I cried, and I won't tell anyone you pulled a Dear Abby."

"Agreed." He stood. "Think about aligning, Lily. I resolved the issues with the Externals, but they won't leave you alone for long. Stefan has it out for you."

I started to speak, maybe shout my refusal, but stopped as Soren turned. A mischievous grin turned his face boyish. "And I have fifty dollars in the pool, so call me when he takes you to dinner."

I scowled, "Get out," and he laughed, shutting the door behind him. I barely heard him talking to someone in the hall before fatigue weighed down my eyelids and I fell back into darkness.

## CHAPTER 57

*I* woke as Moriah threw Kyle out. His weak, "But the Alpha *told* me—" was no match for Moriah's strength or determination.

I waited until she shut the door to lift my head. Moriah sat, and guilt seized me as I saw her reddened eyes and haggard expression. "You're awake," she said.

"Everyone seems surprised by that."

"Well," she said, wiping quickly under her eyes. "You don't know what you looked like when we found you. You were just... there. Anne Marie said you might not wake up, but I didn't believe her until we got you back here and you—"

"Sorry," I said. "The last fight took all I had."

"Anne Marie told Soren the dark witch had you cornered in the basement and would have drained your life force if she hadn't hexed him."

I inhaled to belittle the idea that Anne Marie could ever have saved me when I remembered how I had, in fact, gotten free. Maybe Anne Marie saw me take Sam's magic and knew that would have contaminated me with demon magic, possibly forever, and she wanted to keep that for blackmail purposes. Or maybe she hadn't seen and really believed she saved me. Or maybe, just maybe, she saw and wanted to protect me. I scowled. It was probably the blackmail.

"She said they tortured you and—cut off your fingers." Moriah glanced at my bandaged hand. "And she kept you from telling them what they wanted to know."

Anger burned in my gut; Anne Marie took credit once again. I struggled to keep my voice steady. "What else?"

"She figured out that Tracy was the bad one, and she was the one who confronted and killed Tracy."

Breathing became difficult. I forced my eyes closed, concentrating on the feeling of each breath as I repeated Rosa's mantra. In the grand scheme of things, it didn't matter if Anne Marie took credit. I didn't *want* credit. If Anne Marie ran her yap about it, then the Externals would go after her instead. She helped me by claiming the spotlight.

But still I resented it. She cheapened the fight and Tracy's death and the sacrifices we all made, claiming to have done it all herself. She made me look like a weak, ineffective fool. I was many things, but I was not that. "That's not exactly how it happened."

"Do you want to talk about it?"

"No."

"You'll have to eventually."

"No," I repeated. "Some things I'll take to the grave."

She told me instead about the search after the demons attacked Soren's house. She looked at me sideways as she mentioned Leif, how he'd been Death itself rampaging through the city. Apparently he heard me, begging for help as they tortured me, and it drove him and the wolf insane that he couldn't reach me. My heart hurt to think of the additional pain I'd caused, but there was nothing to do about it after the fact.

Moriah put her feet up on the bed. "We put the wedding off for a few weeks; it didn't seem appropriate to have the ceremony the same week as the pyre. So maybe in a month we'll try again."

"Bet Mimi threw a fit."

"She was hysterical until we found you," Moriah said. "But when we got you back and it was obvious you helped save the coven, she started pestering Soren to allow you at the wedding. Some good may come of this."

I rubbed my eyes. "Soren wants me to align to him," and I repeated Soren's proposal.

Her eyebrows climbed higher with each additional sentence, until she let out a low whistle. "That would really piss the Morrigan off, wouldn't it?"

"To put it mildly."

"Sounds like reason enough to do it," she said, a grin displaying most of her teeth.

I managed a feeble laugh. It hurt my ribs.

"Let me think it over," she said with a more serious expression. "We can plot back at my house; you're coming home with me. A pint of ice cream, a few pints of liquor—everything will be clearer. We'll figure it out. We've got time."

I attempted a smile, "Sure," and lost the rest of my train of thought in a yawn.

She eased to her feet. "Go back to sleep. I'll get some clothes for you. We'll leave for the pyre tomorrow and then on to my house."

The pyre. I couldn't think about that yet.

She said something else before the door closed, but I didn't catch it. The dark water didn't swallow me up like before. Instead I drifted on a gentle wave.

\* \* \*

I WOKE SUDDENLY, stark fear seizing my heart and making the blood pound in my ears. Evil crawled through the room,

475

drenching everything in oil and hate. Sweat broke out on my forehead. *No.*

The memory of a nightmare forced me out of bed, hands shaking as I called up protective wards and surrounded myself as I stared around the room. The magic didn't feel like mine, weak and diluted and shaky. The darkness mocked me. My hand ached as I drew magic through it, the missing pinkie twitching as blue light cast shadows. "Wh-who's there?"

Something lurked in the dark, something breathed deeply and evenly. I shivered, backing into the corner near the bathroom as I cast the entire room in brilliant light. It was hiding somewhere. "I'll hex. I swear. I'll hex."

Panic surged in my throat as the evil grew dense around me, drowning me. I screamed.

The door flew open and normal light flooded the room. Moriah reached for me. "Lily? What's wrong?"

The wards collapsed as I slid down the wall to sit, hugging my knees to my chest, and sobbed. "Something was...was in here."

She searched the room, going to the window and throwing aside the curtains. "What was it?"

"Don't know." Shame crept over me. It was a nightmare. I'd dreamt they tortured me again, using my fingers for dark spells. Some war witch I was, crying over bogeymen and shadows. I ducked my head, humiliated.

She shook her head at someone in the hall, "She's okay," and crouched next to me. "Hey. Let's get you up. I'll stay with you. Just to make sure."

I started to argue, but she shot me a look that brooked no objections. Moriah helped me back into bed before she returned to the half-open door. I caught a glimpse of Leif, his face lined with exhaustion as he growled orders to search the grounds, before Moriah shut the door.

I rolled over, curled around a pillow, as she settled in the chair. The bedside table near the window always held a lamp and an alarm clock, but never before had there been a silver ring with a jade stone.

The ring gleamed as Sam's laughter echoed in my head. I couldn't look away.

I didn't sleep for a long, long time.

# CHAPTER 58

*I* had no recollection of how I traveled to the pyre. They held it far west of the city in an enormous open field, large enough to hold several hundred of the Alliance's top members, with a small stand of trees to the south. Small cairns dotted the field, and a stone fence encircled a wide area. The Alliance traditionally buried its dead in their place of birth, when possible, but laid to rest their heroes in that place, that field.

We arrived last, Moriah and I, the Alliance already assembled in a silent crowd around the pyre. It was a tall wooden structure, according to tradition, and according to tradition, Rosa and Joanne and Andre lay together. They'd fallen in battle together, they would travel onward together. White silk wrapped each of them from head to toe, and I tried not to think of what the silk hid.

Moriah shoved through the crowd until we stood in the front, near Kyle and Anne Marie. Betty took one look at me and hid on the other side of the Morrigan, cowering behind Jacques. Lauren gave me a hard look but inclined her head, and I reconsidered what I thought of her; maybe not a coward, after all. I ignored Leif and Soren, standing across the circle and almost lost behind the wooden beams. Wood and tinder stacked up around the uprights, the coven holding lit torches.

My lip curled in disgust. Wood and a normal fire. Anne Marie knew better. It was not the proper way to send them onward. But the proper way wasn't something she could do. I thought I'd taught her, years ago, but perhaps she'd forgotten. She still looked tired and defeated from her time with the dark witches, and I searched my heart for a charitable thought. Maybe they just didn't have the magic for the right way.

Anne Marie didn't acknowledge me, though it was clear she'd waited. She raised her hands. "We are here to send three loyal war witches on their way. We thank you for your service, Rosa. We thank you for your service, Joanne. We thank you, Andre, for your service."

Her voice broke and she paused. I hated her with an unreasonable rage. I would have done it better. They deserved better.

She bent her head. "You died in service to the Alliance. You died saving junior witches from the claws of a demon, and sacrificed yourselves to protect your coven. You survived ten years of war only to be felled by treachery in the peace. Your deeds, your grace, and your sense of humor will always be remembered. Your deaths will be avenged."

When she looked up, she looked only at me.

Yes. Yes, they would be avenged. They would be avenged in such a blaze that the entire world would feel it. My breath came hard, fast, as rage built with every word. I would create another Remnant in their honor.

Anne Marie didn't look away. "The saints shepherded these witches through the war, and guided their cast in peace. The saints will shelter them, protect and guide them, as they continue on their journey. We should not mourn too deeply."

But we would mourn. They would be mourned.

Anne Marie took a deep breath, bringing her hands

together. "We ask the saints to guard our sisters, Rosa and Joanne, and our brother, Andre. We ask the saints to guide them through the dark. We ask the saints to shelter and lift them up. We ask they be remembered always in the stars."

The coven moved forward with their torches and my heart jumped. Not yet. Saints, no. I couldn't say goodbye yet. It wasn't time.

Anne Marie raised her hand and they froze. Betty flushed, as if embarrassed she'd missed her cue, and I hated the girl more than when she let Rosa die.

Anne Marie faced me, her eyes rimmed with red. "I shared their coven, but you were their friend." Her hand trembled as she gestured at the pyre. "You should send them onward."

Silence echoed through the crowd, so palpable it rippled. I hadn't expected her to admit being the Morrigan, but it was the Morrigan's job to send them on. That she ceded her right meant something. At least, I hoped it meant something.

I dragged my eyes from hers eventually, and looked at the pyre, at the silk-wrapped bodies. I could have said something, could have provoked Anne Marie or challenged her lies. Revealed how I was their Morrigan first. I could have reclaimed my place in the War Coven, seize everything she'd stolen from me six years ago. It would have been my moment.

But it had nothing to do with me. I couldn't see as I stared at the pyre, keeping my eyes wide so I wouldn't embarrass them with tears. It was their journey, not mine.

I brought my hands together to draw power. The sludge from Sam burned away as I dragged deeper. I needed the ocean of power, though only a lake responded. I summoned more and more, until it filled me up, until it built around me and pushed others away. And still I pulled in more magic, attention on a length of silk, rippling in the breeze.

Kyle eyed me askance and shuffled back, catching Moriah's arm to pull her away. Then Anne Marie retreated. The circle widened until everyone stood six feet behind me and I was alone by the pyre.

Until I was alone with Rosa and Joanne and Andre.

There was much to tell them, more than I'd been able to during the reconstruction. Too much for words, really. The magic bubbled and seethed under my control, and I formed it carefully into a spell I hadn't used in five years. Hadn't ever wanted to use again.

"Saints guide your path," I whispered.

The spell blazed in blue-white flames from the base of the pyre. It unfurled in a ladder of fire, consuming everything as it built and built, until the heat burned my cheeks and the roar deafened me. Until it was only a small step into the flames to join them. A very small step. I swayed forward.

I looked through the inferno and found Leif watching.

*Death comes eventually to us all,* Anne Marie whispered in my ear.

The blue fire churned higher, consuming everything until not even ash remained, and reached hungrily into the sky to burn the clouds.

Death comes to us all. But not yet.

I threw my hands apart and the spell severed, the fire rolling up and disappearing into the sky.

The silence was deafening. The fire exposed the bedrock, the ground cracked and scorched. I patted my face, skin tight from the heat. I should have known better than to stand so close. Singed eyebrows certainly didn't do anything to balance the bruises and cuts on my face.

Anne Marie's expression remained stoic as she walked away, coven behind her. The Peacemaker strode over as a crew began unloading white stones from a flatbed. He jumped as heat seeped through his boots from the earth, and he gave the rest of the blackened ground a wide berth. Kyle and Moriah retreated as the Peacemaker confronted me. Leif remained on the other side of the thinning crowd, conferring with Mick.

"What the hell was that?" Soren asked, and I could see him calculating the destructive force for future use.

"Baelfyr," I said. "The only fire for a proper pyre, the only way to guarantee they will find their way."

"Ah," he said, and frowned at something behind me. "I am short four war witches."

"Yes, you are." My knees trembled from using too much magic.

"You are staying with Moriah, I am told."

"Yes."

"Good." Soren smiled, a predatory look sharpening his features. "I know where to find you."

With that, he strode off.

Leif supervised the crew laying stones, but caught me watching. His mouth opened as if he would speak. As if there was more to say.

I flushed and spun around so fast I ran into Moriah. She steadied me. "Those were some impressive fireworks."

She glanced up as Leif stalked past, barking orders as the shifters lugged the stones to where the pyre had been. Moriah watched them as she said, "You should talk to him."

I went rigid. Leif stood close enough that his shifter hearing would catch everything, whispered or not. I took a deep breath. "I..." One of the shifters dropped a stone and I trailed off.

"Go talk to him." She nudged my shoulder. "I know you want to."

"I do," I said, and Leif tensed. I begged his forgiveness. "But I can't."

"Coward." She was only half-joking.

"The witches won't stop until I'm dead. They'll use anyone to get to me. He's already a target because of who he is. I don't want to make him more of a target because of who I am."

"Shouldn't that be his choice?" she asked.

I squared my shoulders against the bone-deep ache of regret. "Maybe. But right now I have too many other things to worry about—and I don't want him to be another thing on my list."

"He asks about you." Moriah grinned as Leif tripped, righting himself with some semblance of dignity, and cuffed a wide-eyed young shifter. She needled the Warder for his blatant eavesdropping. "Tries to be subtle, but..."

"Soren told me," I said, even though it was mostly a lie. I owed Soren some trouble.

My phone vibrated and I checked it: Eric. I made a face at Moriah, "I should take this," and hobbled away before answering it. She could overhear, but we'd gotten good at pretending. "Hello?"

"Hey sis," Eric said, chipper even when using her deep male voice. "Still alive?"

"Barely." I glanced back as Leif harangued Moriah in a red haze of pack magic. "Glad to see you survived. I had my doubts."

"I can run when I need to. But I take it the Warder hasn't caught them?"

"Not yet."

"We're still looking as well," she said. "You're on the list of interesting people we want to talk to, but not at the top. Sorry."

"I'll get over it." My mind wandered as I gazed across the field. She claimed to know others like us, had a plan to gain us safety, if I was really what she claimed. She could teach me about it, show me the way. I could get what I needed from her, enough to control that side of me before it got me killed, and then get the crazy External out of my life. "That...proposal of yours. I'd like to hear more."

"Of course." Glee bubbled in her voice. "But it can wait. You look like death warmed over."

I started to argue, then exhaled my irritation. "How do you know?"

"I'm staring right at you, darling." A light reflected far away in the trees. "You think the Bureau would let pass an opportunity to observe an Alliance gathering? Please. We're human, not stupid."

"And I suppose you saw the fire."

"Mm. Baelfyr," she said. "Impressive. We'd heard of it, but no one had seen it performed. You're not the primary dark witch suspect, but you moved up on a few other lists."

"Can't I say goodbye to my friends without you using it against me?"

"Don't pretend we raided an intimate candlelight vigil. I'm sure if you asked the Warder, he'd seize the tapes, no? We're parked along Woodsall Road, we won't be going anywhere until the shifters leave."

I offered a grudging, "Thanks."

"Don't mention it," she chirped. "And Lil?"

"Yeah?"

"You shouldn't wear green—it really washes you out," and the line went dead.

I hobbled back to where Moriah and Leif argued. "Don't get excited, but there are humans in the trees to the south with recording equipment. You might want to check it out."

Leif wandered away without a word as the white stones piled up. The cairn grew as other shifters nonchalantly dispersed south, radios clicking, and the tension simmered.

Moriah concentrated on the stones. "Do I want to know how you know that?"

"Magic," I said, and she snorted.

I imagined the noose tightening around the Externals, and hoped Leif didn't kill Eric.

Moriah glanced over. "We should go. You look terrible."

"Not yet," I said, hand clenched around a ring in my pocket.

Tracy's black pearl coven ring. Anne Marie didn't know I had it. I'd meant to keep it, add it to the collection of rings I kept in a cigar box, but it didn't feel right. She'd been a good witch for a long time. Part of her died in battle when she fought the temptation of dark magic and lost.

The shifters climbed higher on the cairn, balancing the stones so the wind whistled through in an eerie song.

I didn't look up as startled yells echoed from the trees, supplemented by a lot of growling. "I'm ready."

Moriah put her arm through mine as we walked to the car. "Want to wait for Leif?"

"Yes," I said after hesitating. "But I can't."

She only shook her head as she started the car, and I closed my eyes so we wouldn't have to talk about it.

# CHAPTER 59

*A* week later, I gathered the courage and strength to return to the Skein. I'd been putting it off as I recuperated at Moriah's house, but the black pearl coven ring seemed to find me no matter where I put it. It was bad enough the jade ring felt heavy and malignant; I didn't need a second ring chasing me around.

Moriah didn't like me going back there, so she and half a dozen of the young wolves in her pack went along. They circled through the Slough's tangled trees, searching for danger, and it was only when they declared the whole park empty that Moriah walked with me to the witches' memorial.

She hung back, out of sight, but demanded I use the airhorn she'd given me in case any trouble arose. The wolves wanted a fight, it seemed, because half of the young ones looked excited to face down Externals or dark witches.

If they only knew.

When I was alone in front of the memorial, grief wrapped iron bands around my chest until I could hardly breathe. Most of the trees had been badly burned as I tried to fight the dark witches; there was no way anyone could sneak up on me with

487

all the undergrowth and vegetation burnt to ash. All the beauty and serenity disappeared from the memorial, until only mangled, charred trees remained.

I went to my knees at the edge of the circle and just breathed, searching for a hint of the sacred. Meditation had never been a strength, despite Joanne's guidance and advice, but I leaned back against one of the less-singed trees and tried to find a calm place in my head.

Brandr hadn't been found. Not a trace of him remained at Tracy's house, which still stood but had been condemned due to the damage from the fire as well as dark magic contamination. The wolves, particularly Cold River, searched the entire city for hints of the Old World alpha, and I'd scried for him half a dozen times, but the dark witches hid him well. I believed he lived, despite that Soren wanted to build a cairn for him in the memorial field out west, and every night I Called to him, promising to find him. Asking him to keep fighting. To survive.

I ran cleansing spells on myself for hours at a time, desperate to get rid of every last trace of Sam's magic. I still didn't feel truly clean. Maybe I never would.

Tracy's pearl ring shone in the sunlight that blazed down on the memorial without the leafy umbrella over me. I held it up and took a deep breath. "I'm sorry I didn't stay, that I didn't see when you felt lost. I should have been a better friend."

Only a soft breeze answered.

I pushed to my feet and approached the blackthorn tree, kneeling so I could dig a small hole near the trunk. I put her ring in it and covered it up, patting the dirt firmly in place. "I hope you found some peace, Tracy."

The blackthorn offered a convenient crutch as I hauled myself upright, and I paused to stretch as I stared up at the sky. Hopefully the First Coven had the time and power soon to help tend the memorial, so the foliage re-grew and all the trees healed from the fire. I didn't want to desecrate the memorial with even a hint of Sam's magic. Maybe in a few months, a year —maybe then I'd feel clean.

I frowned as I caught sight of one of the blackthorn branches that should have been brittle from burning, and a spot of green stood out against the ash. Leaves. Tiny buds, growing out of the destruction and devastation.

A tiny speck of hope.

The tree survived, and so did I. We would fight again another day. There was much to do—finding Brandr, killing Sam, freeing myself from the bonds to Soren and Kyle—and there was, as Mother used to say, no use standing around gathering moss.

My missing finger ached as I turned away from the memorial and went to find Moriah. I wasn't the Morrigan anymore, but I was still a war witch—and it was time to go to war.

# ALSO BY LAYLA NASH

Trazzak (The Galaxos Crew Book Three)